SHOW
BOAT

SHOW BOAT

A Facsimile of the 1926 Edition

E D N A   F E R B E R

GRAMERCY BOOKS
NEW YORK

This 2007 edition is published by Gramercy Books, an imprint of
Random House Value Publishing, a division of Random House, Inc.,
New York, by arrangement with the Doubleday Broadway Publishing
Group, both divisions of Random House Inc.

Gramercy is a registered trademark and the colophon
is a trademark of Random House, Inc.

Random House
New York • Toronto • London • Sydney • Auckland
www.valuebooks.com

Printed and bound in the United States.

A catalog record for this title is available
from the Library of Congress.

ISBN: 978-0-517-22993-4

10 9 8 7 6 5 4 3 2 1

To
Winthrop Ames
Who First Said Show Boat
to Me

Edna Ferber's Books

Introduction

"SHOW BOAT" is neither history nor biography, but fiction. This statement is made in the hope that it will forestall such protest as may be registered by demon statisticians against certain liberties taken with characters, places, and events. In the Chicago portion of the book, for example, a character occasionally appears some three or four years after the actual date of his death. Now and then a restaurant or gambling resort is described as running full blast at a time when it had vanished at the frown of civic virtue. This, then, was done, not through negligence in research, but because, in the attempt to give a picture of the time, it was necessary slightly to condense a period of fifteen or twenty years.

E. F.

SHOW

BY EDNA

THE TIME:

From the gilded age of the 1870's, through the '90's up to the present time.

THE SCENE:

The earlier parts of the story take place on the *Cotton Blossom Floating Palace Theatre*, a show boat on the Mississippi. The background aboard *The Cotton Blossom* is panoramic. Twice a year the unwieldy boat was towed up and down the mighty river and its tributaries; it was a familiar sight from New Orleans to the cities of the North, from the coal fields of Pennsylvania to St. Louis, and stirring presentations of "East Lynne," "Tempest and Sunshine," and other old dramatic favourites, by the actors and painted ladies of the *Cotton Blossom* troupe, are still remembered in Paducah, Evansville, Cairo, Cape Girardeau, Natchez, Vicksburg, Baton Rouge, and in many other river towns and cities.

Following the fortunes of the Hawkes-Ravenal family, the story then carries us to the notorious "Gambler's Alley" of earlier Chicago, and then to the modern theatrical centre of America, the Times Square district of New York City.

Published by DOUBLEDAY, PAGE & CO.

BOAT

FERBER

THE PLAYERS:

CAPT. ANDY HAWKS
Mississippi River steamboat captain and
owner of the *Cotton Blossom*

PARTHENIA ANN HAWKS
His wife

MAGNOLIA RAVENAL
Their daughter, later a famous actress
on the variety stage

GAYLORD RAVENAL
Gambler, gentleman of fortune and sometime
actor.   Husband of Magnolia

KIM RAVENAL
Daughter of Gaylord and Magnolia.   Now
the famous Kim Ravenal of the
New York stage

**JULIE, ELLY, STEVE, SCHULTZY, AND
OTHER MEMBERS OF THE
SHOW BOAT TROUPE**

**HABITUÉS OF
OLD SOUTH CLARK STREET
IN CHICAGO**

**ACTORS AND DRAMATIC CRITICS OF THE
PRESENT THEATRICAL WORLD OF NEW YORK CITY**

Garden City, N. Y.

SHOW BOAT

I

BIZARRE as was the name she bore, Kim Ravenal always said she was thankful it had been no worse. She knew whereof she spoke, for it was literally by a breath that she had escaped being called Mississippi.

"Imagine Mississippi Ravenal!" she often said, in later years. "They'd have cut it to Missy, I suppose, or even Sippy, if you can bear to think of anything so horrible. And then I'd have had to change my name or give up the stage altogether. Because who'd go to see—seriously, I mean—an actress named Sippy? It sounds half-witted, for some reason. Kim's bad enough, God knows."

And as Kim Ravenal you doubtless are familiar with her. It is no secret that the absurd monosyllable which comprises her given name is made up of the first letters of three states—Kentucky, Illinois, and Missouri— in all of which she was, incredibly enough, born—if she can be said to have been born in any state at all. Her mother insists that she wasn't. If you were an habitué of old South Clark Street in Chicago's naughty '90s you may even remember her mother, Magnolia Ravenal,

as Nola Ravenal, soubrette—though Nola Ravenal
never achieved the doubtful distinction of cigarette
pictures.   In a day when the stage measured feminine
pulchritude in terms of hips, thighs, and calves, she was
considered much too thin for beauty, let alone for
tights.

It had been this Magnolia Ravenal's respiratory lack
that had saved the new-born girl from being cursed
through life with a name boasting more quadruple
vowels and consonants than any other in the language.
She had meant to call the child Mississippi after the
tawny untamed river on which she had spent so much
of her girlhood, and which had stirred and fascinated
her always.   Her accouchement had been an ordeal
even more terrifying than is ordinarily the case, for Kim
Ravenal had actually been born on the raging turgid
bosom of the Mississippi River itself, when that ram-
pageous stream was flooding its banks and inundating
towns for miles around, at five o'clock of a storm-racked
April morning in 1889.   It was at a point just below
Cairo, Illinois; that region known as Little Egypt,
where the yellow waters of the Mississippi and the olive-
green waters of the Ohio so disdainfully meet and refuse,
with bull-necked pride, to mingle.

From her cabin window on the second deck of the
Cotton Blossom Floating Palace Theatre, Magnolia
Ravenal could have seen the misty shores of three
states—if any earthly shores had interested her at the
moment.   Just here was Illinois, to whose crumbling
clay banks the show boat was so perilously pinioned.
Beyond, almost hidden by the rain veil, was Missouri;

and there, Kentucky. But Magnolia Ravenal lay with her eyes shut because the effort of lifting her lids was beyond her. Seeing her, you would have said that if any shores filled her vision at the moment they were heavenly ones, and those dangerously near. So white, so limp, so spent was she that her face on the pillow was startlingly like one of the waxen blossoms whose name she bore. Her slimness made almost no outline beneath the bedclothes. The coverlet was drawn up to her chin. There was only the white flower on the pillow, its petals closed.

Outside, the redundant rain added its unwelcome measure to the swollen and angry stream. In the ghostly gray dawn the grotesque wreckage of flood-time floated and whirled and jiggled by, seeming to bob a mad obeisance as it passed the show boat which, in its turn, made stately bows from its moorings. There drifted past, in fantastic parade, great trees, uprooted and clutching at the water with stiff dead arms; logs, catapulted with terrific force; animal carcasses dreadful in their passivity; chicken coops; rafts; a piano, its ivory mouth fixed in a death grin; a two-room cabin, upright, and moving in a minuet of stately and ponderous swoops and advances and chassés; fence rails; an armchair whose white crocheted antimacassar stared in prim disapproval at the wild antics of its fellow voyagers; a live sheep, bleating as it came, but soon still; a bed with its covers, by some freak of suction, still snugly tucked in as when its erstwhile occupant had fled from it in fright—all these, and more, contributed to the weird terror of the morning. The Mississippi itself was a tawny tiger, roused, furious, bloodthirsty, lashing out with its great tail, tearing with its cruel claws, and burying its fangs deep in the shore to swallow at a gulp land, houses, trees, cattle—humans, even; and roaring, snarling, howling hideously as it did so.

Inside Magnolia Ravenal's cabin all was snug and warm and bright. A wood fire snapped and crackled cosily in the little pot-bellied iron stove. Over it bent a veritable Sairey Gamp stirring something hot and savoury in a saucepan. She stirred noisily, and talked as she stirred, and glanced from time to time at the mute white figure in the bed. Her own bulky figure was made more ponderous by layer on layer of ill-assorted garments of the kind donned from time to time as night wears on by one who, having been aroused hastily and in emergency, has arrived scantily clad. A gray flannel nightgown probably formed the basis of this costume, for its grizzled cuffs could just be seen emerging from the man's coat whose sleeves she wore turned back from the wrists for comfort and convenience. This coat was of box cut, double-breasted, blue with brass buttons and gold braid, of the sort that river captains wear. It gave her a racy and nautical look absurdly at variance with her bulk and occupation. Peeping beneath and above and around this, the baffled eye could just glimpse oddments and elegancies such as a red flannel dressing gown; a flower-besprigged challis sacque whose frill of doubtful lace made the captain's coat even more incongruous; a brown cashmere skirt, very bustled and bunchy; a pair of scuffed tan kid bedroom slippers (men's) of the sort known as romeos. This lady's back hair was twisted into a knob strictly utilitarian; her front hair bristled with the wired ends of kid curlers assumed, doubtless, the evening before the hasty summons. Her face and head were long and horse-like, at variance with her bulk. This, you sensed immediately, was a person possessed of enormous energy, determination, and the gift of making exquisitely uncomfortable any one who happened to be within hearing radius. She was the sort who rattles anything that can be rattled; slams anything that can be slammed; bumps anything that can be bumped. Her name, by some miracle of fitness, was Parthenia Ann Hawks; wife of Andy Hawks, captain and owner of the Cotton Blossom Floating Palace Theatre; and mother of this Magnolia Ravenal who, having just been delivered of a daughter, lay supine in her bed.

Now, as Mrs. Hawks stirred the mess over which she was bending, her spoon regularly scraped the bottom of the pan with a rasping sound that would have tortured any nerves but her own iron-encased set. She removed the spoon, freeing it of clinging drops by rapping it smartly and metallically against the rim of the basin. Magnolia Ravenal's eyelids fluttered ever so slightly.

"Now then!" spake Parthy Ann Hawks, briskly, in that commanding tone against which even the most spiritless instinctively rebelled, "Now then, young lady, want it or not, you'll eat some of this broth, good and hot and stren'th'ning, and maybe you won't look so much like a wet dish rag." Pan in one hand, spoon in the other, she advanced toward the bed with a tread that jarred the furniture and set the dainty dimity window curtains to fluttering. She brought up against the side of the bed with a bump. A shadow of pain flitted across the white face on the pillow. The eyes still were closed. As the smell of the hot liquid reached her nostrils, the lips of the girl on the bed curled in distaste. "Here, I'll just spoon it right up to you out of the pan, so's it'll be good and hot. Open your mouth! Open your eyes! I say open—— Well, for land's sakes, how do you expect a body to do anything for you if you——"

With a motion shocking in its swift unexpectedness Magnolia Ravenal's hand emerged from beneath the coverlet, dashed aside the spoon with its steaming contents, and sent it clattering to the floor. Then her hand stole beneath the coverlet again and with a little relaxed sigh of satisfaction she lay passive as before. She had not opened her eyes. She was smiling ever so slightly.

"That's right! Act like a wildcat just because I try to get you to sup up a little soup that Jo's been hours cooking, and two pounds of good mutton in it if there's an ounce, besides vegetables and barley, and your pa practically risked his life getting the meat down at Cairo and the water going up by the foot every hour. No, you're not satisfied to get us caught here in the flood, and how we'll ever get out alive or dead, God knows, and me and everybody on the boat up all night long with your goings on so you'd think nobody'd ever had a baby before. Time I had you there wasn't a whimper out of me. Not a whimper. I'd have died, first. I never saw anything as indelicate as the way you carried on, and your own husband in the room." Here Magnolia conveyed with a flutter of the lids that this had not been an immaculate conception. "Well, if you could see yourself now. A drowned rat isn't the word. Now you take this broth, my fine lady, or we'll see who's——" She paused in this dramatic threat to blow a cooling breath on a generous spoonful of the steaming liquid, to sup it up with audible appreciation, and to take another. She smacked her lips. "Now then, no more of your monkey-shines, Maggie Hawks!"

No one but her mother had ever called Magnolia Ravenal Maggie Hawks. It was unthinkable that a name so harsh and unlovely could be applied to this fragile person. Having picked up the rejected spoon and wiped it on the lace ruffle of the challis sacque, that terrible termagant grasped it firmly against surprise in her right hand and, saucepan in left, now advanced a second time toward the bed. You saw the flower on the pillow frosted by an icy mask of utter unyielding-ness; you caught a word that sounded like shenanigans from the woman bending over the bed, when the cabin door opened and two twittering females entered attired in garments strangely akin to the haphazard costume worn by Mrs. Hawks. The foremost of these moved in a manner so bustling as to be unmistakably official. She was at once ponderous, playful, and menacing—this last attribute due, perhaps, to the rather splendid dark moustache which stamped her upper lip. In her arms she carried a swaddled bundle under one flannel flap of which the second female kept peering and uttering strange clucking sounds and words that resembled izzer and yesseris.

"Fine a gal's I ever see!" exclaimed the bustling one. She approached the bed with the bundle. "Mis' Means says the same and so"—she glanced contemptuously over her shoulder at a pale and haggard young man, bearded but boyish, who followed close behind them— "does the doctor."

She paused before the word doctor so that the title, when finally it was uttered, carried with it a poisonous derision. This mysterious sally earned a little snigger from Mis' Means and a baleful snort from Mrs. Hawks. Flushed with success, the lady with the swaddled bundle (unmistakably a midwife and, like all her craft, royally accustomed to homage and applause) waxed more malicious. "Fact is, he says only a minute ago, he never brought a finer baby that he can remember."

At this the sniggers and snorts became unmistakable guffaws. The wan young man became a flushed young man. He fumbled awkwardly with the professionally massive watch chain that so unnecessarily guarded his cheap nickel blob of a watch. He glanced at the flower-like face on the pillow. Its aloofness, its remoteness from the three frowzy females that hovered about it, seemed to lend him a momentary dignity and courage. He thrust his hands behind the tails of his Prince Albert coat and strode toward the bed. A wave of the hand, a slight shove with the shoulder, dismissed the three as nuisances. "One moment, my good woman. . . . *If* you please, Mrs. Hawks. . . . Kindly don't jiggle . . ."

The midwife stepped aside with the bundle. Mrs. Hawks fell back a step, the ineffectual spoon and saucepan in her hands. Mis' Means ceased to cluck and to lean on the bed's footboard. From a capacious inner coat pocket he produced a stethoscope, applied it, listened, straightened. From the waistcoat pocket came the timepiece, telltale of his youth and impecuniosity. He extracted his patient's limp wrist from beneath the coverlet and held it in his own strong spatulate fingers— the fingers of the son of a farmer.

"H'm! Fine!" he exclaimed. "Splendid!"

An unmistakable sniff from the midwife. The boy's florid manner dropped from him. He cringed a little. The sensitive hand he still held in his great grasp seemed to feel this change in him, though Magnolia Ravenal had not opened her eyes even at the entrance of the three. Her wrist slid itself out of his hold and down until her fingers met his and pressed them lightly, reassuringly. The youth looked down, startled. Magnolia Ravenal, white-lipped, was smiling her wide gay gorgeous smile that melted the very vitals of you. It was a smile at once poignant and brilliant. It showed her gums a little, and softened the planes of her high cheek-bones, and subdued the angles of the too-prominent jaw. A comradely smile, an understanding and warming one. Strange that this woman on the bed, so lately torn and racked with the agonies of childbirth, should be the one to encourage the man whose clumsy ministrations had so nearly cost her her life. That she could smile at all was sheer triumph of the spirit over the flesh. And that she could smile in sympathy for and encouragement of this bungling inexpert young medico was incredible. But that was Magnolia Ravenal. Properly directed and managed, her smile, in later years, could have won her a fortune. But direction and management were as futile when applied to her as to the great untamed Mississippi that even now was flouting man-built barriers; laughing at levees that said so far and no farther; jeering at jetties that said do thus and so; for that matter, roaring this very moment in derision of Magnolia Ravenal herself, and her puny pangs and her mortal plans; and her father Captain Andy Hawks, and her mother Parthenia Ann Hawks, and her husband Gaylord Ravenal, and the whole troupe of the show boat, and the Cotton Blossom Floating Palace Theatre itself, now bobbing about like a cork on the yellow flood that tugged and sucked and tore at its moorings.

Two tantrums of nature had been responsible for the present precarious position of the show boat and its occupants. The Mississippi had furnished one; Magnolia Ravenal the other. Or perhaps it might be fairer to fix the blame, not on nature, but on human stupidity that had failed to take into account its vagaries.

Certainly Captain Andy Hawks should have known better, after thirty-five years of experience on keelboats, steamboats, packets, and show boats up and down the great Mississippi and her tributaries (the Indians might call this stream the Father of Waters but your riverman respectfully used the feminine pronoun). The brand-new show boat had done it. Built in the St. Louis shipyards, the new *Cotton Blossom* was to have been

ready for him by February. But February had come
and gone, and March as well. He had meant to be in
New Orleans by this time, with his fine new show boat
and his troupe and his band of musicians in their fresh
glittering red-and-gold uniforms, and the marvellous
steam calliope that could be heard for miles up and down
the bayous and plantations. Starting at St. Louis, he
had planned a swift trip downstream, playing just
enough towns on the way to make expenses. Then,
beginning with Bayou Teche and pushed by the sturdy
steamer *Mollie Able*, they would proceed grandly upstream, calliope screaming, flags flying, band tooting,
to play every little town and landing and plantation
from New Orleans to Baton Rouge, from Baton Rouge
to Vicksburg; to Memphis, to Cairo, to St. Louis, up
and up to Minnesota itself; then over to the coal towns
on the Monongahela River and the Kanawha, and down
again to New Orleans, following the crops as they
ripened—the corn belt, the cotton belt, the sugar cane;
north when the wheat yellowed, following with the sun
the ripening of the peas, the tomatoes, the crabs, the
peaches, the apples; and as the farmer garnered his
golden crops so would shrewd Captain Andy Hawks
gather his harvest of gold.

It was April before the new *Cotton Blossom* was
finished and ready to take to the rivers. Late though
it was, when Captain Andy Hawks beheld her, glittering from texas to keel in white paint with green trimmings, and with Cotton Blossom Floating Palace
Theatre done in letters two feet high on her upper deck,
he was vain enough, or foolhardy enough, or both, to

resolve to stand by his original plan. A little nervous
fussy man, Andy Hawks, with a horrible habit of clawing and scratching from side to side, when aroused or
when deep in thought, at the little mutton-chop whiskers that sprang out like twin brushes just below his
leather-visored white canvas cap, always a trifle too
large for his head, so that it settled down over his ears.
A capering figure, in light linen pants very wrinkled and
baggy, and a blue coat, double-breasted; with a darting
manner, bright brown eyes, and a trick of talking very
fast as he clawed the mutton-chop whiskers first this
side, then that, with one brown hairy little hand. There
was about him something grotesque, something simian.
He beheld the new *Cotton Blossom* as a bridegroom
gazes upon a bride, and frenziedly clawing his whiskers
he made his unwise decision.

"She won't high-water this year till June." He was
speaking of that tawny tigress, the Mississippi; and
certainly no one knew her moods better than he. "Not
much snow last winter, north; and no rain to speak of,
yet. Yessir, we'll just blow down to New Orleans ahead
of French's *Sensation*"—his bitterest rival in the show-
boat business—"and start to work the bayous. Show
him a clean pair of heels up and down the river."

So they had started. And because the tigress lay
smooth and unruffled now, with only the currents playing gently below the surface like muscles beneath the
golden yellow skin, they fancied she would remain com-
plaisant until they had had their way. That was the
first mistake.

The second was as unreasoning. Magnolia Ravenal's

child was going to be a boy. Ma Hawks and the wise
married women of the troupe knew the signs. She felt
thus-and-so. She had such-and-such sensations. She
was carrying the child high. Boys always were slower
in being born than girls. Besides, this was a first child,
and the first child always is late. They got together,
in mysterious female conclave, and counted on the
fingers of their two hands—August, September, October, November, December—why, the end of April,
the soonest. They'd be safe in New Orleans by then,
with the best of doctors for Magnolia, and she on land
while one of the other women in the company played
her parts until she was strong again—a matter of two or
three weeks at most.

No sooner had they started than the rains began.
No early April showers, these, but torrents that blotted
out the river banks on either side and sent the clay
tumbling in great cave-ins, down to the water, jaundic-
ing it afresh where already it seethed an ochreous mass.
Day after day, night after night, the rains came down,
melting the Northern ice and snow, filtering through the
land of the Mississippi basin and finding its way, whether
trickle, rivulet, creek, stream, or river, to the great
hungry mother, Mississippi. And she grew swollen,
and tossed and flung her huge limbs about and shrieked
in labour even as Magnolia Ravenal was so soon to do.

Eager for entertainment as the dwellers were along
the little Illinois and Missouri towns, after a long winter
of dull routine on farm and in store and schoolhouse,
they came sparsely to the show boat. Posters had told
them of her coming, and the news filtered to the back-

country. Town and village thrilled to the sound of the
steam calliope as the Cotton Blossom Floating Palace
Theatre, propelled by the square-cut clucking old
steamer, *Mollie Able*, swept grandly down the river to
the landing. But the back-country roads were im-
passable bogs by now, and growing worse with every
hour of rain. Wagon wheels sank to the hubs in mud.
There were crude signs, stuck on poles, reading, "No
bottom here." The dodgers posted on walls and fences
in the towns were rain-soaked and bleary. And as for
the Cotton Blossom Floating Palace Theatre Ten
Piece Band (which numbered six)—how could it risk
ruin of its smart new red coats, gold-braided and gold-
buttoned, by marching up the water-logged streets of
these little towns whose occupants only stared wistfully
out through storm-blurred windows? It was dreary
even at night, when the show boat glowed invitingly
with the blaze of a hundred oil lamps that lighted the
auditorium seating six hundred (One Thousand Seats!
A Luxurious Floating Theatre within an Unrivalled
Floating Palace!). Usually the flaming oil-flares on
their tall poles stuck in the steep clay banks that led
down to the show boat at the water's edge made a path
of fiery splendour. Now they hissed and spluttered
dismally, almost extinguished by the deluge. Even
when the bill was St. Elmo or East Lynne, those tried
and trusty winners, the announcement of which always
packed the show boat's auditorium to the very last seat
in the balcony reserved for Negroes, there was now only
a damp handful of shuffle-footed men and giggling girls
and a few children in the cheaper rear seats. The

Mississippi Valley dwellers, wise with the terrible wisdom born of much suffering under the dominance of this voracious and untamed monster, so ruthless when roused, were preparing against catastrophe should these days of rain continue.

Captain Andy Hawks clawed his mutton-chop whiskers, this side and that, and scanned the skies, and searched the yellowing swollen stream with his bright brown eyes. "We'll make for Cairo," he said. "Full steam ahead. I don't like the looks of her—the big yella snake."

But full steam ahead was impossible for long in a snag-infested river, as Andy Hawks well knew; and in a river whose treacherous channel shifted almost daily in normal times, and hourly in flood-time. Cautiously they made for Cairo. Cape Girardeau, Gray's Point, Commerce—then, suddenly, near evening, the false sun shone for a brief hour. At once everyone took heart. The rains, they assured each other, were over. The spring freshet would subside twice as quickly as it had risen. Fittingly enough, the play billed for that evening was Tempest and Sunshine, always a favourite. Magnolia Ravenal cheerfully laced herself into the cruel steel-stiffened high-busted corset of the period, and donned the golden curls and the prim ruffles of the part. A goodish crowd scrambled and slipped and slid down the rain-soaked clay bank, torch-illumined, to the show boat, their boots leaving a trail of mud and water up and down the aisles of the theatre and between the seats. It was a restless audience, and hard to hold. There had been an angry sunset, and threatening clouds to the northwest. The crowd shuffled its feet, coughed, stirred constantly. There was in the air something electric, menacing, heavy. Suddenly, during the last act, the north wind sprang up with a whistling sound, and the little choppy hard waves could be heard slapping against the boat's flat sides. She began to rock, too, and pitch, flat though she was and securely moored to the river bank. Lightning, a fusillade of thunder, and then the rain again, heavy, like drops of molten lead, and driven by the north wind. The crowd scrambled up the perilous clay banks, slipping, falling, cursing, laughing, frightened. To this day it is told that the river rose seven feet in twenty-four hours. Captain Andy Hawks, still clawing his whiskers, still bent on making for Cairo, cast off and ordered the gangplank in as the last scurrying villager clawed his way up the slimy incline whose heights the river was scaling inch by inch.

"The Ohio's the place," he insisted, his voice high and squeaky with excitement. "High water at Cincinnati, St. Louis, Evansville, or even Paducah don't have to mean high water on the Ohio. It's the old yella serpent making all this kick-up. But the Ohio's the river gives Cairo the real trouble. Yessir! And she don't flood till June. We'll make for the Ohio and stay on her till this comes to a stand, anyway."

Then followed the bedlam of putting off. Yells, hoarse shouts, bells ringing, wheels churning the water to foam. Lively now! Cramp her down! Snatch her! SNATCH her!

Faintly, above the storm, you heard the cracked

falsetto of little Captain Andy Hawks, a pilot for years, squeaking to himself in his nervousness the orders that river etiquette forbade his actually giving that ruler, that ultimate sovereign, the pilot, old Mark Hooper, whose real name was no more Mark than Twain's had been: relic of his leadsmen days, with the cry of, "Mark three! Mark three! Half twain! Quarter twain! M-A-R-K twain!" gruffly shouted along the hurricane deck.

It was told, on the rivers, that little Andy Hawks had been known, under excitement, to walk off the deck into the river and to bob afloat there until rescued, still spluttering and shrieking orders in a profane falsetto.

Down the river they went, floating easily over bars that in normal times stood six feet out of the water; clattering through chutes; shaving the shores. Thunder, lightning, rain, chaos outside. Within, the orderly routine of bedtime on the show boat. Mis' Means, the female half of the character team, heating over a tiny spirit flame a spoonful of goose grease which she would later rub on her husband's meagre cough-racked chest; Maudie Rainger, of the general business team, sipping her bedtime cup of coffee; Bert Forbush, utility man, in shirt sleeves, check pants, and carpet slippers, playing a sleep-inducing game of canfield—all this on the stage, bare now of scenery and turned into a haphazard and impromptu lounging room for the members of this floating theatrical company. Mrs. Hawks, in her fine new cabin on the second deck, off the gallery, was putting her sparse hair in crimpers as she would do if this were the night before Judgment Day. Flood, storm, danger—

all part of river show-boat life. Ordinarily, it is true, they did not proceed down river until daybreak. After the performance, the show boat and its steamer would stay snug and still alongside the wharf of this little town or that. By midnight, company and crew would have fallen asleep to the sound of the water slap-slapping gently against the boat's sides.

To-night there probably would be little sleep for some of the company, what with the storm, the motion, the unwonted stir, and the noise that came from the sturdy *Mollie Able*, bracing her cautious bulk against the flood's swift urging; and certainly none for Captain Andy Hawks, for pilot Mark Hooper and the crew of the *Mollie Able*. But that, too, was all part of the life.

Midnight had found Gaylord Ravenal, in nightshirt and dressing gown, a handsome and distraught figure, pounding on the door of his mother-in-law's cabin. From the cabin he had just left came harrowing sounds —whimpers, and little groans, and great moans, like an animal in agony. Magnolia Ravenal was not one of your silent sufferers. She was too dramatic for that. Manœuvred magically by the expert Hooper, they managed to make a perilous landing just above Cairo. The region was scoured for a doctor, without success, for accident had followed on flood. Captain Andy had tracked down a stout and reluctant midwife who consented only after an enormous bribe to make the perilous trip to the levee, clambering ponderously down the slippery bank with many groanings and forebodings, and being sustained, both in bulk and spirit, by the agile and vivacious little captain much as a tiny fussy river tug guides a gigantic and unwieldy ocean liner. He was almost frantically distraught, for between Andy Hawks and his daughter Magnolia Ravenal was that strong bond of affection and mutual understanding that always exists between the henpecked husband and the harassed offspring of a shrew such as Parthy Ann Hawks.

When, an hour later, Gaylord Ravenal, rain-soaked and mud-spattered, arrived with a white-faced young doctor's assistant whose first obstetrical call this was, he found the fat midwife already in charge and inclined to elbow about any young medical upstart who might presume to dictate to a female of her experience.

It was a sordid and ravaging confinement which, at its climax, teetered for one dreadful moment between tragedy and broad comedy. For at the crisis, just before dawn, the fat midwife, busy with ministrations, had said to the perspiring young doctor, "D'you think it's time to snuff her?"

Bewildered, and not daring to show his ignorance, he had replied, judicially, "Uh—not just yet. No, not just yet."

Again the woman had said, ten minutes later, "Time to snuff her, I'd say."

"Well, perhaps it is." He watched her, fearfully, wondering what she might mean; cursing his own lack of knowledge. To his horror and amazement, before he could stop her, she had stuffed a great pinch of strong snuff up either nostril of Magnolia Ravenal's delicate nose. And thus Kim Ravenal was born into the world on the gust of a series of convulsive a-CHOOs!

"God almighty, woman!" cried the young medico, in a frenzy. "You've killed her."

"Run along, do!" retorted the fat midwife, testily, for she was tired by now, and hungry, and wanted her coffee badly. "H'm! It's a gal. And they had their minds all made up to a boy. Never knew it to fail." She turned to Magnolia's mother, a ponderous and unwieldy figure at the foot of the bed. "Well, now, Mis'—Hawks, ain't it?—that's right—Hawks. Well, now, Mis' Hawks, we'll get this young lady washed up and then I'd thank you for a pot of coffee and some breakfast. I'm partial to a meat breakfast."

All this had been a full hour ago. Magnolia Ravenal still lay inert, unheeding. She had not even looked at her child. Her mother now uttered bitter complaint to the others in the room.

"Won't touch a drop of this good nourishing broth. Knocked the spoon right out of my hand, would you believe it! for all she lays there looking so gone. Well! I'm going to open her mouth and pour it down."

The young doctor raised a protesting palm. "No, no, I wouldn't do that." He bent over the white face on the pillow. "Just a spoonful," he coaxed, softly. "Just a swallow?"

She did not vouchsafe him another smile. He glanced at the irate woman with the saucepan; at the two attendant vestals. "Isn't there somebody——?"

The men of the company and the crew were out, he well knew, with pike poles in hand, working to keep the drifting objects clear of the boats. Gaylord Ravenal would be with them. He had been in and out a score of times through the night, his handsome young face (too handsome, the awkward young doctor had privately decided) twisted with horror and pity and self-reproach. He had noticed, too, that the girl's cries had abated not a whit when the husband was there. But when he took her writhing fingers, and put one hand on her wet forehead, and said, in a voice that broke with agony, "Oh, Nola! Nola! Don't. I didn't know it was like . . . Not like this. . . . Magnolia . . ."—she had said, through clenched teeth and white lips, surprisingly enough, with a knowledge handed down to her through centuries of women writhing in childbirth, "It's all right, Gay. . . . Always . . . like this . . . damn it. . . . Don't you worry. . . . It's . . . all . . ." And the harassed young doctor had then seen for the first time the wonder of Magnolia Ravenal's poignant smile.

So now when he said, shyly, "Isn't there somebody else——" he was thinking that if the young and handsome husband could be spared for but a moment from his pike pole it would be better to chance a drifting log sent crashing against the side of the boat by the flood than that this white still figure on the bed should be allowed to grow one whit whiter or more still.

"Somebody else's fiddlesticks!" exploded Mrs. Hawks, inelegantly. They were all terribly rude to him, poor lad, except the one who might have felt justified in being so. "If her own mother can't——" She had reheated the broth on the little iron stove, and now made a third advance, armed with spoon and saucepan. The midwife had put the swaddled bundle on the pillow so that it lay just beside Magnolia Ravenal's arm. It was she who now interrupted Mrs. Hawks, and abetted her.

"How in time d'you expect to nurse," she demanded, "if you don't eat!"

Magnolia Ravenal didn't know and, seemingly, didn't care.

A crisis was imminent. It was the moment for drama. And it was furnished, obligingly enough, by the opening of the door to admit the two whom Magnolia Ravenal loved in all the world. There came first the handsome, haggard Gaylord Ravenal, actually managing, in some incredible way, to appear elegant, well-dressed, dapper, at a time, under circumstances, and in a costume which would have rendered most men unsightly, if not repulsive. But his gifts were many, and not the least of them was the trick of appearing sartorially and tonsorially flawless when dishevelment and a stubble were inevitable in any other male. Close behind him trotted Andy Hawks, just as he had been twenty-four hours before—wrinkled linen pants, double-breasted blue coat, oversize visored cap, mutton-chop whiskers and all. Together he and Ma Hawks, in her blue brass-buttoned coat that was a twin of his, managed to give the gathering quite a military aspect. Certainly Mrs. Hawks' manner was martial enough at the moment. She raised her voice now in complaint.

"Won't touch her broth. Ain't half as sick as she lets on or she wouldn't be so stubborn. Wouldn't have the strength to be, 's what I say."

Gaylord Ravenal took from her the saucepan and the

spoon. The saucepan he returned to the stove. He espied a cup on the washstand; with a glance at Captain Andy he pointed silently to this. Andy Hawks emptied its contents into the slop jar, rinsed it carefully, and half filled it with the steaming hot broth. The two men approached the bedside. There was about both a clumsy and touching but magically effective tenderness. Gay Ravenal slipped his left arm under the girl's head with its hair all spread so dank and wild on the pillow. Captain Andy Hawks leaned forward, cup in hand, holding it close to her mouth. With his right hand, delicately, Gay Ravenal brought the first hot revivifying spoonful to her mouth and let it trickle slowly, drop by drop, through her lips. He spoke to her as he did this, but softly, softly, so that the others could not hear the words. Only the cadence of his voice, and that was a caress. Another spoonful, and another, and another. He lowered her again to the pillow, his arm still under her head. A faint tinge of palest pink showed under the waxen skin. She opened her eyes; looked up at him. She adored him. Her pain-dulled eyes even then said so. Her lips moved. He bent closer. She was smiling almost mischievously.

"Fooled them."

"What's she say?" rasped Mrs. Hawks, fearfully, for she loved the girl.

Over his shoulder he repeated the two words she had whispered.

"Oh," said Parthy Ann Hawks, and laughed. "She means fooled 'em because it's a girl instead of a boy."

But at that Magnolia Ravenal shook her head ever so

slightly, and looked up at him again and held up one slim forefinger and turned her eyes toward the corners with a listening look.   And in obedience he held up his hand then, a warning for silence, though he was as mystified as they.   And in the stillness of the room you heard the roar and howl and crash of the great river whose flood had caught them and shaken them and brought Magnolia Ravenal to bed ahead of her time. And now he knew what she meant.   She wasn't thinking of the child that lay against her arms.   Her lips moved again.   He bent closer.   And what she said was:

"The River."

II

SURELY no little girl had ever had a more fantastic little girlhood than this Magnolia Ravenal who had been Magnolia Hawks. By the time she was eight she had fallen into and been fished out of practically every river in the Mississippi Basin from the Gulf of Mexico to Minnesota. The ordinary routine of her life, in childhood, had been made up of doing those things that usually are strictly forbidden the average child. She swam muddy streams; stayed up until midnight; read the lurid yellow-backed novels found in the cabins of the women of the company; went to school but rarely; caught catfish; drank river water out of the river itself; roamed the streets of strange towns alone; learned to strut and shuffle and buck-and-wing from the Negroes whose black faces dotted the boards of the Southern wharves as thickly as grace notes sprinkle a bar of lively music. And all this despite constant watchfulness, nagging, and admonition from her spinster-like mother; for Parthy Ann Hawks, matron though she was, still was one of those women who, confined as favourite wife in the harem of a lascivious Turk, would have remained a spinster at heart and in manner. And though she lived on her husband's show boat season after season, and tried to rule it from pilot house to cook's galley, she was always an incongruous figure in the gay, careless vagabond life of this band of floating players. The very fact of her presence on the boat was a paradox. Life, for Parthy Ann Hawks, was meant to be made up of crisp white dimity curtains at kitchen windows; of bi-weekly bread bakings; of Sunday morning service and Wednesday night prayer meeting; of small gossip rolled evilly under the tongue. The male biped, to her, was a two-footed animal who tracked up a clean kitchen floor just after it was scoured and smoked a pipe in defiance of decency. Yet here she was—and had been for ten years—leading an existence which would have made that of the Stratford strollers seem orderly and prim by comparison.

She had been a Massachusetts school teacher, living with a henpecked fisherman father, and keeping house expertly for him with one hand while she taught school with the other. The villagers held her up as an example of all the feminine virtues, but the young males of the village were to be seen walking home from church with this or that plump twitterer who might be a notoriously bad cook but who had an undeniable way of tying a blue sash about a tempting waist. Parthenia Ann, prayer book clasped in mitted hands, walked sedately home with her father. The vivacious little Andy Hawks, drifting up into Massachusetts one summer, on a visit to fishermen kin, had encountered the father, and, through him, the daughter. He had eaten her light flaky biscuit, her golden-brown fries; her ruddy jell; her succulent pickles; her juicy pies. He had stood in her kitchen doorway, shyly yet boldly watching her as she moved briskly from table to stove,

from stove to pantry. The sleeves of her crisp print
dress were rolled to the elbow, and if those elbows were
not dimpled they were undeniably expert in batter-
beating, dough-kneading, pan-scouring. Her sallow
cheeks were usually a little flushed with the heat of the
kitchen and the energy of her movements, and, perhaps,
with the consciousness of the unaccustomed masculine
eye so warmly turned upon her. She looked her bustling
best, and to little impulsive warm-hearted Andy she
represented all he had ever known and dreamed, in his
roving life, of order, womanliness, comfort. She was
seven years older than he. The intolerance with which
women of Parthenia Ann's type regard all men was
heightened by this fact to something resembling contempt. Even before their marriage, she bossed him
about much as she did her old father, but while she
nagged she also fed them toothsome viands, and the
balm of bland, well-cooked food counteracted the acid
of her words. Then, too, Nature, the old witch-
wanton, had set the yeast to working in the flabby
dough of Parthy Ann's organism. Andy told her that
his real name was André and that he was descended,
through his mother, from a long line of Basque fisher
folk who had lived in the vicinity of St. Jean-de-Luz,
Basses-Pyrénées. It probably was true, and certainly
accounted for his swarthy skin, his bright brown eyes,
his impulsiveness, his vivacious manner. The first
time he kissed this tall, raw-boned New England woman
he was startled at the robustness with which she met
and returned the caress. They were married and went
to Illinois to live in the little town of Thebes, on the

Mississippi. In the village from which she had married it was said that, after she left, her old father, naturally neat and trained through years of nagging to super-neatness, indulged in an orgy of disorder that lasted days. As other men turn to strong drink in time of exuberance or relief from strain, so the tidy old septua-genarian strewed the kitchen with dirty dishes and scummy pots and pans; slept for a week in an unmade bed; padded in stocking feet; chewed tobacco and spat where he pleased; smoked the lace curtains brown; was even reported by a spying neighbour to have been seen seated at the reedy old cottage organ whose palsied pipes had always quavered to hymn tunes, picking out with one gnarled forefinger the chorus of a bawdy song. He lived one free, blissful year and died of his own cook-ing.

As pilot, river captain, and finally, as they thrived, owner and captain of a steamer accommodating both passengers and freight, Captain Andy was seldom in a position to be guilty of tracking the white-scoured kitchen floor or discolouring with pipe smoke the stiff folds of the window curtains. The prim little Illinois cottage saw him but rarely during the season when river navigation was at its height. For many months in the year Parthy Ann Hawks was free to lead the spinsterish existence for which nature had so evidently planned her Her window panes glittered, her linen was immaculate, her floors unsullied. When Captain Andy came home there was constant friction between them. Sometimes her gay, capering little husband used to look at this woman as at a stranger. Perhaps his nervous habit of clawing at his mutton-chop whiskers had started as a gesture of puzzlement or despair.

The child Magnolia was not born until seven years after their marriage. That Parthy Ann Hawks could produce actual offspring was a miracle to give one renewed faith in certain disputed incidents recorded in the New Testament. The child was all Andy—manner, temperament, colouring. Between father and daughter there sprang up such a bond of love and understanding as to make their relation a perfect thing, and so sturdy as successfully to defy even the destructive forces bent upon it by Mrs. Hawks. Now the little captain came home whenever it was physically possible, sacrificing time, sleep, money—everything but the safety of his boat and its passengers—for a glimpse of the child's piquant face, her gay vivacious manner, her smile that wrung you even then.

It was years before Captain Andy could persuade his wife to take a river trip with him on his steamer down to New Orleans and back again, bringing the child. It was, of course, only a ruse for having the girl with him. River captains' wives were not popular on the steamers their husbands commanded. And Parthy Ann, from that first trip, proved a terror. It was due only to tireless threats, pleadings, blandishments, and actual bribes on the part of Andy that his crew did not mutiny daily. Half an hour after embarking on that first trip, Parthy Ann poked her head into the cook's galley and told him the place was a disgrace. The cook was a woolly-headed black with a rolling protuberant eye and the quick temper of his calling.

Furthermore, though a capable craftsman, and in good standing on the river boats, he had come aboard drunk, according to time-honoured custom; not drunk to the point of being quarrelsome or incompetent, but entertaining delusions of grandeur, varied by ominous spells of sullen silence. In another twelve hours, and for the remainder of the trip, he would be sober and himself. Captain Andy knew this, understood him, was satisfied with him.

Now one of his minions was seated on an upturned pail just outside the door, peeling a great boiler full of potatoes with almost magic celerity and very little economy.

Parthy Ann's gimlet eye noted the plump peelings as they fell in long spirals under the sharp blade. She lost no time.

"Well, I declare! Of all the shameful waste I ever clapped my eyes on, that's the worst."

The black at the stove turned to face her, startled and uncomprehending. Visitors were not welcome in the cook's galley. He surveyed without enthusiasm the lean figure with the long finger pointing accusingly at a quite innocent pan of potato parings.

"Wha' that you say, missy?"

"Don't you missy me!" snapped Parthy Ann Hawks. "And what I said was that I never saw such criminal waste as those potato parings. An inch thick if they're a speck, and no decent cook would allow it."

A simple, ignorant soul, the black man, and a somewhat savage; as mighty in his small domain as Captain Andy in his larger one. All about him now were his helpers, black men like himself, with rolling eyes and great lips all too ready to gash into grins if this hard-visaged female intruder were to worst him.

"Yo-all passenger on this boat, missy?"

Parthy Ann surveyed disdainfully the galley's interior, cluttered with the disorder attendant on the preparation of the noonday meal.

"Passenger! H'mph! No, I'm not. And passenger or no passenger, a filthier hole I never saw in my born days. I'll let you know that I shall make it my business to report this state of things to the Captain. Good food going to waste——"

A red light seemed to leap then from the big Negro's eyeballs. His lips parted in a kind of savage and mirthless grin, so that you saw his great square gleaming teeth and the blue gums above them. Quick as a panther he reached down with one great black paw into the pan of parings, straightened, and threw the mass, wet and slimy as it was, full at her. The spirals clung and curled about her—on her shoulders, around her neck, in the folds of her gown, on her head, Medusa-like.

"They's something for you take to the Captain to show him, missy."

He turned sombrely back to his stove. The other blacks were little less grave than he. They sensed something sinister in the fury with which this garbage-hung figure ran screaming to the upper deck. The scene above decks must have been a harrowing one.

They put him off at Memphis and shipped another cook there, and the big Negro, thoroughly sobered now, went quite meekly down the gangplank and up the levee, his carpet bag in hand. In fact, it was said that, when he had learned it was the Captain's wife whom he had treated thus, he had turned a sort of ashen gray and had tried to jump overboard and swim ashore. The gay little Captain Andy was a prime favourite with his crew. Shamefaced though the Negro was, there appeared something akin to pity in the look he turned on Captain Andy as he was put ashore. If that was true, then the look on the little captain's face as he regarded the miscreant was certainly born of an inward and badly concealed admiration. It was said, too, but never verified, that something round and gold and gleaming was seen to pass from the Captain's hairy little brown hand to the big black paw.

For the remainder of the trip Mrs. Hawks constituted herself a sort of nightmarish housekeeper, prowling from corridor to cabins, from dining saloon to pantry. She made life wretched for the pert yellow wenches who performed the cabin chamber-work. She pounced upon them when they gathered in little whispering groops, gossiping. Thin-lipped and baleful of eye, she withered the very words they were about to utter to a waiter or deck-hand, so that the flowers of coquetry became ashes on their tongues. She regarded the female passengers with suspicion and the males with contempt. This was the latter '70s, and gambling was as much a part of river-boat life as eating and drinking. Professional gamblers often infested the boats. It was no uncommon sight to see a poker game that had started in the saloon in the early evening still in progress when sunrise reddened the river. It was the day of the flowing moustache, the broad-brimmed hat, the open-faced collar, and the diamond stud. It constituted masculine America's last feeble flicker of the picturesque before he sank for ever into the drab ashes of uniformity. A Southern gentleman, particularly, clad thus, took on a dashing and dangerous aspect. The rakish angle of the hat with its curling brim, the flowing ends of the string tie, the movement of the slender virile fingers as they stroked the moustache, all were things to thrill the feminine beholder. Even that frigid female, Parthenia Ann Hawks, must have known a little flutter of the senses as she beheld these romantic and—according to her standards—dissolute passengers seated, silent, wary, pale, about the gaming table. But in her stern code, that which thrilled was wicked. She belonged to the tribe of the Knitting Women; of the Salem Witch Burners; of all fanatics who count nature as an enemy to be suppressed; and in whose veins the wine of life runs vinegar. If the deep seepage of Parthy Ann's mind could have been brought to the surface, it would have analyzed chemically thus: "I find these men beautiful, stirring, desirable. But that is an abomination. I must not admit to myself that I am affected thus. Therefore I think and I say that they are disgusting, ridiculous, contemptible."

Her attitude was somewhat complicated by the fact that, as wife of the steamer's captain, she was treated with a courtly deference on the part of these very gentlemen whom she affected to despise; and with a gracious cordiality by their ladies. The Southern men, especially, gave an actual effect of plumes on their wide-brimmed soft hats as they bowed and addressed her in their soft drawling vernacular.

"Well, ma'am, and how are you enjoying your trip on your good husband's magnificent boat?" It sounded much richer and more flattering as they actually said it. " . . . Yo' trip on yo' good husband's ma-a-a-yg-nif'cent . . ." They gave one the feeling that they were really garbed in satin, sword, red heels, lace ruffles.

Parthenia Ann, whose stays always seemed, somehow, to support her form more stiffly than did those of any other female, would regard her inquirers with a cold and fishy eye.

"The boat's well enough, I suppose. But what with the carousing by night and the waste by day, a Christian soul can hardly look on at it without feeling that some dreadful punishment will overtake us all before we arrive at the end of our journey." From her tone you would almost have gathered that she hoped it.

He of the broad-brimmed hat, and his bustled, basqued alpaca lady, would perhaps exchange a glance not altogether amused. Collisions, explosions, snag-founderings were all too common in the river traffic of the day to risk this deliberate calling down of wrath.

Moving away, the soft-tongued Southern voices would be found to be as effective in vituperation as in flattery. "Pole cat!" he of the phantom plumes would say, aside, to his lady.

Fortunately, Parthy Ann's dour misgivings did not materialize. The trip downstream proved a delightful one, and as tranquil as might be with Mrs. Hawks on board. Captain Andy's steamer, though by no means as large as some of the so-called floating palaces that plied the Mississippi, was known for the excellence of its table, the comfort of its appointments, and the affability of its crew. So now the passengers endured the irritation of Mrs. Hawks' presence under the balm of appetizing food and good-natured service. The crew suffered her nagging for the sake of the little captain, whom they liked and respected; and for his wages, which were generous.

Though Parthenia Ann Hawks regarded the great river—if, indeed, she noticed it at all—merely as a moist highway down which one travelled with ease to New Orleans; untouched by its mystery, unmoved by its majesty, unsubdued by its sinister power, she must still, in spite of herself, have come, however faintly and remotely, under the spell of its enchantment. For this trip proved, for her, to be the first of many, and led, finally, to her spending seven months out of the twelve, not only on the Mississippi, but on the Ohio, the Missouri, the Kanawha, the Big Sandy. Indeed, her liking for the river life, together with her zeal for reforming it, became so marked that in time river travellers began to show a preference for steamers other than Captain Andy's, excellently though they fared thereon.

Perhaps the attitude of the lady passengers toward the little captain and the manner of the little captain as he addressed the lady passengers did much to feed the flame of Parthy Ann's belligerence. Until the coming of Andy Hawks she had found favour in no man's eyes.

Cut in the very pattern of spinsterhood, she must actually have had moments of surprise and even incredulity at finding herself a wife and mother. The art of coquetry was unknown to her; because the soft blandishments of love had early been denied her she now repudiated them as sinful; did her hair in a knob; eschewed flounces; assumed a severe demeanour; and would have been the last to understand that any one of these repressions was a confession. All about her—and Captain Andy—on the steamship were captivating females, full of winning wiles; wives of Southern planters; cream-skinned Creoles from New Orleans, indolent, heavy-lidded, bewitching; or women folk of prosperous Illinois or Iowa merchants, lawyers, or manufacturers making a pleasure jaunt of the Southern business trip with husband or father.

And, "Oh, Captain Hawks!" they said; and, "Oh, Captain Andy! Do come here like a nice man and tell us what it means when that little bell rings so fast? . . . And why do they call it the hurricane deck? . . . Oh, Captain Hawks, is that a serpent tattooed on the back of your hand! I declare it is! Look, Emmaline! Emmaline, look! This naughty Captain Andy has a serpent . . ."

Captain Andy's social deportment toward women was made up of that most devastating of combinations, a deferential manner together with an audacious tongue. A tapering white finger, daringly tracing a rosy nail over the blue coils of the tattooed serpent, would find itself gently imprisoned beneath the hard little brown paw that was Andy's free hand.

"After this," the little captain would say, thoughtfully, "it won't be long before that particular tattoo will be entirely worn away. Yes, ma'am! No more serpent."

"But why?"

"Erosion, ma'am."

"E—but I don't understand. I'm so stupid. I——"

Meltingly, the wicked little monkey, "I'll be so often kissing the spot your lovely finger has traced, ma'am."

"Oh-h-h-h!" A smart tap of rebuke with her palm-leaf fan. "You *are* a saucy thing. Emmaline, did you hear what this wicked captain said!"

Much of the freedom that Magnolia enjoyed on this first trip she owed to her mother's quivering preoccupation with these vivacious ladies.

If the enchantment of the river had been insidious enough to lure even Mrs. Hawks, certainly the child Magnolia fell completely under its magic spell. From that first trip on the Mississippi she was captive in its coils. Twenty times daily, during that leisurely journey from St. Louis to New Orleans, Mrs. Hawks dragged her child, squirming and protesting, from the pilot house perched atop the steamer or from the engine room in its bowels. Refurbished, the grime removed from face and hands, dressed in a clean pinafore, she was thumped on one of the red plush fauteuils of the gaudy saloon. Magnolia's hair was almost black and without a vestige of natural curl. This last was a great cross to Mrs. Hawks, who spent hours wetting and twining the long dank strands about her forefinger with a fine-toothed comb in an unconvincing attempt to make a swan out of her duckling. The rebellious little figure stood clamped between her mother's relentless knees. Captured thus, and made fresh, her restless feet in their clean white stockings and little strapped black slippers sticking straight out before her, her starched skirts stiffly spread, she was told to conduct herself as a young lady of her years and high position should.

"Listen to the conversation of the ladies and gentlemen about you," Mrs. Hawks counselled her, severely, "instead of to the low talk of those greasy engineers and pilots you're always running off to. I declare I don't know what your father is thinking of, to allow it. . . . Or read your book. . . . Then where is it? Where is the book I bought you especially to read on this trip? You haven't opened it, I'll be bound. . . . Go get it and come back directly."

A prissy tale about a female Rollo so prim that Magnolia was sure she turned her toes out even in her sleep. When she returned with a book (if she returned at all) it was likely to be of a quite different sort—a blood-curdling tale of the old days of river-banditry—a story, perhaps, of the rapacious and brutal Murrel and his following of ten hundred cut-throats sworn to do his evil will; and compared to whom Jesse James was a philanthropist. The book would have been loaned her by one of the crew. She adored these bloody tales and devoured them with the avidity that she always showed for any theme that smacked of the river. It was snatched away soon enough when it came under her mother's watchful eye.

Magnolia loathed the red plush and gilt saloon except at night, when its gilding and mirrors took on a false glitter and richness from the kerosene lamps that filled wall brackets and chandeliers. Then it was that the lady passengers, their daytime alpacas and serges replaced by silks, sat genteelly conversing, reading, or embroidering. Then, if ever, the gentlemen twirled their mustachios most fiercely so that the diamond on the third finger of the right hand sparkled entrancingly. Magnolia derived a sensory satisfaction from the scene. The rich red of the carpet fed her, and the yellow glow of the lamps. In her best cashmere dress of brown with the polonaise cut up the front and around the bottom in deep turrets she sat alertly watching the elaborate posturings of the silken ladies and the broadcloth gentlemen.

Sometimes one of the ladies sang to the hoarse accompaniment of the ship's piano, whose tones always sounded as though the Mississippi River mist had lodged permanently in its chords. The Southern ladies rendered tinkling and sentimental ballads. The Midwestern wives were wont to deliver themselves of songs of a somewhat sterner stuff. There was one song in particular, sung by a plain and falsetto lady hailing from Iowa, that aroused in Magnolia a savage (though quite reasoning) loathing. It was entitled Waste Not, Want Not; Or: You Never Miss The Water Till The Well Runs Dry. Not being a psychologist, Magnolia did not know why, during the rendition of the first verse and the chorus, she always longed to tear her best

dress into ribbons and throw a barrel of flour and a
dozen hams into the river. The song ran:

> When a child I lived at Lincoln,
> With my parents at the farm,
> The lessons that my mother taught,
> To me were quite a charm.
> She would often take me on her knee,
> When tired of childish play,
> And as she press'd me to her breast,
> I've heard my mother say:

Chorus: Waste not, want not, is a maxim I would teach——

Escape to the decks or the pilot house was impossible
of accomplishment by night. She extracted what
savour she could from the situation. This, at least,
was better than being sent off to bed. All her disorderly
life Magnolia went to bed only when all else failed.
Then, too, once in her tiny cabin she could pose and
swoop before the inadequate mirror in pitiless imitation
of the arch alpacas and silks of the red plush saloon;
tapping an imaginary masculine shoulder with a phantom fan; laughing in an elegant falsetto; grimacing
animatedly as she squeaked, "Deah, yes!" and "Deah,
no!" moistening a forelock of her straight black hair
with a generous dressing of saliva wherewith to paste
flat to her forehead the modish spit-curl that graced the
feminine adult coiffure.

But during the day she and her father often contrived
to elude the maternal duenna. With her hand in that
of the little captain, she roamed the boat from stem to
stern, from bunkers to pilot house. Down in the engine
room she delightedly heard the sweating engineer

denounce the pilot, decks above him, as a goddam Pittsburgh brass pounder because that monarch, to achieve a difficult landing, had to ring more bells than the engineer below thought necessary to an expert. But best of all Magnolia loved the bright, gay, glass-enclosed pilot house high above the rest of the boat and reached by the ultimate flight of steep narrow stairs. From this vantage point you saw the turbulent flood of the Mississippi, a vast yellow expanse, spread before you and all around you; for ever rushing ahead of you, no matter how fast you travelled; sometimes whirling about in its own tracks to turn and taunt you with your unwieldy ponderosity; then leaping on again. Sometimes the waters widened like a sea so that one could not discern the dim shadow of the farther shore; again they narrowed, snake-like, crawling so craftily that the side-wheeler boomed through the chutes with the willows brushing the decks. You never knew what lay ahead of you—that is, Magnolia never knew. That was part of the fascination of it. The river curved and twisted and turned and doubled. Mystery always lay just around the corner of the next bend. But her father knew. And Mr. Pepper, the chief pilot, always knew. You couldn't believe that it was possible for any human brain to remember the things that Captain Andy and Mr. Pepper knew about that treacherous, shifting, baffling river. Magnolia delighted to test them. She played a game with Mr. Pepper and with her father, thus:

"What's next?"

"Kinney's woodpile."

"Now what?"

"Ealer's Bend."

"What'll be there, when we come round that corner?"

"Patrie's Plantation."

"What's around that bend?"

"An old cottonwood with one limb hanging down, struck by lightning."

"What's coming now?"

"A stump sticking out of the water at Higgin's Point."

They always were right. It was magic. It was incredible. They knew, too, the depth of the water. They could point out a spot and say, "That used to be an island—Buckle's Island."

"But it's water! It couldn't be an island. It's water. We're—why, we're riding on it now."

Mr. Pepper would persist, unmoved. "Used to be an island." Or, pointing again, "Two years ago I took her right down through there where that point lays."

"But it's dry land. You're just fooling, aren't you, Mr. Pepper? Because you couldn't take a boat on dry land. It's got things growing on it! Little trees, even. So how could you?"

"Water there two years ago—good eleven foot."

Small wonder Magnolia was early impressed with this writhing monster that, with a single lash of its tail, could wipe a solid island from the face of the earth, or with a convulsion of its huge tawny body spew up a tract of land where only water had been.

Mr. Pepper had respect for his river. "Yessir, the Mississippi and this here Nile, over in Egypt, they're a couple of old demons. I ain't seen the Nile River,

myself. Don't expect to. This old river's enough for
one man to meet up with in his life. Like marrying.
Get to learn one woman's ways real good, you know
about all there is to women and you got about all you
can do one lifetime."

Not at all the salty old graybeard pilot of fiction,
this Mr. Pepper. A youth of twenty-four, nerveless,
taciturn, gentle, profane, charming. His clear brown
eyes, gazing unblinkingly out upon the river, had tiny
golden flecks in them, as though something of the river
itself had taken possession of him, and become part of
him. Born fifty years later, he would have been the
steel stuff of which aviation aces are made.

Sometimes, in deep water, Mr. Pepper actually permitted Magnolia to turn the great pilot wheel that
measured twice as high as she. He stood beside her, of
course; or her father, if he chanced to be present, stood
behind her. It was thrilling, too, when her father took
the wheel in an exciting place—where the water was
very shoal, perhaps; or where the steamer found a stiff
current pushing behind her, and the tricky dusk coming
on. At first it puzzled Magnolia that her father,
omnipotent in all other parts of the *Creole Belle*, should
defer to this stripling; should actually be obliged, on
his own steamer, to ask permission of the pilot to take
the wheel. They were both beautifully formal and
polite about it.

"What say to my taking her a little spell, Mr. Pepper?"

"Not at all, Captain Hawks. Not at all, sir," Mr.
Pepper would reply, cordially if ambiguously. His

gesture as he stepped aside and relinquished the wheel was that of one craftsman who recognizes and respects the ability of another. Andy Hawks had been a crack Mississippi River pilot in his day. And then to watch Captain Andy skinning the wheel—climbing it round and round, hands and feet, and looking for all the world like a talented little monkey.

Magnolia even learned to distinguish the bells by tone. There was the Go Ahead, soprano-voiced. Mr. Pepper called it the Jingle. He explained to Magnolia: "When I give the engineer the Jingle, why, he knows I mean for him to give her all she's got." Strangely enough, the child, accustomed to the sex of boats and with an uncannily quick comprehension of river jargon, understood him, nodded her head so briskly that the hand-made curls jerked up and down like bell-ropes. "Sometimes it's called the Soprano. Then the Centre Bell—the Stopping Bell—that's middle tone. About alto. This here, that's the Astern Bell—the backup bell. That's bass. The Boom-Boom, you call it. Here's how you can remember them: The Jingle, the Alto, and the Boom-Boom."

A charming medium through which to know the river, Mr. Pepper. An enchanting place from which to view the river, that pilot house. Magnolia loved its shining orderliness, disorderly little creature that she was. The wilderness of water and woodland outside made its glass-enclosed cosiness seem the snugger. Oilcloth on the floor. You opened the drawer of the little table and there lay Mr. Pepper's pistol, glittering and sinister; and Mr. Pepper's Pilot Rules. Magnolia

lingered over the title printed on the brick-coloured
paper binding:

PILOT RULES
FOR THE
RIVERS WHOSE WATERS FLOW INTO THE GULF OF
MEXICO AND THEIR TRIBUTARIES
AND FOR
THE RED RIVER OF THE NORTH

The Red River of the North! There was something in
the words that thrilled her; sent little delicious prickles
up and down her spine.

There was a bright brass cuspidor. The expertness
with which Mr. Pepper and, for that matter, Captain
Hawks himself, aimed for the centre of this glittering receptacle and sustained a one-hundred-per-cent.
record was as fascinating as any other feature of this
delightful place. Visitors were rarely allowed up there.
Passengers might peer wistfully through the glass en-
closure from the steps below, but there they were confronted by a stern and forbidding sign which read:
No Visitors Allowed. Magnolia felt very superior and
slightly contemptuous as she looked down from her
vantage point upon these unfortunates below. Sometimes, during mid-watch, a very black texas-tender in a
very white starched apron would appear with coffee
and cakes or ices for Mr. Pepper. Magnolia would have
an ice, too, shaving it very fine to make it last; licking
the spoon luxuriously with little lightning flicks of her
tongue and letting the frozen sweet slide, a slow delicious trickle, down her grateful throat.

"Have another cake, Miss Magnolia," Mr. Pepper would urge her. "A pink one, I'd recommend, this time."

"I don't hardly think my mother——"

Mr. Pepper, himself, surprisingly enough, the father of twins, was sure her mother would have no objection; would, if present, probably encourage the suggestion. Magnolia bit quickly into the pink cake. A wild sense of freedom flooded her. She felt like the river, rushing headlong on her way.

To be snatched from this ecstatic state was agony. The shadow of the austere and disapproving maternal figure loomed always just around the corner. At any moment it might become reality. The knowledge that this was so made Magnolia's first taste of Mississippi River life all the more delicious.

III

GRIM force though she was, it would be absurd to fix upon Parthy Ann Hawks as the sole engine whose relentless functioning cut down the profits of Captain Andy's steamboat enterprise. That other metal monster, the railroad, with its swift-turning wheels and its growing network of lines, was weaving the doom of river traffic. The Prince Albert coats and the alpaca basques were choosing a speedier, if less romantic, way to travel from Natchez to Memphis, or from Cairo to Vicksburg. Illinois, Minnesota, and Iowa business men were favouring a less hazardous means of transporting their merchandise. Farmers were freighting their crops by land instead of water. The river steamboat was fast becoming an anachronism. The jig, Captain Andy saw, was up. Yet the river was inextricably interwoven with his life—was his life, actually. He knew no other background, was happy in no other surroundings, had learned no other trade. These streams, large and small of the North, the Mid-west, the South, with their harsh yet musical Indian names—Kaskaskia, Cahokia, Yazoo, Monongahela, Kanawha—he knew in every season: their currents, depths, landings, banks, perils. The French strain in him on the distaff side did not save him from pronouncing the foreign names of Southern rivers as

murderously as did the other rivermen. La Fourche
was the Foosh. Bayou Teche was Bayo Tash. As
for names such as Plaquemine, Paincourteville, and
Thibodaux—they emerged mutilated beyond recognition, with entire syllables lopped off, and flat vowels
protruding everywhere. Anything else would have
been considered affected.

Captain Andy thought only in terms of waterways.
Despite the prim little house in Thebes, home, to Andy,
was a boat. Towns and cities were to him mere sources
of supplies and passengers, set along the river banks
for the convenience of steamboats. He knew every
plank in every river-landing from St. Paul to Baton
Rouge. As the sky is revealed, a printed page, to the
astronomer, so Andy Hawks knew and interpreted every
reef, sand bar, current, and eddy in the rivers that
drained the great Mississippi Basin. And of these he
knew best of all the Mississippi herself. He loved her,
feared her, respected her. Now her courtiers and lovers
were deserting her, one by one, for an iron-throated,
great-footed, brazen-voiced hussy. Andy, among the
few, remained true.

To leave the river—to engage, perforce, in some
landlubberly pursuit was to him unthinkable. On the
rivers he was a man of consequence. As a captain and
pilot of knowledge and experience his opinion was deferred to. Once permanently ashore, penduluming pro-
saically between the precise little household and some
dull town job, he would degenerate and wither until
inevitably he who now was Captain Andy Hawks,
owner and master of the steamboat *Creole Belle*, would

be known merely as the husband of Parthy Ann Hawks, that Mistress of the Lace Curtains, Priestess of the Parlour Carpet, and Keeper of the Kitchen Floor. All this he did not definitely put into words; but he sensed it.

He cast about in his alert mind, and made his plans craftily, and put them warily, for he knew the force of Parthenia's opposition.

"I see here where old Ollie Pegram's fixing to sell his show boat." He was seated in the kitchen, smoking his pipe and reading the local newspaper. "*Cotton Blossom*, she's called."

Parthy Ann was not one to simulate interest where she felt none. Bustling between stove and pantry she only half heard him. "Well, what of it?"

Captain Andy rattled the sheet he was holding, turned a page leisurely, meanwhile idly swinging one leg, as he sat with knees crossed. Each movement was calculated to give the effect of casualness.

"Made a fortune in the show-boat business, Ollie has. Ain't a town on the river doesn't wait for the *Cotton Blossom*. Yessir. Anybody buys that outfit is walking into money."

"Scallywags." Thus, succinctly, Parthenia thought to dismiss the subject while voicing her opinion of water thespians.

"Scallywags nothing! Some of the finest men on the river in the show-boat business. Look at Pegram! Look at Finnegan! Look at Hosey Watts!"

It was Mrs. Hawks' habit to express contempt by reference to a ten-foot pole, this being an imaginary implement of disdain and a weapon of defence which was her Excalibur. She now announced that not only would she decline to look at the above-named gentlemen, but that she could not be induced to touch any of them with a ten-foot pole. She concluded with the repetitious "Scallywags!" and evidently considered the subject closed.

Two days later, the first pang of suspicion darted through her when Andy renewed the topic with an assumption of nonchalance that failed to deceive her this time. It was plain to this astute woman that he had been thinking concentratedly about show boats since their last brief conversation. It was at supper. Andy should have enjoyed his home-cooked meals more than he actually did. They always were hot, punctual, palatable. Parthenia had kept her cooking hand. Yet he often ate abstractedly and unappreciatively. Perhaps he missed the ceremony, the animation, the sociability that marked the meal hours in the dining saloon of the *Creole Belle*. The Latin in him, and the unconsciously theatrical in him, loved the mental picture of himself in his blue coat with brass buttons and gold braid, seated at the head of the long table while the alpacas twittered, "Do you think so, Captain Hawks?" and the Prince Alberts deferred to him with, "What's your opinion, sir?" and the soft-spoken black stewards in crackling white jackets bent over him with steaming platters and tureens.

Parthenia did not hold with conversation at meal time. Andy and Magnolia usually carried on such talk as occurred at table. Strangely enough, there was in his tone toward the child none of the usual patronizing attitude of the adult. No what-did-you-learn-at-school; no have-you-been-a-good-girl-to-day. They conversed like two somewhat rowdy grown-ups, constantly chafed by the reprovals of the prim Parthenia. It was a habit of Andy seldom to remain seated in his chair throughout a meal. Perhaps this was due to the fact that he frequently was called away from table while in command of his steamer. At home his jumpiness was a source of great irritation to Mrs. Hawks. Her contributions to the conversation varied little.

"Pity's sake, Hawks, sit still! That's the third time you've been up and down, and supper not five minutes on the table. . . . Eat your potato, Magnolia, or not a bite of cup cake do you get. . . . That's a fine story to be telling a child, I must say, Andy Hawks. . . . Can't you talk of anything but a lot of good-for-nothing drunken river roustabouts! . . . Drink your milk, Maggie. . . . Oh, stop fidgeting, Hawks! . . . Don't cut away all the fat like that, Magnolia. No wonder you're so skinny I'm ashamed of you and the neighbours think you don't get enough to eat."

Like a swarm of maddening mosquitoes, these admonitions buzzed through and above and around the conversation of the man and the child.

To-night Andy's talk dwelt on a dramatic incident that had been told him that day by the pilot of the show boat *New Sensation*, lately burned to the water's edge. He went on vivaciously, his bright brown eyes sparkling with interest and animation. Now and then, he jumped up from the table the better to illustrate a situation. Magnolia was following his every word and gesture with spellbound attention. She never had been permitted to see a show-boat performance. When one of these gay water travellers came prancing down the river, band playing, calliope tooting, flags flying, towboat puffing, bringing up with a final flare and flourish at the landing, there to tie up for two or three days, or even, sometimes, for a week, Magnolia was admonished not to go near it. Other children of the town might swarm over it by day, enchanted by its mystery, enthralled by its red-coated musicians when the band marched up the main street; might even, at night, witness the performance of a play and actually stay for the song-and-dance numbers which comprised the "concert" held after the play, and for which an additional charge of fifteen cents was made.

Magnolia hungered for a glimpse of these forbidden delights. The little white house at Thebes commanded a view up the river toward Cape Girardeau. At night from her bedroom window she could see the lights shining golden yellow through the boat's many windows, was fired with excitement at sight of the kerosene flares stuck in the river bank to light the way of the lucky, could actually hear the beat and blare of the band. Again and again, in her very early childhood, the spring nights when the show boats were headed downstream and the autumn nights when they were returning up river were stamped indelibly on her mind as she knelt in her nightgown at the little window of the dark room that faced the river with its dazzling and for-

bidden spectacle. Her bare feet would be as icy as her
cheeks were hot. Her ears were straining to catch the
jaunty strains of the music, and her eyes tried to discern
the faces that passed under the weird glow of the torch
flares. Usually she did not hear the approaching
tread of discovery until the metallic, "Magnolia Hawks,
get into your bed this very minute!" smote cruelly on
her entranced ears. Sometimes she glimpsed men
and women of the show-boat troupe on Front Street
or Third Street, idling or shopping. Occasionally you
saw them driving in a rig hired from Deffler's Livery
Stable. They were known to the townspeople as Show
Folks, and the term carried with it the sting of oppro-
brium. You could mark them by something different
in their dress, in their faces, in the way they walked.
The women were not always young. Magnolia noticed
that often they were actually older than her mother
(Parthy was then about thirty-nine). Yet they looked
lively and somehow youthful, though their faces bore
wrinkles. There was about them a certain care-free
gaiety, a jauntiness. They looked, Magnolia decided,
as if they had just come from some interesting place and
were going to another even more interesting. This was
rather shrewd of her. She had sensed that the dulness
of village and farm life, the look that routine, drudgery,
and boredom stamp indelibly on the countenance of the
farm woman or the village housewife, were absent in
these animated and often odd faces. Once she had
encountered a little group of three—two women and a
man—strolling along the narrow plank sidewalk near
the Hawks house. They were eating fruit out of a bag,

sociably, and spitting out the seeds, and laughing and chatting and dawdling. One of the women was young and very pretty, and her dress, Magnolia thought, was the loveliest she had ever seen. Its skirt of navy blue was kilted in the back, and there were puffs up each side edged with passementerie. On her head, at a saucy angle, was a chip bonnet of blue, trimmed with beaded lace, and ribbon, and adorable pink roses. The other woman was much older. There were queer deep lines in her face—not wrinkles, though Magnolia could not know this, but the scars left when the gashes of experience have healed. Her eyes were deep, and dark, and dead. She was carelessly dressed, and the box-pleated tail of her flounced black gown trailed in the street, so that it was filmed with a gray coating of dust. The veil wound round her bonnet hung down her back, imparting a Spanish and mysterious look. The man, too, though young and tall and not bad-looking, wore an unkempt look. His garments were ill assorted. His collar boasted no cravat. But all three had a charming air of insouciance as they strolled up the tree-shaded village street, laughing and chatting and munching and spitting out cherry stones with a little childish ballooning of the cheeks. Magnolia hung on the Hawks fence gate and stared. The older woman caught her eye and smiled, and immediately Magnolia decided that she liked her better than she did the pretty, young one, so after a moment's grave inspection she smiled in return her sudden, brilliant wide smile.

"Look at that child," said the older woman. "All of a sudden she's beautiful."

The other two surveyed her idly. Magnolia's smile
had vanished now. They saw a scrawny sallow little
girl, big-eyed, whose jaw conformation was too plainly
marked, whose forehead was too high and broad, and
whose black hair deceived no one into believing that its
dank curls were other than tortured.

"You're crazy, Julie," remarked the pretty girl, without heat; and looked away, uninterested.

But between Magnolia and the older woman a fila-
ment of live liking had leaped. "Hello, little girl,"
said the older woman.

Magnolia continued to stare, gravely; said nothing.

"Won't you say hello to me?" the woman persisted;
and smiled again. And again Magnolia returned her
smile. "There!" the woman exclaimed, in triumph.
"What did I tell you!"

"Cat's got her tongue," the sloppy young man remarked as his contribution to the conversation.

"Oh, come on," said the pretty girl; and popped
another cherry into her mouth.

But the woman persisted. She addressed Magnolia
gravely. "When you grow up, don't smile too often;
but smile whenever you want anything very much, or
like any one, or want them to like you. But I guess
maybe you'll learn that without my telling you. . . .
Listen, won't you say hello to me? H'm?"

Magnolia melted. "I'm not allowed," she explained.

"Not——? Why not? Pity's sake!"

"Because you're show-boat folks. My mama won't
let me talk to show-boat folks."

"Damned little brat," said the pretty girl, and spat out a cherry stone. The man laughed.

With a lightning gesture the older woman took off her hat, stuffed it under the man's arm, twisted her abundant hair into a knob off her face, pulled down her mouth and made a narrow line of her lips, brought her elbows sharply to her side, her hands clasped, her shoulders suddenly pinched.

"Your mama looks like this," she said.

"Why, how did you know!" cried Magnolia, amazed. The three burst into sudden loud laughter. And at that Parthy Hawks appeared at the door, bristling, protective.

"Maggie Hawks, come into the house this minute!"

The laughter of the three then was redoubled. The quiet little village street rang with it as they continued their leisurely care-free ramble up the sun-dappled leafy path.

Now her father, at supper, had a tale to tell of these forbidden fascinators. The story had been told him that afternoon by Hard Harry Swager, river pilot, just in at the landing after a thrilling experience.

"Seems they were playing at China Grove, on the Chappelia. Yessir. Well, this girl—La Verne, her name was, or something—anyway, she was on the stage singing, he says. It was the concert, after the show. She comes off and the next thing you know there's a little blaze in the flies. Next minute she was afire and no saving her." To one less initiated it might have been difficult to differentiate in his use of the pronoun, third person, feminine. Sometimes he referred to the girl, sometimes to the boat. "Thirty years old if she's a day and burns like greased paper. Went up in ten minutes. Hard Harry goes running to the pilot house to get his clothes. Time he reaches the boiler deck, fire has cut off the gangway. He tries to lower himself twelve feet from the boiler deck to the main, and falls and breaks his leg. By that time they were cutting the tow-boat away from the *Sensation* to save her. Did save her, too, finally. But the *Sensation* don't last long's it takes to tell it. Well, there he was, and what did they have to do but send four miles inland for a doctor, and when he comes, the skunk, guess what?"

"What!" cries Magnolia not merely to be obliging in this dramatic crisis, but because she is frantic to know. Captain Andy is on his feet by this time, fork in hand.

"When the doc comes he takes a look around, and there they all are in any kind of clothes they could grab or had on. So he says he won't set the leg unless he's paid in advance, twenty-five dollars. 'Oh, you won't, won't you!' says Hard Harry, laying there with his broken leg. And draws. 'You'll set it or I'll shoot yours off so you won't ever walk again, you son of a bitch!'"

"Captain Andy Hawks!"

He has acted it out. The fork is his gun. Magnolia is breathless. Now both gaze, stricken, at Mrs. Hawks. Their horror is not occasioned by the word spoken but by the interruption.

"Go on!" shouts Magnolia; and bounces up and down in her chair. "Go *on!*"

But the first fine histrionic flavour has been poisoned

by that interruption. Andy takes his seat at table. He resumes the eating of his pork steak and potatoes, but listlessly. Perhaps he is a little ashamed of the extent to which he has been carried away by his own recital. "Slipped out," he mumbled.

"Well, I should say as much!" Parthy retorted, ambiguously. "What kind of language can a body expect, you hanging around show-boat riff-raff."

Magnolia would not be cheated of her dénouement. "But did he? Did he shoot it off, or did he fix it, or what? What did he do?"

"He set it, all right. They gave him his twenty-five and told him to get the h—— to get out of there, and he got. But they had to get the boat out—the towboat they'd saved—and no pilot but Hard Harry. So next day they put him on the hurricane deck, under a tarpaulin because the rain was pouring the way it does down there worse than any place in the world, just about. And with two men steering, he brings the boat to Baton Rouge seventy-five miles through bayou and Mississippi. Yessir."

Magnolia breathed again.

"And who's this," demanded Mrs. Hawks, "was telling you all this fol-de-rol, did you say?"

"Swager himself. Harry. Hard Harry Swager, they call him." (You could see the ten-foot pole leap of itself into Mrs. Hawks' hand as her fingers drummed the tablecloth.) "I was talking to him to-day. Here of late he's been with the *New Sensation*. He piloted the *Cotton Blossom* for years till Pegram decided to quit. Well, sir! He says five hundred people a night on the show boat was nothing, and eight hundred on Saturday nights in towns with a good back-country. Let me tell you right here and now that runs into money. Say a quarter of 'em's fifty centers, a half thirty-five, and the rest twenty-five. The niggers all twenty-five up in the gallery, course. Naught . . . five times five's . . . five and carry the two . . . five times two's ten carry the one . . . five . . ."

Parthy was no fool. She sensed that here threatened a situation demanding measures even more than ordinarily firm.

"I may not know much"—another form of locution often favoured by her. The tone in which it was spoken utterly belied the words; the tone told you that not only did she know much, but all. "I may not know much, but this I do know. You've got something better to do with your time than loafing down at the landing like a river rat with that scamp Swager. Hard Harry! He comes honestly enough by that name, I'll be bound, if he never came honestly by anything else in his life. And before the child, too. Show boats! And language!"

"What's wrong with show boats?"

"Everything, and more, too. A lot of loose-living worthless scallywags, men *and* women. Scum, that's what. Trollops!" Parthy could use a good old Anglo-Saxon word herself, on occasion.

Captain Andy made frantic foray among the whiskers. He clawed like a furious little monkey—always the sign of mental disturbance in him. "No more scum than your own husband, Mrs. Hawks, ma'am. I used to be with a show-boat troupe myself."

"Pilot, yes."

"Pilot be damned." He was up now and capering like a Quilp. "Actor, Mrs. Hawks, and pretty good I was, too, time I was seventeen or eighteen. You ought to've seen me in the after-piece. Red Hot Coffee it was called. I played the nigger. Doubled in brass, too. I pounded the bass drum in the band, and it was bigger than me."

Magnolia was enchanted. She sprang up, flew round to him. "Were you really? An actor? You never told me. Mama, did you know? Did you know Papa was an actor on a show boat?"

Parthy Ann rose in her wrath. Always taller than her husband, she seemed now to tower above him. He defied her, a terrier facing a mastiff.

"What kind of talk is this, Andy Hawks! If you're making up tales to tease me before the child I'm surprised at you, that thought nothing you could do would ever surprise me again."

"It's the truth. The *Sunny South*, she was called. Captain Jake Bofinger, owner. Married ten times, old Jake was. A pretty rough lot we were in those days, let me tell you. I remember time we——"

"Not another word, Captain Hawks. And let me tell you it's a good thing for you that you kept it from me all these years. I'd never have married you if I'd known. A show-boat actor!"

"Oh, yes, you would, Parthy. And glad of the chance."

Words. Bickering. Recriminations. Finally, "I'll thank you not to mention show boats again in front of the child. You with your La Vernes and your Hard Harrys and your concerts and broken legs and fires and ten wives and language and what not! I don't want to be dirtied by it, nor the child. . . . Run out and play, Magnolia. . . . And let this be the last of show-boat talk in this house."

Andy breathed deep, clung with both hands to his whiskers, and took the plunge. "It's far from being the last of it, Parthy. I've bought the *Cotton Blossom* from Pegram."

IV

MANY quarrels had marked their married life, but this one assumed serious proportions. It was a truly sinister note in the pageant of mismating that passed constantly before Magnolia's uncomprehending eyes in childhood. Parthenia had opposed him often, and certainly always when a new venture or plan held something of the element of unconventionality. But now the Puritan in her ran rampant. He would disgrace her before the community. He was ruining the life of his child. She would return to her native New England. He would not see Magnolia again. He had explained to her—rather, it had come out piecemeal—that his new project would necessitate his absence from home for months at a time. He would be away, surely, from April until November. If Parthy and the child would live with him on the show boat part of that time—summers—easy life—lots to see—learn the country——

The storm broke, raged, beat about his head, battered his diminutive frame. He clutched his whiskers and hung on for dear life. In the end he won.

All that Parthy ever had in her life of colour, of romance, of change, he brought her. But for him she would still be ploughing through the drifts or mud of the New England road on her way to and from the frigid little schoolhouse. But for him she would still be living her barren spinster life with her salty old father in the grim coast town whence she had come. She was to trail through the vine-hung bayous of Louisiana; float down the generous rivers of the Carolinas, of Tennessee, of Mississippi, with the silver-green weeping willows misting the water's edge. She was to hear the mellow plaintive voices of Negroes singing on the levees and in cabin doorways as the boat swept by. She would taste exotic fruits; see stirring sights; meet the fantastic figures that passed up and down the rivers like shadows drifting in and out of a weird dream. Yet always she was to resent loveliness; fight the influence of each new experience; combat the lure of each new face. Tight-lipped, belligerent, she met beauty and adventure and defied them to work a change in her.

For three days, then, following Andy's stupendous announcement, Parthenia threatened to leave him, though certainly, in an age that looked upon the marriage tie as well-nigh indissoluble by any agent other than death, she could not have meant it, straight-laced as she was. For another three days she refused to speak to him, conveying her communications to him through a third person who was, perforce, Magnolia. "Tell your father thus-and-so." This in his very presence. "Ask your father this-and-that."

Experience had taught Magnolia not to be bewildered by these tactics; she was even amused, as at a game. But finally the game wearied her; or perhaps, child though she was, an instinctive sympathy between her and her father made her aware of the pain twisting the face of the man. Suddenly she stamped her foot, issued her edict. "I won't tell him another single word for you. It's silly. I thought it was kind of fun, but it isn't. It's silly for a great big grown-up person like you that's a million years old."

Andy was absent from home all day long, and often late into the night. The *Cotton Blossom* was being overhauled from keel to pilot house. She was lying just below the landing; painters and carpenters were making her ship-shape. Andy trotted up and down the town and the river bank, talking, gesticulating, capering excitedly. There were numberless supplies to be ordered; a troupe to be assembled. He was never without a slip of paper on which he figured constantly. His pockets and the lining of his cap bristled with these paper scraps.

One week following their quarrel Parthy Ann began to evidence interest in these negotiations. She demanded details. How much had he paid for that old mass of kindling wood? (meaning, of course, the *Cotton Blossom*). How many would its theatre seat? What did the troupe number? What was their route? How many deck-hands? One cook or two? Interspersed with these questions were grumblings and dire predictions anent money thrown away; poverty in old age; the advisability of a keeper being appointed for people whose minds had palpably given way. Still, her curiosity was obviously intense.

"Tell you what," suggested Andy with what he fancied to be infinite craft. "Get your hat on come on down and take a look at her."

"Never," said Parthenia; and untied her kitchen apron.

"Well, then, let Magnolia go down and see her. She likes boats, don't you, Nola? Same's her pa."

"H'm! Likely I'd let her go," sniffed Parthy.

Andy tried another tack. "Don't you want to come and see where your papa's going to live all the months and months he'll be away from you and ma?"

At which Magnolia, with splendid dramatic sense, began to cry wildly and inconsolably. Parthy remained grim. Yet she must have been immediately disturbed, for Magnolia wept so seldom as to be considered a queer child on this count, among many others.

"Hush your noise," commanded Parthy.

Great sobs racked Magnolia. Andy crudely followed up his advantage. "I guess you'll forget how your papa looks time he gets back."

Magnolia, perfectly aware of the implausibility of any such prediction, now hurled herself at her father, wrapped her arms about him, and howled, jerking back her head, beating a tattoo with her heels, interspersing the howls with piteous supplications not to be left behind. She wanted to see the show boat; and, with the delightful memory of the *Creole Belle* trip fresh in her mind, she wanted to travel on the *Cotton Blossom* as she had never wanted anything in her life. Her eyes were staring and distended; her fingers clutched; her body writhed; her moans were heart-breaking. She gave a magnificent performance.

Andy tried to comfort her. The howls increased. Parthy tried stern measures. Hysteria. The two united then, and alarm brought pleadings, and pleadings promises, and finally the three sat intertwined, Andy's arm about Magnolia and Parthenia; Parthenia's arm embracing Andy and Magnolia; Magnolia clinging to both.

"Come get your hair combed.   Mama'll change your dress.   Now stop that crying."   Magnolia had been shaken by a final series of racking sobs, real enough now that the mechanics had been started.   Her lower lip quivered at intervals as the wet comb chased the strands of straight black hair around Mrs. Hawks' expert forefinger.   When finally she appeared in starched muslin petticoats and second-best plaid serge, there followed behind her Parthy Ann herself bonneted and cloaked for the street.   The thing was done.   The wife of a showman.   The Puritan in her shivered, but her curiosity was triumphant even over this.   They marched down Oak Street to the river landing, the child skipping and capering in her excitement.   There was, too, something of elation in Andy's walk.   If it had not been for the grim figure at his side and the restraining hand on his arm, it is not unlikely that the two—father and child— would have skipped and capered together down to the water's edge.   Mrs. Hawks' tread and mien were those of a matronly Christian martyr on her way to the lions. As they went the parents talked of unimportant things to which Magnolia properly paid no heed, having had her way. . . .   Gone most of the time. . . .   It wouldn't hurt her any, I tell you. . . .   Learn more in a week than she would in a year out of books. . . . But they *ain't*, I tell you.   Decent folks as you'd ever

want to see. Married couples, most of 'em. . . .
What do you think I'm running? A bawdy-boat? . . .
Oh, language be damned! . . . Now, Parthy,
you've got this far, don't start all over again. . . .
There she is! Ain't she pretty! Look, Magnolia!
That's where you're going to live. . . . Oh, all
right, all right! I was just talking . . .

The *Cotton Blossom* lay moored to great stobs.
Long, and wide and plump and comfortable she looked,
like a rambling house that had taken perversely to the
nautical life and now lay at ease on the river's broad
breast. She had had two coats of white paint with green
trimmings; and not the least of these green trimmings
comprised letters, a foot high, that smote Parthy's an-
guished eye, causing her to groan, and Magnolia's delighted gaze, causing her to squeal. There it was in all
the finality of painter's print:

CAPT. ANDY HAWKS COTTON BLOSSOM FLOATING PALACE THEATRE

Parthy gathered her dolman more tightly about her,
as though smitten by a chill. The clay banks of the
levee were strewn with cinders and ashes for a foothold.
The steep sides of a river bank down which they would
scramble and up which they would clamber were to be
the home path for these three in the years to come.

An awninged upper deck, like a cosy veranda, gave the
great flat boat a curiously homelike look. On the main
deck, too, the gangplank ended in a forward deck which
was like a comfortable front porch. Pillars, adorned
with scroll-work, supported this. And there, its mouth
open in a half-oval of welcome, was the ticket window

through which could be seen the little box office with its desk and chair and its wall rack for tickets. There actually were tickets stuck in this, purple and red and blue. Parthy shut her eyes as at a leprous sight. A wide doorway led into the entrance hall. There again double doors opened to reveal a stairway.

"Balcony stairs," Andy explained, "and upper boxes. Seat hundred and fifty to two hundred, easy. Niggers mostly, upstairs, of course." Parthy shuddered. An aisle to the right, an aisle to the left of this stairway, and there was the auditorium of the theatre itself, with its rows of seats and its orchestra pit; its stage, its boxes, its painted curtain raised part way so that you saw only the lower half of the Venetian water scene it depicted; the legs of gondoliers in wooden attitudes; faded blue lagoon; palace steps. Magnolia knew a pang of disappointment. True, the boxes bore shiny brass railings and boasted red plush upholstered seats.

"But I thought it would be all light and glittery and like a fairy tale," she protested.

"At night," Andy assured her. He had her warm wriggling little fingers in his. "At night. That's when it's like a fairy tale. When the lamps are lighted; and all the people; and the band playing."

"Where's the kitchen?" demanded Mrs. Hawks.

Andy leaped nimbly down into the orchestra pit, stooped, opened a little door under the stage, and beckoned. Ponderously Parthy followed. Magnolia scampered after. Dining room and cook's galley were under the stage. Great cross-beams hung so low that even Andy was forced to stoop a little to avoid battering

his head against them. Magnolia could touch them
quite easily with her finger-tips. In time it came to
seem quite natural to see the company and crew of the
Cotton Blossom entering the dining room at meal time
humbly bent as though in a preliminary attitude of
grace before meat.

There were two long tables, each accommodating
perhaps ten; and at the head of the room a smaller table
for six.

"This is our table," Andy announced, boldly, as he
indicated the third. Parthy snorted; but it seemed to
the sensitive Andy that in this snort there was just a
shade less resentment than there might have been.
Between dining room and kitchen an opening, the size
of a window frame, had been cut in the wall, and the
base of this was a broad shelf for convenience in conveying hot dishes from stove to table. As the three passed
from dining room to kitchen, Andy tossed over his
shoulder further information for the possible approval of
the bristling Parthy. "Jo and Queenie—she cooks
and he waits and washes up and one thing another—
they promised to be back April first, sure. Been with
the *Cotton Blossom*, those two have, ten years and more.
Painters been cluttering up here, and what not. And
will you look at the way the kitchen looks, spite of 'em.
Slick's a whistle. Look at that stove!" Crafty Andy.

Parthenia Ann Hawks looked at the stove. And
what a stove it was! Broad-bosomed, ample, vast, like
a huge fertile black mammal whose breast would suckle
numberless eager sprawling bubbling pots and pans.
It shone richly. Gazing upon this generous expanse

you felt that from its source could emerge nothing that was not savoury, nourishing, satisfying. Above it, and around the walls, on hooks, hung rows of pans and kettles of every size and shape, all neatly suspended by their pigtails. Here was the wherewithal for boundless cooking. You pictured whole hams, sizzling; fowls neatly trussed in rows; platoons of brown loaves; hampers of green vegetables; vast plateaus of pies. Crockery, thick, white, coarse, was piled, plate on plate, platter on platter, behind the neat doors of the pantry. A supplementary and redundant kerosene stove stood obligingly in the corner.

"Little hot snack at night, after the show," Andy explained. "Coffee or an egg, maybe, and no lighting the big wood burner."

There crept slowly, slowly over Parthy's face a look of speculation, and this in turn was replaced by an expression that was, paradoxically, at once eager and dreamy. As though aware of this she tried with words to belie her look. "All this cooking for a crowd. Take a mint of money, that's what it will."

"Make a mint," Andy retorted, blithely. A black cat, sleek, lithe, at ease, paced slowly across the floor, stood a moment surveying the two with wary yellow eyes, then sidled toward Parthy and rubbed his arched back against her skirts. "Mouser," said Andy.

"Scat!" cried Parthy; but her tone was half-hearted, and she did not move away. In her eyes gleamed the unholy light of the housewife who beholds for the first time the domain of her dreams. Jo and Queenie to boss. Wholesale marketing. Do this. Do that.

Perhaps Andy, in his zeal, had even overdone the thing a little. Suddenly, "Where's that child! Where's—— Oh, my goodness, Hawks!" Visions of Magnolia having fallen into the river. She was, later, always to have visions of Magnolia having fallen into rivers so that Magnolia sometimes fell into them out of sheer perversity as other children, cautioned to remain in the yard, wilfully run away from home.

Andy darted out of the kitchen, through the little rabbit-hutch door. Mrs. Hawks gathered up her voluminous skirts and flew after; scrambled across the orchestra pit, turned at the sound of a voice, Magnolia's, and yet not Magnolia's, coming from that portion of the stage exposed below the half-raised curtain. In tones at once throaty, mincing, and falsely elegant—that arrogant voice which is childhood's unconscious imitation of pretence in its elders—Magnolia was reciting nothing in particular, and bringing great gusto to the rendition. The words were palpably made up as she went along—"Oh, do you rully think so! . . . My little girl is very naughty . . . we are rich, oh dear me yes, ice cream every day for breakfast, dinner, and supper. . . ." She wore her mother's dolman which that lady had unclasped and left hanging over one of the brass railings of a box. From somewhere she had rummaged a bonnet whose jet aigrette quivered with the earnestness of its wearer's artistic effort. The dolman trailed in the dust of the floor. Magnolia's right hand was held in a graceful position, the little finger elegantly crooked.

"Maggie Hawks, will you come down out of there this

instant!" Parthy whirled on Andy. "There! That's
what it comes to, minute she sets foot on this sink of
iniquity. Play acting!"

Andy clawed his whiskers, chuckling. He stepped to
the proscenium and held out his arms for the child and
she stood looking down at him, flushed, smiling, radiant.
"You're about as good as your pa was, Nola. And
that's no compliment." He swung her to the floor, a
whirl of dolman, short starched skirt and bonnet askew.
Then, as Parthy snatched the dolman from her and
glared at the bonnet, he saw that he must create again a
favourable impression—contrive a new diversion—or
his recent gain was lost. A born showman, Andy.

"Where'd you get that bonnet, Magnolia?"

"In there." She pointed to one of a row of doors
facing them at the rear of the stage. "In one of those
little bedrooms—cabins—what are they, Papa?"

"Dressing rooms, Nola, and bedrooms, too. Want to
see them, Parthy?" He opened a little door leading
from the right-hand box to the stage, crossed the stage
followed by the reluctant Parthenia, threw open one of
the doors at the back. There was revealed a tiny cabin
holding a single bed, a diminutive dresser, and washstand. Handy rows of shelves were fastened to the
wall above the bed. Dimity curtains hung at the window. The window itself framed a view of river and
shore. A crudely coloured calendar hung on the wall,
and some photographs and newspaper clippings, time-
yellowed. There was about the little chamber a cosiness, a snugness, and, paradoxically enough, a sense of
space. That was the open window, doubtless, with its

vista of water and sky giving the effect of freedom.

"Dressing rooms during the performance," Andy explained, "and bedrooms the rest of the time. That's the way we work it."

Mrs. Hawks, with a single glance, encompassed the tiny room and rejected it. "Expect me to live in a cubby-hole like that!" It was, unconsciously, her first admission.

Magnolia, behind her mother's skirts, was peering, wide-eyed, into the room. "Why, I *love* it! Why, I'd love to live in it. Why, look, there's a little bed, and a dresser, and a——"

Andy interrupted hastily. "Course I don't expect you to live in a cubby-hole, Parthy. No, nor the child, neither. Just you step along with me. Now don't say anything; and stop your grumbling till you see. Put that bonnet back, Nola, where you got it. That's wardrobe. Which room 'd you get it out of?"

Across the stage, then, up the aisle to the stairway that led to the balcony, Andy leading, Mrs. Hawks following funereally, Magnolia playing a zigzag game between the rows of seats yet managing mysteriously to arrive at the foot of the stairs just as they did. The balcony reached, Magnolia had to be rescued from the death that in Mrs. Hawks' opinion inevitably would result from her leaning over the railing to gaze enthralled on the auditorium and stage below. "Hawks, will you look at that child! I declare, if I ever get her off this boat alive I'll never set foot on it again."

But her tone somehow lacked conviction. And when she beheld those two upper bedrooms forward, leading off the balcony—those two square roomy bedrooms, as large, actually, as her bedroom in the cottage, she was lost. The kitchen had scored. But the bedrooms won. They were connected by a little washroom. Each had two windows. Each held bed, dresser, rocker, stove. Bedraggled dimity curtains hung at the windows. Matting covered the floors. Parthy did an astonishing —though characteristic—thing. She walked to the dresser, passed a practised forefinger over its surface, examined the finger critically, and uttered that universal tongue-and-tooth sound indicating disapproval. "An inch thick," she then said. "A sight of cleaning this boat will take, I can tell you. Not a curtain in the place but'll have to come down and washed and starched and ironed."

Instinct or a superhuman wisdom cautioned Andy to say nothing. From the next room came a shout of joy. "Is this my room? It's got a chair that rocks and a stove with a res'vore and I can see my whole self in the looking glass, it's so big. Is this my room? Is it? Mama!"

Parthy passed into the next room. "We'll see. We'll see. We'll see." Andy followed after, almost a-tiptoe; afraid to break the spell with a sudden sound.

"But is it? I want to know. Papa, make her tell me. Look! The window here is a little door. It's a door and I can go right out on the upstairs porch. And there's the whole river."

"I should say as much, and a fine way to fall and drown without anybody being the wiser."

But the child was beside herself with excitement and

suspense. She could endure it no longer; flew to her stern parent and actually shook that adamantine figure in its dolman and bonnet. "Is it? Is it? Is it?"

"We'll see." A look, then, of almost comic despair flashed between father and child—a curiously adult look for one of Magnolia's years. It said: "What a woman this is! Can we stand it? I can only if you can."

Andy tried suggestion. "Could paint this furniture any colour Nola says——"

"Blue," put in Magnolia, promptly.

"—and new curtains, maybe, with ribbons to match ——" He had, among other unexpected traits, a keen eye for colour and line; a love for fabrics.

Parthy said nothing. Her lips were compressed. The look that passed between Andy and Magnolia now was pure despair, with no humour to relieve it. So they went disconsolately out of the door; crossed the balcony, clumped down the stairs, like mutes at a funeral. At the foot of the stairs they heard voices from without— women's voices, high and clear—and laughter. The sounds came from the little porch-like deck forward. Parthy swooped through the door; had scarcely time to gaze upon two sprightly females in gay plumage before both fell upon her lawful husband Captain Andy Hawks and embraced him. And the young pretty one kissed him on his left-hand mutton-chop whisker. And the older plain one kissed him on the right-hand mutton-chop whisker. And, "Oh, dear Captain Hawks!" they cried. "Aren't you surprised to see us! And happy! Do say you're happy. We drove over from Cairo specially to see you and the *Cotton Blossom*. Doc's with us."

Andy flung an obliging arm about the waist of each and gave each armful a little squeeze. "Happy ain't the word." And indeed it scarcely seemed to cover the situation; for there stood Parthy viewing the three entwined, and as she stood she seemed to grow visibly taller, broader, more ominous, like a menacing cloud. Andy's expression was a protean thing in which bravado and apprehension battled.

Magnolia had recognized them at once as the pretty young woman in the rose-trimmed hat and the dark woman who had told her not to smile too often that day when, in company with the sloppy young man, they had passed the Hawks house, laughing and chatting and spitting cherry stones idly and comfortably into the dust of the village street. So she now took a step forward from behind her mother's voluminous skirts and made a little tentative gesture with one hand toward the older woman. And that lively female at once said, "Why, bless me! Look, Elly! It's the little girl!"

Elly looked. "What little girl?"

"The little girl with the smile." And at that, quite without premeditation, and to her own surprise, Magnolia ran to her and put her hand in hers and looked up into her strange ravaged face and smiled. "There!" exclaimed the woman, exactly as she had done that first time.

"Maggie Hawks!" came the voice.

And, "Oh, my God!" exclaimed the one called Elly,

"it's the——" sensed something dangerous in the air, laughed, and stopped short.

Andy extricated himself from his physical entanglements and attempted to do likewise with the social snarl that now held them all.

"Meet my wife Mrs. Hawks. Parthy, this is Julie Dozier, female half of our general business team and one of the finest actresses on the river besides being as nice a little lady as you'd meet in a month of Sundays. . . . This here little beauty is Elly Chipley—Lenore La Verne on the bills. Our ingénue lead and a favourite from Duluth to New Orleans. . . . Where's Doc?"

At which, with true dramatic instinct, Doc appeared scrambling down the cinder path toward the boat; leaped across the gangplank, poised on one toe, spread his arms and carolled, "Tra-da!" A hard-visaged man of about fifty-five, yet with kindness, too, written there; the deep-furrowed, sad-eyed ageless face of the circus shillaber and showman.

"Girls say you drove over. Must be flush with your spondulicks, Doc. . . . Parthy, meet Doc. He's got another name, I guess, but nobody's ever used it. Doc's enough for anybody on the river. Doc goes ahead of the show and bills us and does the dirty work, don't you, Doc?"

"That's about the size of it," agreed Doc, and sped sadly and accurately a comet of brown juice from his lips over the boat's side into the river. "Pleased to make your acquaintance."

Andy indicated Magnolia. "Here's my girl Magnolia you've heard me talk about."

"Well, well! Lookit them eyes! They oughtn't to go bad in the show business, little later." A sound from Parthy who until now had stood a graven image, a portent. Doc turned to her, soft-spoken, courteous. "Fixin' to take a little ride with us for good luck I hope, ma'am, our first trip out with Cap here?"

Mrs. Hawks glanced then at the arresting face of Julie Dozier, female half of our general business team and one of the finest actresses on the river. Mrs. Hawks looked at Elly Chipley (Lenore La Verne on the bills) the little beauty, and favourite from Duluth to New Orleans. She breathed deep.

"Yes. I am." And with those three monosyllables Parthenia Ann Hawks renounced the ties of land, of conventionality; forsook the staid orderliness of the little white-painted cottage at Thebes; shut her ears to the scandalized gossip of her sedate neighbours; yielded grimly to the urge of the river and became at last its unwilling mistress.

V

WHEN April came, and the dogwood flashed its spectral white in the woods, the show boat started. It was the most leisurely and dreamlike of journeys. In all the hurried harried country that still was intent on repairing the ravages of a Civil War, they alone seemed to be leading an enchanted existence, suspended on another plane. Miles—hundreds—thousands of miles of willow-fringed streams flowing aquamarine in the sunlight, olive-green in the shade. Wild honeysuckle clambering over black tree trunks. Mules. Negroes. Bare unpainted cabins the colour of the sandy soil itself. Sleepy little villages blinking drowsily down upon a river which was some almost forgotten offspring spawned years before by the Mississippi. The nearest railroad perhaps twenty-five miles distant.

They floated down the rivers. They floated down the rivers. Sometimes they were broad majestic streams rolling turbulently to the sea, and draining a continent. Sometimes they were shallow narrow streams little more than creeks, through which the *Cotton Blossom* picked her way as cautiously as a timid girl picking her way among stepping stones. Behind them, pushing them maternally along like a fat puffing

duck with her silly little gosling, was the steamboat
Mollie Able.

To the people dwelling in the towns, plantations, and
hamlets along the many tributaries of the Mississippi
and Ohio, the show boat was no longer a novelty. It
had been a familiar and welcome sight since 1817 when
the first crude barge of that type had drifted down the
Cumberland River. But familiarity with these craft
had failed to dispel their glamour. To the farmers and
villagers of the Midwest; and to the small planters—
black and white—of the South, the show boat meant
music, romance, gaiety. It visited towns whose leafy
crypts had never echoed the shrill hoot of an engine
whistle. It penetrated settlements whose backwoods
dwellers had never witnessed a theatrical performance
in all their lives—simple child-like credulous people to
whom the make-believe villainies, heroics, loves, adventures of the drama were so real as sometimes to
cause the *Cotton Blossom* troupe actual embarrassment.
Often quality folk came to the show boat. The perfume and silks and broadcloth of the Big House took
frequent possession of the lower boxes and the front
seats.

That first summer was, to Magnolia, a dream of pure
delight. Nothing could mar it except that haunting
spectre of autumn when she would have to return to
Thebes and to the ordinary routine of a little girl in a
second-best pinafore that was donned for school in the
morning and thriftily replaced by a less important pinafore on her return from school in the late afternoon.
But throughout those summer months Magnolia was a

fairy princess. She was Cinderella at the ball. She shut her mind to the horrid certainty that the clock would inevitably strike twelve.

Year by year, as the spell of the river grew stronger and the easy indolence of the life took firmer hold, Mrs. Hawks and the child spent longer and longer periods on the show boat; less and less time in the humdrum security of the cottage ashore. Usually the boat started in April. But sometimes, when the season was mild, it was March. Mrs. Hawks would announce with a good deal of firmness that Magnolia must finish the school term, which ended in June. Later she and the child would join the boat wherever it happened to be showing at the time.

"Couple of months missed won't hurt her," Captain Andy would argue, loath as always to be separated from his daughter. "May's the grandest month on the rivers—and April. Everything coming out fresh. Outdoors all day. Do her good."

"I may not know much, but this I do know, Andy Hawks: No child of mine is going to grow up an ignoramus just because her father has nothing better to do than go galumphing around the country with a lot of riff-raff."

But in the end, when the show boat started its leisurely journey, there was Mrs. Hawks hanging fresh dimity curtains; bickering with Queenie; preventing, by her acid presence, the possibility of a too-saccharine existence for the members of the *Cotton Blossom* troupe. In her old capacity as school teacher, Parthy undertook the task of carrying on Magnolia's education during these truant spring months. It was an acrimonious and painful business ending, almost invariably, in temper, tears, disobedience, upbraidings. Unconsciously Andy Hawks had done much for the youth of New England when he ended Parthy's public teaching career.

"Nine times seven, I said. . . . No, it isn't! Just because fifty-six was the right answer last time it isn't right every time. That was seven times eight and I'll thank you to look at the book and not out of the window. I declare, Maggie Hawks, sometimes I think you're downright simple."

Magnolia's under lip would come out. Her brow was lowering. She somehow always looked her plainest and sallowest during these sessions with her mother. "I don't care what nine times seven is. Elly doesn't know, either. I asked her and she said she never had nine of anything, much less nine times seven of anything; and Elly's the most beautiful person in the world, except Julie sometimes—and me when I smile. And my name isn't Maggie Hawks, either."

"I'd like to know what it is if it isn't. And if you talk to me like that again, young lady, I'll smack you just as sure as I'm sitting here."

"It's Magnolia—Magnolia—uh—something beauti-ful—I don't know what. But not Hawks. Magnolia —uh——" a gesture with her right hand meant to con-vey some idea of the exquisiteness of her real name.

Mrs. Hawks clapped a maternal hand to her daugh-ter's somewhat bulging brow, decided that she was feverish, needed a physic, and promptly administered one.

As for geography, if Magnolia did not learn it, she lived it. She came to know her country by travelling up and down its waterways. She learned its people by meeting them, of all sorts and conditions. She learned folkways; river lore; Negro songs; bird calls; pilot rules; profanity; the art of stage make-up; all the parts in the *Cotton Blossom* troupe's repertoire including East Lynne, Lady Audley's Secret, Tempest and Sunshine, Spanish Gipsy, Madcap Margery, and Uncle Tom's Cabin.

There probably was much that was sordid about the life. But to the imaginative and volatile little girl of ten or thereabouts it was a combination playhouse, make-believe theatre, and picnic jaunt. Hers were days of enchantment—or would have been were it not for the practical Parthy who, iron woman that she was, saw to it that the child was properly fed, well clothed, and sufficiently refreshed by sleep. But Parthy's interests now were too manifold and diverse to permit of her accustomed concentration on Magnolia. She had an entire boatload of people to boss—two boatloads, in fact, for she did not hesitate to investigate and criticize the manners and morals of the crew that manned the towboat *Mollie Able*. A man was never safe from her as he sat smoking his after-dinner pipe and spitting contemplatively into the river. It came about that Magnolia's life was infinitely more free afloat than it had ever been on land.

Up and down the rivers the story went that the *Cotton Blossom* was the sternest-disciplined, best-managed, and most generously provisioned boat in the business. And it was notorious that a sign back-stage and in each dressing room read: "No lady of the company allowed on deck in a wrapper." It also was known that drunkenness on the *Cotton Blossom* was punished by instant dismissal; that Mrs. Captain Andy Hawks was a holy terror; that the platters of fried chicken on Sunday were inexhaustible. All of this was true.

Magnolia's existence became a weird mixture of lawlessness and order; of humdrum and fantasy. She slipped into the life as though she had been born to it. Parthy alone kept her from being utterly spoiled by the members of the troupe.

Mrs. Hawks' stern tread never adjusted itself to the leisurely rhythm of the show boat's tempo. This was obvious even to Magnolia. The very first week of their initial trip she had heard her mother say briskly to Julie, "What time is it?" Mrs. Hawks was marching from one end of the boat to the other, intent on some fell domestic errand of her own. Julie, seated in a low chair on deck, sewing and gazing out upon the yellow turbulence of the Mississippi, had replied in her deep indolent voice, without glancing up, "What does it matter?"

The four words epitomized the divinely care-free existence of the *Cotton Blossom* show-boat troupe.

Sometimes they played a new town every night. Sometimes, in regions that were populous and that boasted a good back-country, they remained a week. In such towns, as the boat returned year after year until it became a recognized institution, there grew up between the show-boat troupe and the townspeople a sort of friendly intimacy. They were warmly greeted on their arrival; sped regretfully on their departure. They almost never travelled at night. Usually they went to bed with the sound of the water slap-slapping gently against the boat's flat sides, and proceeded down river at daybreak. This meant that constant warfare raged between the steamboat crew of the *Mollie Able* and the show-boat troupe of the *Cotton Blossom*. The steamer crew, its work done, retired early, for it must be up and about at daybreak. It breakfasted at four-thirty or five. The actors never were abed before midnight or one o'clock and rose for a nine o'clock breakfast. They complained that the steamer crew, with its bells, whistles, hoarse shouts, hammerings, puffings, and general to-do attendant upon casting off and getting under way, robbed them of their morning sleep. The crew grumbled and cursed as it tried to get a night's rest in spite of the noise of the band, the departing audience, the midnight sociability of the players who, still at high tension after their night's work, could not yet retire meekly to bed.

"Lot of damn scenery chewers," growled the crew, turning in sleep.

"Filthy roustabouts," retorted the troupers, disturbed at dawn. "Yell because they can't talk like human beings."

They rarely mingled, except such members of the crew as played in the band; and never exchanged civilities. This state of affairs lent spice to an existence that might otherwise have proved too placid for comfort. The bickering acted as a safety valve.

It all was, perhaps, the worst possible environment

for a skinny, high-strung, and sensitive little girl who was one-quarter French. But Magnolia thrived on it. She had the solid and lumpy Puritanism of Parthy's presence to counteract the leaven of her volatile father. This saved her from being utterly consumed.

The life was at once indolent and busy. Captain Andy, scurrying hither and thither, into the town, up the river bank, rushing down the aisle at rehearsal to squeak a false direction to the hard-working company, driving off into the country to return in triumph laden with farm produce, was fond of saying, "We're just like one big happy family."

Captain Andy knew and liked good food (the Frenchman in him). They ate the best that the countryside afforded—not a great deal of meat in the height of summer when they were, perhaps, playing the hot humid Southern river towns, but plenty of vegetables and fruit—great melons bought from the patch with the sun still hot on their rounded bulging sides, and then chilled to dripping deliciousness before eating; luscious yams; country butter and cream. They all drank the water dipped out of the river on which they happened to be floating. They quaffed great dippersful of the Mississippi, the Ohio, and even the turbid Missouri, and seemed none the worse for it. At the stern was the settling barrel. Here the river water, dipped up in buckets, was left to settle before drinking. At the bottom of this receptacle, after it was three-quarters empty, one might find a rich layer of Mississippi silt intermingled with plummy odds and ends of every description including, sometimes, a sizable catfish.

In everything but actual rehearsing and playing, Magnolia lived the life of the company. The boat was their home. They ate, slept, worked, played on it. The company must be prompt at meal time, at rehearsals, and at the evening performances. There all responsibility ended for them.

Breakfast was at nine; and under Parthy's stern régime this meant nine. They were a motley lot as they assembled. In that bizarre setting the homely, everyday garb of the men and women took on a grotesque aspect. It was as though they were dressed for a part. As they appeared in the dining room, singly, in couples, or in groups, with a cheerful or a dour greeting, depending on the morning mood of each, an onlooker could think only of the home life of the Vincent Crummleses. Having seen Elly the night before as Miss Lenore La Verne in the golden curls, short skirts, and wide-eyed innocence of Bessie, the backwoodsman's daughter, who turned out, in the last act, to be none other than the Lady Clarice Trelawney, carelessly mislaid at birth, her appearance at breakfast was likely to have something of the shock of disillusionment. The baby stare of her great blue eyes was due to near-sightedness to correct which she wore silver-rimmed spectacles when not under the public gaze. Her breakfast jacket, though frilly, was not of the freshest, and her kid curlers were not entirely hidden by a silk-and-lace cap. Elly was, despite these grotesqueries, undeniably and triumphantly pretty, and thus arrayed gave the effect of a little girl mischievously tricked out in her grandmother's wardrobe. Her husband, known as Schultzy in private and Harold Westbrook on the bills, acted as director of the company. He was what is known in actor's parlance as a raver, and his method of acting was designated in the show-boat world as spitting scenery. A somewhat furtive young man in very tight pants and high collar always a trifle too large. He was a cuff-shooter, and those cuffs were secured and embellished with great square shiny chunks of quartz-like stuff which he frequently breathed upon heavily and then rubbed with his handkerchief. Schultzy played juvenile leads opposite his wife's ingénue rôles; had a real flair for the theatre.

Sometimes they were in mid-river when the breakfast bell sounded; sometimes tied to a landing. The view might be plantation, woods, or small town—it was all one to the *Cotton Blossom* company, intent on coffee and bacon. Long before white-aproned Jo, breakfast bell in hand, emerged head first from the little doorway beneath the stage back of the orchestra pit, like an amiable black python from its lair, Mrs. Hawks was on the scene, squinting critically into cream jugs, attacking flies as though they were dragons, infuriating Queenie with the remark that the biscuits seemed soggy this morning. Five minutes after the bell was brandished, Jo had placed the breakfast on the table, hot: oatmeal, steaming pots of coffee, platters of fried eggs with ham or bacon, stacks of toast, biscuits fresh from the oven. If you were prompt you got a hot breakfast; tardy, you took it cold.

Parthy, whose breakfast cap, designed to hide her curl papers, always gave the effect, somehow, of a martial helmet, invariably was first at the small table that stood at the head of the room farthest from the little doorway. So she must have sat at her school-house desk during those New England winters, awaiting the tardy morning arrival of reluctant and chilblained urchins. Magnolia was one of those children whom breakfast does not interest. Left to her own devices, she would have ignored the meal altogether. She usually entered late, her black hair still wet from the comb, her eyes wide with her eagerness to impart the day's first bit of nautical news.

"Doc says there's a family going down river on a bumboat, and they've got a teensy baby no bigger than a——"

"Drink your milk."

"——doll and he says it must have been born on the boat and he bets it's not more than a week old. Oh, I hope they'll tie up somewhere near——"

"Eat your toast with your egg."

"Do I have to eat my egg?"

"Yes."

If Magnolia was late, Andy was always later. He ate quickly and abstractedly. As he swallowed his coffee you could almost see his agile mind darting here and there, so that you wondered how his electric little body resisted following it as a lesser force follows a greater—up into the pilot house, down in the engine room, into the town, leaping ahead to the next landing; dickering with storekeepers for supplies. He was always the first to finish and was off at a quick trot, clawing the mutton-chop whiskers as he went.

Early or late, Julie and Steve came in together, Steve's great height ludicrously bent to avoid the low rafters of the dining room. Julie and Steve were the character team—Julie usually cast as adventuress, older sister, foil for Elly, the ingénue. Julie was a natural and intuitive actress, probably the best in the company. Sometimes she watched Elly's unintelligent work, heard her slovenly speech and her silly inflections, and a little contemptuous look would come into her face.

Steve played villains and could never have kept the job, even in that uncritical group, had it not been for Julie. He was very big and very fair, and almost entirely lacking in dramatic sense. A quiet gentle giant, he always seemed almost grotesquely miscast, his blondeur and his trusting faithful blue eyes belying the sable hirsuteness of villainy. Julie coached him patiently, tirelessly. The result was fairly satisfactory. But a nuance, an inflection, was beyond him.

"Who has a better right!" his line would be, perhaps. Schultzy, directing at rehearsal, would endeavour fruitlessly to convey to him its correct reading. After rehearsal, Julie could be heard going over the line again and again.

"Who has a better *right!*" Steve would thunder, dramatically.

"No, dear. The accent is on 'better.' Like this: 'Who has a *better* right!'"

Steve's blue eyes would be very earnest, his face red with effort. "Oh, I see. Come down hard on 'better,' huh? 'Who has a better *right!*'"

It was useless.

The two were very much in love. The others in the
company sometimes teased them about this, but not
often. Julie and Steve did not respond to this badinage
gracefully. There existed between the two a relation
that made the outsider almost uncomfortable. When
they looked at each other, there vibrated between them
a current that sent a little shiver through the beholder.
Julie's eyes were deep-set and really black, and there
was about them a curious indefinable quality. Magnolia liked to look into their soft and mournful depths.
Her own eyes were dark, but not like Julie's. Perhaps
it was the whites of Julie's eyes that were different.

Magnolia had once seen them kiss. She had come
upon them quietly and unexpectedly, on deck, in the
dusk. Certainly she had never witnessed a like passage
of love between her parents; and even her recent familiarity with stage romance had not prepared her for it.
It was long before the day of the motion picture fade-
out. Olga Nethersole's famous osculation was yet to
shock a Puritan America. Steve had held Julie a long
long minute, wordlessly. Her slimness had seemed to
melt into him. Julie's eyes were closed. She was
quite limp as he tipped her upright. She stood thus a
moment, swaying, her eyes still shut. When she opened
them they were clouded, misty, as were his. The two
then beheld a staring and fascinated little girl quite
palpably unable to move from the spot. Julie had
laughed a little low laugh. She had not flushed, exactly.
Her sallow colouring had taken on a tone at once deeper
and clearer and brighter, like amber underlaid with
gold. Her eyes had widened until they were enormous

in her thin dark glowing face. It was as though a lamp
had been lighted somewhere behind them.

"What makes you look like that?" Magnolia had
demanded, being a forthright young person.

"Like what?" Julie had asked.

"Like you do. All—all shiny."

"Love," Julie had answered, quite simply. Magnolia had not in the least understood; but she remembered. And years later she did understand.

Besides Elly, the ingénue, Schultzy, juvenile lead,
Julie and Steve, character team, there were Mr. and
Mrs. Means, general business team, Frank, the heavy,
and Ralph, general utility man. Elly and Schultzy sat
at table with the Hawkses, the mark of favour customary to their lofty theatrical eminence. The others of
the company, together with Doc, and three of the band
members, sat at the long table in the centre of the
room. Mrs. Means played haughty dowagers, old
Kentucky crones, widows, mothers, and middle-aged
females. Mr. Means did bankers, Scrooges, old hunters
and trappers, comics, and the like.

At the table nearest the door and the kitchen sat
the captain and crew of the *Mollie Able*. There were
no morning newspapers to read between sips of coffee;
no mail to open. They were all men and women of experience. They had knocked about the world. In their
faces was a lived look, together with an expression that
had in it a curiously child-like quality. Captain Andy
was not far wrong in his boast that they were like one
big family—a close and jealous family needing no outside stimulus for its amusement. They were extraor-

dinarily able to amuse themselves. Their talk was racy, piquant, pungent. The women were, for the most part, made of sterner stuff than the men—that is, among the actors. That the men had chosen this drifting, carefree, protected life, and were satisfied with it, proved that. Certainly Julie was a force stronger than Steve; Elly made a slave of Schultzy; Mrs. Means was a sternly maternal wife to her weak-chested and drily humorous little husband.

Usually they lingered over their coffee. Jo, padding in from the kitchen, would bring on a hot potful.

Julie had a marmoset which she had come by in NewOrleans, where it had been brought from equatorial waters by some swarthy earringed sailor. This she frequently carried to the table with her, tucked under her arm, its tiny dark head with the tragic mask of a face peering out from beneath her elbow. To Mrs. Hawks' intense disgust, Julie fed the tiny creature out of her own dish. In her cabin its bed was an old sealskin muff from whose depths its mournful dark eyes looked appealingly out from a face that was like nothing so much as that of an old old baby.

"I declare," Parthy would protest, almost daily, "it fairly turns a body's stomach to see her eating out of the same dish with that dirty little rat."

"Why, Mama! it isn't a rat any such thing! It's a monkey and you know it. Julie says maybe Schultzy can get one for me in New Orleans if I promise to be very very careful of it."

"I'd like to see her try," grimly putting an end to that dream.

The women took care of their own cabins. The detail of this occupied them until mid-morning. Often there was a rehearsal at ten that lasted an hour or more. Schultzy announced it at breakfast.

ₜAs they swept up a river, or floated down, their approach to the town was announced by the shrill iron-throated calliope, pride of Captain Andy's heart. Its blatant voice heralded the coming of the show boat long before the boat itself could be seen from the river bank. It had solid brass keys and could plainly be heard for five miles. George, who played the calliope, was also the pianist. He was known, like all calliope players, as the Whistler. Magnolia delighted in watching him at the instrument. He wore a slicker and a slicker hat and heavy gloves to protect his hands, for the steam of the whistles turned to hot raindrops and showered his hands and his head and shoulders as he played. As they neared the landing, the band, perched atop the show boat, forward, alternated with the calliope. From the town, hurrying down the streets, through the woods, dotting the levee and the landing, came eager figures, black and white. Almost invariably some magic-footed Negro, overcome by the music, could be seen on the wharf executing the complicated and rhythmic steps of a double shuffle, his rags flapping grotesquely about him, his mouth a gash of white. By nine o'clock in the morning every human being within a radius of five miles knew that the Cotton Blossom Floating Palace Theatre had docked at the waterfront.

By half-past eleven the band, augmented by two or three men of the company who doubled in brass, must

be ready for the morning concert on the main street
corner. Often, queerly enough, the town at which they
made their landing was no longer there. The Mississippi, in prankish mood, had dumped millions of tons of
silt in front of the street that faced the river. Year by
year, perhaps, this had gone on, until now that which
had been a river town was an inland town, with a mile
of woodland and sandy road between its main street and
the waterfront. The old serpent now stretched its
sluggish yellow coils in another channel.

By eleven o'clock the band would have donned its
scarlet coats with the magnificent gold braid and brass
buttons. The nether part of these costumes always
irritated Magnolia. Her colour-loving eye turned
away from them, offended. For while the upper costume was splendidly martial, the lower part was composed merely of such everyday pants as the band members might be wearing at the time of the concert hour,
and were a rude shock to the ravished eye as it travelled
from the gay flame and gold of the jacket and the dashing impudence of the cap. Especially in the drum
major did this offend her. He was called the baton
spinner and wore, instead of the scarlet cap of the other
band members, an imposing (though a slightly mangy)
fur shako, very black and shaggy and fierce-looking,
and with a strap under the chin. Pete, the bass drummer, worked in the engine room. Usually, at the last
minute, he washed up hastily, grabbed his drum,
buttoned on his coat, and was dazzlingly transformed
from a sooty crow into a scarlet tanager.

Up the levee they scrambled—two cornets, a clarinet,

a tuba, an alto (called a peck horn. Magnolia loved its
ump-a ump-a ta-ta-ta-ta, ump-a ump-a ta-ta-ta-ta), a
snare drummer who was always called a "sticks," and
the bass drum, known as the bull.

When the landing was a waterfront town, the band
concert was a pleasant enough interval in the day's light
duties. But when a mile or more of dusty road lay
between the show boat and the main street it became a
real chore. Carrying their heavy instruments, their
scarlet coats open, their caps in their hands, they would
trudge, tired, hot, and sweating, the long dusty road
that led through the woods. When the road became a
clearing and they emerged abruptly into the town, they
would button their coats, mop their hot faces, adjust
cap or shako, stiffen their drooping shoulders. Their
gait would change from one of plodding weariness to a
sprightly strut. Their pepper-and-salt, or brown, or
black trousered legs would move with rhythmic precision in time to the music. From tired, sticky, wilted
plodders, they would be transformed into heroic and
romantic figures. Up came the chest of the baton
spinner. His left hand rested elegantly on his hip, his
head and shoulders were held stiffly, arrogantly; his
right hand twirled the glittering baton until it dazzled
the eyes like a second noonday sun. Hotel waitresses,
their hearts beating high, scurried to the windows:
children rushed pell-mell from the school yard into the
street; clerks in their black sateen aprons and straw
sleevelets stood in the shop doorways; housewives left
their pots a-boil as they lingered a wistful moment on

the front porch, shading their eyes with a work-seamed hand; loafers spilled out of the saloons and stood agape and blinking. And as the music blared and soared, the lethargic little town was transformed for an hour into a gay and lively scene. Even the old white fly-bitten nags in the streets stepped with a jerky liveliness in their spring-halted gait, and a gleam came into their lack-lustre eyes as they pricked up their ears to the sound. Seeking out the busiest corner of the dull little main street, the band would take their stand, bleating and blaring, the sun playing magnificently on the polished brass of their instruments.

Although he never started with them, at this point Captain Andy always turned up, having overtaken them in some mysterious way. Perhaps he swung from tree to tree through the woods. There he was in his blue coat, his wrinkled baggy linen pants, his white canvas cap with the leather visor; fussy, nervous, animated, bright-eyed, clawing the mutton-chop whiskers from side to side. Under his arm he carried a sheaf of play-bills announcing the programmes and extolling the talents of the players. After the band had played two lively numbers, he would make his speech, couched in the absurd grandiloquence of the showman. He talked well. He made his audience laugh, bizarre yet strangely appealing little figure that he was. "Most magnificent company of players every assembled on the rivers . . . unrivalled scenery and costumes . . . Miss Lenore La Verne . . . dazzling array of talent . . . fresh from triumphs in the East . . . concert

after the show . . . singing and dancing . . .
bring the children . . . come one, come all. . . .
Cotton Blossom troupe just one big happy family. . . ."

The band would strike up again. Captain Andy would whisk through the crowd with uncanny swiftness distributing his playbills, greeting an acquaintance met on previous trips, chucking a child under the chin, extolling the brilliance and gaiety of the performance scheduled for that evening. At the end of a half hour the band would turn and march playing down the street. In the dispersing crowd could be discerned Andy's agile little figure darting, stooping, swooping as he thriftily collected again the playbills that, once perused, had been dropped in the dust by careless spectators.

Dinner was at four, a hearty meal. Before dinner, and after, the *Cotton Blossom* troupe was free to spend its time as it would. The women read or sewed. There were always new costumes to be contrived, or old ones to mend and refurbish. The black-hearted adventuress of that morning's rehearsal sat neatly darning a pair of her husband's socks. There was always the nearby town to visit; a spool of thread to be purchased, a stamp, a sack of peppermint drops, a bit of muslin, a toothbrush. The indolence of the life was such that they rarely took any premeditated exercise. Sometimes they strolled in the woods at springtime when the first tender yellow-green hazed the forest vistas. They fished, though the catch was usually catfish. On hot days the more adventuresome of them swam. The river was their front yard, grown as accustomed as a stretch of lawn. They were extraordinarily able to amuse themselves. Hardly one that did not play piano, violin, flute, banjo, mandolin.

By six o'clock a stir—a little electric unrest—an undercurrent of excitement could be sensed aboard the show boat. They came sauntering back from the woods, the town, the levee. They drifted down the aisles and in and out of their dressing rooms. Years of trouping failed to still in them the quickened pulse that always came with the approach of the evening's performance.

Down in the orchestra pit the band was tuning up. They would play atop the show boat on the forward deck before the show, alternating with the calliope, as in the morning. The daytime lethargy had vanished. On the stage the men of the company were setting the scene. Hoarse shouts. Lift 'er up there! No—down a little. H'ist her up. Back! Closer! Dressing-room doors opened and shut. Calls from one room to another. Twilight came on. Doc began to light the auditorium kerosene lamps whose metal reflectors sent back their yellow glow. Outside the kerosene search-light, cunningly rigged on top of the *Mollie Able's* pilot hoüse, threw its broad beam up the river bank to the levee.

Of all the hours in the day this was the one most be-loved of Magnolia's heart. She enjoyed the stir, the colour, the music, the people. Anything might happen on board the Cotton Blossom Floating Palace Theatre between the night hours of seven and eleven. And then it was that she was banished to bed. There was a nightly struggle in which, during the first months of their life on the rivers, Mrs. Hawks almost always won. Infrequently, by hook or crook, Magnolia managed to evade the stern parental eye.

"Let me just stay up for the first act—where Elly shoots him."

"Not a minute."

"Let me stay till the curtain goes up, then."

"You march yourself off to bed, young lady, or no trip to the pirate's cave to-morrow with Doc, and so I tell you."

Doc's knowledge of the gruesome history of river banditry and piracy provided Magnolia with many a goose-skinned hour of delicious terror. Together they went excursioning ashore in search of the blood-curdling all the way from Little Egypt to the bayous of Louisiana.

Lying there in her bed, then, wide-eyed, tense, Magnolia would strain her ears to catch the words of the play's dialogue as it came faintly up to her through the locked door that opened on the balcony; the almost incredibly naïve lines of a hackneyed play that still held its audience because of its full measure of fundamental human emotions. Hate, love, revenge, despair, hope, joy, terror.

"I will bring you to your knees yet, my proud beauty!"

"Never. I would rather die than accept help from your blood-stained hand."

Once Parthy, warned by some maternal instinct, stole softly to Magnolia's room to find the prisoner flown. She had managed to undo the special lock with which Mrs. Hawks had thought to make impossible her little daughter's access to the upper veranda deck just off her room. Magnolia had crept around the perilously narrow ledge enclosed by a low railing just below the upper deck and was there found, a shawl over her nightgown, knitted bed-slippers on her feet, peering in at the upper windows together with adventuresome and indigent urchins of the town who had managed somehow to scramble to this uncertain foothold.

After fitting punishment, the ban was gradually removed; or perhaps Mrs. Hawks realized the futility of trying to bring up a show-boat child according to Massachusetts small-town standards. With natural human perversity, thereafter, Magnolia frequently betook herself quietly to bed of her own accord the while the band blared below, guns were fired, love lost, villains foiled, beauty endangered, and blood spilled. Curiously enough, she never tired of watching these simple blood-and-thunder dramas. Automatically she learned every part in every play in the Cotton Blossom's repertoire, so that by the time she was thirteen she could have leaped on the stage at a moment's notice to play anything from Simon Legree to Lena Rivers.

But best of all she liked to watch the audience assembling. Unconsciously the child's mind beheld the moving living drama of a nation's peasantry. It was such an audience as could be got together in no other kind of theatre in all the world. Farmers, labourers, Negroes; housewives, children, yokels, lovers; roustabouts, dock wallopers, backwoodsmen, rivermen, gamblers. The coal-mining regions furnished the roughest audiences. The actors rather dreaded the coal towns of West Virginia or Pennsylvania. They knew that when they played the Monongahela River or the Kanawha there were likely to be more brawls and bloodshed off the stage than on.

By half-past six the levee and landing were already dotted with the curious, the loafers, the impecunious, the barefoot urchins who had gathered to snatch such crumbs as could be gathered without pay. They fed richly on the colour, the crowds, the music, the glimpses they caught of another world through the show boat's glowing windows.

Up the river bank from the boat landing to the top of the bluff flared kerosene torches suspended on long spikes stuck in the ground. Magnolia knew they were only kerosene torches, but their orange and scarlet flames never failed to excite her. There was something barbaric and splendid about them against the dusk of the sky and woods beyond, the sinister mystery of the river below. Something savage and elemental stirred in her at sight of them; a momentary reversion to tribal days, though she could not know that. She did know that she liked the fantastic dancing shadows cast by their vivid tongues on the figures that now teetered and slid and scrambled down the steep clay bank to the boat landing. They made a weird spectacle of the commonplace. The whites of the Negroes' eyes gleamed whiter. The lights turned their cheeks to copper and bronze and polished ebony. The swarthy coal miners and their shawled and sallow wives, the farmers of the corn and wheat lands, the backwoods poor whites, the cotton pickers of Tennessee, Louisiana, Mississippi, the small-town merchants, the shambling loafers, the lovers two by two were magically transformed into witches, giants, princesses, crones, gnomes, Nubians, genii.

At the little ticket window sat Doc, the astute, or Captain Andy. Later Mrs. Hawks was found to possess a grim genius for handling ticket-seeking crowds and the intricacies of ticket rack and small coins. Those dimes, quarters, and half dollars poured so willingly into the half-oval of the ticket window's open mouth found their way there, often enough, through a trail of pain and sweat and blood. It was all one to Parthy. Black faces. White faces. Hands gnarled. Hands calloused. Men in jeans. Women in calico. Babies. Children. Gimme a ticket. I only got fifteen. How much for her here? Many of them had never seen a theatre or a play. It was a strangely quiet crowd, usually. Little of laughter, of shouting. They came to the show boat timid, wide-eyed, wondering, like children. Two men of the steamboat crew or two of the musicians acted as ushers. After the first act was over they had often to assure these simple folk that the play was not yet ended. "This is just a recess. You come back to your seat in a couple of minutes. No, it isn't over. There's lots more to the show."

After the play there was the concert. Doc, Andy, and the ushers passed up and down between the acts selling tickets for this. They required an additional fifteen cents. Every member of the *Cotton Blossom* troupe must be able to sing, dance, play some musical instrument, or give a monologue—in some way contribute to the half hour of entertainment following the regular performance.

Now the band struck up. The kerosene lamps on the walls were turned low. The scuffling, shuffling, coughing audience became quiet, quiet. There was in that stillness something of fright. Seamed faces. Furrowed faces. Drab. Bitter. Sodden. Childlike. Weary. Sometimes, startlingly clear-cut in that half light, could be glimpsed a profile of some gaunt Southern labourer, or backwoodsman; and it was the profile of a portrait seen in some gallery or in the illustration of a book of history. A nose high-bred, aquiline; a sensitive, haughty mouth; eyes deep-set, arrogant. Spanish, French, English? The blood of a Stuart, a Plantagenet? Some royal rogue or adventurer of many many years ago whose seed, perhaps, this was.

The curtain rose. The music ceased jerkily, in mid-bar. They became little children listening to a fairy tale. A glorious world of unreality opened before their eyes. Things happened. They knew that in life things did not happen thus. But here they saw, believed, and were happy. Innocence wore golden curls. Wickedness wore black. Love triumphed, right conquered, virtue was rewarded, evil punished.

They forgot the cotton fields, the wheatfields, the cornfields. They forgot the coal mines, the potato patch, the stable, the barn, the shed. They forgot the labour under the pitiless blaze of the noonday sun; the bitter marrow-numbing chill of winter; the blistered skin; the frozen road; wind, snow, rain, flood. The women forgot for an hour their washtubs, their kitchen stoves, childbirth pains, drudgery, worry, disappointment. Here were blood, lust, love, passion. Here were warmth, enchantment, laughter, music. It was Anodyne. It was Lethe. It was Escape. It was the Theatre.

VI

I T WAS the theatre, perhaps, as the theatre was meant to be. A place in which one saw one's dreams come true. A place in which one could live a vicarious life of splendour and achievement; winning in love, foiling the evildoer; a place in which one could weep unashamed, laugh aloud, give way to emotions long pent-up. When the show was over, and they had clambered up the steep bank, and the music of the band had ceased, and there was left only the dying glow of the kerosene flares, you saw them stumble a little and blink, dazedly, like one rudely awakened to reality from a lovely dream.

By eleven the torches had been gathered in. The show-boat lights were dimmed. Troupers as they were, no member of the *Cotton Blossom* company could go meekly off to sleep once the work day was over. They still were at high tension. So they discussed for the thousandth time the performance that they had given a thousand times. They dissected the audience.

"Well, they were sitting on their hands to-night, all right. Seemed they never would warm up."

"I got a big laugh on that new business with the pillow. Did you notice?"

"Notice! Yeh, the next time you introduce any new business you got a right to leave me know beforehand.

I went right up. If Schultzy hadn't thrown me my line where'd I been!"

"I never thought of it till that minute, so help me! I just noticed the pillow on the sofa and that minute it came to me it'd be a good piece of business to grab it up like it was a baby in my arms. I didn't expect any such laugh as I got on it. I didn't go to throw you off."

From Schultzy, in the rôle of director: "Next time you get one of those inspirations you try it out at rehearsal first."

"God, they was a million babies to-night. Cap, I guess you must of threw a little something extra into your spiel about come and bring the children. They sure took you seriously and brought 'em, all right. I'd just soon play for a orphan asylum and be done with it."

Julie was cooking a pot of coffee over a little spirit lamp. They used the stage as a common gathering place. Bare of scenery now, in readiness for next night's set, it was their living room. Stark and shadowy as it was, there was about it an air of coziness, of domesticity. Mrs. Means, ponderous in dressing gown and slippers, was heating some oily mess for use in the nightly ministrations on her frail little husband's delicate chest. Usually Andy, Parthy, Elly, and Schultzy, as the *haute monde*, together with the occasional addition of the *Mollie Able's* captain and pilot, supped together at a table below-stage in the dining room, where Jo and Queenie had set out a cold collation— cheese, ham, bread, a pie left from dinner. Parthy cooked the coffee on the kerosene stove. On stage the women of the company hung their costumes care-

fully away in the tiny cubicles provided for such purpose
just outside the dressing-room doors. The men smoked
a sedative pipe. The lights of the little town on the
river bank had long been extinguished. Even the
saloons on the waterfront showed only an occasional
glow. Sometimes George at the piano tried out a
new song for Elly or Schultzy or Ralph, in preparation
for to-morrow night's concert. The tinkle of the piano,
the sound of the singer's voice drifted across the river.
Up in the little town in a drab cottage near the waterfront a restless soul would turn in his sleep and start
up at the sound and listen between waking and sleeping;
wondering about these strange people singing on their
boat at midnight; envying them their fantastic vagabond life.

A peaceful enough existence in its routine, yet a
curiously crowded and colourful one for a child. She
saw town after town whose waterfront street was a solid
block of saloons, one next the other, open day and
night. Her childhood impressions were formed of
stories, happenings, accidents, events born of the rivers.
Towns and cities and people came to be associated in
her mind with this or that bizarre bit of river life. The
junction of the Ohio and Big Sandy rivers always was
remembered by Magnolia as the place where the Black
Diamond Saloon was opened on the day the *Cotton
Blossom* played Catlettsburg. Catlettsburg, typical
waterfront town of the times, was like a knot that drew
together the two rivers. Ohio, West Virginia, and
Kentucky met just there. And at the junction of the
rivers there was opened with high and appropriate

ceremonies the Black Diamond Saloon, owned by those picturesque two, Big Wayne Damron and Little Wayne Damron. From the deck of the *Cotton Blossom* Magnolia saw the crowd waiting for the opening of the Black Diamond doors—free drinks, free lunch, river town hospitality. And then Big Wayne opened the doors, and the crowd surged back while their giant host, holding the key aloft in his hand, walked down to the river bank, held the key high for a moment, then hurled it far into the yellow waters of the Big Sandy. The Black Diamond Saloon was open for business.

The shifting colourful life of the rivers unfolded before her ambient eyes. She saw and learned and remembered. Rough sights, brutal sights; sights of beauty and colour; deeds of bravery; dirty deeds. Through the wheat lands, the corn country, the fruit belt, the cotton, the timber region. The river life flowed and changed like the river itself. Shanty boats. Bumboats. Side-wheelers. Stern-wheelers. Fussy packets, self-important. Races ending often in death and disaster. Coal barges. A fleet of rafts, log-laden. The timber rafts, drifting down to Louisville, were steered with great sweeps. As they swept down the Ohio, the timbermen sang their chantey, their great shoulders and strong muscular torsos bending, straightening to the rhythm of the rowing song. Magnolia had learned the words from Doc, and when she espied the oarsmen from the deck of the *Cotton Blossom* she joined in the song and rocked with their motion out of sheer dramatic love of it:

"The river is up,
The channel is deep,
The wind blows steady and strong.
Oh, Dinah's got the hoe cake on,
So row your boat along.
Down the river,
Down the river,
Down the O-hi-o.
Down the river,
Down the river,
Down the O-
            hi-
                O!"

Three tremendous pulls accompanied those last three long-drawn syllables. Magnolia found it most invigorating. Doc had told her, too, that the Ohio had got its name from the time when the Indians, standing on one shore and wishing to cross to the other, would cup their hands and send out the call to the opposite bank, loud and high and clear, "O-*HE*-O!"

"Do you think it's true?" Magnolia would say; for Mrs. Hawks had got into the way of calling Doc's stories stuff-and-nonsense. All those tales, it would seem, to which Magnolia most thrilled, turned out, according to Parthy, to be stuff-and-nonsense. So then, "Do you think it's true?" she would demand, fearfully.

"Think it! Why, pshaw! I know it's true. Sure as shootin'."

It was noteworthy and characteristic of Magnolia that she liked best the rampant rivers. The Illinois, which had possessed such fascination for Tonti, for

Joliet, for Marquette—for countless *coureurs du bois*
who had frequented this trail to the southwest—left
her cold. Its clear water, its gentle current, its fretless
channel, its green hillsides, its tidy bordering grain
fields, bored her. From Doc and from her father she
learned a haphazard and picturesque chronicle of its
history, and that of like rivers—a tale of voyageurs and
trappers, of flatboat and keelboat men, of rafters in the
great logging days, of shanty boaters, water gipsies,
steamboats. She listened, and remembered, but was
unmoved. When the *Cotton Blossom* floated down the
tranquil bosom of the Illinois Magnolia read a book.
She drank its limpid waters and missed the mud-tang
to be found in a draught of the Mississippi.

"If I was going to be a river," she announced, "I
wouldn't want to be the Illinois, or like those. I'd
want to be the Mississippi."

"How's that?" asked Captain Andy.

"Because the Illinois, it's always the same. But
the Mississippi is always different. It's like a person
that you never know what they're going to do next,
and that makes them interesting."

Doc was oftenest her cicerone and playmate ashore.
His knowledge of the countryside, the rivers, the dwellers along the shore and in the back country, was almost
godlike in its omniscience. At his tongue's end were
tales of buccaneers, of pirates, of adventurers. He
told her of the bloodthirsty and rapacious Murrel who,
not content with robbing and killing his victims, ripped
them open, disembowelled them, and threw them into
the river.

"Oh, my!" Magnolia would exclaim, inadequately; and peer with some distaste into the water rushing past the boat's flat sides. "How did he look? Like Steve when he plays Legree?"

"Not by a jugful, he didn't. Dressed up like a parson, and used to travel from town to town, giving sermons. He had a slick tongue, and while the congregation inside was all stirred up getting their souls saved, Murrel's gang outside would steal their horses."

Stories of slaves stolen, sold, restolen, resold, and murdered. Murrel's attempted capture of New Orleans by rousing the blacks to insurrection against the whites. Tales of Crenshaw, the vulture; of Mason, terror of the Natchez road. On excursions ashore, Doc showed her pirates' caves, abandoned graveyards, ancient robber retreats along the river banks or in the woods. They visited Sam Grity's soap kettle, a great iron pot half hidden in a rocky unused field, in which Grity used to cache his stolen plunder. She never again saw an old soap kettle sitting plumply in some Southern kitchen doorway, its sides covered with a handsome black velvet coat of soot, that she did not shiver deliciously. Strong fare for a child at an age when other little girls were reading the Dotty Dimple Series and Little Prudy books.

Doc enjoyed these sanguinary chronicles in the telling as much as Magnolia in the listening. His lined and leathery face would take on the changing expressions suitable to the tenor of the tale. Cunning, cruelty, greed, chased each other across his mobile countenance. Doc had been a show-boat actor himself at some time back in his kaleidoscopic career. So together he and Magnolia and his ancient barrel-bellied black-and-white terrier Catchem roamed the woods and towns and hills and fields and churchyards from Cairo to the Gulf.

Sometimes, in the spring, she went with Julie, the indolent. Elly almost never walked and often did not leave the *Cotton Blossom* for days together. Elly was extremely neat and fastidious about her person. She was for ever heating kettles and pans of water for bathing, for washing stockings and handkerchiefs. She had a knack with the needle and could devise a quite plausible third-act ball gown out of a length of satin, some limp tulle, and a yard or two of tinsel. She never read. Her industry irked Julie as Julie's indolence irritated her.

Elly was something of a shrew (Schultzy had learned to his sorrow that your blue-eyed blondes are not always doves). "Pity's sake, Julie, how you can sit there doing nothing, staring out at that everlasting river's more than I can see. I should think you'd go plumb crazy."

"What would you have me do?"

"Do! Mend the hole in your stocking, for one thing."

"I should say as much," Mrs. Hawks would agree, if she chanced to be present. She had no love for Elly; but her own passion for industry and order could not but cause her to approve a like trait in another.

Julie would glance down disinterestedly at her long slim foot in its shabby shoe. "Is there a hole in my stocking?"

"You know perfectly well there is, Julie Dozier.

You must have seen it the size of a half dollar when
you put it on this morning. It was there yesterday,
same's to-day."

Julie smiled charmingly. "I know. I declare to
goodness I hoped it wouldn't be. When I woke up this
morning I thought maybe the good fairies would have
darned it up neat's a pin while I slept." Julie's voice
was as indolent as Julie herself. She spoke with a
Southern drawl. Her I was Ah. Ah declah to goodness—or approximately that.

Magnolia would smile in appreciation of Julie's
gentle raillery. She adored Julie. She thought Elly,
with her fair skin and china-blue eyes, as beautiful as
a princess in a fairy tale, as was natural in a child of
her sallow colouring and straight black hair. But the
two were antipathetic. Elly, in ill-tempered moments,
had been known to speak of Magnolia as "that brat,"
though her vanity was fed by the child's admiration of
her beauty. But she never allowed her to dress up in
her discarded stage finery, as Julie often did. Elly
openly considered herself a gifted actress whose talent
and beauty were, thanks to her shiftless husband,
pearls cast before the river-town swinery. Pretty
though she was, she found small favour in the eyes of
men of the company and crew. Strangely enough, it
was Julie who drew them, quite without intent on her
part. There was something about her life-scarred face,
her mournful eyes, her languor, her effortlessness, her
very carelessness of dress that seemed to fascinate and
hold them. Steve's jealousy of her was notorious. It
was common boat talk, too, that Pete, the engineer of

the *Mollie Able*, who played the bull drum in the band, was openly enamoured of her and had tried to steal her from Steve. He followed Julie into town if she so much as stepped ashore. He was found lurking in corners of the *Cotton Blossom* decks; loitering about the stage where he had no business to be. He even sent her presents of imitation jewellery and gaudy handkerchiefs and work boxes, which she promptly presented to Queenie, first urging that mass of ebon royalty to bedeck herself with her new gifts when dishing up the dinner. In that close community the news of the disposal of these favours soon reached Pete's sooty ears. There had even been a brawl between Steve and Pete—one of those sudden tempestuous battles, animal-like in its fierceness and brutality. An oath in the darkness; voices low, ominous; the thud of feet; the impact of bone against flesh; deep sob-like breathing; a high weird cry of pain, terror, rage. Pete was overboard and floundering in the swift current of the Mississippi. Powerful swimmer though he was, they had some trouble in fishing him out. It was well that the *Cotton Blossom* and the *Mollie Able* were lying at anchor. Bruised and dripping, Pete had repaired to the engine room to dry, and to nurse his wounds, swearing in terms ridiculously like those frequently heard in the second act of a *Cotton Blossom* play that he would get his revenge on the two of them. He had never, since then, openly molested Julie, but his threats, mutterings, and innuendoes continued. Steve had forbidden his wife to leave the show boat unaccompanied. So it was that when spring came round, and the dogwood gleaming white among the black trunks of the pines and firs was like a bride and her shining attendants in a great cathedral, Julie would tie one of her floppy careless hats under her chin and, together with Magnolia, range the forests for wild flowers. They would wander inland until they found trees other than the willows, the live oaks, and the elms that lined the river banks. They would come upon wild honeysuckle, opalescent pink. In autumn they went nutting, returning with sackfuls of hickory and hazel nuts—anything but the black walnut which any show-boat dweller knows will cause a storm if brought aboard. Sometimes they experienced the shock of gay surprise that follows the sudden sight of gentian, a flash of that rarest of flower colours, blue; almost poignant in its beauty. It always made Magnolia catch her breath a little.

Julie's flounces trailing in the dust, the two would start out sedately enough, though to the accompaniment of a chorus of admonition and criticism.

From Mrs. Hawks: "Now keep your hat pulled down over your eyes so's you won't get all sunburned, Magnolia. Black enough as 'tis. Don't run and get all overheated. Don't eat any berries or anything you find in the woods, now. . . . Back by four o'clock the latest . . . poison ivy . . . snakes . . . lost . . . gipsies. . . ."

From Elly, trimming her rosy nails in the cool shade of the front deck: "Julie, your placket's gaping. And tuck your hair in. No, there, on the side."

So they made their way up the bank, across the little town, and into the woods. Once out of sight of the

boat the two turned and looked back. Then, without
a word, each would snatch her hat from her head; and
they would look at each other, and Julie would smile
her wide slow smile, and Magnolia's dark plain pointed
little face would flash into sudden beauty. From some
part of her person where it doubtless was needed Julie
would extract a pin and with it fasten up the tail of
her skirt. Having thus hoisted the red flag of rebellion,
they would plunge into the woods to emerge hot, sticky,
bramble-torn, stained, flower-laden, and late. They
met Parthy's upbraidings and Steve's reproaches with
cheerful unconcern.

Often Magnolia went to town with her father, or
drove with him or Doc into the back country. Andy
did much of the marketing for the boat's food, frequently hampered, supplemented, or interfered with
by Parthy's less openhanded methods. He loved good
food, considered it important to happiness, liked to
order it and talk about it; was himself an excellent cook,
like most boatmen, and had been known to spend a
pleasant half hour reading the cook book. The but-
chers, grocers, and general store keepers of the river
towns knew Andy, understood his fussy ways, liked
him. He bought shrewdly but generously, without
haggling; and often presented a store acquaintance of
long standing with a pair of tickets for the night's performance. When he and Magnolia had time to range
the countryside in a livery rig, Andy would select the
smartest and most glittering buggy and the liveliest
nag to be had. Being a poor driver and jerky, with no
knowledge of a horse's nerves and mouth, the ride was

likely to be exhilarating to the point of danger. The animal always was returned to the stable in a lather, the vehicle spattered with mud-flecks to the hood. Certainly, it was due to Andy more than Parthy that the *Cotton Blossom* was reputed the best-fed show boat on the rivers. He was always bringing home in triumph a great juicy ham, a side of beef. He liked to forage the season's first and best: a bushel of downy peaches, fresh-picked; watermelons; little honey-sweet seckel pears; a dozen plump broilers; new corn; a great yellow cheese ripe for cutting.

He would plump his purchases down on the kitchen table while Queenie surveyed his booty, hands on ample hips. She never resented his suggestions, though Parthy's offended her. Capering, Andy would poke a forefinger into a pullet's fat sides. "Rub 'em over with a little garlic, Queenie, to flavour 'em up. Plenty of butter and strips of bacon. Cover 'em over till they're tender and then give 'em a quick brown the last twenty minutes."

Queenie, knowing all this, still did not resent his direction. "That shif'less no-'count Jo knew 'bout cookin' like you do, Cap'n Andy, Ah'd git to rest mah feet now an' again, Ah sure would."

Magnolia liked to loiter in the big, low-raftered kitchen. It was a place of pleasant smells and sights and sounds. It was here that she learned Negro spirituals from Jo and cooking from Queenie, both of which accomplishments stood her in good stead in later years. Queenie had, for example, a way of stuffing a ham for baking. It was a fascinating process to behold, and

one that took hours.   Spices—bay, thyme, onion, clove,
mustard, allspice, pepper—chopped and mixed and
stirred together.   A sharp-pointed knife plunged deep
into the juicy ham.   The incision stuffed with the
spicy mixture.   Another plunge with the knife.   Another filling.   Again and again and again until the
great ham had grown to twice its size.   Then a heavy
clean white cloth, needle and coarse thread.   Sewed up
tight and plump in its jacket the ham was immersed in a
pot of water and boiled.   Out when tender, the jacket
removed; into the oven with it.   Basting and basting
from Queenie's long-handled spoon.   The long sharp
knife again for cutting, and then the slices, juicy and
scented, with the stuffing of spices making a mosaic
pattern against the pink of the meat.   Many years
later Kim Ravenal, the actress, would serve at the
famous little Sunday night suppers that she and her
husband Kenneth Cameron were so fond of giving a
dish that she called ham *à la* Queenie.

"How does your cook do it!" her friends would say—
Ethel Barrymore or Kit Cornell or Frank Crownin-
shield or Charley Towne or Woollcott.   "I'll bet it
isn't real at all.   It's painted on the platter."

"It is not!   It's a practical ham, stuffed with all
kinds of devilment.   The recipe is my mother's.   She
got it from an old Southern cook named Queenie."

"Listen, Kim.   You're among friends.   Your dear
public is not present.   You don't have to pretend any
old Southern aristocracy Virginia belle mammy stuff
with *us*."

"Pretend, you great oaf!   I was born on a show

boat on the Mississippi, and proud of it.   Everybody knows that."

Mrs. Hawks, bustling into the show-boat kitchen with her unerring gift for scenting an atmosphere of mellow enjoyment, and dissipating it, would find Magnolia perched on a chair, both elbows on the table, her palms propping her chin as she regarded with round-eyed fascination Queenie's magic manipulations.   Or perhaps Jo, the charming and shiftless, would be singing for her one of the Negro plantation songs, wistful with longing and pain; the folk songs of a wronged race, later to come into a blaze of popularity as spirituals.

For some nautical reason, a broad beam, about six inches high and correspondingly wide, stretched across the kitchen floor from side to side, dividing the room. Through long use Jo and Queenie had become accustomed to stepping over this obstruction, Queenie ponderously, Jo with an effortless swing of his lank legs. On this Magnolia used to sit, her arms hugging her knees, her great eyes in the little sallow pointed face fixed attentively on Jo.   The kitchen was very clean and shining and stuffy.   Jo's legs were crossed, one foot in its great low shapeless shoe hooked in the chair rung, his banjo cradled in his lap.   The once white parchment face of the instrument was now almost as black as Jo's, what with much strumming by work-stained fingers.

"Which one, Miss Magnolia?"

"I Got Shoes," Magnolia would answer, promptly.

Jo would throw back his head, his sombre eyes half shut:

The longing of a footsore, ragged, driven race expressed in the tragically childlike terms of shoes, white robes, wings, and the wise and simple insight into hypocrisy: "Ev'rybody talkin 'bout Heav'n ain't goin' there. . . ."

"Now which one?" His fingers still picking the strings, ready at a word to slip into the opening chords of the next song.

"Go Down, Moses."

She liked this one—at once the most majestic and supplicating of all the Negro folk songs—because it always made her cry a little. Sometimes Queenie, busy at the stove or the kitchen table, joined in with her high rich camp-meeting voice. Jo's voice was a reedy tenor, but soft and husky with the indescribable Negro vocal quality. Magnolia soon knew the tune and the words of every song in Jo's repertoire. Unconsciously, being an excellent mimic, she sang as Jo and Queenie sang, her head thrown slightly back, her eyes rolling or half closed, one foot beating rhythmic time to the music's cadence. Her voice was true, though mediocre; but she got into this the hoarsely sweet Negro overtone—purple velvet muffling a flute.

Between Jo and Queenie flourished a fighting affection, deep, true, and lasting. There was some doubt as to the actual legal existence of their marriage, but the union was sound and normal enough. At each season's close they left the show boat the richer by three hundred dollars, clean new calico for Queenie, and proper jeans for Jo. Shoes on their feet. Hats on their heads. Bundles in their arms. Each spring they returned penniless, in rags, and slightly liquored. They had had a magnificent time. They did not drink again while the *Cotton Blossom* kitchen was their home. But the next winter the programme repeated itself. Captain Andy liked and trusted them. They were as faithful to him as their childlike vagaries would permit.

So, filled with the healthy ecstasy of song, the Negro man and woman and the white child would sit in deep contentment in the show-boat kitchen. The sound of a door slammed. Quick heavy footsteps. Three sets of nerves went taut. Parthy.

"Maggie Hawks, have you practised to-day?"

"Some."

"How much?"

"Oh, half an hour—more."

"When?"

"''Smorning."

"I didn't hear you."

The sulky lower lip out. The high forehead wrinkled by a frown. Song flown. Peace gone.

"I did so. Jo, didn't you hear me practising?"

"Ah suah did, Miss Magnolia."

"You march right out of here, young lady, and practise another half hour. Do you think your father's made of money, that I can throw fifty-cent pieces away on George for nothing? Now you do your exercises fifteen minutes and the Maiden's Prayer fifteen. . . . Idea!"

Magnolia marched. Out of earshot Parthy expressed her opinion of nigger songs. "I declare I don't know where you get your low ways from! White people aren't good enough for you, I suppose, that you've got to run with blacks in the kitchen. Now you sit yourself down on that stool."

Magnolia was actually having music lessons. George, the Whistler and piano player, was her teacher, receiving fifty cents an hour for weekly instruction. Driven by her stern parent, she practised an hour daily on the tinny old piano in the orchestra pit, a rebellious, skinny, pathetic little figure strumming painstakingly away in the great emptiness of the show-boat auditorium. She must needs choose her time for practice when a rehearsal of the night's play was not in progress on the stage or when the band was not struggling with the music of a new song and dance number. Incredibly enough, she actually learned something of the mechanics of music, if not of its technique. She had an excellent rhythm sense, and this was aided by none other than Jo, whose feeling for time and beat and measure and pitch was flawless. Queenie lumped his song gift in with his general shiftlessness. Born fifty years later he might have known brief fame in some midnight revue or Club Alabam' on Broadway. Certainly Magnolia unwittingly learned more of real music from black Jo and many another Negro wharf minstrel than she did from hours of the heavy-handed and unlyrical George.

That Mrs. Hawks could introduce into the indolent tenor of show-boat life anything so methodical and humdrum as five-finger exercises done an hour daily was triumphant proof of her indomitable driving force. Life had miscast her in the rôle of wife and mother. She was born to be a Madam Chairman. Committees, Votes, Movements, Drives, Platforms, Gavels, Reports all showed in her stars. Cheated of these, she had to be content with such outlet of her enormous energies as the *Cotton Blossom* afforded. Parthy had never heard the word Feminist, and wouldn't have recognized it if she had. One spoke at that time not of Women's Rights but of Women's Wrongs. On these Parthenia often waxed tartly eloquent. Her housekeeping fervour was the natural result of her lack of a more impersonal safety valve. The *Cotton Blossom* shone like a Methodist Sunday household. Only Julie and Windy, the *Mollie Able* pilot, defied her. She actually indulged in those most domestic of rites, canning and preserving, on board the boat. Donning an all-enveloping gingham apron, she would set frenziedly to work on two bushels of peaches or seckel pears; baskets of tomatoes; pecks of apples. Pickled pears, peach marmalade, grape jell in jars and pots and glasses filled shelves and cupboards. Queenie found a great deal of satisfaction in the fact that occasionally, owing to some culinary accident or to the unusual motion of the flat-bottomed *Cotton Blossom* in the rough waters of an open bay, one of these jars was found smashed on the floor, its rich purple or amber contents mingling with splinters of glass. No one—not even Parthy—ever dared connect Queenie with these quite explicable mishaps.

Parthy was an expert needlewoman. She often assisted Julie or Elly or Mis' Means with their costumes. To see her stern implacable face bent over a heap of frivolous stuffs while her industrious fingers swiftly sent the needle flashing through unvarying seams was to receive the shock that comes of beholding the incongruous. The enormity of it penetrated even her blunt sensibilities.

"If anybody'd ever told me that I'd live to see the day when I'd be sewing on costumes for show folks!"

"Run along, Parthy. You like it," Andy would say.

But she never would admit that. "Like it or lump it, what can I do! Married you for better or worse, didn't I!" Her tone leaving no doubt as to the path down which that act had led her. Actually she was having a rich, care-free, and varied life such as she had never dreamed of and of which she secretly was enamoured.

Dwellers in this or that river town loitering down at the landing to see what manner of sin and loose living went on in and about this show boat with its painted

women and play-acting men would be startled to hear
sounds and sniff smells which were identical with those
which might be issuing that very moment from their
own smug and godly dwellings ashore. From out the
open doors of the Cotton Blossom Floating Palace
Theatre came the unmistakable and humdrum sounds
of scales and five-finger exercises done painfully and
unwillingly by rebellious childish hands. Ta-ta-ta—
TA—ta-ta-ta. From below decks there floated up the
mouth-watering savour of tomato ketchup, of boiling
vinegar and spices, or the perfumed aroma of luscious
fruits seething in sugary kettles.

"Smells for all the world like somebody was doing
up sweet pickles." One village matron to another.

"Well, I suppose they got to eat like other folks."
Ta-ta-ta—*TA*—ta-ta-ta.

It was inevitable, however, that the ease and indolence of the life, as well as the daily contact with odd and
unconventional characters must leave some imprint on
even so adamantine an exterior as Parthy's. Little by
little her school-teacherly diction dropped from her.
Slowly her vowels began to slur, her aren'ts became
ain'ts, her crisp new England utterance took on something of the slovenly Southern drawl, her consonants
were missing from the end of a word here and there.
True, she still bustled and nagged, managed and
scolded, drove and reproached. She still had the power
to make Andy jump with nervousness. Whether con-
sciously or unconsciously, the influence of this virago
was more definitely felt than that of any other one of
the *Cotton Blossom's* company and crew. Of these only

Julie Dozier, and Windy, the pilot (so called because he almost never talked) actually triumphed over Mrs. Hawks. Julie's was a negative victory. She never voluntarily spoke to Parthy and had the power to aggravate that lady to the point of frenzy by remaining limp, supine, and idle when Parthy thought she should be most active; by raising her right eyebrow quizzically in response to a more than usually energetic tirade; by the habitual disorder of the tiny room which she shared with Steve; by the flagrant carelessness and untidiness of her own gaunt graceful person.

"I declare, Hawks, what you keep that slatternly yellow cat around this boat for beats me."

"Best actress in the whole caboodle, that's why." Something fine in little Captain Andy had seen and recognized the flame that might have glorified Julie had it not instead consumed her. "That girl had the right backing she'd make her mark, and not in any show boat, either. I've been to New York. I've seen 'em down at Wallack's and Daly's and around."

"A slut, that's what she is. I had my way she'd leave this boat bag and baggage."

"Well, this is one time you won't have your way, Mrs. Hawks, ma'am." She had not yet killed the spirit in Andy.

"Mark my words, you'll live to regret it. The way she looks out of those black eyes of hers! Gives me the creeps."

"What would you have the girl look out of," retorted Andy, not very brilliantly. "Her ears?"

Julie could not but know of this antagonism toward

her. Some perverse streak in her otherwise rich and gentle make-up caused her to find a sinister pleasure in arousing it.

Windy's victory was more definitely dramatic, though his defensive method against Parthy's attacks resembled in sardonic quiet and poise Julie's own. Windy was accounted one of the most expert pilots on the Mississippi. He knew every coil and sinew and stripe of the yellow serpent. River men used his name as a synonym for magic with the pilot's wheel. Starless night or misty day; shoal water or deep, it was all one to Windy. Though Andy's senior by more than fifteen years, the two had been friends for twenty. Captain Andy had enormous respect for his steersmanship; was impressed by his taciturnity (being himself so talkative and vivacious); enjoyed talking with him in the bright quiet security of the pilot house. He was absolute czar of the *Mollie Able* and the *Cotton Blossom*, as befitted his high accomplishments. No one ever dreamed of opposing him except Parthy. He was slovenly of person, careless of habit. These shortcomings Parthy undertook to correct early in her show-boat career. She met with defeat so prompt, so complete, so crushing as to cause her for ever after to leave him unmolested.

Windy had muddy boots. They were, it seemed, congenitally so. He would go ashore in mid-afternoon of a hot August day when farmers for miles around had been praying for rain these weeks past and return in a downpour with half the muck and clay of the countryside clinging to his number eleven black square-toed elastic-side boots. A tall, emaciated drooping old man,

Windy; with long gnarled muscular hands whose en-
larged knuckles and leathery palms were the result of
almost half a century at the wheel. His pants were
always grease-stained; his black string tie and gray
shirt spattered with tobacco juice; his brown jersey
frayed and ragged. Across his front he wore a fine
anchor watch chain, or "log" chain, as it was called.
And gleaming behind the long flowing tobacco-splotched
gray beard that reached almost to his waist could be
glimpsed a milkily pink pearl stud like a star behind a
dirty cloud-bank. The jewel had been come by, doubtless, in payment of some waterfront saloon gambling
debt. Surely its exquisite curves had once glowed
upon fine and perfumed linen.

It was against this taciturn and omnipotent conquerer
of the rivers that Parthy raised the flag of battle.

"Traipsin' up and down this boat and the *Mollie Able*,
spitting his filthy tobacco and leaving mud tracks like an
elephant that's been in a bog. If I've had those steps
leading up to the pilot house scrubbed once, I've had 'em
scrubbed ten times this week, and now look at them! I
won't have it, and so I tell you. Why can't he go up
the side of the boat the way a pilot is supposed to do!
What's that side ladder for, I'd like to know! He's
supposed to go up it; not the steps."

"Now, Parthy, you can't run a boat the way you
would a kitchen back in Thebes. Windy's no hired
man. He's the best pilot on the rivers, and I'm lucky
to have him. A hundred jobs better than this ready to
jump at him if he so much as crooks a finger. He's
pulled this tub through good many tight places where

any other pilot'd landed us high and dry on a sand bar. And don't you forget it."

"He's a dirty old man. And I won't have it. Muddying up my clean . . ."

Parthy was not one of your scolds who takes her grievances out in mere words. With her, to threaten was to act. That very morning, just before the *Cotton Blossom* was making a late departure from Greenville, where they had played the night before, to Sunnisie Side Landing, twelve miles below, this formidable woman, armed with hammer and nails, took advantage of Windy's temporary absence below decks to nail down the hatch above the steps leading to the pilot house. She was the kind of woman who can drive a nail straight. She drove ten of them, long and firm and deep. A pity that no one saw her. It was a sight worth seeing, this accomplished and indomitable virago in curl papers, driving nails with a sure and steady stroke.

Below stairs Windy, coming aboard from an early morning look around, knocked the ashes out of his pipe, sank his great yellow fangs into a generous wedge of Honest Scrap, and prepared to climb the stairs to the *Cotton Blossom* pilot house, there to manipulate wheel and cord that would convey his orders to Pete in the engine room.

Up the stairs, leaving a mud spoor behind. One hand raised to lift the hatch; wondering, meanwhile, to find it closed. A mighty heave; a pounding with the great fist; another heave, then, with the powerful old shoulder.

"Nailed," said Windy aloud to himself, mildly.
Then, still mildly, "The old hell cat." He spat, then,
on the hatchway steps and clumped leisurely down
again. He leaned over the boat rail, looking benignly
down at the crowd of idlers gathered at the wharf to
watch the show boat cast off. Then he crossed the
deck again to where a capacious and carpet-seated easy
chair held out its inviting arms. Into this he sank
with a grunt of relaxation. From his pocket he took
the pipe so recently relinquished, filled it, tamped it,
lighted it. From another pocket he took a month-old
copy of the New Orleans *Times-Democrat*, turned to the
column marked Shipping News, and settled down, apparently, for a long quiet day with literature.

Up came the anchor. In came the hawser. Chains
clanked. The sound of the gangplank drawn up.
The hoarse shouts from land and water that always
attend the departure of a river boat. "Throw her over
there! Lift 'er! Heh, Pete! Gimme hand here!
Little to the left. Other side! Hold on! Easy!"

The faces of the crowd ashore turned expectantly
toward the boat. Everything shipshape. Pete in the
engine room. Captain Andy scampering for the texas.
Silence. No bells. No steam. No hoarse shouts of
command. God A'mighty, where's Windy? Windy!
Windy!

Windy lowers his shielding newspaper and mildly
regards the capering captain and bewildered crew and
startled company. He is wearing his silver-rimmed
reading spectacles slightly askew on his biblical-looking

hooked nose.   Andy rushes up to him, all the Basque
in him bubbling.   "God's sake, Windy, what's . . .
why don't you take her!   We're going."

Windy chewed rhythmically for a moment, spat a long
brown jet of juice, wiped his hairy mouth with the back
of one gnarled hand.   "We ain't going, Cap'n Hawks,
because she can't go till I give her the go-ahead.   And I
ain't give her the go-ahead.   I'm the pilot of this here
boat."

"But why?   What the . . . Wh——"

"The hatch is nailed down above the steps leading
to the pilot house, Cap'n Andy.   Till that hatchway's
open, I don't climb up to no pilot house.   And till I
climb up to the pilot house, she don't get no go-ahead.
And till I give her the go-ahead, she don't go, not if we
stay here alongside this landing till the *Cotton Blossom*
rots."

He looked around benignly and resumed his reading
of the New Orleans *Times-Democrat*.

Profanity, frowned upon under Parthy's régime, now
welled up in Andy and burst from him in spangled
geysers.   Words seethed to the surface and exploded
like fireworks.   Twenty-five years of river life had
equipped him with a vocabulary rich, varied, purple.
He neglected neither the heavens above nor the earth
beneath.   Revolt and rage shook his wiry little frame.
Years of henpecking, years of natural gaiety suppressed,
years of mincing when he wished to stride, years of
silence when he wished to sing, now were wiped away
by the stream of undiluted rage that burst from Captain
Andy Hawks.   It was a torrent, a flood, a Mississippi

of profanity in which hells and damns were mere drops in the mighty roaring mass.

"Out with your crowbars there. Pry up that hatch! I'm captain of this boat, by God, and anybody, man or woman, who nails down that hatch again without my orders gets put off this boat wherever we are, and so I say."

Did Parthenia Ann Hawks shrink and cower and pale under the blinding glare of this pyrotechnic profanity? Not that indomitable woman. The picture of outraged virtue in curl papers, she stood her ground like a Roman matron. She had even, when the flood broke, sent Magnolia indoors with a gesture meant to convey protection from the pollution of this verbal stream.

"Well, Captain Hawks, a fine example you have set for your company and crew I must say."

"*You* must say! You——! Let me tell you, Mrs. Hawks, ma'am, the less you say the better. And I repeat, anybody touches that hatchway again——"

"Touch it!" echoed Parthy in icy disdain. "I wouldn't touch it, nor the pilot house, nor the pilot either, if you'll excuse my saying so, with a ten-foot pole."

And swept away with as much dignity as a *Cotton Blossom* early morning costume would permit. Her head bloody but unbowed.

VII

JULIE was gone. Steve was gone. Tragedy had stalked into Magnolia's life; had cast its sable mantle over the *Cotton Blossom*. Pete had kept his promise and revenge had been his. But the taste of triumph had not, after all, been sweet in his mouth. There was little of the peace of satisfaction in his sooty face stuck out of the engine-room door. The arm that beat the bull drum in the band was now a listless member, so that a hollow mournful thump issued from that which should have given forth a rousing boom.

The day the *Cotton Blossom* was due to play Lemoyne, Mississippi, Julie Dozier took sick. In show-boat troupes, as well as in every other theatrical company in the world, it is an unwritten law that an actor must never be too sick to play. He may be sick. Before the performance he may be too sick to stand; immediately after the performance he may collapse. He may, if necessary, die on the stage and the curtain will then be lowered. But no real trouper while conscious will ever confess himself too sick to go on when the overture ends and the lights go down.

Julie knew this. She had played show boats for years, up and down the rivers of the Middle West and the South. She had a large and loyal following.

Lemoyne was a good town, situated on the river, prosperous, sizable.

Julie lay on her bed in her darkened room, refusing all offers of aid. She did not want food. She did not want cold compresses on her head. She did not want hot compresses on her head. She wanted to be left alone—with Steve. Together the two stayed in the darkened room, and when some member of the company came to the door with offers of aid or comfort, there came into their faces a look that was strangely like one of fear, followed immediately by a look of relief.

Queenie sent Jo to the door with soup, her panacea for all ailments, whether of the flesh or the spirit. Julie made a show of eating it, but when Jo had clumped across the stage and down to his kitchen Julie motioned to Steve. He threw the contents of the bowl out of the window into the yellow waters of the Mississippi.

Doc appeared at Julie's door for the tenth time though it was only mid-morning. "Think you can play all right, to-night, though, don't you, Julie?"

In the semi-darkness of her shaded room Julie's eyes glowed suddenly wide and luminous. She sat up in bed, pushing her hair back from her forehead with a gesture so wild as to startle the old trouper.

"No!" she cried, in a sort of terror. "No! I can't play to-night. Don't ask me."

Blank astonishment made Doc's face almost ludicrous. For an actress to announce ten hours before the time set for the curtain's rising that she would not be able to go on that evening—an actress who had not

suffered decapitation or an amputation—was a thing
unheard of in Doc's experience.

"God a'mighty, Julie! If you're sick as all that,
you'd better see a doctor. Steve, what say?"

The great blond giant seated at the side of Julie's
bed did not look round at his questioner. His eyes
were on Julie's face. "Julie's funny that way. She's
set against doctors. Won't have one, that's all. Don't
coax her. It'll only make her worse."

Inured as he was to the vagaries of woman, this apparently was too much for Doc. Schultzy appeared
in the doorway; peered into the dimness of the little
room.

"Funny thing. I guess you must have an admirer
in this town, Jule. Somebody's stole your picture,
frame and all, out of the layout in the lobby there.
First I thought it might be that crazy Pete, used to
be so stuck on you. . . . Now, now, Steve! Keep
your shirt on! Keep your shirt on! . . . I asked
him, straight, but he was surprised all right. He ain't
good enough actor to fool me. He didn't do it. Must
be some town rube all right, Julie, got stuck on your
shape or something. I put up another one." He
stood a moment, thoughtfully. Elly came up behind
him, hatted and gloved.

"I'm going up to town, Julie. Can I fetch you something? An orange, maybe? Or something from the
drug store?"

Julie's head on the pillow moved a negative. "She
says no, thanks," Steve answered for her, shortly. It
was as though both laboured under a strain. The

three in the doorway sensed it. Elly shrugged her shoulders, though whether from pique or indifference it was hard to say. Doc still stood puzzled, bewildered. Schultzy half turned away. "S'long's you're all right by to-night," he said cheerfully.

"Says she won't be," Doc put in, lowering his voice.

"Won't be!" repeated Schultzy, almost shrilly. "Why, she ain't *sick*, is she! I mean, sick!"

Schultzy sent his voice shrilling from Julie's little bedroom doorway across the bare stage, up the aisles of the empty auditorium, so that it penetrated the box office at the far end of the boat, where Andy, at the ticket window, was just about to be relieved by Parthy.

"Heh, Cap! Cap! Come here. Julie's sick. Julie's too sick to go on. Says she's too sick to . . ."

"Here," said Andy, summarily, to Parthy; and left her in charge of business. Down the aisle with the light quick step that was almost a scamper; up the stage at a bound. "Best advance sale we've had since we started out. We never played this town before. License was too high. But here it is, not eleven o'clock, and half the house gone already." He peered into the darkened room.

From its soft fur nest in the old sealskin muff the marmoset poked its tragic mask and whimpered like a sick baby. This morning there was a strange resemblance between the pinched and pathetic face on the pillow and that of the little sombre-eyed monkey.

By now there was quite a little crowd about Julie's door. Mis' Means had joined them and could be heard murmuring about mustard plasters and a good hot something or other. Andy entered the little room with the freedom of an old friend. He looked sharply down at the face on the pillow. The keen eyes plunged deep into the tortured eyes that stared piteously up at him. Something he saw there caused him to reach out with one brown paw, none too immaculate, and pat that other slim brown hand clutching the coverlet so tensely. "Why, Jule, what's—— Say, s'pose you folks clear out and let me and Jule and Steve here talk things over quiet. Nobody ain't going to get well with this mob scene you're putting on. Scat!" Andy could distinguish between mental and physical anguish.

They shifted—Doc, Elly, Schultzy, Mis' Means, Catchem the torpid. Another moment and they would have moved reluctantly away. But Parthy, torn between her duty at the ticket window and her feminine curiosity as to the cause of the commotion at Julie's door became, suddenly, all woman. Besides—demon statistician that she was—she suddenly had remembered a curious coincidence in connection with this sudden illness of Julie's. She slammed down the ticket window, banged the box-office door, sailed down the aisle. As she approached Doc was saying for the dozenth time:

"Person's too sick to play, they're sick enough to have a doctor's what I say. Playing Xenia to-morrow. Good a stand's we got. Prolly won't be able to open there, neither, if you're sick's all that."

"I'll be able to play to-morrow!" cried Julie, in a high strained voice. "I'll be able to play to-morrow. To-morrow I'll be all right."

"How do you know?" demanded Doc.

Steve turned on him in sudden desperation. "She'll be all right, I tell you. She'll be all right as soon as she gets out of this town."

"That's a funny thing," exclaimed Parthy. She swept through the little crowd at the door, seeming to mow them down with the energy of her progress. "That's a funny thing."

"What?" demanded Steve, his tone belligerent. "What's funny?"

Captain Andy raised a placating palm. "Now, Parthy, now, Parthy. Sh-sh!"

"Don't shush *me*, Hawks. I know what I'm talking about. It came over me just this minute. Julie took sick at this very town of Lemoyne time we came down river last year. Soon as you and Doc decided we wouldn't open here because the license was too high she got well all of a sudden, just like that!" She snapped a thumb and forefinger.

Silence, thick, uncomfortable, heavy with foreboding, settled down upon the little group in the doorway.

"Nothing so funny about that," said Captain Andy, stoutly; and threw a sharp glance at the face on the pillow. "This hot sticky climate down here after the cold up north is liable to get anybody to feeling queer. None too chipper myself, far's that goes. Affects some people that way." He scratched frenziedly at the mutton-chop whiskers, this side and that.

"Well, I may not know *much*——" began Parthy.

Down the aisle skimmed Magnolia, shouting as she came, her child's voice high and sharp with excitement. "Mom! Mom! Look. What do you think! Julie's picture's been stolen again right out of the front of the lobby. Julie, they've taken your picture again. Somebody took one and Schultzy put another in and now it's been stolen too."

She was delighted with her news; radiant with it. Her face fell a little at the sight of the figure on the bed, the serious group about the doorway that received her news with much gravity. She flew to the bed then, all contrition. "Oh, Julie darling, I'm so sorry you're sick." Julie turned her face away from the child, toward the wall.

Captain Andy, simulating fury, capered a threatening step toward the doorway crowd now increased by the deprecating figure of Mr. Means and Ralph's tall shambling bulk. "Will you folks clear out of here or will I have to use force! A body'd think a girl didn't have the right to feel sick. Doc, you get down and 'tend to that ticket window, or Parthy. If we can't show to-night we got to leave 'em know. Ralph, you write out a sign and get it pasted up at the post office. . . . Sure you won't be feeling better by night time, are you, Julie?" He looked doubtfully down at the girl on the bed.

With a sudden lithe movement Julie flung herself into Steve's arms, clung to him, weeping. "No!" she cried, her voice high, hysterical. "No! No! No! Leave me alone, can't you! Leave me alone!"

"Sure," Andy motioned, then, fiercely to the company. "Sure we'll leave you alone, Julie."

But Tragedy, having stalked her victim surely, relentlessly, all the morning, now was about to close in upon her. She had sent emissary after emissary down the show-boat aisle, and each had helped to deepen the look of terror in Julie's eyes. Now sounded the slow shambling heavy tread of Windy the pilot, bearded, sombre, ominous as the figure of fate itself. The little group turned toward him automatically, almost absurdly, like a badly directed mob scene in one of their own improbable plays.

He clumped up the little flight of steps that led from the lower left-hand box to the stage. Clump, clump, clump. Irresistibly Parthy's eyes peered sharply in pursuit of the muddy tracks that followed each step. She snorted indignantly. Across the stage, his beard waggling up and down as his jaws worked slowly, rhythmically on a wedge of Honest Scrap. As he approached Julie's doorway he took off his cap and rubbed his pate with his palm, sure sign of great mental perturbation in this monumental old leviathan. The yellow skin of his knobby bald dome-like head shone gold in the rays of the late morning sun that came in through the high windows at the side of the stage.

He stood a moment, chewing, and peering mildly into the dimness of the bedroom, Sphinx-like, it seemed that he never would speak. He stood, champing. The *Cotton Blossom* troupe waited. They had not played melodrama for years without being able to sense it when they saw it. He spoke. "Seems that skunk Pete's up to something." They waited. The long tobacco-stained beard moved up and down, up and down. "Skinned out half an hour back streaking toward town like possessed. He yanked that picture of Julie out of the hall there. Seen him. I see good deal goes on around here."

Steve sprang to his feet with a great ripping river oath. "I'll kill him this time, the ——"

"Seen you take that first picture out, Steve." The deep red that had darkened Steve's face and swelled the veins on his great neck receded now, leaving his china-blue eyes staring out of a white and stricken face.

"I never did! I never did!"

Julie sat up, clutching her wrapper at the throat. She laughed shrilly. "What would he want to steal my picture for! His own wife's picture. Likely!"

"So nobody in this town'd see it, Julie," said Windy, mildly. "Listen. Fifty years piloting on the rivers, you got to have pretty good eyesight. Mine's as good to-day as it was time I was twenty. I just stepped down from the texas to warn you I see Pete coming along the levee with Ike Keener. Ike's the sheriff. He'll be in here now any minute."

"Let him," Andy said, stoutly. "Our license is paid. Sheriff's as welcome around this boat as anybody. Let him."

But no one heard him; no one heeded him. A strange and terrible thing was happening. Julie had sprung from her bed. In her white nightgown and her wrapper, her long black hair all tumbled and wild about her face, a stricken and hunted thing, she clung to Steve, and he to her. There came a pounding at the door that led into the show-boat auditorium from the fore deck. Steve's eyes seemed suddenly to sink far back in his head. His cheek-bones showed gaunt and sharp as

Julie's own. His jaw was set so that a livid ridge stood out on either side like bars of white-hot steel. He loosened Julie's hold almost roughly. From his pocket he whipped a great clasp-knife and opened its flashing blade. Julie did not scream, but the other women did, shriek on shriek. Captain Andy sprang for him, a mouse attacking a mastodon. Steve shook him off with a fling of his powerful shoulders.

"I'm not going to hurt her, you fool. Leave me be. I know what I'm doing." The pounding came again, louder and more insistent. "Somebody go down and let him in—but keep him there a minute."

No one stirred. The pounding ceased. The doors opened. The boots of Ike Keener, the sheriff, clattered down the aisle of the *Cotton Blossom*.

"Stop those women screeching," Steve shouted. Then, to Julie, "It won't hurt much, darling." With incredible swiftness he seized Julie's hand in his left one and ran the keen glittering blade of his knife firmly across the tip of her forefinger. A scarlet line followed it. He bent his blond head, pressed his lips to the wound, sucked it greedily. With a little moan Julie fell back on the bed. Steve snapped the blade into its socket, thrust the knife into his pocket. The boots of Sheriff Ike Keener were clattering across the stage now. The white faces clustered in the doorway—the stricken, bewildered, horrified faces—turned from the two within the room to the one approaching it. They made way for this one silently. Even Parthy was dumb. Magnolia clung to her, wide-eyed, uncomprehending, sensing tragedy though she had never before encountered it.

The lapel of his coat flung back, Ike Keener confronted the little cowed group on the stage. A star shone on his left breast. The scene was like a rehearsal of a *Cotton Blossom* thriller.

"Who's captain of this here boat?"

Andy, his fingers clutching his whiskers, stepped forward. "I am. What's wanted with him? Hawks is my name—Captain Andy Hawks, twenty years on the rivers."

He looked the sheriff of melodrama, did Ike Keener— boots, black moustaches, wide-brimmed black hat, flowing tie, high boots, and all. Steve himself, made up for the part, couldn't have done it better. "Well, Cap, kind of unpleasant, but I understand there's a miscegenation case on board."

"What?" whispered Magnolia. "What's that? What does he mean, Mom?"

"Hush!" hissed Parthy, and jerked the child's arm.

"How's that?" asked Andy, but he knew.

"Miscegenation. Case of a Negro woman married to a white man. Criminal offense in this state, as you well know."

"No such thing," shouted Andy. "No such thing on board this boat."

Sheriff Ike Keener produced a piece of paper. "Name of the white man is Steve Baker. Name of the negress"— he squinted again at the slip of paper—"name of the negress is Julie Dozier." He looked around at the group. "Which one's them?"

"Oh, my God!" screamed Elly. "Oh, my God! Oh, my God!"

"Shut up," said Schultzy, roughly.

Steve stepped to the window and threw up the shade, letting the morning light into the crowded disorderly little cubicle. On the bed lay Julie, her eyes enormous in her sallow pinched face.

"I'm Steve Baker. This is my wife."

Sheriff Ike Keener tucked the paper in his pocket. "You two better dress and come along with me."

Julie stood up. She looked an old woman. The marmoset whimpered and whined in his fur nest. She put out a hand, automatically, and plucked it from the muff and held it in the warm hollow of her breast. Her great black eyes stared at the sheriff like the wide-open unseeing eyes of a sleep walker.

Steve Baker grinned—rather, his lips drew back from his teeth in a horrid semblance of mirth. He threw a jovial arm about Julie's shrinking shoulder. For once she had no need to coach him in his part. He looked Ike Keener in the eye. "You wouldn't call a man a white man that's got Negro blood in him, would you?"

"No, I wouldn't; not in Mississippi. One drop of nigger blood makes you a nigger in these parts."

"Well, I got more than a drop of—nigger blood in me, and that's a fact. You can't make miscegenation out of that."

"You ready to swear to that in a court of law?"

"I'll swear to it any place. I'll swear it now." Steve took a step forward, one hand outstretched. "I'll do more than that. Look at all these folks here. There ain't one of them but can swear I got Negro blood in me this minute. That's how white I am."

Sheriff Ike Keener swept the crowd with his eye. Perhaps what he saw in their faces failed to convince him. "Well, I seen fairer men than you was niggers. Still, you better tell that——"

Mild, benevolent, patriarchal, the figure of old Windy stepped out from among the rest. "Guess you've known me, Ike, better part of twenty-five years. I was keelboatin' time you was runnin' around, a barefoot on the landin'. Now I'm tellin' you—me, Windy McKlain—that that white man there's got nigger blood in him. I'll take my oath to that."

Having thus delivered himself of what was, perhaps, the second longest speech in his career, he clumped off again, across the stage, down the stairs, up the aisle, looking, even in that bizarre environment, like something out of Genesis.

Sheriff Ike Keener was frankly puzzled. "If it was anybody else but Windy—but I got this straight from—from somebody ought to know."

"From who?" shouted Andy, all indignation. "From a sooty-faced scab of a bull-drumming engineer named Pete. And why? Because he's been stuck on Julie here I don't know how long, and she wouldn't have anything to do with him."

"Is that right?"

"Yes, it is," Steve put in, quickly. "He was after my wife. Anybody in the company 'll bear me out. He wouldn't leave her alone, though she hated the sight of him, and Cap here give him a talking—didn't you, Cap? So finally, when he wouldn't quit, then there was nothing for it but lick him, and I licked him good, and soused him in the river to get his dirty face clean. He crawls out swearing he'll get me for it. Now you know."

Keener now addressed himself to Julie for the first time. "He says—this Pete—that you was born here in Lemoyne, and that your pop was white and your mammy black. That right?"

Julie moistened her lips with the tip of her tongue. "Yes," she said. "That's—right."

A sudden commotion in the group that had been so still. Elly's voice, shrill with hysteria. "I will! I'll tell right out. The wench! The lying black——"

Suddenly stifled, as though a hand had been clapped none too gently across her mouth. Incoherent blubberings; a scuffle. Schultzy had picked Elly up like a sack of meal, one hand still firmly held over her mouth; had carried her into her room and slammed the door.

"What's she say?" inquired Keener.

Again Andy stepped into the breach. "That's our ingénue lead. She's kind of high strung. You see, she's been friends with this—with Julie Dozier, here— without knowing about her—about her blood, and like that. Kind of give her a shock, I guess. Natural."

It was plain that Sheriff Ike Keener was on the point of departure, puzzled though convinced. He took off his broad-brimmed hat, scratched his head, replaced the hat at an angle that spelled bewilderment. His eye, as he turned away, fell on the majestic figure of Parthenia Ann Hawks, and on Magnolia cowering, wide-eyed, in the folds of her mother's ample skirts.

"You look like a respectable woman, ma'am."

Imposing enough at all times, Parthy now grew visibly taller. Cold sparks flew from her eyes. "I am."

"That your little girl?"

Andy did the honours. "My wife, Sheriff. My little girl, Magnolia. What do you say to the Sheriff, Magnolia?"

Thus urged, Magnolia spoke that which had been seething within her. "You're bad!" she shouted, her face twisted with the effort to control her tears. "You're a bad mean man, that's what! You called Julie names and made her look all funny. You're a——"

The maternal hand stifled her.

"If I was you, ma'am, I wouldn't bring up no child on a boat like this. No, nor stay on it, neither. Fine place to rear a child!"

Whereupon, surprisingly enough, Parthy turned defensive. "My child's as well brought up as your own, and probably better, and so I tell you. And I'll thank you to keep your advice to yourself, Mr. Sheriff."

"Parthy! Parthy!" from the alarmed Andy.

But Sheriff Ike Keener was a man of parts. "Well, women folks are all alike. I'll be going. I kind of smell a nigger in the woodpile here in more ways than one. But I'll take your word for it." He looked Captain Andy sternly in the eye. "Only let me tell you this, Captain Hawks. You better not try to give your show in this town to-night. We got some public-spirited folks here in Lemoyne and this fix you're in has kind of leaked around. You go to work and try to give your show with this mixed blood you got here and first thing you know you'll be riding out of town on something don't sit so easy as a boat."

His broad-brimmed hat at an angle of authority, his coat tails flirting as he strode, he marched up the aisle then and out.

The little huddling group seemed visibly to collapse. It was as though an unseen hand had removed a sustaining iron support from the spine of each. Magnolia would have flown to Julie, but Parthy jerked her back. Whispering then; glance of disdain.

"Well, Julie, m'girl," began Andy Hawks, kindly. Julie turned to him.

"We're going," she said, quietly.

The door of Elly's room burst open. Elly, a rumpled, distraught, unlovely figure, appeared in Julie's doorway, Schultzy trying in vain to placate her.

"You get out of here!" She turned in a frenzy to Andy. "She gets out of here with that white trash she calls her husband or I go, and so I warn you. She's black! She's black! God, I was a fool not to see it all the time. Look at her, the nasty yellow——" A stream of abuse, vile, obscene, born of the dregs of river talk heard through the years, now welled to Elly's lips, distorting them horribly.

"Come away from here," Parthy said, through set lips, to Magnolia. And bore the child, protesting, up the aisle and into the security of her own room forward.

"I want to stay with Julie! I want to stay with Julie!" wailed Magnolia, overwrought, as the inexorable hand dragged her up the stairs.

In her tiny disordered room Julie was binding up her

wild hair with a swift twist. She barely glanced at Elly. "Shut that woman up," she said, quietly. "Tell her I'm going." She began to open boxes and drawers.

Steve approached Andy, low-voiced. "Cap, take us down as far as Xenia, will you, for God's sake! Don't make us get off here."

"Down as far as Xenia you go," shouted Captain Andy at the top of his voice, "and anybody in this company don't like it they're free to git, bag and baggage, now. We'll pull out of here now. Xenia by afternoon at four, latest. And you two want to stay the night on board you're welcome. I'm master of this boat, by God!"

They left, these two, when the *Cotton Blossom* docked at Xenia in the late afternoon. Andy shook hands with them, gravely; and Windy clumped down from the pilot house to perform the same solemn ceremony. You sensed unseen peering eyes at every door and window of the *Cotton Blossom* and the *Mollie Able*.

"How you fixed for money?" Andy demanded, bluntly.

"We're fixed all right," Julie replied, quietly. Of the two of them she was the more composed. "We've been saving. You took too good care of us on the *Cotton Blossom*. No call to spend our money." The glance from her dark shadow-encircled eyes was one of utter gratefulness. She took up the lighter pieces of luggage. Steve was weighed down with the others— bulging boxes and carpet bags and bundles—their clothing and their show-boat wardrobe and their pitifully few trinkets and personal belongings. A pin cushion, very lumpy, that Magnolia had made for her at Christmas a year ago. Photographs of the *Cotton Blossom*. A book of pressed wild flowers. Old newspaper clippings.

Julie lingered. Steve crossed the gangplank, turned, beckoned with his head. Julie lingered. An unspoken question in her eyes.

Andy flushed and scratched the mutton-chop whiskers this side and that. "Well, you know how she is, Julie. She don't mean no harm. But she didn't let on to Magnolia just what time you were going. Told her to-morrow, likely. Women folks are funny, that way. She don't mean no harm."

"That's all right," said Julie; picked up the valises, was at Steve's side. Together the two toiled painfully up the steep river bank, Steve turning to aid her as best he could. They reached the top of the levee. They stood a moment, breathless; then turned and trudged down the dusty Southern country road, the setting sun in their faces. Julie's slight figure was bent under the weight of the burden she carried. You saw Steve's fine blond head turned toward her, tender, concerned, encouraging.

Suddenly from the upper deck that fronted Magnolia's room and Parthy's came the sound of screams, a scuffle, a smart slap, feet clattering pell-mell down the narrow wooden balcony stairs. A wild little figure in a torn white frock, its face scratched and tear-stained, its great eyes ablaze in the white face, flew past Andy, across the gangplank, up the levee, down the road. Behind her, belated and panting, came Parthy. Her hand on her heart, her bosom heaving, she leaned against the inadequate support offered by Andy's right arm, threatening momentarily to topple him, by her own dead weight, into the river.

"To think that I should live to see the day when—my own child—she slapped me—her mother! I saw them out of the window, so I told her to straighten her bureau drawers—a sight! All of a sudden she heard that woman's voice, low as it was, and she to the window. When she saw her going she makes for the door. I caught her on the steps, but she was like a wildcat, and raised her hand against me—her own mother— and tore away, with me holding this in my hand." She held out a fragment of torn white stuff. "Raised her hand against her own——"

Andy grinned. "Good for her."

"What say, Andy Hawks!"

But Andy refused to answer. His gaze followed the flying little figure silhouetted against the evening sky at the top of the high river bank. The slim sagging figure of the woman and the broad-shouldered figure of the man trudged down the road ahead. The child's voice could be heard high and clear, with a note of hysteria in it. "Julie! Julie! Wait for me! I want to say good- bye! Julie!"

The slender woman in the black dress turned and made as though to start back and then, with a kind of crazy fear in her pace, began to run away from the pur- suing little figure—away from something that she had not the courage to face. And when she saw this Mag- nolia ran on yet a little while, faltering, and then she

stopped and buried her head in her hands and sobbed.
The woman glanced over her shoulder, fearfully. And
at what she saw she dropped her bags and bundles in
the road and started back toward her, running fleetly
in spite of her long ruffled awkward skirts; and she held
out her arms long before they were able to reach her.
And when finally they came together, the woman
dropped on her knees in the dust of the road and gathered the weeping child to her and held her close, so that
as you saw them sharply outlined against the sunset the
black of the woman's dress and the white of the child's
frock were as one.

VIII

MAGNOLIA, at fifteen, was a gangling gawky child whose eyes were too big for her face and whose legs were too long for her skirts. She looked, in fact, all legs, eyes, and elbows. It was a constant race between her knees and her skirt hems. Parthy was for ever lengthening frocks. Frequently Magnolia, looking down at herself, was surprised, like Alice in Wonderland after she had eaten the magic currant cake, to discover how far away from her head her feet were. Being possessed of a natural creamy pallor which her mother mistook for lack of red corpuscles, she was dosed into chronic biliousness on cod liver oil, cream, eggs, and butter, all of which she loathed. Then suddenly, at sixteen, legs, elbows, and eyes assumed their natural proportions. Overnight, seemingly, she emerged from adolescence a rather amazing looking young creature with a high broad forehead, a wide mobile mouth, great dark liquid eyes, and a most lovely speaking voice which nobody noticed. Her dress was transformed, with Cinderella-like celerity, from the pinafore to the bustle variety. She was not a beauty. She was, in fact, considered rather plain by the un-noticing. Being hipless and almost boyishly flat of bust in a day when the female form was a thing not only of curves but of loops, she was driven by her mother into wearing all sorts of pads and ruffled corset covers and contrivances which somehow failed to conceal the slimness of the frame beneath. She was, even at sixteen, what might be termed distinguished-looking. Merely by standing tall, pale, dark-haired, next to Elly, that plump and pretty ingénue was transformed into a dumpy and rather dough-faced blonde in whose countenance selfishness and dissatisfaction were beginning to etch telltale lines.

She had been now almost seven years on the show boat. These seven years had spread a tapestry of life and colour before her eyes. Broad rivers flowing to the sea. Little towns perched high on the river banks or cowering flat and fearful, at the mercy of the waters that often crept like hungry and devouring monsters, stealthily over the levee and into the valley below. Singing Negroes. Fighting whites. Spawning Negroes. A life fantastic, bizarre, peaceful, rowdy, prim, eventful, calm. On the rivers anything might happen and everything did. She saw convict chain gangs working on the roads. Grisly nightmarish figures of striped horror, manacled leg to leg. At night you heard them singing plantation songs in the fitful glare of their camp fires in the woods; simple songs full of hope. Didn't My Lord Deliver Daniel? they sang. Swing Low Sweet Chariot, Comin' for to Carry Me Home. In the Louisiana bayou country she saw the Negroes perform that weird religious rite known as a ring shout, semi-savage, hysterical, mesmerizing.

Iowa, Illinois, and Missouri small-town housewives came to be Magnolia's friends, and even Parthy's. The coming of the show boat was the one flash of blazing colour in the drab routine of their existence. To them Schultzy was the John Drew of the rivers, Elly the Lillian Russell. You saw them scudding down the placid tree-shaded streets in their morning ginghams and calicoes, their bits of silver clasped in their work-seamed hands, or knotted into the corner of a handkerchief. Fifty cents for two seats at to-night's show.

"How are you, Mis' Hawks? . . . And the little girl? . . . My! Look at the way she's shot up in a year's time! Well, you can't call her little girl any more. . . . I brought you a glass of my home-made damson preserve. I take cup of sugar to cup of juice. Real rich, but it is good if I do say so. . . . I told Will I was coming to the show every night you were here, and he could like it or lump it. I been saving out of the housekeeping money."

They brought vast chocolate cakes; batches of cookies; jugs of home-brewed grape wine; loaves of fresh bread; jars of strained honey; stiff tight bunches of garden flowers. Offerings on the shrine of Art.

Periodically Parthy threatened to give up this roving life and take Magnolia with her. She held this as a weapon over Andy's head when he crossed her will, or displeased her. Immediately boarding schools, convents, and seminaries yawned for Magnolia.

Perhaps Parthy was right. "What kind of a life is this for a child!" she demanded. And later, "A fine kind of a way for a young lady to be living—slopping up and down these rivers, seeing nothing but loafers and gamblers and niggers and worse. What about her

Future?" Future, as she pronounced it, was spelled with a capital F and was a thin disguise for the word husband.

"Future'll take care of itself," Andy assured her, blithely.

"If that isn't just like a man!"

It was inevitable that Magnolia should, sooner or later, find herself through force of circumstance treading the boards as an actress in the Cotton Blossom Floating Theatre company. Not only that, she found herself playing ingénue leads. She had been thrown in as a stop-gap following Elly's defection, and had become, quite without previous planning, a permanent member of the troupe. Strangely enough, she developed an enormous following, though she lacked that saccharine quality which river towns had come to expect in their show-boat ingénues. True, her long legs were a little lanky beneath the short skirts of the woodman's pure daughter, but what she lacked in one extremity she made up in another. They got full measure when they looked at her eyes, and her voice made the small-town housewives weep. Yet when their husbands nudged them, saying, "What you sniffling about?" they could only reply, "I don't know." And no more did they.

Elly was twenty-eight when she deserted Schultzy for a gambler from Mobile. For three years she had been restless, fault-finding, dissatisfied. Each autumn she would announce to Captain Andy her intention to forsake the rivers and bestow her talents ashore. During the winter she would try to get an engagement through the Chicago booking offices contrary to the custom of show-boat actors whose habit it was to hibernate in the winter on the savings of a long and economical summer. But the Chicago field was sparse and uncertain. She never had the courage or the imagination to go as far as New York. April would find her back on the *Cotton Blossom*. Between her and Schultzy the bickerings and the quarrels became more and more frequent. She openly defied Schultzy as he directed rehearsals. She refused to follow his suggestions though he had a real sense of direction. Everything she knew he had taught her. She invariably misread a line and had to be coached in it, word by word; inflection; business; everything.

Yet now, when Schultzy said, "No! Listen. You been kidnapped and smuggled on board this rich fella's yacht, see. And he thinks he's got you in his power. He goes to grab you. You're here, see. Then you point toward the door back of him, see, like you saw something there scared the life out of you. He turns around and you grab the gun off the table, see, and cover him, and there's your big speech. *So* and so and *so* and so and *so* and so and *so* and so——" the *ad lib.* directions that have held since the day of Shakespeare.

Elly would deliberately defy him. Others in the company—new members—began to take their cue from her.

She complained about her wardrobe; refused to interest herself in it, though she had been an indefatigable needlewoman. Now, instead of sewing, you saw her looking moodily out across the river, her hands idle, her brows black. An unintelligent and unresourceful woman turned moody and thoughtful must come to mischief, for within herself she finds no solace.

At Mobile, then, she was gone. It was, they all knew, the black-moustached gambler who had been following the show boat down the river since they played Paducah, Kentucky. Elly had had dozens of admirers in her show-boat career; had received much attention from Southern gallants, gamblers, loafers, adventurers —all the romantic beaux of the river towns of the '80s. Her attitude toward them had been puritanical to the point of sniffiness, though she had enjoyed their homage and always displayed any amorous missives or gifts that came her way.

True to the melodramatic tradition of her environment, she left a note for Schultzy, written in a flourishing Spencerian hand that made up, in part, for the spelling. She was gone. He need not try to follow her or find her or bring her back. She was going to star at the head of her own company and play Camille and even Juliet. He had promised her. She was good and sick and tired of this everlasting flopping up and down the rivers. She wouldn't go back to it, no matter what. Her successor could have her wardrobe. They had bookings through Iowa, Illinois, Missouri, and Kansas. She might even get to New York. (Incredibly enough, she did actually play Juliet through the Mid-west, to audiences of the bewildered yokelry.) She was sorry to leave Cap in the lurch like this. And she would close, and begged to remain his loving Wife (this inked out but still decipherable)—begged to remain, his truly, Elly Chipley. Just below this signature the added one of Lenore La Verne, done in tremendous sable down-strokes and shaded curlecues, especially about the L's.

It was a crushing blow for Schultzy, who loved her. Stricken, he thought only of her happiness. "She can't get along without me," he groaned. Then, in a stunned way, "Juliet!" There was nothing of bitterness or rancour in his tone; only a dumb despairing wonder. "Juliet! And she couldn't play Little Eva without making her out a slut." He pondered this a moment. "She's got it into her head she's Bernhardt, or something. . . . Well, she'll come back."

"Do you mean to say you'd take her back!" Parthy demanded.

"Why, sure," Schultzy replied, simply. "She never packed a trunk in her life, or anything. I done all those things for her. Some ways she's a child. I guess that's how she kept me so tight. She needed me all the time. . . . Well, she'll come back."

Captain Andy sent to Chicago for an ingénue lead. It was then, pending her arrival, that Magnolia stepped into the breach—the step being made, incidentally, over what was practically Parthy's dead body. For at Magnolia's calm announcement that she knew every line of the part and all the business, her mother stormed, had hysterics, and finally took to her bed (until nearly time for the rise of the curtain). The bill that night was The Parson's Bride. Show-boat companies to this day still tell the story of what happened during that performance on the Cotton Blossom.

They had two rehearsals, one in the morning, another that lasted throughout the afternoon. Of the company,

Magnolia was the calmest. Captain Andy seemed to swing, by invisible pulleys, from the orchestra pit below to Parthy's chamber above. One moment he would be sprawled in the kerosene footlights, his eyes deep in wrinkles of delight, his little brown paws scratching the mutton-chop whiskers in a frenzy of excitement.

"That's right. That's the stuff! Elly never give it half the——'Scuse me, Schultzy—I didn't go for to hurt your feelings, but by golly, Nollie! I wouldn't of believed you had it in you, not if your own mother told——" Then, self-reminded, he would cast a fearful glance over his shoulder, that shoulder would droop, he would extricate himself from the welter of footlights and music racks and prompt books in which he squatted, and scamper up the aisle. The dim outline of a female head in curl papers certainly could not have been seen peering over the top of the balcony rail as he fancied, for when he had clattered up the balcony stairs and had gently turned the knob of the bedroom door, there lay the curl-papered head on the pillow of the big bed, and from it issued hollow groans, and plastered over one cheek of it was a large moist white cloth soaked in some pungent and nostril-pricking stuff. The eyes were closed. The whole figure was shaken by shivers. Mortal agony, you would have said (had you not known Parthy), had this stricken and monumental creature in its horrid clutches.

In a whisper—"Parthy!"

A groan, hollow, heartrending, mortuary.

He entered, shut the door softly, tiptoed over to the bed, laid a comforting brown paw on the shivering

shoulder. The shoulder became convulsive, the shivers
swelled to heaves. "Now, now, Parthy! What you
taking on so for? God A'mighty, person'd think she'd
done something to shame you instead of make you
mighty proud. If you'd see her! Why, say, she's a
born actress."

The groans now became a wail. The eyes unclosed.
The figure raised itself to a sitting posture. The sopping
rag rolled limply off. Parthy rocked herself to and fro.
"My own daughter! An actress! That I should have
lived to see this day! . . . Rather have . . .
in her grave . . . why I ever allowed her to set
foot on this filthy scow . . ."

"Now, Parthy, you're just working yourself up.
Matter of fact, that time Mis' Means turned her ankle
and we thought she couldn't step on it, you was all for
going on in her part, and I bet if Sophy Means hadn't
tied up her foot and gone on like a soldier she is, we'd
of had you acting that night. You was rarin' to. I
watched you."

"Me! Acting on the stage! Not that I couldn't
play better than any Sophy Means, and that's no
compliment. A poor stick if I couldn't." But her
defence lacked conviction. Andy had surprised a
secret ambition in this iron-armoured bosom.

"Now, come on! Cheer up! Ought to be proud
your own daughter stepping in and saving us money
like this. We'd of closed. Had to. God knows when
that new baggage'll get here, if she gets here at all.
What do you think of that Chipley! Way I've treated
that girl, if she'd been my own daughter—well! . . .

How'd you like a nice little sip of whisky, Parthy?
Then you come on down give Nollie a hand with her
costumes. Chipley's stuff comes up on her like ballet
skirts.—Now, now, now! I didn't say she—— Oh, my
God!"

Parthy had gone off again into hysterics. "My own
daughter! My little girl!"

The time for severe measures had come. Andy had
not dealt with actresses for years without learning something of the weapons with which to fight hysteria.

"All right. I'll give you something to screech for.
The boys paraded this noon with a banner six feet long
and red letters a foot high announcing the Appearance
Extraordinaire of Magnolia the Mysterious Comedy
Tragedienne in The Parson's Bride. I made a special
spiel on the corner. We got the biggest advance sale
we had this season. Yessir! Doc's downstairs raking
it in with both hands and you had the least bit of gump-
tion in you, instead of laying here whining and carrying
on, you'd——"

"What's the advance?" spake up Parthy, the box-
office expert.

"Three hundred; and not anywheres near four
o'clock."

With one movement Parthy had flung aside the
bedclothes and stepped out of bed revealing, rather in-
explicably, a complete lower costume including shoes.

Andy was off, down the stairs, up the aisle, into the
orchestra pit just in time to hear Magnolia say,
"Schultzy, *please!* Don't throw me the line like that,
I know it. I didn't stop because I was stuck."

"What'd you stop for, then, and look like you'd seen spooks!"

"I stopped a-purpose.   She sees her husband that she hates and that she thought was dead for years come sneaking in, and she wouldn't start right in to talk. She'd just stand there, kind of frozen and stiff, staring at him."

"All right, if you know so much about directing go ahead and di——"

She ran to him, threw her arms about him, hugged him, all contrition. "Oh, Schultzy, don't be mad.   I didn't go to boss.   I just wanted to act it like I felt. And I'm awfully sorry about Elly and everything.   I'll do as you say, only I just can't help thinking, Schultzy dear, that she'd stand there, staring kind of silly, almost."

"You're right.   I guess my mind ain't on my work. I ought to know how right you are.   I got that letter Elly left for me, I just stood there gawping with my mouth open, and never said a word for I don't know how long—— Oh, my God!"

"There, there, Schultzy."

By a tremendous effort (the mechanics of which were not entirely concealed) Schultzy, the man, gave way to Harold Westbrook, the artist.

"You're right, Magnolia.   That'll get 'em.   You standing there like that, stunned and pale."

"How'll I get pale, Schultzy?"

"You'll feel pale inside and the audience'll think you are."   (The whole art of acting unconsciously expressed by Schultzy.)   "Then Frank here has his

sneery speech—*so* and so and *so* and so and *so* and so—
and thought you'd marry the parson, huh? And then
you open up with your big scene—*so* and so and *so* and
so and *so* and so——"

Outwardly calm, Magnolia took only a cup of coffee
at dinner, and Parthy, for once, did not press her to eat.
That mournful matron, though still occasionally shaken
by a convulsive shudder, managed her usual heartening
repast and actually spent the time from four to seven
lengthening Elly's frocks for Magnolia and taking them
in to fit the girl's slight frame.

Schultzy made her up, and rather overdid it so that,
as the deserted wife and school teacher and, later, as
the Parson's prospective bride, she looked a pass
between a healthy Camille and Cleopatra just before
she applied the asp. In fact, in their effort to bridge
the gap left by Elly's sudden flight, the entire company
overdid everything and thus brought about the cataclysmic moment which is theatrical show-boat history.

Magnolia, so sure of her lines during rehearsal,
forgot them a score of times during the performance
and, had it not been for Schultzy, who threw them to her
unerringly and swiftly, would have made a dismal failure of this, her first stage appearance. They were
playing Vidallia, always a good show-boat town. The
house was filled from the balcony boxes to the last row
downstairs near the door, from which point very little
could be seen and practically nothing heard. Something of the undercurrent of excitement which pervaded
the *Cotton Blossom* troupe seemed to seep through the
audience; or perhaps even an audience so unsophisti-

cated as this could not but sense the unusual in this performance. Every one of the troupe—Schultzy, Mis' Means, Mr. Means, Frank, Ralph, the Soapers (Character Team that had succeeded Julie and Steve) —all were trembling for Magnolia. And because they were fearful for her they threw themselves frantically into their parts. Magnolia, taking her cue (literally as well as figuratively) from them, did likewise. As ingénue lead, her part was that of a young school mistress earning her livelihood in a little town. Deserted some years before by her worthless husband, she learns now of his death. The town parson has long been in love with her, and she with him. Now they can marry. The wedding gown is finished. The guests are invited.

This is her last day as school teacher. She is alone in the empty schoolroom. Farewell, dear pupils. Farewell, dear schoolroom, blackboard, erasers, water-bucket, desk, etc. She picks up her key. But what is this evil face in the doorway! Who is this drunken, leering tramp, grisly in rags, repulsive—— My God! You! My husband!

(Never was villain so black and diabolical as Frank. Never was heroine so lovely and frail and trembling and helpless and white—as per Schultzy's directions. As for Schultzy himself, the heroic parson, very heavily made up and pure yet brave withal, it was a poor stick of a maiden who wouldn't have contrived to get into some sort of distressing circumstance just for the joy of being got out of it by this godly yet godlike young cleric.)

Frank, then: "I reckon you thought I was dead.

Well, I'm about the livest corpse you ever saw." A diabolical laugh. "Too damn bad you won't be able to wear that new wedding dress."

Pleadings, agony, despair.

Now his true villainy comes out. A thousand dollars, then, and quick, or you don't walk down the aisle to the music of no wedding march.

"I haven't got it."

"No! Where's the money you been saving all these years?"

"I haven't a thousand dollars. I swear it."

"So!" Seizes her. Drags her across the room. Screams. His hand stifles them.

Unfortunately, in their very desire to help Magnolia, they all exaggerated their villainy, their heroism, their business. Being a trifle uncertain of her lines, Magnolia, too, sought to cover her deficiencies by stressing her emotional scenes. When terror was required her face was distorted with it. Her screams of fright were real screams of mortal fear. Her writhings would have wrung pity from a fiend. Frank bared his teeth, chortled like a maniac. He wound his fingers in her long black hair and rather justified her outcry. In contrast, Schultzy's nobility and purity stood out as crudely and unmistakably as white against black. Nuances were not for show-boat audiences.

So then, screams, protestations, snarls, ha-ha's, pleadings, agony, cruelty, anguish.

Something—intuition—or perhaps a sound from the left upper box made Frank, the villain, glance up. There, leaning over the box rail, his face a mask of

hatred, his eyes glinting, sat a huge hairy backwoodsman. And in his hand glittered the barrel of a businesslike gun. He was taking careful aim. Drama had
come late into the life of this literal mind. He had,
in the course of a quick-shooting rough-and-tumble
career, often seen the brutal male mishandling beauty
in distress. His code was simple. One second more
and he would act on it.

Frank's hand released his struggling victim. Gentle-
ness and love overspread his features, dispelling their
villainy. To Magnolia's staring and open-mouthed
amazement he made a gesture of abnegation. "Well,
Marge, I ain't got nothin' more to say if you and the
parson want to get married." After which astounding
utterance he slunk rapidly off, leaving the field to what
was perhaps the most abject huddle of heroism that
every graced a show-boat stage.

The curtain came down. The audience, intuitively
glancing toward the upper box, ducked, screamed, or
swore. The band struck up. The backwoodsman,
a little bewildered but still truculent, subsided somewhat. A trifle mystified, but labouring under the
impression that this was, perhaps, the ordinary routine
of the theatre, the audience heard Schultzy, in front
of the curtain, explaining that the villain was taken
suddenly ill; that the concert would now be given free
of charge; that each and every man, woman, and child
was invited to retain his seat. The backwoodsman,
rather sheepish now, took a huge bite of Honest Scrap
and looked about him belligerently. Out came Mr.
Means to do his comic Chinaman. Order reigned on

one side of the footlights at least, though behind the heaving Venetian lagoon was a company saved from collapse only by a quite human uncertainty as to whether tears or laughter would best express their state of mind.

The new ingénue lead, scheduled to meet the *Cotton Blossom* at Natchez, failed to appear. Magnolia, following her trial by firearms, had played the absent Elly's parts for a week. There seemed to be no good reason why she should not continue to do so at least until Captain Andy could engage an ingénue who would join the troupe at New Orleans.

A year passed. Magnolia was a fixture in the company. Now, as she, in company with Parthy or Mis' Means or Mrs. Soaper, appeared on the front street of this or that little river town, she was stared at and commented on. Round-eyed little girls, swinging on the front gate, gazed at her much as she had gazed, not so many years before, at Elly and Julie as they had sauntered down the shady path of her own street in Thebes.

She loved the life. She worked hard. She cherished the admiration and applause. She took her work seriously. Certainly she did not consider herself an apostle of art. She had no illusions about herself as an actress. But she did thrive on the warm electric current that flowed from those river audiences made up of miners, farmers, Negroes, housewives, harvesters, backwoodsmen, villagers, over the footlights, to her. A naïve people, they accepted their theatre without question, like children. That which they saw they believed. They hissed the villain, applauded the heroine, wept over the plight of the wronged. The plays were as naïve as the audience. In them, on-rushing engines were cheated of their victims; mill wheels were stopped in the nick of time; heroes, bound hand and foot and left to be crushed under iron wheels, were rescued by the switchman's ubiquitous daughter. Sheriffs popped up unexpectedly in hidden caves. The sound of horses' hoofs could always be heard when virtue was about to be ravished. They were the minstrels of the rivers, these players, telling in terms of blood, love, and adventure the crude saga of a new country.

Frank, the Heavy, promptly fell in love with Magnolia. Parthy, quick to mark the sheep's eyes he cast in the direction of the ingénue lead, watched him with a tigress glare, and though he lived on the *Cotton Blossom*, as did Magnolia; saw her all day, daily; probably was seldom more than a hundred feet removed from her, he never spoke to her alone and certainly never was able to touch her except in the very public glare of the footlights with some hundreds of pairs of eyes turned on the two by the *Cotton Blossom* audiences. He lounged disconsolately after her, a large and somewhat splay-footed fellow whose head was too small for his shoulders, giving him the look of an inverted exclamation point.

His unrequited and unexpressed passion for Magnolia would have bothered that young lady and her parents very little were it not for the fact that his emotions began to influence his art. In his scenes on the stage with her he became more and more uncertain of his lines. Not only that, his attitude and tone as villain of the piece took on a tender note most mystifying to the audience, accustomed to seeing villainy black, with no half tones. When he should have been hurling Magnolia into the mill stream or tying her brutally to the track, or lashing her with a horsewhip or snarling at her like a wolf, he became a cooing dove. His blows were caresses. His baleful glare became a simper of adoration.

"Do you intend to speak to that sheep, or shall I?" demanded Parthy of her husband.

"I'll do it," Andy assured her, hurriedly. "Leave him be till we get to New Orleans. Then, if anything busts, why, I can always get some kind of a fill-in there."

They had been playing the Louisiana parishes—little Catholic settlements between New Orleans and Baton Rouge, their inhabitants a mixture of French and Creole. Frank had wandered disconsolately through the miniature cathedral which each little parish boasted and, returning, had spoken darkly of abandoning the stage for the Church.

New Orleans meant mail for the *Cotton Blossom* troupe. With that mail came trouble. Schultzy, white but determined, approached Captain Andy, letter in hand.

"I got to go, Cap. She needs me."

"Go!" squeaked Andy. His squeak was equivalent to a bellow in a man of ordinary stature. "Go where? What d'you mean, she?" But he knew.

Out popped Parthy, scenting trouble.

Schultzy held out a letter written on cheap paper, lined, and smelling faintly of antiseptic. "She's in the hospital at Little Rock. Says she's had an operation. He's left her, the skunk. She ain't got a cent."

"I'll take my oath on that," Parthy put in, pungently.

"You can't go and leave me flat now, Schultzy."

"I got to go, I tell you. Frank can play leads till you get somebody, or till I get back. Old Means can play utility at a pinch, and Doc can do general business."

"Frank," announced Parthy, with terrible distinctness, "will play no leads in this company, and so I tell you, Hawks."

"Who says he's going to! A fine-looking lead he'd make, with that pin-head of his, and those elephant's hoofs. . . . Now looka here, Schultzy. You been a trouper long enough to know you can't leave a show in the ditch like this. No real show-boat actor'd do it, and you know it."

"Sure I know it. I wouldn't do it for myself, no matter what. But it's her. I wrote her a letter, time she left. I got her bookings. I said if the time comes you need me, leave me know, and I'll come. And she needs me, and she left me know, and I'm coming."

"How about us!" demanded Parthy. "Leaving us in the lurch like that, first Elly and now you after all these years. A fine pair, the two of you."

"Now, Parthy!"

"Oh, I've no patience with you, Hawks. Always letting people get the best of you."

"But I told you," Schultzy began again, almost tearfully, "it's for her, not me. She's sick. You can pick up somebody here in New Orleans. I bet there's a dozen better actors than me laying around the docks this minute. I got to talking to a fellow while ago, down on the wharf. The place was all jammed up with freight, and I was waiting to get by so's I could come aboard. I said I was an actor on the *Cotton Blossom*, and he said he'd acted and that was a life he'd like."

"Yes," snapped Parthy. "I suppose he would. What does he think this is! A bumboat! Plenty of wharf rats in New Orleans'd like nothing better——"

Schultzy pointed to where a slim figure leaned indolently against a huge packing case—one of hundreds of idlers dotting the great New Orleans plank landing.

Andy adjusted the pair of ancient binoculars through which he recently had been scanning the wharf and the city beyond the levee. He surveyed the graceful lounging figure.

"I'd go ashore and talk to him, I was you," advised Schultzy.

Andy put down the glasses and stared at Schultzy in amazement. "Him! Why, I couldn't go up and talk to him about acting on no show boat. He's a gentleman."

"Here," said Parthy, abruptly, her curiosity piqued. She in turn trained the glasses on the object of the discussion. Her survey was brief but ample. "He may be a gentleman. But nobody feels a gentleman with a crack in his shoe, and he's got one. I can't say I like the looks of him, specially.   But with Schultzy playing us this dirty trick—well, that's what it amounts to, and there's no sense trying to prettify it—we can't be choosers.   I'd just step down talk to him if I was you, Hawks."

IX

THIS, then, turned out to be Magnolia's first glimpse of Gaylord Ravenal—an idle elegant figure in garments whose modish cut and fine material served, at a distance, to conceal their shabbiness. Leaning moodily against a tall packing case dumped on the wharf by some freighter, he gazed about him and tapped indolently the tip of his shining (and cracked) boot with an exquisite little ivory-topped malacca cane. There was about him an air of distinction, an atmosphere of richness. On closer proximity you saw that the broadcloth was shiny, the fine linen of the shirt front and cuffs the least bit frayed, the slim boots undeniably split, the hat (a delicate gray and set a little on one side) soiled as a pale gray hat must never be. From the *Cotton Blossom* deck you saw him as the son, perhaps, of some rich Louisiana planter, idling a moment at the water's edge. Waiting, doubtless, for one of the big river packets—the floating palaces of the Mississippi—to bear him luxuriously away up the river to his plantation landing.

The truth was that Gaylord Ravenal was what the river gamblers called broke. Stony, he would have told you. No one had a better right to use the term than he. Of his two possessions, save the sorry clothes he had on, one was the little malacca cane. And though

he might part with cuff links, shirt studs and, if necessary, shirt itself, he would always cling to that little
malacca cane, emblem of good fortune, his mascot.
It had turned on him temporarily. Yet his was the
gambler's superstitious nature. To-morrow the cane
would bring him luck.

Not only was Gaylord Ravenal broke; he had just
politely notified the Chief of Police of New Orleans that
he was in town. The call was not entirely one of social
obligation. It had a certain statutory side as well.

In the first place, Chief of Police Vallon, in a sudden
political spasm of virtue, endeavouring to clear New
Orleans of professional gamblers, had given them all
twenty-four hours' shrift. In the second place, this
particular visitor would have come under the head of
New Orleans undesirables on his own private account,
even though his profession had been that of philanthropist. Gaylord Ravenal had one year-old notch to
his gun.

It had not been murder in cold blood or in rage,
but a shot fired in self-defence just the fraction of a
second before the other man could turn the trick. The
evidence proved this, and Ravenal's final vindication
followed. But New Orleans gathered her civic skirts
about her and pointed a finger of dismissal toward the
door. Hereafter, should he enter, his first visit must be
to the Chief of Police; and twenty-four hours—no more
—must be the limit of his stay in the city whose pom-
pano and crayfish and Creoles and roses and Ramos gin
fizzes he loved.

The evening before, he had stepped off the river

packet *Lady Lee*, now to be seen lying alongside the New Orleans landing together with a hundred other craft. His twenty-four hours would expire this evening.

Certainly he had not meant to find himself in New Orleans. He had come aboard the *Lady Lee* at St. Louis, his finances low, his hopes high, his erstwhile elegant garments in their present precarious state. He had planned, following the game of stud poker in which he immediately immersed himself, to come ashore at Memphis or, at the latest, Natchez, with his finances raised to the high level of his hopes. Unfortunately his was an honest and over-eager game. His sole possession, beside the little slim malacca cane (itself of small tangible value) was a singularly clear blue-white diamond ring which he never wore. It was a relic of luckier days before his broadcloth had become shiny, his linen frayed, his boots split. He had clung to it, as he had to the cane, through almost incredible hazards. His feeling about it was neither sentimental nor superstitious. The tenuous streak of canniness in him told him that, possessed of a clear white diamond, one can hold up one's head and one's hopes, no matter what the state of coat, linen, boots, and hat. It had never belonged, fiction-fashion, to his sainted (if any) mother, nor was it an old Ravenal heirloom. It was a relic of winnings in luckier days and represented, he knew, potential hundreds. In the trip that lasted, unexpectedly, from St. Louis to New Orleans, he had won and lost that ring six times. When the *Lady Lee* had nosed her way into the Memphis landing, and again at Natchez, it had been out of his possession. He had stayed on board, perforce. Half an hour before coming into New Orleans he had had it again, and had kept it. The game of stud poker had lasted days, and he rose from it the richer by exactly nothing at all.

He had glanced out of the *Lady Lee's* saloon window, his eyes bloodshot from sleeplessness, his nerves jangling, his hands twitching, his face drawn; but that face shaven, those hands immaculate. Gaylord Ravenal, in luck or out, had the habits and instincts of a gentleman.

"Good God!" he exclaimed now, "this looks like— it is New Orleans!" It was N'Yawlins as he said it.

"What did you think it was?" growled one of the players, who had temporarily owned the diamond several times during the journey down river. "What did you think it was? Shanghai?"

"I wish it was," said Gaylord Ravenal. Somewhat dazedly he walked down the *Lady Lee's* gangplank and retorted testily to a beady-eyed giant-footed gentleman who immediately spoke to him in a low and not unfriendly tone, "Give me time, can't you! I haven't been twenty-four hours stepping from the gangplank to this wharf, have I? Well, then!"

"No offence, Gay," said the gentleman, his eyes still searching the other passengers as they filed across the narrow gangplank. "Just thought I'd remind you, case of trouble. You know how Vallon is."

Vallon had said, briefly, later, "That's all right, Gay. But by this time to-morrow evening——" He had eyed Ravenal's raiment with a comprehending eye. "Cigar?" The weed he proffered was slim, pale, and

frayed as the man who stood before him. Gaylord
Ravenal's jangling nerves ached for the solace of tobacco; but he viewed this palpably second-hand gift
with a glance of disdain that was a triumph of the spirit
over the flesh. Certainly no man handicapped by his
present sartorial and social deficiencies was justified
in raising a quizzical right eyebrow in the manner
employed by Ravenal.

"What did you call it?" said he now.

Vallon looked at it. He was not a quick-witted
gentleman. "Cigar."

"Optimist." And strolled out of the chief's office,
swinging the little malacca cane.

So then, you now saw him leaning moodily against a
wooden case on the New Orleans plank wharf, distinguished, shabby, dapper, handsome, broke, and twenty-
four.

It was with some amusement that he had watched the
crew of the *Mollie Able* bring the flat unwieldy bulk of
the *Cotton Blossom* into the wharfside in the midst of the
confusion of packets, barges, steamboats, tugs, flats,
tramp boats, shanty boats. He had spoken briefly and
casually to Schultzy while that bearer of evil tidings,
letter in hand, waited impatiently on the dock as the
Cotton Blossom was shifted to a landing position farther
upstream. He had seen these floating theatres of the
Mississippi and the Ohio many times, but he had never
before engaged one of their actors in conversation.

"Juvenile lead!" he had exclaimed, unable to hide
something of incredulity in his voice. Schultzy, an
anxious eye on the *Mollie Able's* tedious manœuvres,

had just made clear to Ravenal his own position in the *Cotton Blossom* troupe. Ravenal, surveying the furrowed brow, the unshaven cheeks, the careless dress, the lack-lustre eye, had involuntarily allowed to creep into his tone something of the astonishment he felt.

Schultzy made a little deprecating gesture with his hands, his shoulders. "I guess I don't look like no juvenile lead, and that's a fact. But I'm all shot to pieces. Took a drink the size of this"—indicating perhaps five fingers—"up yonder on Canal Street; straight whisky. No drinking allowed on the show boat. Well, sir, never felt it no more'n it had been water. I just got news my wife's sick in the hospital."

Ravenal made a little perfunctory sound of sympathy. "In New Orleans?"

"Little Rock, Arkansas. I'm going. It's a dirty trick, but I'm going."

"How do you mean, dirty trick?" Ravenal was mildly interested in this confiding stranger.

"Leave the show flat like that. I don't know what they'll do. I——" He saw that the *Cotton Blossom* was now snugly at ease in her new position, and that her gangplank had again been lowered. He turned away abruptly, without a good-bye, went perhaps ten paces, came back five and called to Ravenal. "You ever acted?"

"Acted!"

"On the stage. Acted. Been an actor."

Ravenal threw back his handsome head and laughed as he would have thought, ten minutes ago, he never could laugh again. "Me! An actor! N—" then,

suddenly sober, thoughtful even—"Why, yes. Yes."
And eyeing Schultzy through half-shut lids he tapped
the tip of his shiny shabby boot with the smart little
malacca cane. Schultzy was off again toward the
Cotton Blossom.

If Ravenal was aware of the scrutiny to which he was
subjected through the binoculars, he gave no sign as he
lounged elegantly on the wharf watching the busy
waterside scene with an air of indulgent amusement
that would have made the onlooker receive with incredulity the information that the law was even then
snapping at his heels.

Captain Andy Hawks scampered off the *Cotton
Blossom* and approached this figure, employing none of
the finesse that the situation called for.

"I understand you've acted on the stage."

Gaylord Ravenal elevated the right eyebrow and
looked down his aristocratic nose at the capering little
captain. "I am Gaylord Ravenal, of the Tennessee
Ravenals. I failed to catch your name."

"Andy Hawks, captain and owner of the Cotton
Blossom Floating Palace Theatre." He jerked a thumb
over his shoulder at the show boat.

"Ah, yes," said Ravenal, with polite unenthusiasm.
He allowed his patrician glance to rest idly a moment on
the *Cotton Blossom*, lying squat and dumpy alongside
the landing.

Captain Andy found himself suddenly regretting
that he had not had her painted and overhauled. He
clutched his whiskers in embarrassment, and, under
stress of that same emotion, blurted the wrong thing.

"I guess Parthy was mistaken." The Ravenal eyebrow became interrogatory. Andy floundered on. "She said that no man with a crack in the shoe——" he stopped, then, appalled.

Gaylord Ravenal looked down at the footgear under discussion. He looked up at the grim and ponderous female figure on the forward deck of the show boat. Parthy was wearing one of her most uncompromising bonnets and a gown noticeably bunchy even in that day of unsymmetrical feminine fashions. Black was not becoming to Mrs. Hawks' sallow colouring. Lumpy black was fatal. If anything could have made this figure less attractive than it actually was, Ravenal's glance would seem to have done so. "That—ah—lady?"

"My wife," said Andy. Then, mindful of the maxim of the sheep and the lamb, he went the whole way. "We've lost our juvenile lead. Fifteen a week and found. Chance to see the world. No responsibility. Schultzy said you said . . . I said . . . Parthy said . . ." Hopelessly entangled, he stopped.

"Am I to understand that I am being offered the position of—ah—juvenile lead on the—" the devastating glance upward—"Cotton Blossom Floating Palace——"

"That's the size of it," interrupted Andy, briskly. After all, even this young man's tone and manner could not quite dispel that crack in the boot. Andy knew that no one wears a split shoe from choice.

"No responsibility," he repeated. "A chance to see life."

"I've seen it," in the tone of one who did not care

for what he has beheld. His eyes were on a line with the *Cotton Blossom's* deck. His gaze suddenly became concentrated. A tall slim figure in white had just appeared on the upper deck, forward—the bit of deck that looked for all the world like a nautical veranda. It led off Magnolia's bedroom. The slim white figure was Magnolia. Prepatory to going ashore she was taking a look at this romantic city which she always had loved, and which she, in company with Andy or Doc, had roamed a dozen times since her first early childhood trip on the *Creole Belle*.

Her dress was bunchy, too, as the mode demanded. But where it was not bunchy it was very tight. And its bunchiness thus only served to emphasize the slimness of the snug areas. Her black hair was drawn smoothly away from the temples and into a waterfall at the back. Her long fine head and throat rose exquisitely above the little pleated frill that finished the neckline of her gown. She carried her absurd beribboned and beflowered high-crowned hat in her hand. A graceful, pliant, slim young figure in white, surveying the pandemonium that was the New Orleans levee. Columns of black rose from a hundred steamer stacks. Freight barrels and boxes went hurtling through the air, or were shoved or carried across the plank wharf to the accompaniment of shouting and sweating and swearing. Negroes everywhere. Band boxes, carpet bags, babies, drays, carriages, wheelbarrows, carts. Beyond the levee rose the old salt warehouses. Beyond these lay Canal Street. Magnolia was going into town with her father and her mother. Andy had promised her supper at Antoine's and an evening at the old French theatre. She knew scarcely ten words of French. Andy, if he had known it in his childhood, had quite forgotten it now. Parthy looked upon it as the language of sin and the yellow-back paper novels. But all three found enjoyment in the grace and colour and brilliance of the performance and the audience—both of a sort to be found nowhere else in the whole country. Andy's enjoyment was tinged and heightened by a vague nostalgia; Magnolia's was that of one artist for the work of another; Parthy's was the enjoyment of suspicion. She always hoped the play's high scenes were going to be more risqué than they actually were.

From her vantage point Magnolia stood glancing alertly about her, enjoying the babel that was the New Orleans plank wharves. She now espied and recognized the familiarly capering little figure below with its right hand scratching the mutton-chop whiskers this side and that. She was impatient to be starting for their jaunt ashore. She waved at him with the hand that held the hat. The upraised arm served to enhance the delicate curve of the pliant young figure in its sheath of white.

Andy, catching sight of her, waved in return.

"Is that," inquired Gaylord Ravenal, "a member of your company?"

Andy's face softened and glowed. "That? That's my daughter Magnolia."

"Magnolia. Magnol—— Does she—is she a——"

"I should smile she is! She's our ingénue lead, Magnolia is. Plays opposite the juvenile lead. But if you've been a trouper you know that, I guess." A sudden suspicion darted through him. "Say, young man—what's your name?—oh, yes, Ravenal. Well, Ravenal, you a quick study? That's what I got to know, first off. Because we leave New Orleans to-night to play the bayous. Bayou Teche to-morrow night in Tempest and Sunshine. . . . You a quick study?"

"Lightning," said Gaylord Ravenal.

Five minutes later, bowing over her hand, he did not know whether to curse the crack in his shoe for shaming him before her, or to bless it for having been the cause of his being where he was.

That he and Magnolia should become lovers was as inevitable as the cosmic course. Certainly some force greater than human must have been at work on it, for it overcame even Parthy's opposition. Everything conspired to bring the two together, including their being kept forcibly apart. Himself a picturesque, mysterious, and romantic figure, Gaylord Ravenal, immediately after joining the *Cotton Blossom* troupe, became the centre of a series of dramatic episodes any one of which would have made him glamorous in Magnolia's eyes, even though he had not already assumed for her the glory of a Galahad.

She had never before met a man of Ravenal's stamp. In this dingy motley company he moved aloof, remote, yet irresistibly attracting all of them—except Parthy. She, too, must have felt drawn to this charming and magnetic man, but she fought the attraction with all the strength of her powerful and vindictive nature. Sensing that here lay his bitterest opposition, Ravenal

deliberately set about exercising his charm to win
Parthy to friendliness. For the first time in his life he
received rebuff so bristling, so unmistakable, as to cause
him temporarily to doubt his own gifts.

Women had always adored Gaylord Ravenal. He
was not a villain. He was, in fact, rather gentle, and
more than a little weak. His method, coupled with
strong personal attractiveness, was simple in the ex-
treme. He made love to all women and demanded
nothing of them. Swept off their feet, they waited,
trembling deliciously, for the final attack. At its
failure to materialize they looked up, wondering, to see
his handsome face made more handsome by a certain
wistful sadness. At that their hearts melted within
them. That which they had meant to defend they now
offered. For the rest, his was a paradoxical nature.
A courtliness of manner, contradicted by a bluff boyish-
ness. A certain shy boldness. He was not an especially
intelligent man. He had no need to be. His upturned
glance at a dining-room waitress bent over him was in
no way different from that which he directed straight at
Parthy now; or at the daughter of a prosperous Southern
lawyer, or at that daughter's vaguely uneasy mama.
It wasn't deliberate evil in him or lack of fastidiousness.
He was helpless to do otherwise.

Certainly he had never meant to remain a member of
this motley troupe, drifting up and down the rivers.
He had not, for that matter, meant to fall in love with
Magnolia, much less marry her. Propinquity and opposition, either of which usually is sufficient to fan
the flame, together caused the final conflagration. For

weeks after he came on board, he literally never spoke to Magnolia alone. Parthy attended to that. He saw her not only daily but almost hourly. He considered himself lucky to be deft enough to say, "Lovely day, isn't it, Miss Magn——" before Mrs. Hawks swept her offspring out of earshot. Parthy was wise enough to see that this handsome, graceful, insidious young stranger would appear desirable and romantic in the eyes of women a hundredfold more sophisticated than the child-like and unawakened Magnolia. She took refuge in the knowledge that this dangerous male was the most impermanent of additions to the *Cotton Blossom* troupe. His connection with them would end on Schultzy's return.

Gaylord Ravenal was, in the meantime, a vastly amused and prodigiously busy young man. To learn the juvenile leads in the plays that made up the *Cotton Blossom* troupe's repertoire was no light matter. Not only must he memorize lines, business, and cues of the regular bills—Uncle Tom's Cabin, East Lynne, Tempest and Sunshine, Lady Audley's Secret, The Parson's Bride, The Gambler, and others— but he must be ready to go on in the concert afterpiece, whatever it might be —sometimes A Dollar for a Kiss, sometimes Red Hot Coffee. The company rehearsed day and night; during the day they rehearsed that night's play; after the performance they rehearsed next night's bill. With some astonishment the *Cotton Blossom* troupe realized, at the end of two weeks, that Gaylord Ravenal was acting as director. It had come about naturally and inevitably. Ravenal had a definite theatre sense—a feeling for tempo, rhythm, line, grouping, inflection, characterization—any, or all, of these. The atmosphere had freshness for him; he was interested; he wished to impress Andy and Parthy and Magnolia; he considered the whole business a gay adventure; and an amusing interlude. For a month they played the bayous and plantations of Louisiana, leaving behind them a whole countryside whose planters, villagers, Negroes had been startled out of their Southern lethargy. These had known show boats and show-boat performances all their lives. They had been visited by this or that raffish, dingy, slap-dash, or decent and painstaking troupe. The *Cotton Blossom* company had the reputation for being the last-named variety, and always were patronized accordingly. The plays seldom varied. The performance was, usually, less than mediocre. They were, then, quite unprepared for the entertainment given them by the two handsome, passionate, and dramatic young people who now were cast as ingénue and juvenile lead of the Cotton Blossom Floating Palace Theatre company. Here was Gaylord Ravenal, fresh, young, personable, aristocratic, romantic of aspect. Here was Magnolia, slim, girlish, ardent, electric, lovely. Their make-believe adventures as they lived them on the stage became real; their dangers and misfortunes set the natives to trembling; their love-making was a fragrant and exquisite thing. News of this troupe seeped through from plantation to plantation, from bayou to bayou, from settlement to settlement, in some mysterious underground way. The *Cotton Blossom* did a record-breaking business in

a region that had never been markedly profitable.
Andy was jubilant, Parthy apprehensive, Magnolia
starry-eyed, tremulous, glowing. Her lips seemed to
take on a riper curve. Her skin was, somehow, softly
radiant as though lighted by an inner glow, as Julie's
amber colouring, in the years gone by, had seemed to
deepen into golden brilliance. Her eyes were enormous,
luminous. The gangling, hobbledehoy, sallow girl of
seventeen was a woman of eighteen, lovely, and in love.

Back again in New Orleans there was a letter from
Schultzy, a pathetic scrawl; illiterate; loyal. Elly was
out of the hospital, but weak and helpless. He had a
job, temporarily, whose nature he did not indicate.
("Porter in a Little Rock saloon, I'll be bound," ven-
tured Parthy, shrewdly, "rubbing up the brass and the
cuspidors.") He had met a man who ran a rag-front
carnival company. He could use them for one attraction called The Old Plantation; or, The South Before
the War. They were booked through the Middle
West. In a few weeks, if Elly was stronger . . .

He said nothing about money. He said nothing of
their possible return to the *Cotton Blossom*. That,
Andy knew, was because of Elly. Unknown to Parthy,
he sent Schultzy two hundred dollars. Schultzy never
returned to the rivers. It was, after all, oddly enough,
Elly who, many many years later, completed the circle
which brought her again to the show boat.

Together, Andy, Parthy, and Doc went into consul-
tation. They must keep Ravenal. But Ravenal obviously was not of the stuff of show-boat actors. He
had made it plain, when first he came aboard, that he

was the most impermanent of troupers; that his connection with the *Cotton Blossom* would continue, at
the latest, only until Schultzy's return. He meant to
leave them, not at New Orleans, as they had at first
feared, but at Natchez, on the up trip.

"Don't tell him Schultzy ain't coming back," Doc
offered, brilliantly.

"Have to know it some time," was Andy's obvious
reply.

"Person'd think," said Parthy, "he was the only
juvenile lead left in the world. Matter of fact, I can't
see where he's such great shakes of an actor. Rolls
those eyes of his a good deal, and talks deep-voiced, but
he's got hands white's a woman's and fusses with his
nails. I'll wager if you ask around in New Orleans
you'll find something queer, for all he talks so high about
being a Ravenal of Tennessee and his folks governors in
the old days, and slabs about 'em in the church, and
what not. Shifty, that's what he is. Mark my words."

"Best juvenile lead ever played the rivers. And I
never heard that having clean finger nails hurt an actor
any."

"Oh, it isn't just clean finger nails," snapped Parthy.
"It's everything."

"Wouldn't hold that against him, either," roared
Doc. The two men then infuriated the humourless
Mrs. Hawks by indulging in a great deal of guffawing
and knee-slapping.

"That's right, Hawks. Laugh at your own wife.
And you, too, Doc."

"You ain't my wife," retorted Doc, with the privilege of sixty-odd. And roared again.

The gossamer thread that leashed Parthy's temper dissolved now. "I can't bear the sight of him. Palavering and soft-soaping. Thinks he can get round a woman my age. Well, I'm worth a dozen of him when it comes to smart." She leaned closer to Andy, her face actually drawn with fear and a sort of jealousy. "He looks at Magnolia, I tell you."

"A fool if he didn't."

"Andy Hawks, you mean to tell me you'd sit there and see your own daughter married to a worthless tramp of a wharf rat, or worse, that hadn't a shirt to his back when you picked him up!"

"Oh, God A'mighty, woman, can't a man look at a girl without having to marry her!"

"*Having* to marry her, Captain Hawks! *Having*—— Well, what can a body expect when her own husband talks like that, and before strangers, too. Having——!"

Doc rubbed his leathery chin a trifle ruefully. "Stretching a point, Mrs. Hawks, ma'am, calling me a stranger, ain't you?"

"All right. Keep him with the show, you two. Who warned you about that yellow-skinned Julie! And what happened! If sheriffs is what you want, I'll wager you could get them fast enough if you spoke his name in certain parts of this country. Wait till we get back to New Orleans. I intend to do some asking around, and so does Frank."

"What's Frank got to do with it?"

But at this final exhibition of male obtuseness Parthy flounced out of the conference.

On their return from the bayous the *Cotton Blossom* lay idle a day at the New Orleans landing. Early on the morning of their arrival Gaylord Ravenal went ashore. On his stepping off the gangplank he spoke briefly to that same gimlet-eyed gentleman who was still loitering on the wharf. To the observer, the greeting between them seemed amiable enough.

"Back again, Gay!" he of the keen gaze had exclaimed. "Seems like you can't keep away from the scene of the——"

"Oh, go to hell," said Ravenal.

He returned to the *Cotton Blossom* at three o'clock. At his appearance the idler who had accosted him (and who was still mysteriously lolling at the waterside) shut his eyes and then opened them quickly as though to dispel a vision.

"Cripes, Ravenal! Robbed a bank?"

From the tip of his shining shoes to the top of his pale gray hat, Ravenal was sartorial perfection, nothing less. The boots were hand-made, slim, aristocratic. The cloth of his clothes was patently out of England, and tailored for no casual purchaser, but for Ravenal's figure alone. The trousers tapered elegantly to the instep. The collar was moulded expertly so that it hugged the neck. The linen was of the finest and whitest, and cunning needlecraft had gone into the embroidering of the austere monogram that almost escaped showing in one corner of the handkerchief that peeped above his left breast pocket. The malacca stick seemed to take

on a new lustre and richness now that it found itself
once more in fitting company. With the earnings of
his first two weeks on the *Cotton Blossom* enclosed as
evidence of good faith, and future payment assured,
Gaylord Ravenal had sent by mail from the Louisiana
bayous to Plumbridge, the only English tailor in New
Orleans, the order which had resulted in his present
splendour.

He now paused a moment to relieve himself of that
which had long annoyed him in the beady-eyed one.
"Listen to me, Flat Foot. The *Cotton Blossom* dropped
anchor at seven o'clock this morning at the New Orleans dock. I came ashore at nine. It is now three.
I am free to stay on shore or not, as I like, until nine
to-morrow morning. Until then, if I hear any more
of your offensive conversation, I shall have to punish
you."

Flat Foot, thus objurgated, stared at Ravenal with
an expression in which amazement and admiration
fought for supremacy. "By God, Ravenal, with any
luck at all, that gall of yours ought to get you a million
some day."

"I wouldn't be bothered with any sum so vulgar."
From an inside pocket he drew a perfecto, long, dark,
sappy. "Have a smoke." He drew out another.
"And give this to Vallon when you go back to report.
Tell him I wanted him to know the flavour of a decent
cigar for once in his life."

As he crossed the gangplank he encountered
Mrs. Hawks and Frank, the lumbering heavy, evidently
shore-bound together. He stepped aside with a courtli-

ness that the Ravenals of Tennessee could not have excelled in the days of swords, satins, and periwigs.

Mrs. Hawks was, after all, a woman; and no woman could look unmoved upon the figure of cool elegance that now stood before her. "Sakes alive!" she said, inadequately. Frank, whose costumes, ashore or afloat, always were négligée to the point of causing the beholder some actual nervousness, attempted to sneer without the aid of makeup and made a failure of it.

Ravenal now addressed Mrs. Hawks. "You are not staying long ashore, I hope?"

"And why not?" inquired Mrs. Hawks, with her usual delicacy.

"I had hoped that perhaps you and Captain Hawks and Miss Magnolia might do me the honour of dining with me ashore and going to the theatre afterward. I know a little restaurant where——"

"Likely," retorted Parthy, by way of polite refusal; and moved majestically down the gangplank, followed by the gratified heavy.

Ravenal continued thoughtfully on his way. Captain Andy was in the box office just off the little forward deck that served as an entrance to the show boat. With him was Magnolia—Magnolia minus her mother's protecting wings. After all, even Parthy had not the power to be in more than one place at a time. At this moment she was deep in conversation with Flat Foot on the wharf.

Magnolia was evidently dressed for a festive occasion. The skirt of her light écru silk dress was a polonaise draped over a cream-white surah silk, and the front of the tight bodice-basque was of the same cream-white stuff. Her round hat of Milan straw, with its modishly high crown, had an artful brim that shaded her fine eyes, and this brim was faced with deep rose velvet, and a bow of deep rose flared high against the crown. The black of her hair was all the blacker for this vivid colour. An écru parasol and long suède gloves completed the costume. She might have stepped out of *Harper's Bazaar*—in fact, she had. The dress was a faithful copy of a costume which she had considered particularly fetching as she pored over the pages of that book of fashion.

Andy was busy at his desk. Ranged in rows on that desk were canvas sacks, plump, squat; canvas sacks limp, lop-sided; canvas sacks which, when lifted and set down again, gave forth a pleasant clinking sound. Piled high in front of these were neat packets of greenbacks, ones and ones and ones, in bundles of fifty, each bound with a tidy belt of white paper pinned about its middle. Forming a kind of Chinese wall around these were stacked half dollars, quarters, dimes, and nickels, with now and then a campanile of silver dollars. In the midst of this Andy resembled an amiable and highly solvent gnome stepped out of a Grimm's fairy tale. The bayou trip had been a record-breaking one in point of profit.

". . . And fifty's six hundred and fifty," Andy was crooning happily, as he jotted figures down on a sheet of yellow lined paper, ". . . and fifty's seven hundred, and twenty-five's seven hundred twenty-five and twenty-five's . . ."

"Oh, Papa!" Magnolia exclaimed impatiently, and turned toward the little window through which one saw New Orleans lying so invitingly in the protecting arms of the levee. "It's almost four, and you haven't even changed your clothes, and you keep counting that old money, and Mama's gone on some horrid business with that sneaky Frank. I know it's horrid because she looked so pleased. And you promised me. We won't see New Orleans again for a whole year. You said you'd get a carriage and two horses and we'd drive out to Lake Pontchartrain, and have dinner, and drive back, and go to the theatre, and now it's almost four and you haven't even changed your clothes and you keep counting that old money, and Mama's——" After all, in certain ways, Magnolia the ingénue lead had not changed much from that child who had promptly had hysterics to gain her own ends that day in Thebes many years before.

"Minute," Andy muttered, absently. "Can't leave this money laying around like buttons, can I? Germania National's letting me in the side door as a special favour after hours, as 'tis, just so's I can deposit. . . . And fifty's eight-fifty, and fifty's nine . . ."

"I don't *care!*" cried Magnolia, and stamped her foot. "It's downright mean of you, Papa. You promised. And I'm all dressed. And you haven't even changed your——"

"Oh, God A'mighty, Nollie, you ain't going to turn out an unreasonable woman like your ma, are you! Here I sit, slaving away——"

"Oh! How beautiful you look!" exclaimed Magnolia now, to Andy's bewilderment. He looked up at her. Her gaze was directed over his head at someone standing in the doorway. Andy creaked hastily around in the ancient swivel chair. Ravenal, of course, in the doorway. Andy pursed his lips in the sky-rocket whistle, starting high and ending low, expressive of surprise and admiration.

"How beautiful you look!" said Magnolia again; and clasped her hands like a child.

"And you, Miss Magnolia," said Ravenal; and advanced into the cubby hole that was the office, and took one of Magnolia's surprised hands delicately in his, and bent over it, and kissed it. Magnolia was an excellent enough actress, and sufficiently the daughter of the gallant and Gallic Andy, to acknowledge this salute with a little gracious inclination of the head, and no apparent surprise whatever. Andy himself showed nothing of astonishment at the sight of this suave and elegant figure bent over his daughter's hand. He looked rather pleased than otherwise. But suddenly then the look on his face changed to one of alarm. He jumped to his feet. He scratched the mutton-chop whiskers, sure evidence of perturbation.

"Look here, Ravenal! That ain't a sign you're leaving, is it? Those clothes, and now kissing Nollie's hand. God A'mighty, Ravenal, you ain't leaving us!"

Ravenal flicked an imaginary bit of dust from the cuff of his flawless sleeve. "These are my ordinary clothes, Captain Hawks, sir. I mean to say, I usually

am attired as you now see me. When first we met I was
in temporary difficulties. The sort of thing that can
happen to any gentleman."

"Certainly can," Andy agreed, heartily and hastily.
"Sure can. Well, you gave me a turn. I thought you
come in to give me notice. And while we're on it, you're
foolish to quit at Natchez like you said, Ravenal. I
don't know what you been doing, but you're cut out for
a show-boat actor, and that's the truth. Stick with us
and I'll raise you to twenty—" as Ravenal shook his
head—"twenty-five—" again the shake of the head—
"thirty! And, God A'mighty, they ain't a juvenile
lead on the rivers ever got anywheres near that."

Ravenal held up one white shapely hand. "Let's not
talk money now, Captain. Though if you would care
to advance me a fifty, I . . . Thanks . . . I
was going to say I came in to ask if you and Mrs. Hawks
and Miss Magnolia here would do me the honour to
dine with me ashore this evening, and go to the theatre.
I know a little French restaurant——"

"Papa!" She swooped down upon little Andy then,
enveloping him in her ruffles, in her surah silk, her rose
velvet, her perfume. Her arms were about his neck.
Her fresh young cheek pressed the top of his grizzled
head. Her eyes were enormous—and they looked into
Ravenal's eyes. "Papa!"

But years of contact with the prim Parthy had taught
him caution. "Your ma——" he began, feebly.

Magnolia deserted him, flew to Ravenal, clutched his
arm. Her lovely eyes held tears. Involuntarily his
free hand covered her hand that clung so appealingly to

his sleeve. "He promised me. And now, because he's got all that money to count because Doc was delayed at Baton Rouge and didn't meet us here like he expected he would this afternoon and Mama's gone ashore and we were to drive to Lake Pontchartrain and have dinner and he hasn't even changed his clothes and it's almost four o'clock—probably is four by now—and he keeps counting that old money——"

"Magnolia!" shouted Andy in a French frenzy, clutching the whiskers as though to raise himself by them from the floor.

Magnolia must have been enjoying the situation. Here were two men, both of whom adored her, and she them. She therefore set about testing their love. Her expression became tragic—but not so tragic as to mar her delightful appearance. To the one who loved her most deeply and unselfishly she said:

"You don't care anything about me or my happiness. It's all this old boat, and business, and money. Haven't I worked, night after night, year in, year out! And now, when I have a chance to enjoy myself—it isn't as if you hadn't promised me——"

"We're going, I tell you, Nollie. But your ma isn't even here. And how did I know Doc was going to be stuck at Baton Rouge! We got plenty of time to have dinner ashore and go to the theatre, but we'll have to give up the drive to Pontchartrain——"

A heartbroken wail from Magnolia. Her great dark eyes turned in appeal to Ravenal. "It's the drive I like better than anything in the world. And horses. I'm crazy about horses, and I don't get a chance to drive

—oh, well—" at an objection from Andy—"sometimes; but what kind of horses do they have in those little towns! And here you can get a splendid pair, all shiny, and their nostrils working, and a victoria and lovely long tails and a clanky harness and fawn cushions and the lake and soft-shell crabs——" She was becoming incoherent, but remained as lovely as ever, and grew more appealing by the moment.

Ravenal resisted a mad urge to take her in his arms. He addressed himself earnestly to the agonized Andy. "If you will trust me, Captain Hawks, I have a plan which I have just thought of. I know New Orleans very well and I am—uh—very well known in New Orleans. Miss Magnolia has set her heart on this little holiday. I know where I can get a splendid turnout. Chestnuts—very high steppers, but quite safe." An unadult squeal of delight from Magnolia. "If we start immediately, we can enjoy quite a drive—Miss Magnolia and I. If you like, we can take Mrs. Means with us, or Mrs. Soaper——"

"No," from the brazen beauty.

"—and return in time to meet you and Mrs. Hawks at, say, Antoine's for dinner."

"Oh, Papa!" cried Magnolia now. "Oh, Papa!"

"Your ma——" began Andy again, feebly. The stacks and piles still lay uncounted on the desk. This thing must be settled somehow. He scuttled to the window, scanned the wharf, the streets that led up from it. "I don't know where she's got to." He turned from the window to survey the pair, helplessly. Something about them—the very fitness of their standing there together, so young, so beautiful, so eager, so alive, so vibrant—melted the romantic heart within him. Magnolia in her holiday garb; Ravenal in his tailored perfection. "Oh, well, I don't see how it'll hurt any. Your ma and I will meet you at Antoine's at, say, half-past six——"

They were off. It was as if they had been lifted bodily and blown together out of the little office, across the gangplank to the landing. Flat Foot stared after them almost benignly.

Andy returned to his desk. Resumed his contented crooning. Four o'clock struck. Half-past four. His pencil beat a rat-a-tat-tat as he jotted down the splendid figures. A gold mine, this Ravenal. A fine figger of a boy. Cheap at thirty. Rat-a-tat-tat. And fifty's one thousand. And twenty-five's one thousand twenty-five. And fifty's—and fifty's—twelve twenty-five—gosh a'mighty!——

A shriek. A bouncing across the gangplank and into the cubby hole just as Andy was rounding, happily, into thirteen hundred. A hand clutching his shoulder frantically, whirling him bodily out of the creaking swivel chair. Parthy, hat awry, bosom palpitating, eyes starting, mouth working.

"On Canal Street!" she wheezed. It was as though the shriek she had intended were choked in her throat by the very force of the feeling behind it, so that it emerged a strangled thing. "Canal Street! The two of them . . . with my own eyes . . . driving . . . in a . . . in a——"

She sank into a chair. There seemed to be no pretense about this.   Andy, for once, was alarmed.   The tall shambling figure of Frank, the heavy, passed the little ticket window, blocked the low doorway.   He stared, open-mouthed, at the almost recumbent Parthy. He was breathing heavily and looked aggrieved.

"She ran away from me," he said.   "Sees 'em in the crowd, driving, and tries to run after the carriage on Canal, with everybody thinking she's gone loony. Then she runs down here to the landing, me after her. Woman her age.   What d'yah take me for, anyway!"

But Parthy did not hear him.   He did not exist.   Her face was ashen.   "He's a murderer!" she now gasped.

Andy's patience, never too long-suffering, snapped under the strain of the afternoon's happenings.   "What's wrong with you, woman!   Have you gone clean crazy! Who's a murderer!   Frank?   Who's he murdered? For two cents I'd murder the both of you, come howling in here when a man's trying to run his business *like* a business and not like a yowling insane asylum——"

Parthy stood up, shaking.   Her voice was high and quavering.   "Listen to me, you fool.   I talked to the man on the docks—the one he was talking to—and he wouldn't tell me anything and he said I could ask the chief of police if I wanted to know about anybody, and I went to the chief of police, and a perfect gentleman if there ever was one, and he's killed a man."

"The chief of police!   Killed a man!   What man!"

"No!" shrieked Parthy.   "Ravenal!   Ravenal's killed a man."

"God A'mighty, when!"   He started as though to rescue Magnolia.

"A year ago. A year ago, in this very town."

The shock of relief was too much for Andy. He was furious. "They didn't hang him for it, did they?"

"Hang who?" asked Parthy, feebly.

"Who! Ravenal! They didn't hang him?"

"Why, no, they let him go. He said he shot him in self——"

"He killed a man and they let him go. What does that prove? He'd a right to. All right. What of it!"

"What of it! Your own daughter is out driving in an open carriage this minute with a murderer, that's what, Andy Hawks. I saw them with my own eyes. There I was, out trying to protect her from contamination by finding out . . . and I saw her the minute my back was turned . . . your doings . . . your own daughter driving in the open streets in an open carriage with a murderer——"

"Oh, open murderer be damned!" squeaked Andy in his falsetto of utter rage. "I killed a man when I was nineteen, Mrs. Hawks, ma'am, and I've been twenty-five years and more as respected a man as there is on the rivers, and that's the truth if you want to talk about mur——"

But Parthenia Ann Hawks, for the first time in her vigorous life, had fainted.

X

GAYLORD RAVENAL had not meant to fall in love. Certainly he had not dreamed of marrying. He was not, he would have told you, a marrying man. Yet Natchez had come and gone, and here he was, still playing juvenile leads on the *Cotton Blossom;* still planning, days ahead, for an opportunity to outwit Mrs. Hawks and see Magnolia alone. He was thoroughly and devastatingly in love. Alternately he pranced and cringed. To-day he would leave this dingy scow. What was he, Gaylord Ravenal, doing aboard a show boat, play-acting for a miserable thirty dollars a week! He who had won (and lost) a thousand a night at poker or faro. To-morrow he was resolved to give up gambling for ever; to make himself worthy of this lovely creature; to make himself indispensable to Andy; to find the weak chink in Parthy's armour.

He had met all sorts of women in his twenty-four years. He had loved some of them, and many of them had loved him. He had never met a woman like Magnolia. She was a paradoxical product of the life she had led. The contact with the curious and unconventional characters that made up the *Cotton Blossom* troupe; the sights and sounds of river life, sordid, romantic, homely, Rabelaisian, tragic, humorous; the tolerant and meaty wisdom imbibed from her sprightly little father; the spirit of *laissez faire* that pervaded the whole atmosphere about her, had given her a flavour, a mellowness, a camaraderie found usually only in women twice her age and a hundredfold more experienced. Weaving in and out of this was an engaging primness directly traceable to Parthy. She had, too, a certain dignity that was, perhaps, the result of years of being deferred to as the daughter of a river captain. Sometimes she looked at Ravenal with the wide-eyed gaze of a child. At such times he wished that he might leap into the Mississippi (though muddy) and wash himself clean of his sins as did the pilgrims in the River Jordan.

On that day following Parthy's excursion ashore at New Orleans there had been between her and Captain Andy a struggle, brief and bitter, from which Andy had emerged battered but victorious.

"That murdering gambler goes or I go," Parthy had announced, rashly. It was one of those pronunciamentos that can only bring embarrassment to one who utters it.

"He stays." Andy was iron for once.

He stayed. So did Parthy, of course.

You saw the two—Parthy and Ravenal—eyeing each other, backs to the wall, waiting for a chance to lunge and thrust.

Cotton Blossom business was booming. News of the show boat's ingénue and juvenile lead filtered up and down the rivers. During the more romantic scenes of this or that play Parthy invariably stationed herself in the wings and glowered and made muttering sounds to which the two on stage—Magnolia starry-eyed as the

heroine, Ravenal ardent and passionate as the lover—
were oblivious. It was their only opportunity to express to each other what they actually felt. It probably was, too, the most public and convincing love-
making that ever graced the stage of this or any other
theatre.

Ravenal made himself useful in many ways. He took
in hand, for example, the *Cotton Blossom's* battered
scenery. It was customary on all show boats to use
both sides of a set. One canvas side would represent,
perhaps, a drawing room. Its reverse would show the
greens and browns of leaves and tree trunks in a forest
scene. Both economy and lack of stage space were responsible for this. Painted by a clumsy and unimag-
inative hand, each leaf daubed as a leaf, each inch of
wainscoting drawn to scale, the effect of any *Cotton
Blossom* set, when viewed from the other side of the
footlights, was unconvincing even to rural and inexperienced eyes. Ravenal set to work with paint and
brush and evolved two sets of double scenery which
brought forth shrieks of ridicule and protest from the
company grouped about the stage.

"It isn't supposed to look like a forest," Ravenal
explained, slapping on the green paint with a lavish
hand. "It's supposed to give the effect of a forest.
The audience isn't going to sit on the stage, is it? Well,
then! Here—this is to be a gate. Well, there's no use
trying to paint a flat thing with slats that nobody will
ever believe looks like a gate. I'll just do this . . .
and this . . ."

"It does!" cried Magnolia from the middle of the house where she had stationed herself, head held critically on one side. "It does make you think there's a gate there, without its actually being . . . Look, Papa! . . . And the trees. All those lumpy green spots we used to have somehow never looked like leaves."

All unconsciously Ravenal was using in that day, and in that crude milieu, a method which was to make a certain Bobby Jones famous in the New York theatre of a quarter of a century later.

"Where did you learn to——" some one of the troupe would marvel; Magnolia, perhaps, or Mis' Means, or Ralph.

"Paris," Ravenal would reply, briefly. Yet he had never spoken of Paris.

He often referred thus casually to a mysterious past.

"Paris fiddlesticks!" rapped out Parthy, promptly. "No more Paris than he's a Ravenal of Tennessee, or whatever rascally highfalutin story he's made up for himself."

Whereupon, when they were playing Tennessee, weeks later, he strolled one day with Magnolia and Andy into the old vine-covered church of the village, its churchyard fragrant and mysterious with magnolia and ilex; its doorstep worn, its pillars sagging. And there, in a glass case, together with a tattered leather-bound Bible a century and a half old, you saw a time-yellowed document. The black of the ink strokes had, perhaps, taken on a tinge of gray, but the handwriting, clear and legible, met the eye.

WILL OF JEAN BAPTISTA RAVENAL.

I, Jean Baptista Ravenal, of this Province, being through the mercy of Almighty God of sound mind and memory do make, appoint, declare and ordain this and this only to be my last Will and Testament. It is my will that my sons have their estates delivered to them as they severally arrive at the age of twenty and one years, the eldest being Samuel, the second Jean, the third Gaylord.

I will that my slaves be kept to work on my lands that my estate be managed to the best advantage so as my sons may have as liberal an education as the profits thereof will afford. Let them be taught to read and write and be introduced into the practical part of Arithmetic, not too hastily hurrying them to Latin and Grammar. To my sons, when they arrive at age I recommend the pursuit and study of some profession or business (I would wish one to ye Law, the other to Merchandise).

"The other?" cried Magnolia softly then, looking up very bright-eyed and flushed from the case over which she had been bending. "But the third? Gaylord? It doesn't say——"

"The black sheep. My great-grandfather. There always was a Gaylord. And he always was the black sheep. My grandfather, Gaylord Ravenal and my father Gaylord Ravenal, and——" he bowed.

"Black too, are you?" said Andy then, drily.

"As pitch."

Magnolia bent again to the book, her brow thoughtful, her lips forming the words and uttering them softly as she deciphered the quaint script.

I give and bequeath unto my son Samuel the lands called Ashwood, which are situated, lying and being on the South Side of the

Cumberland River, together with my other land on the North side
of said River. . . .

I give and bequeath unto my son Jean, to him and his heirs and
assigns for ever a tract of land containing seven hundred and forty
acres lying on Stumpy Sound . . . also another tract containing one thousand acres . . .

I give and bequeath to my son Samuel four hundred and fifty
acres lying above William Lowrie's plantation on the main branch
of Old Town Creek . . .

Magnolia stood erect. Indignation blazed in her
fine eyes. "But, Gaylord!" she said.

"Yes!" Certainly she had never before called him
that.

"I mean this Gaylord. I mean the one who came
after Samuel and Jean. Why isn't—why didn't——"

"Naughty boy," said Ravenal, with his charming
smile.

She actually yearned toward him then. He could
not have said anything more calculated to bind his enchantment for her. They swayed toward each other
over the top of the little glass-encased relic. Andy
coughed hastily. They swayed gently apart. They
were as though mesmerized.

"Folks out here in the churchyard?" inquired Andy,
briskly, to break the spell. "Ravenal kin?"

"Acres of 'em," Gaylord assured him, cheerfully.
"Son of . . . and daughter of . . . and be-
loved father of. . . . For that matter, there's one
just beside you."

Andy side-stepped hastily, with a little exclamation.
He cast a somewhat fearful glance at the spot toward
which Ravenal so carelessly pointed. A neat gray stone

slab set in the wall. Andy peered at the lettering it
bore; stooped a little. "Here—you read it, Nollie.
You've got young eyes."

Her fresh young cheek so near the cold gray slab,
she read in her lovely flexible voice:

Here lies the body of M^{rs}. Suzanne Ravenal, wife of Jean Baptista
Ravenal Esqr., one of his Majesty's Council and Surveyor General
of the Lands of this Province, who departed this life Octr 19^c 1765.
Aged 37 Years. After labouring ten of them under the severest
Bodily afflictions brought on by Change of Climate, and tho' she
went to her native land received no relief but returned and bore them
with uncommon Resolution and Resignation to the last.

Magnolia rose, slowly, from the petals of her flounced
skirt spread about her as she had stooped to read.
"Poor darling!" Her eyes were soft with pity. Again
the two seemed to sway a little toward each other, as
though blown by a gust of passion. And this time little
Captain Andy turned his back and clattered down the
aisle. When they emerged again into the sunshine
they found him, a pixie figure, leaning pensively against
the great black trunk of a live oak. He was smoking a
pipe somewhat apologetically, as though he hoped the
recumbent Ravenals would not find it objectionable.

"I guess," he remarked, as Magnolia and Ravenal
came up to him, "I'll have to bring your ma over.
She's partial to history, her having been a schoolma'am,
and all."

Like the stage sets he so cleverly devised for the show
boat, Gaylord Ravenal had a gift for painting about
himself the scenery of romance. These settings, too,
did not bear the test of too close scrutiny. But in a

favourable light, and viewed from a distance, they were charmingly effective and convincing.

His sense of the dramatic did not confine itself to the stage. He was the juvenile lead, on or off. Audiences adored him. Mid-western village housewives, good mothers and helpmates for years, were, for days after seeing him as the heroic figure of some gore-and-glory drama, mysteriously silent and irritably waspish by turn. Disfavour was writ large on their faces as they viewed their good commonplace dull husbands across the midday table set with steaming vegetables and meat.

"Why'n't you shave once in a while middle of the week," they would snap, "'stead of coming to the table looking like a gorilla?"

Mild surprise on the part of the husband. "I shaved Sat'dy, like always."

"Lookit your hands!"

"Hands? . . . Say, Bella, what in time's got into you, anyway?"

"Nothing." A relapse into moody silence on the part of Bella.

Mrs. Hawks fought a good fight, but what chance had her maternal jealousy against youth and love and romance? For a week she would pour poison into Magnolia's unwilling ear. Only making a fool of you . . . probably walk off and leave the show any day . . . common gambler . . . look at his eyes . . . murderer and you know it . . . rather see you in your grave. . . .

Then, in one brief moment, Ravenal, by some act of

courage or grace or sheer deviltry, would show Parthy
that all her pains were for nothing.

That night, for example, when they were playing
Kentucky Sue. Ravenal's part was what is known as
a blue-shirt lead—the rough brave woodsman, with
the uncouth speech and the heart of gold. Magnolia,
naturally, was Sue. They were playing Gains Landing,
always a tough town, often good for a fight. It was a
capacity audience and a surprisingly well-behaved and
attentive. Midway in the play's progress a drawling
drunken voice from the middle of the house began a
taunting and ridiculous chant whose burden was, "Is
'at so!" After each thrilling speech; punctuating each
flowery period, "Is 'at so!" came the maddening and dis-
rupting refrain. You had to step carefully at Gains
Landing. The *Cotton Blossom* troupe knew that. One
word at the wrong moment, and knives flashed, guns
popped. Still, this could not go on.

"Don't mind him," Magnolia whispered fearfully to
Ravenal. "He's drunk. He'll stop. Don't pay any
attention."

The scene was theirs. They were approaching the
big moment in the play when the brave Kentuckian re-
nounces his love that Kentucky Sue may be happy with
her villainous bridegroom-to-be (Frank, of course).
Show-boat audiences up and down the rivers had known
that play for years; had committed the speech word
for word, through long familiarity. "Sue," it ran, "ef
he loves yuh and you love him, go with him. Ef he
h'ain't good to yuh, come back where there's honest

hearts under homespun shirts. Back to Kaintucky and home!"

Thus the speech ran. But as they approached it the blurred and mocking voice from the middle of the house kept up its drawling skepticism. "Is *'at* so! Is *'at* so!"

"Damned drunken lout!" said Ravenal under his breath, looking unutterable love meanwhile at the languishing Kentucky Sue.

"Oh, dear!" said Magnolia, feeling Ravenal's muscles tightening under the blue shirt sleeves; seeing the telltale white ridge of mounting anger under the grease paint of his jaw line. "Do be careful."

Ravenal stepped out of his part. He came down to the footlights. The house, restless and irritable, suddenly became quiet. He looked out over the faces of the audience. "See here, pardner, there's others here want to hear this, even if you don't."

The voice subsided. There was a little desultory applause from the audience and some cries of, "That's right! Make him shut up." They refused to manhandle one of their own, but they ached to see someone else do it.

The play went on. The voice was silent. The time approached for the big speech of renunciation. It was here. "Sue, ef he loves yuh and you love him, go with him. Ef he——"

"Is *'at* so!" drawled the amused voice, with an element of surprise in it now. "Is *'at* so!"

Ravenal cast Kentucky Sue from him. "Well, if you will have it," he threatened, grimly. He sprang over the footlights, down to the piano top, to the keyboard, to the piano stool, all in four swift strides, was up the aisle, had plucked the limp and sprawling figure out of his seat by the collar, clutched him then firmly by this collar hold and the seat of his pants, and was up the aisle again to the doorway, out of the door, across the gangplank, and into the darkness. He was down the aisle then in a moment, spatting his hands briskly as he came; was up on the piano stool, on to the piano keyboard, on the piano top, over the footlights, back in position. There he paused a moment, breathing fast. Nothing had been said. There had actually been no sound other than his footsteps and the discordant jangle of protest that the piano keyboard had emitted when he had stepped on its fingers. Now a little startled expression came into Ravenal's face.

"Let's see," he said, aloud. "Where was I——"

And as one man the audience chanted, happily, "Sue, ef he loves yuh and you love him——"

What weapon has a Parthenia against a man like that? And what chance a Frank?

Drama leaped to him. There was, less than a week later, the incident of the minister. He happened to be a rather dirty little minister in a forlorn little Kentucky river town. He ran a second-hand store on the side, was new to the region, and all unaware of the popularity and good-will enjoyed by the members of the *Cotton Blossom* troupe. To him an actor was a burning brand. Doc had placarded the little town with dodgers and handbills. There was one, especially effective even in that day of crude photography, showing Magnolia in the angelic part of the ingénue lead in Tempest and Sunshine. These might be seen displayed in the windows of such ramshackle stores as the town's river front street boasted. Gaylord Ravenal, strolling disdainfully up into the sordid village that was little more than a welter of mud and flies and mules and Negroes, stopped aghast as his eye chanced to fall upon the words scrawled beneath a picture of Magnolia amidst the dusty disorderly mélange of the ministerial second-hand window. There was the likeness of the woman he loved looking, starry-eyed, out upon the passer-by. And beneath it, in the black fanatic penmanship of the itinerant parson:

A LOST SOUL

In his fine English clothes, swinging the slim malacca cane, Gaylord Ravenal, very narrow-eyed, entered the fusty shop and called to its owner to come forward. From the cobwebby gloom of the rear reaches emerged the merchant parson, a tall, shambling large-knuckled figure of the anaconda variety. You thought of Uriah Heep and of Ichabod Crane, experiencing meanwhile a sensation of distaste.

Ravenal, very elegant, very cool, very quiet, pointed with the tip of his cane. "Take that picture out of the window. Tear it up. Apologize."

"I won't do anything of the kind," retorted the holy man. "You're a this-and-that, and a such-and-such, and a so-and-so, and she's another, and the whole boat-load of you ought to be sunk in the river you contaminate."

"Take off your coat," said Ravenal, divesting himself neatly of his own faultless garment as he spoke.

A yellow flame of fear leaped into the man's eyes. He edged toward the door. With a quick step Ravenal blocked his way. "Take it off before I rip it off. Or fight with your coat on."

"You touch a man of God and I'll put the law on you. The sheriff's office is just next door. I'll have you——"

Ravenal whirled him round, seized the collar of his grimy coat, peeled it dexterously off, revealing what was, perhaps, as maculate a shirt as ever defiled the human form. The Ravenal lip curled in disgust.

"If cleanliness is next to godliness," he remarked, swiftly turning back his own snowy cuffs meanwhile, "you'll be shovelling coal in hell." And swung. The minister was taller and heavier than this slight and dandified figure. But Ravenal had an adrenal advantage, being stimulated by the fury of his anger. The godly one lay, a soiled heap, among his soiled wares. The usual demands of the victor.

"Take that thing out of the window! . . . Apologize to me! . . . Apologize publicly for defaming a lady!"

The man crept groaning to the window, plucked the picture, with its offensive caption, from amongst the miscellany there, handed it to Ravenal in response to a gesture from him. "Now then, I think you're pretty badly bruised, but I doubt that anything's broken. I'm going next door to the sheriff. You will write a public apology in letters corresponding to these and place it in your filthy window. I'll be back."

He resumed his coat, picked up the malacca cane, blithely sought out the sheriff, displayed the sign, heard that gallant Kentuckian's most Southern expression of regard for Captain Andy Hawks, his wife and gifted daughter, together with a promise to see to it that the written apology remained in the varmint's window throughout the day and until the departure of the *Cotton Blossom*. Ravenal then went his elegant and unruffled way up the sunny sleepy street.

By noon the story was known throughout the village, up and down the river for a distance of ten miles each way, and into the back country, all in some mysterious word-of-mouth way peculiar to isolated districts. Ravenal, returning to the boat, was met by news of his own exploit. Business, which had been booming for this month or more, grew to phenomenal proportions. Ravenal became a sort of legendary figure on the rivers. Magnolia went to her mother. "I am never allowed to talk to him. I won't stand it. You treat him like a criminal."

"What else is he?"

"He's the——" A long emotional speech, ringing with words such as hero, gentleman, wonderful, honourable, nobility, glorious—a speech such as Schultzy, in his show-boat days as director, would have designated as a so-and-so-and-so-and-so-and-so-and-so.

Ravenal went to Captain Andy. I am treated as an outcast. I'm a Ravenal. Nothing but the most honourable conduct. A leper. Never permitted to speak to your daughter. Humiliation. Prefer to discontinue connection which can only be distasteful to the Captain and Mrs. Hawks, in view of your conduct. Leaving the *Cotton Blossom* at Cairo.

In a panic Captain Andy scampered to his lady and declared for a more lenient chaperonage.

"Willing to sacrifice your own daughter, are you, for the sake of a picking up a few more dollars here and there with this miserable upstart!"

"Sacrificing her, is it, to tell her she can speak civilly to as handsome a young feller and good-mannered as I ever set eyes on, or you either!"

"Young squirt, that's what he is."

"I was a girl like Nollie I'd run off with him, by God, and that's the truth. She had any spirit left in her after you've devilled her these eighteen years past, she'd do it."

"That's right! Put ideas into her head! How do you know who he is?"

"He's a Rav——"

"He says he is."

"Didn't he show me the church——"

"Oh, Hawks, you're a zany. I could show you grave-stones. I could say my name was Bonaparte and show you Napoleon's tomb, but that wouldn't make him my grandfather, would it!"

After all, there was wisdom in what she said. She may even have been right, as she so often was in her shrewish intuition. Certainly they never learned more of this scion of the Ravenal family than the meagre information gleaned from the chronicles of the village church and graveyard.

Grudgingly, protestingly, she allowed the two to con-

verse genteelly between the hours of five and six, after
dinner.   But no oriental princess was ever more heavily
chaperoned than was Magnolia during these prim meet-
ings.   For a month, then, they met on the port side of
the upper deck, forward.   Their chairs were spaced well
apart.   On the starboard side, twenty-five feet away,
sat Parthy in her chair, grim, watchful; radiating opposition.

Magnolia, feeling the gimlet eye boring her spine,
would sit bolt upright, her long nervous fingers tightly
interwoven, her ankles neatly crossed, the pleats and
flounces of her skirts spread sedately enough yet seeming to vibrate with an electric force that gave them the
effect of standing upright, a-quiver, like a kitten's fur
when she is agitated.

He sat, one arm negligently over the back of his chair,
facing the girl.   His knees were crossed.   He seemed at
ease, relaxed.   Yet a slim foot in its well-made boot
swung gently to and fro.   And when Parthy made one
of her sudden moves, as was her jerky habit, or when she
coughed raspingly by way of emphasizing her presence,
he could be felt, rather than seen, to tighten in all his
nerves and muscles, and the idly swinging foot took a
clonic leap.

The words they spoke with their lips and the words
they spoke with their eyes were absurdly at variance.

"Have you really been in Paris, Mr. Ravenal!   How
I should love to see it!"   (How handsome you are,
sitting there like that.   I really don't care anything
about Paris.   I only care about you.)

"No doubt you will, some day, Miss Magnolia."

(You darling! How I should like to take you there. How I should like to take you in my arms.)

"Oh, I've never even seen Chicago. Only these river towns." (I love the way your hair grows away from your temples in that clean line. I want to put my finger on it, and stroke it. My dear.)

"A sordid kind of city. Crude. Though it has some pleasant aspects. New York——" (What do I care if that old tabby is sitting there! What's to prevent me from getting up and kissing you a long long while on your lovely pomegranate mouth.)

Lowering, inflexible, sat Parthy. "She'll soon enough tire of that sort of popinjay talk," she told herself. She saw the bland and almost vacuous expression on the countenance of the young man, and being ignorant of the fact that he was famous from St. Louis to Chicago for his perfect poker face, was equally ignorant of the tides that were seething and roaring within him now.

They were prisoners on this boat; together, yet miles apart. Guarded, watched. They had their scenes together on the stage. These were only aggravations. The rather high planes of Magnolia's cheek-bones began to show a trifle too flat. Ravenal, as he walked along the grass-grown dusty streets of this or that little river town, switched viciously at weed and flower stalks with the slim malacca cane.

They hit upon a pathetic little scheme whereby they might occasionally, if lucky, steal the ecstasy of a good-night kiss. After the performance he would stroll carelessly out to the stern where stood the settling barrel. Ostensibly he was taking a bedtime drink of water.

Magnolia was, if possible, to meet him there for a brief
and perilous moment. It was rarely accomplished.
The signal to him was the slamming of the screen door.
But often the screen door slammed as he stood there, a
tense quivering figure in the velvet dark of the Southern
night, and it was Frank, or Mrs. Soaper, or Mis' Means,
or puny Mr. Means, coughing his bronchial wheeze.
Crack! went the screen door. Disappointment. Often
he sloshed down whole gallons of river water before she
came—if she came at all.

He had managed to save almost a hundred dollars.
He was restless, irritable. Except for a mild pinochle
game now and then with the men of the company, he
had not touched a card in weeks. If he could get into
a real game, somehow; manage a sweepstakes. Chicago. St. Louis, even. These little rotten river towns.
No chance here. If he could with luck get together
enough to take her away with him. Away from the
old hell-cat, and this tub, and these damned eternal
rivers. God, but he was sick of them!

They were playing the Ohio River—Paducah, Kentucky. He found himself seated at mid-afternoon
round a table in the back room of a waterfront saloon.
What time is it? Five. Plenty of time. Just for that
raise you five. A few hundred dollars would do it.
Six o'clock. Seven. Seven-thirty. Eight. Half-past
—Who said half past! Ralph in the doorway. Can't
be! Been looking everywhere for you. This's a fine
way . . . Come on outa here you. . . . Christ!
. . . Ten dollars in his pocket. The curtain up at
eight. Out, the shouts of the men echoing in his ears.

Down to the landing. A frantic company, Andy clawing at his whiskers. Magnolia in tears, Parthy grim
but triumphant, Frank made up to go on in Ravenal's
part.

He dashed before the curtain, raised his shaking hand
to quiet the cat-calling angry audience.

"Ladies and gentlemen, I ask your patience. There
has been an unfortunate but unavoidable delay. The
curtain will rise in exactly five minutes. In the name
of the management I wish to offer you all apologies.
We hope, by our performance, to make up for the in-
convenience you have suffered. I thank you." A
wave of his hand.

The band.

Parthy in the wings. "Well, Captain Hawks, I
guess this settles it. Maybe you'll listen to your wife,
after this. In a saloon—that's where he was—gambling. If Ralph hadn't found him—a pretty kettle of fish.
Years building up a reputation on the rivers and then
along comes a soft-soaping murdering gambler . . ."

Ravenal had got into his costume with the celerity of
a fireman, and together he and Magnolia were giving a
performance that was notable for its tempo and a certain
vibratory quality. The drama that unrolled itself before the Paducah gaze was as nothing compared to the
one that was being secretly enacted.

Between the lines of her part she whispered between
immovable lips: "Oh, Gay, why did you do it?"

A wait, perhaps, of ten minutes before the business
of the play brought him back within whispering distance
of her.

"Money" (very difficult to whisper without moving the lips. It really emerged, "Uh-ney," but she understood). "For you. Marry you. Take you away."

All this while the lines of the play went on. When they stood close together it was fairly easy.

Magnolia (in the play): What! Have all your friends deserted you! (Mama'll make Andy send you away.)

Ravenal: No, but friendship is too cold a passion to stir my heart now. (Will you come with me?)

Magnolia: Oh, give me a friend in preference to a sweetheart. (But how can I?)

Ravenal: My dear Miss Brown—Miss Lucy—— (Marry me).

Magnolia: Oh, please don't call me Miss Brown. (When?)

Ravenal: Lucy! (Where do we play to-morrow? Marry me there.)

Magnolia: Defender of the fatherless! (Metropolis. I'm frightened.)

Ravenal: Will you be a poor man's bride? (Darling!)

For fear of arousing suspicion, she did not dare put on her best dress in which to be married. One's best dress does not escape the eye of a Parthy at ten o'clock in the morning, when the landing is Metropolis. With a sigh Magnolia donned her second best—the reseda sateen, basqued, its overskirt caught up coquettishly at the side. She determined on her Milan hat trimmed with the grosgrain ribbon and pink roses. After all, Parthy or no Parthy, if one has a hat with pink roses, the time to wear it is at one's wedding, or never.

Ravenal vanished beyond the river bank immediately

after breakfast next day; a meal which he had eaten in haste and in silence. He did not, the general opinion ran, look as crushed as his misdemeanour warranted. He had, after all, been guilty of the crime of crimes in the theatre, be it a Texas tent show or an all-star production on Broadway; he had held up the performance. For once the *Cotton Blossom* troupe felt that Mrs. Hawks' bristling attitude was justified. All through the breakfast hour the stern ribbon bow on her breakfast cap had quivered like a seismographic needle registering the degree of her inward upheaval.

"I think," said Magnolia, drinking her coffee in very small sips, and eating nothing, "I'll just go to town and match the ribbon on my grosgrain striped silk——"

"You'll do nothing of the kind, miss, and so I tell you."

"But, Mama, why? You'd think I was a child instead of a——"

"You are, and no more. I can't go with you. So you'll stop at home."

"But Mis' Means is going with me. I promised her I'd go. She wants to get some ointment for Mr. Means' chest. And a yard of elastic. And half a dozen oranges. . . . Papa, don't you think it's unreasonable to make me suffer just because everybody's in a bad temper this morning? I'm sure I haven't done anything. I'm sure I——"

Captain Andy clawed his whiskers in a frenzy. "Don't come to me with your yards of elastic and your oranges. God A'mighty!" He rushed off, a distraught little figure, as well he might be after a wretched night

during which Mrs. Hawks had out-caudled Mrs. Cau-
dle. When finally he had dropped off to sleep to the
sound of the monotonously nagging voice, it was to
dream of murderous gamblers abducting Magnolia who
always turned out to be Parthy.

In her second best sateen and the Milan with the
pink roses Magnolia went off to town at a pace that
rather inconvenienced the short-breathed Mis' Means.

"What's your hurry!" wheezed that lady, puffing up
the steep cinder path to the levee.

"We're late."

"Late! Late for what? Nothing to do all day till
four, far's I know."

"Oh, I just meant—uh—I mean we started kind of
late——" her voice trailed off, lamely.

Fifteen minutes later Mis' Means stood in indecision
before a counter crawling with unwound bolts of elastic
that twined all about her like garter snakes. The little
general store smelled of old apples and broom straw and
kerosene and bacon and potatoes and burlap and mice.
Sixteen minutes later she turned to ask Magnolia's advice. White elastic half an inch wide? Black elastic
three quarters of an inch wide? Magnolia had vanished
from her side. Mis' Means peered through the dimness
of the fusty little shop. Magnolia! White elastic in
one hand, black in the other, Mis' Means scurried to the
door. Magnolia had gone.

Magnolia had gone to be married in her second best
dress and her hat with the pink roses. She flew down
the street. Mis' Means certainly could have achieved
no such gait; much less could she have bettered it to the

extent of overtaking Magnolia. Magnolia made such speed that when her waiting bridegroom, leaning against the white picket fence in front of the minister's house next the church, espied her and came swiftly to meet her, she was so breathless a bride that he could make nothing out of her panted—"Elastic . . . Mis' Means . . . ran away . . ."

She leaned against the picket fence to catch her breath, a lovely flushed figure, and not a little frightened. And though it was early April with Easter just gone, there was a dogwood in bridal bloom in the minister's front yard, and a magnolia as well. And along the inside of the picket fence tulips and jonquils lifted their radiant heads. She looked at Gaylord Ravenal then and smiled her wide and gorgeous smile. "Let's go," she said, "and be married. I've caught my breath."

"All right," said Ravenal. Then he took from his pocket the diamond ring that was much too large for her. "Let's be engaged first, while we go up the path." And slipped it on her finger.

"Why, Gay! It's a diamond! Look what the sun does to it! Gay!"

"That's nothing compared to what the sun does to you," he said; and leaned toward her.

"Right at noon, in the minister's front yard!"

"I know. But I've had only those few moments in the dark by the settling barrel—it's been terrible."

The minister's wife opened the door. She looked at the two.

"I saw you from the parlour window. We were wondering—I thought maybe you'd like to be married in the church. The Easter decorations are still up. It looks lovely, all palms and lilies and smilax, too, from down South, sent up. The altar's banked with it. Mr. Seldon's gone there."

"Oh, I'd love to be married in church. Oh, Gay, I'd love to be married in church."

The minister's wife smoothed the front of her dress with one hand, and the back of her hair with the other, and, having made these preparations for the rôle of bridal attendant, conducted them to the little flower-banked church next door.

Magnolia never did remember very clearly the brief ceremony that followed. There were Easter lilies—whole rows of them—and palms and smilax, as the minister's wife had said. And the sun shone, picture-book fashion, through the crude yellows and blues and scarlets of the windows. And there was the Reverend Something-or-other Seldon, saying solemn words. But these things, strangely enough, seemed unimportant. Two little pig-tailed girls, passing by from school, had seen them enter the church and had tiptoed in, scenting a wedding. Now they were up in the choir loft, tittering hysterically. Magnolia could hear them above the Reverend Seldon's intonings. In sickness and in health—tee–hee–hee—for richer, for poorer—tee–hee–hee—for better, for worse—tee–hee–hee.

They were kneeling. Ravenal was wearing his elegantly sharp-pointed shoes. As he knelt his heels began to describe an arc—small at first, then wider and wider as he trembled more and more, until, at the end, they were all but striking the floor from side to side. Outwardly Magnolia was the bride of tradition, calm and pale.

. . . . pronounce you man and wife.

Ravenal had a ten-dollar bill—that last ten-dollar bill—all neatly folded in his waistcoat pocket. This he now transferred to the Reverend Seldon's somewhat surprised palm.

"And," the minister's wife was saying, "while it isn't much—we're church mice, you see—you're welcome to it, and we'd be happy to have you take your wedding dinner with us. Veal loaf, I'm afraid, and butter beets——"

So Magnolia Ravenal was married in church, as proper as could be. And had her wedding dinner with the minister vis-à-vis. And when she came out of the church, the two little giggling girls, rather bold and rather frightened, but romantically stirred, pelted her with flowers. Pelted may be rather an exaggeration, because one threw a jonquil at her, and one a tulip, and both missed her. But it helped, enormously. They went to the minister's house and ate veal loaf and buttered beets and bread pudding, or ambrosia or whatever it was. And so they lived h—— and so they lived . . . ever after.

XI

EVEN after she had seen the Atlantic in a January hurricane, Kim Ravenal always insisted that the one body of water capable of striking terror to her was the Mississippi River. Surely she should have known. She had literally been born on that turbid torrent. All through her childhood her mother, Magnolia Ravenal, had told her tales of its vagaries, its cruelties, its moods; of the towns along its banks; of the people in those towns; of the boats that moved upon it and the fantastic figures that went up and down in those boats. Her grandfather, Captain Andy Hawks, had lost his life in the treacherous swift current of its channel; her grandmother, Parthenia Ann Hawks was, at eighty, a living legend of the Mississippi; the Flying Dutchman of the rivers, except that the boat touched many ports. One heard strange tales about Hawks' widow. She had gone on with the business after his tragic death. She was the richest show-boat owner on the rivers. She ran the boat like a female seminary. If an actor uttered so much as a damn, he was instantly dismissed from the troupe. Couples in the company had to show a marriage certificate. Every bill—even such innocuous old-timers as East Lynne and The Gambler's Daughter and Tempest and Sunshine—were subject to a purifying process before the stern-visaged female owner of the new *Cotton Blossom* would sanction their performance on her show boat.

Kim herself remembered many things about the Mississippi, though after her very early childhood she did not see it for many years; and her mother rarely spoke of it. She even shook her head when Kim would ask her for the hundredth time to tell her the story of how she escaped being named Mississippi.

"Tell about the time the river got so high, and all kinds of things floated on it—animals and furniture and houses, even—and you were so scared, and I was born, and you wanted to call me Mississippi, but you were too sleepy or something to say it. And the place was near Kentucky and Illinois and Missouri, all at once, so they made up a name from the letters K and I and M, just till you could think of a real name. And you never did. And it stayed Kim. . . . People laugh when I tell them my name's Kim. Other girls are named Ellen and Mary and Elizabeth. . . . Tell me about that time on the Mississippi. And the Cotton Blossom Floating Palace Theatre."

"But you know all about it. You've just told me."

"I like to hear you tell it."

"Your father doesn't like to have me talk so much about the rivers and the show boat."

"Why not?"

"He wasn't very happy on them. I wasn't, either, after Grandpa Hawks——"

Kim knew that, too. She had heard her father say, "God's sake, Nola, don't fill the kid's head full of that stuff about the rivers and the show boat. The **way**

you tell it, it sounds romantic and idle and picturesque."

"Well, wasn't——?"

"No. It was rotten and sordid and dull. Flies on
the food and filthy water to drink and yokels to play to.
And that old harridan——"

"Gay!"

He would come over to her, kiss her tenderly, contrite-
ly. "Sorry, darling."

Kim knew that her mother had a strange deep feeling
about the rivers. The ugly wide muddy ruthless rushing rivers of the Middle West.

Kim Ravenal's earliest river memories were bizarre
and startling flashes. One of these was of her mother
seated in a straight-backed chair on the upper deck of
the *Cotton Blossom*, sewing spangles all over a high-
busted corset. It was a white webbed corset with a
pinched-in waist and high full bosom and flaring hips.
This humdrum garment Magnolia Ravenal was covering
with shining silver spangles, one overlapping the other
so that the whole made a glittering basque. She took
quick sure stitches that jerked the fantastic garment in
her lap, and when she did this the sun caught the brilliant heap aslant and turned it into a blaze of gold and
orange and ice-blue and silver.

Kim was enchanted. Her mother was a fairy princess. It was nothing to her that the spangle-covered
basque, modestly eked out with tulle and worn with
astonishingly long skirts for a bareback rider, was to serve
as Magnolia's costume in The Circus Clown's Daughter.

Kim's grandmother had scolded a good deal about

that costume. But then, she had scolded a good deal about everything. It was years before Kim realized that all grandmothers were not like that. At three she thought that scolding and grandmothers went together, like sulphur and molasses. The same was true of fun and grandfathers, only they went together like ice cream and cake. You called your grandmother grandma. You called your grandfather Andy, or, if you felt very roguish, Cap'n. When you called him that, he cackled and squealed, which was his way of laughing, and he clawed his delightful whiskers this side and that. Kim would laugh then, too, and look at him knowingly from under her long lashes. She had large eyes, deep-set like her mother's and her mother's wide mobile mouth. For the rest, she was much like her father—a Ravenal, he said. His fastidious ways (highfalutin, her grandmother called them); his slim hands and feet; his somewhat drawling speech, indirect though strangely melting glance, calculatedly impulsive and winning manner.

Another childhood memory was that of a confused and terrible morning. Asleep in her small bed in the room with her father and mother, she had been wakened by a bump, followed by a lurch, a scream, shouts, bells, clamour. Wrapped in her comforter, hastily snatched up from her bed by her mother, she was carried to the deck in her mother's arms. Gray dawn. A misty morning with fog hanging an impenetrable curtain over the river, the shore. The child was sleepy, bewildered. It was all one to her—the confusion, the shouting, the fog, the bells. Close in her mother's arms, she did not in the least understand what had happened when the confusion became pandemonium; the shouts rose to screams. Her grandfather's high squeaky voice that had been heard above the din—"La'berd lead there! Sta'berd lead! Snatch her! *SNATCH HER!*" was heard no more. Something more had happened. Someone was in the water, hidden by the fog, whirled in the swift treacherous current. Kim was thrown on her bed like a bundle of rags, all rolled in her blanket. She was left there, alone. She had cried a little, from fright and bewilderment, but had soon fallen asleep again. When she woke up her mother was bending over her, so wild-eyed, so frightening with her black hair streaming about her face and her face swollen and mottled with weeping, that Kim began to cry again in sheer terror. Her mother had snatched her to her. Curiously enough the words Magnolia Ravenal now whispered in a ghastly kind of agony were the very words she had whispered after the agony of Kim's birth—though the child could not know that.

"The river!" Magnolia said, over and over. Gaylord Ravenal came to her, flung an arm about her shoulder, but she shook him off wildly. "The river! The river!"

Kim never saw her grandfather again. Because of the look it brought to her mother's face, she soon learned not to say, "Where's Andy?" or—the roguish question that had always made him appear, squealing with delight: "Where's Cap'n?"

Baby though she was, the years—three or four—just preceding her grandfather's tragic death were indelibly stamped on the infant's mind. He had adored her;

made much of her. Andy, dead, was actually a more vital figure than many another alive.

It had been a startling but nevertheless actual fact that Parthenia Ann Hawks had not wanted her daughter Magnolia to have a child. Parthy's strange psychology had entered into this, of course—a pathological twist. Of this she was quite unaware.

"How're you going to play ingénue lead, I'd like to know, if you—when you—while you——" She simply could not utter the word "pregnant" or say, "while you are carrying your child," or even the simpering evasion of her type and class—"in the family way."

Magnolia laughed a little at that. "I'll play as long as I can. Toward the end I'll play ruffly parts. Then some night, probably between the second and third acts—though they may have to hold the curtain for five minutes or so—I'll excuse myself——"

Mrs. Hawks declared that she had never heard anything so indelicate in her life. "Besides, a show boat's no place to bring up a child."

"You brought me up on one."

"Yes," said Mrs. Hawks, grimly. Her tone added, "And now look at you!"

Even before Kim's birth the antagonism between Parthy and her son-in-law deepened to actual hatred. She treated him like a criminal; regarded Magnolia's quite normal condition as a reproach to him.

"Look here, Magnolia, I can't stand this, you know. I'm so sick of this old mud-scow and everything that goes with it."

"Gay! Everything!"

"You know what I mean. Let's get out of it. I'm no actor. I don't belong here. If I hadn't happened to see you when you stepped out on deck that day at New Orleans——"

"Are you sorry?"

"Darling! It's the only luck I ve ever had that lasted."

She looked thoughtfully down at the clear colourful brilliance of the diamond on her third finger. Always too large for her, it now hung so loosely on her thin hand that she had been obliged to wind it with a great pad of thread to keep it from dropping off, though hers were the large-knuckled fingers of the generous and resourceful nature. It was to see much of life, that ring.

She longed to say to him, "Where do you belong, Gay? Who are you? Don't tell me you're a Ravenal. That isn't a profession, is it? You can't live on that."

But she knew it was useless. There was a strange deep streak of the secretive in him; baffling, mystifying. Questioned, he would say nothing. It was not a moody silence, or a resentful one. He simply would not speak. She had learned not to ask.

"We can't go away now, Gay dear. I can't go. You don't want to go without me, do you? You wouldn't leave me! Maybe next winter, after the boat's put up, we can go to St. Louis, or even New Orleans—that would be nice, wouldn't it? The winter in New Orleans."

One of his silences.

He never had any money—that is, he never had it for long. It vanished. He would have one hundred dollars. He would go ashore at some sizable town and return with five hundred—a thousand. "Got into a little game with some of the boys," he would explain, cheerfully. And give her three hundred of it, four hundred, five. "Buy yourself a dress, Nola. Something rich, with a hat to match. You're too pretty to wear those home-made things you're always messing with."

Some woman wisdom in her told her to put by a portion of these sums. She got into the habit of tucking away ten dollars, twenty, fifty. At times she reproached herself for this; called it disloyal, sneaking, underhand. When she heard him say, as he frequently did, "I'm strapped. If I had fifty dollars I could turn a trick that would make five hundred out of it. You haven't got fifty, have you, Nola? No, of course not."

She wanted then to give him every cent of her tiny hoard. It was the tenuous strain of her mother in her, doubtless—the pale thread of the Parthy in her make-up—that caused her to listen to an inner voice. "Don't do it," whispered the voice, nudging her, "keep it. You'll need it badly by and by."

It did not take many months for her to discover that her husband was a gambler by profession—one of those smooth and plausible gentry with whom years of river life had made her familiar. It was, after all, not so much a discovery as a forced admission. She knew, but refused to admit that she knew. Certainly no one could have been long in ignorance with Mrs. Hawks in possession of the facts.

Ten days after Magnolia's marriage to Ravenal (and what a ten days those had been! Parthy alone crowded

into them a lifetime of reproach), Mrs. Hawks came to
her husband, triumph in her mien, portent in her voice:
"Well, Hawks, I hope you're satisfied now." This
was another of Parthy's favourite locutions. The im-
plication was that the unfortunate whom she addressed
had howled heaven-high his demands for hideous mis-
fortune and would not be content until horror had piled
upon horror. "I hope you're satisfied now, Hawks.
Your son-in-law is a gambler, and no more. A common
barroom gambler, without a cent to his trousers longer'n
it takes to transfer his money from his pocket to the
table. That's what your only daughter has married.
Understand, I'm not saying he gambles, and that's all.
I say he's a gambler by calling. That's the way he
made his living before he came aboard this boat. I
wish he had died before he ever set foot on the *Cotton
Blossom* gangplank, and so I tell you, Hawks. A
smooth-tongued, oily, good-for-nothing; no better than
the scum Elly ran off with."

"Now, Parthy, what's done's done. Why'n't you
try to make the best of things once in a while, instead of
the worst? Magnolia's happy with him."

"She ain't lived her life out with him yet. Mark my
words. He's got a roving eye for a petticoat."

"Funny thing, Parthy. Your father was a man, and
so's your husband, and your son-in-law's another.
Yet seems you never did get the hang of a man's ways."

Andy liked Ravenal. There was about the fellow a
grace, an ease, a certain elegance that appealed to the
æsthetic in the little Gallic captain. When the two men
talked together sometimes. after dinner, it was amiably,

in low tones, with an air of leisure and relaxation. Two
gentlemen enjoying each other's company. There
existed between the two a sound respect and liking.

Certainly Ravenal's vogue on the rivers was tremendous. Andy paid him as juvenile lead a salary that was
unheard of in show-boat records. But he accounted
him worth it. Shortly after Kim's birth, Andy spoke
of giving Ravenal a share in the *Cotton Blossom*. But
this Mrs. Hawks fought with such actual ferocity that
Andy temporarily at least relinquished the idea.

Magnolia had learned to dread the idle winter
months. During this annual period of the *Cotton
Blossom's* hibernation the Hawks family had, before
Magnolia's marriage, gone back to the house near
the river at Thebes. Sometimes Andy had urged
Parthy to spend these winter months in the South,
evading the harsh Illinois climate for a part of the
time at least in New Orleans, or one of the towns of
southern Mississippi where one might have roses instead of holly for Christmas. He sometimes envied
black Jo and Queenie their period of absence from the
boat. In spite of the disreputable state in which they
annually returned to the *Cotton Blossom* in the early
spring, they always looked as if they had spent
the intervening months seated in the dappled shade,
under a vine, with the drone of insects in the air, and
the heavy scent of white-petalled blossoms; eating fruit
that dripped juice between their fingers; sleeping,
slack-jawed and heavily content, through the heat of the
Southern mid-afternoon; supping greasily and plentifully
on fried catfish and corn bread; watching the moon

come up to the accompaniment of Jo's coaxing banjo.

"We ought to lazy around more, winters," Andy said to his energetic wife. She was, perhaps, setting the Thebes house to rights after their long absence; thwacking pillows, pounding carpets, sloshing pails, scouring tables, hanging fresh curtains, flapping drapes, banging bureau drawers. A towel wrapped about her head, turban-wise, her skirts well pinned up, she would throw a frenzy of energy into her already exaggerated housewifeliness until Andy, stepping fearfully out of the way of mop and broom and pail, would seek waterfront cronies for solace.

"Lazy! I've enough of lazying on that boat of yours month in month out all summer long. No South for me, thank you. Eight months of flies and niggers and dirty mud-tracking loafers is enough for me, Captain Hawks. I'm thankful to get back for a few weeks where I can live like a decent white woman." Thwack! Thump! Bang!

After one trial lasting but a few days, the Thebes house was found by Magnolia to be impossible for Gaylord Ravenal. That first winter after their marriage they spent in various towns and cities. Memphis for a short time; a rather hurried departure; St. Louis; Chicago. That brief glimpse of Chicago terrified her, but she would not admit it. After all, she told herself, as the astounding roar and din and jangle and clatter of State Street and Wabash Avenue beat at her ears, this city was only an urban Mississippi. The cobblestones were the river bed. The high grim buildings the river banks. The men, women, horses, trucks, drays, carriages, street cars that surged through those streets; creating new channels where some obstacle blocked their progress; felling whole sections of stone and brick and wood and sweeping over that section, obliterating all trace of its former existence; lifting other huge blocks and sweeping them bodily downstream to deposit them in a new spot; making a boulevard out of what had been a mud swamp—all this, Magnolia thought, was only the Mississippi in another form and environment; ruthless, relentless, Gargantuan, terrible. One might think to know its currents and channels ever so well, but once caught unprepared in the maelstrom, one would be sucked down and devoured as Captain Andy Hawks had been in that other turbid hungry flood.

"You'll get used to it," Ravenal told his bride, a trifle patronizingly, as one who had this monster tamed and fawning. "Don't be frightened. It's mostly noise."

"I'm not frightened, really. It's just the kind of noise that I'm not used to. The rivers, you know, all these years—so quiet. At night and in the morning."

That winter she lived the life of a gambler's wife. Streak o' lean, streak o' fat. Turtle soup and terrapin at the Palmer House to-day. Ham and eggs in some obscure eating house to-morrow. They rose at noon. They never retired until the morning hours. Gay seemed to know a great many people, but to his wife he presented few of these.

"Business acquaintance," he would say. "You wouldn't care for him."

Hers had been a fantastic enough life on the show boat. But always there had been about it an orderli-

ness, a routine, due, perhaps, to the presence of the
martinet, Parthenia Ann Hawks. Indolent as the days
appeared on the rivers, they still bore a methodical
aspect. Breakfast at nine. Rehearsal. Parade. Dinner at four. Make-up. Curtain. Wardrobe to mend
or refurbish; parts to study; new songs to learn for the
concert. But this new existence seemed to have no
plot or plan. Ravenal was a being for the most part
unlike the lover and husband of *Cotton Blossom* days.
Expansive and secretive by turn; now high-spirited, now
depressed; frequently absent-minded. His manner toward her was always tender, courteous, thoughtful.
He loved her as deeply as he was capable of loving.
She knew that. She had to tell herself all this one
evening when she sat in their hotel room, dressed and
waiting for him to take her to dinner and to the theatre.
They were going to McVicker's Theatre, the handsome
new auditorium that had risen out of the ashes of the
old (to quote the owner's florid announcement).
Ravenal was startled to learn how little Magnolia knew
of the great names of the stage. He had told her something of the history of McVicker's, in an expansive burst
of pride in Chicago. He seemed to have a definite feeling about this great uncouth giant of a city.

"When you go to McVicker's," Ravenal said, "you
are in the theatre where Booth has played, and Sothern,
and Lotta, and Kean, and Mrs. Siddons."

"Who," asked Magnolia, "are they?"

He was so much in love that he found this ignorance
of her own calling actually delightful. He laughed, of
course, but kissed her when she pouted a little, and ex-

plained to her what these names meant, investing them
with all the glamour and romance that the theatre—
the theatre of sophistication, that is—had for him; for
he had the gambler's love of the play. It must have
been something of that which had held him so long to
the *Cotton Blossom*. Perhaps, after all, his infatuation
for Magnolia alone could not have done it.

And now she was going to McVicker's. And she had
on her dress with the open-throated basque, which she
considered rather daring, though now that she was a
married woman it was all right. She was dressed long
before the time when she might expect him back. She
had put out fresh linen for him. He was most fastidious about his dress. Accustomed to the sloppy desha-
bille of the show boat's male troupers, this sartorial
niceness in Ravenal had impressed her from the first.

She regarded herself in the mirror now. She knew
she was not beautiful. She affected, in fact, to despise
her looks; bemoaned her high forehead and prominent
cheek-bones, her large-knuckled fingers, her slenderness,
her wide mouth. Yet she did not quite believe these
things she said about herself; loved to hear Ravenal say
she was beautiful. As she looked at her reflection now
in the long gilt-framed mirror of the heavy sombre
walnut bedroom, she found herself secretly agreeing with
him. This was the first year of her marriage. She was
pregnant. It was December. The child was expected
in April. There was nothing distorted about her figure
or her face. As is infrequently the case, her condition
had given her an almost uncanny radiance of aspect.
Her usually pallid skin showed a delicious glow of rosy

colouring; her eyes were enormous and strangely luminous; tiny blue veins were faintly, exquisitely etched against the cream tint of her temples; her rather angular slimness was replaced by a delicate roundness; she bore herself well, her shoulders back, her head high. A happy woman, beloved, and in love.

Six o'clock. A little late, but he would be here at any moment now. Half-past six. She was opening the door every five minutes to peer up the red-carpeted corridor. Seven. Impatience had given way to fear, fear to terror, terror to certain agony. He was dead. He had been killed. She knew by now that he frequented the well-known resorts of the city, that he played cards in them. "Just for pastime," he told her. "Game of cards to while away the afternoon. What's the harm in that? Now, Nola! Don't look like your mother. Please!"

She knew about them. Red plush and gilt, mahogany and mirrors. Food and drink. River-front saloons and river-front life had long ago taught her not to be squeamish. She was not a foolish woman, nor an intolerant. She was, in fact, in many ways wise beyond her years. But this was 1888. The papers had been full of the shooting of Simeon Peake, the gambler, in Jeff Hankins' place over on Clark Street. The bullet had been meant for someone else—a well-known newspaper publisher, in fact. But a woman, hysterical, crazed, revengeful, had fired it. It had gone astray. Ravenal had known Simeon Peake. The shooting had been a shock to him. It had, indeed, thrown him so much off his guard that he had talked to Magnolia about it for relief. Peake had had a young daughter Selina. She was left practically penniless.

Now the memory of this affair came rushing back to her. She was frantic. Half-past seven. It was too late, now, for the dinner they had planned for the gala evening—dinner at the Wellington Hotel, down in the white marble café. The Wellington was just across the street from McVicker's. It would make everything simple and easy; no rush, no hurrying over that last delightful sweet sip of coffee.

Eight o'clock. He had been killed. She no longer merely opened the door to peer into the corridor. She left the room door open and paced from room to hall, from hall to room, wildly; down the corridor. Finally, in desperation, down to the hotel lobby into which she had never stepped in the evening without her husband. There were two clerks at the office desk. One was an ancient man, flabby and wattled, as much a part of the hotel as the stones that paved the lobby. He had soft wisps of sparse white hair that seemed to float just above his head instead of being attached to it; and little tufts of beard, like bits of cotton stuck on his cheeks. He looked like an old baby. The other was a glittering young man; his hair glittered, his eyes, his teeth, his nails, his shirt-front, his cuffs. Both these men knew Ravenal; had greeted him on their arrival; had bowed impressively to her. The young man had looked flattering things; the old man had pursed his soft withered lips.

Magnolia glanced from one to the other. There were

people at the clerks' desk, leaning against the marble
slab. She waited, nervous, uncertain. She would
speak to the old man. She did not want, somehow, to
appeal to the glittering one. But he saw her, smiled,
left the man to whom he was talking, came toward her.
Quickly she touched the sleeve of the old man—leaned
forward over the marble to do it—jerked his sleeve,
really, so that he glanced up at her testily.

"I—I want—may I speak to you?"

"A moment, madam. I shall be free in a moment."

The sparkler leaned toward her. "What can I do
for you, Mrs. Ravenal?"

"I just wanted to speak to this gentleman——"

"But I can assist you, I'm sure, as well as——"

She glanced at him and he was a row of teeth, all
white and even, ready to bite. She shook her head
miserably; glanced appealingly at the old man. The
sparkler's eyebrows came up. He gave the effect of
stepping back, courteously, without actually doing so.
Now that the old clerk faced her, questioningly, she
almost regretted her choice.

She blushed, stammered; her voice was little more
than a whisper. "I . . . my husband . . .
have been . . . he hasn't returned . . . worried . . . killed or . . . theatre . . ."

The old baby cupped one hand behind his ear.
"What say?"

Her beautiful eyes, in their agony, begged the sparkler now to forgive her for having been rude. She
needed him. She could not shout this. He stepped

forward, but the teeth were hidden. After all, a chief clerk is a chief clerk. Miraculously, he had heard the whisper.

"You say your husband——?"

She nodded. She was terribly afraid that she was going to cry. She opened her eyes very wide and tried not to blink. If she so much as moved her lids she knew the mist that was making everything swim in a rainbow haze would crystallize into tears.

"He is terribly late. I—I've been so worried. We were going to the—to McVicker's—and dinner—and now it's after seven——"

"After eight," wheezed cotton whiskers, peering at the clock on the wall.

"—after eight," she echoed, wretchedly. There! She had winked. Two great drops plumped themselves down on the silk bosom of her bodice with the open-throated neck line. It seemed to her that she heard them splash.

"H'm!" cackled the old man.

The glittering one leaned toward her. She was enveloped in a waft of perfume. "Now, now, Mrs. Ravenal! There's absolutely nothing to worry about. Your husband has been delayed. That's all. Unavoidably delayed."

She snatched at this. "Do you think—? Are you sure? But he always is back by six, at the latest. Always. And we were going to dinner—and Mc——"

"You brides!" smiled the young man. He actually patted her hand, then. Just a touch. "Now you just have a bite of dinner, like a sensible little woman."

"Oh, I couldn't eat a bite! I couldn't!"

"A cup of tea. Let me send up a cup of tea."

The old one made a sucking sound with tongue and teeth, rubbed his chin, and proffered his suggestion in a voice that seemed to Magnolia to echo and reëcho through the hotel lobby. "Why'n't you send a messenger around for him, madam?"

"Messenger? Around? Where?"

Sparkler made a little gesture—a tactful gesture. "Perhaps he's having a little game of—uh—cards; and you know how time flies. I've done the same thing myself. Look up at the clock and first thing you know it's eight. Now if I were you, Mrs. Ravenal——"

She knew, then. There was something so sure about this young man; and so pitying. And suddenly she, too, was sure. She recalled in a flash that time when they were playing Paducah, and he had not come. They had held the curtain until after eight. Ralph had searched for him. He had been playing poker in a waterfront saloon. Send around for him! Not she. The words of a popular sentimental song of the day went through her mind, absurdly.

Father, dear father, come home with me now.
The clock in the steeple strikes one.

She drew herself up, now. The actress. She even managed a smile, as even and sparkling and toothy as the sparkler's own. "Of course. I'm very silly. Thank you so . . . I'll just have a bit of supper in my room. . . ." She turned away with a little gracious bow. The eyes very wide again.

"H'm!" The old man. Translated it meant, "Little idiot!"

She took off the dress with the two dark spots on the silk of the basque. She put away his linen and his shiny shoes. She took up some sewing. But the mist interfered with that. She threw herself on the bed. An agony of tears. That was better. Ten o'clock. She fell asleep, the gas lights burning. At a little before midnight he came in. She awoke with a little cry. Queerly enough, the first thing she noticed was that he had not his cane—the richly mottled malacca stick that he always carried. She heard herself saying, ridiculously, half awake, half asleep, "Where's your cane?"

His surprise at this matter-of-fact reception made his expression almost ludicrous. "Cane! Oh, that's so. Why I left it. Must have left it."

In the years that followed she learned what the absence of the malacca stick meant. It had come to be a symbol in every pawnshop on Clark Street. Its appearance was bond for a sum a hundred times its actual value. Gaylord Ravenal always paid his debts.

She finished undressing, in silence. Her face was red and swollen. She looked young and helpless and almost ugly. He was uncomfortable and self-reproachful. "I'm sorry, Nola. I was detained. We'll go to the theatre to-morrow night."

She almost hated him then. Being, after all, a normal woman, there followed a normal scene—tears, reproaches, accusations, threats, pleadings, forgiveness. Then:

"Uh—Nola, will you let me take your ring—just for a day or two?"

"Ring?" But she knew.

"You'll have it back. This is Wednesday. You'll have it by Saturday. I swear it."

The clear white diamond had begun its travels with the malacca stick.

He had spoken the truth when he said that he had been unavoidably detained.

She had meant not to sleep. She had felt sure that she would not sleep. But she was young and healthy and exhausted from emotion. She slept. As she lay there by his side she thought, before she slept, that life was very terrible—but fascinating. Even got from this a glow of discovery. She felt old and experienced and married and tragic. She thought of her mother. She was much, much older and more married, she decided, than her mother ever had been.

They returned to Thebes in February. Magnolia longed to be near her father. She even felt a pang of loneliness for her mother. The little white cottage near the river, at Thebes, looked like a toy house. Her bedroom was doll-size. The town was a miniature village, like a child's Christmas set. Her mother's bonnet was a bit of grotesquerie. Her father's face was etched with lines that she did not remember having seen there when she left. The home-cooked food, prepared by Parthy's expert hands, was delicious beyond belief. She was a traveller returned from a far place.

Captain Andy had ordered a new boat. He talked of nothing else. The old *Cotton Blossom*, bought from

Pegram years before, was to be discarded. The new boat was to be lighted by some newfangled gas arrangement instead of the old kerosene lamps. Carbide or some such thing Andy said it was. There were to be special footlights, new scenery, improved dressing and sleeping rooms. She was being built at the St. Louis shipyards.

"She's a daisy!" squeaked Andy, capering. He had just returned from a trip to the place of the *Cotton Blossom's* imminent birth. Of the two impending ac couchements—that which was to bring forth a grand child and that which was to produce a new show boat— it was difficult to say which caused him keenest anticipation. Perhaps, secretly, it was the boat, much as he loved Magnolia. He was, first, the river man; second, the showman; third, the father.

"Like to know what you want a new boat for!" Parthy scolded. "Take all the money you've earned these years past with the old tub and throw it away on a new one."

"Old one a'n't good enough."

"Good enough for the riff-raff we get on it."

"Now, Parthy, you know's well's I do you couldn't be shooed off the rivers now you've got used to 'em. Any other way of living'd seem stale to you."

"I'm a woman loves her home and asks for nothing better."

"Bet you wouldn't stay ashore, permanent, if you had the chance."

He won the wager, though he had to die to do it.

The new *Cotton Blossom* and the new grandchild had
a trial by flood on their entrance into life. The Mississippi, savage mother that she was, gave them both a
baptism that threatened for a time to make their entrance into and their exit from the world a simultaneous
act. But both, after some perilous hours, were piloted
to safety; the one by old Windy, who swore that this
was his last year on the rivers; the other by a fat midwife and a frightened young doctor. Through storm
and flood was heard the voice of Parthenia Ann Hawks,
the scold, berating Captain Hawks her husband, and
Magnolia Ravenal her daughter, as though they, and
not the elements, were responsible for the predicament
in which they now found themselves.

There followed four years of war and peace. The
strife was internal. It raged between Parthy and her
son-in-law. The conflict of the two was a chemical
thing. Combustion followed inevitably upon their
meeting. The biting acid of Mrs. Hawks' discernment
cut relentlessly through the outer layers of the young
man's charm and grace and melting manner and revealed
the alloy. Ravenal's nature recoiled at sight of a
woman who employed none of the arts of her sex and despised and penetrated those of the opposite sex. She
had no vanity, no coquetry, no reticences, no respect
for the reticence of others; treated compliment as insult,
met flattery with contempt.

A hundred times during those four years he threatened
to leave the *Cotton Blossom*, yet he was held to his wife
Magnolia and to the child Kim by too many tender ties.

His revolt usually took the form of a gambling spree
ashore during which he often lost every dollar he had
saved throughout weeks of enforced economy. There
was no opportunity to spend money legitimately in the
straggling hamlets to whose landings the *Cotton Blossom*
was so often fastened. Then, too, the easy indolence of
the life was beginning to claim him—its effortlessness,
its freedom from responsibility. Perhaps a new part to
learn at the beginning of the season—that was all.
River audiences liked the old plays. Came to see them
again and again. It was Ravenal who always made the
little speech in front of the curtain. Wish to thank you
one and all . . . always glad to come back to the
old . . . to-morrow night that thrilling comedy-
drama entitled . . . each and every one . . .
concert after the show . . .

Never had the *Cotton Blossom* troupe so revelled in
home-baked cakes, pies, cookies; home-brewed wine;
fruits of tree and vine. The female population of the
river towns from the Great Lakes to the Gulf beheld in
him the lover of their secret dreams and laid at his feet
burnt offerings and shewbread. Ravenal, it was said
by the *Cotton Blossom* troupe, could charm the gold out
of their teeth.

Perhaps, with the passing of the years, he might have
grown quite content with this life. Sometimes the little
captain, when the two men were conversing quietly
apart, dropped a word about the future.

"When I'm gone—you and Magnolia—the boat'll be
yours, of course."

Ravenal would laugh. Little Captain Andy looked

so very much alive, his bright brown eyes glancing here
and there, missing nothing on land or shore, his brown
paw scratching the whiskers that showed so little of gray,
his nimble legs scampering from texas to gangplank,
never still for more than a minute.

"No need to worry about that for another fifty years,"
Ravenal assured him.

The end had in it, perhaps, a touch of the ludicrous,
as had almost everything the little capering captain did.
The *Cotton Blossom*, headed upstream on the Mississippi,
bound for St. Louis, had struck a snag in Cakohia Bend,
three miles from the city. It was barely dawn, and a
dense fog swathed the river. The old *Cotton Blossom*
probably would have sunk midstream. The new boat
stood the shock bravely. In the midst of the pandemonium that followed the high shrill falsetto of the
little captain's voice could be heard giving commands
which he, most of all, knew he had no right to give.
The pilot only was to be obeyed under such conditions.
The crew understood this, as did the pilot. It was, in
fact, a legend that more than once in a crisis Captain
Andy on the upper deck had screamed his orders in a
kind of dramatic frenzy of satisfaction, interspersing
these with picturesque and vivid oaths during which he
had capered and bounced his way right off the deck and
into the river, from which damp station he had continued to screech his orders and profanities in cheerful
unconcern until fished aboard again. Exactly this happened. High above the clamour rose the voice of Andy.
His little figure whirled like that of a dervish. Up,
down, fore, aft—suddenly he was overboard unseen in

the dimness, in the fog, in the savage swift current of the Mississippi, wrapped in the coils of the old yellow serpent, tighter, tighter, deeper, deeper, until his struggles ceased. She had him at last.

"The river," Magnolia had said, over and over. "The river. The river."

XII

"THEBES?" echoed Parthenia Ann Hawks, widow. The stiff crêpe of her weeds seemed to bristle. "I'll do nothing of the kind, miss! If you and that fine husband of yours think to rid yourself of me *that* way——"

"But, Mama, we're not trying to rid ourselves of you. How can you think of such things! You've always said you hated the boat. Always. And now that Papa— now that you needn't stay with the show any longer, I thought you'd want to go back to Thebes to live."

"Indeed! And what's to become of the *Cotton Blossom*, tell me that, Maggie Hawks!"

"I don't know," confessed Magnolia, miserably. "I don't—know. That's what I think we ought to talk about." The *Cotton Blossom*, after her tragic encounter with the hidden snag in the Mississippi, was in for repairs. The damage to the show boat had been greater than they had thought. The snag had, after all, inflicted a jagged wound. So, too, had it torn and wounded something deep and hidden in Magnolia's soul. Suddenly she had a horror of the great river whose treacherous secret fangs had struck so poisonously. The sight of the yellow turbid flood sickened her; yet held her hypnotized. Now she thought that she must run from it, with her husband and her child, to safety.

Now she knew that she never could be content away from it. She wanted to flee. She longed to stay. This, if ever, was her chance. But the river had Captain Andy. Somewhere in its secret coils he lay. She could not leave him. On the rivers the three great mysteries—Love and Birth and Death—had been revealed to her. All that she had known of happiness and tragedy and tranquillity and adventure and romance and fulfilment was bound up in the rivers. Their willow-fringed banks framed her world. The motley figures that went up and down upon them or that dwelt on their shores were her people. She knew them; was of them. The Mississippi had her as surely as it had little Andy Hawks.

"Well, we're talking about it, ain't we?" Mrs. Hawks now demanded.

"I mean—the repairs are going to be quite expensive. She'll be laid up for a month or more, right in the season. Now's the time to decide whether we're going to try to run her ourselves just as if Papa were still——"

"I can see you've been talking things over pretty hard and fast with Ravenal. Well, I'll tell you what we're going to do, miss. We're going to run her ourselves—leastways, I am."

"But, Mama!"

"Your pa left no will. Hawks all over. I've as must say-so as you have. More. I'm his widow. You won't see me willing to throw away the good-will of a business that it's taken years to build up. The boat's insurance'll take care of the repairs. Your pa's life insurance is paid up, and quite a decent sum—for him.

I saw to that. You'll get your share, I'll get mine. The boat goes on like it always has. No Thebes for me. You'll go on playing ingénue leads; Ravenal juvenile. Kim——"

"No!" cried Magnolia much as Parthy had, years before. "Not Kim."

"Why not?"

There was about the Widow Hawks a terrifying and invincible energy. Her black habiliments of woe billowed about her like the sable wings of a destroying angel. With Captain Andy gone, she would appoint herself commander of the Cotton Blossom Floating Palace Theatre. Magnolia knew that. Who, knowing Parthy, could imagine it otherwise? She would appoint herself commander of their lives. Magnolia was no weakling. She was a woman of mettle. But no mettle could withstand the sledge-hammer blows of Parthy Ann Hawks' iron.

It was impossible that such an arrangement could hold. From the first Ravenal rejected it. But Magnolia's pleadings for at least a trial won him over, but grudgingly.

"It won't work, Nola, I tell you. We'll be at each other's throats. She's got all kinds of plans. I can see them whirling around in her eye."

"But you will try to be patient, won't you, Gay? For my sake and Kim's?"

But they had not been out a week before mutiny struck the *Cotton Blossom*. The first to go was Windy. Once his great feet were set toward the gangplank there was no stopping him. He was over seventy now, but he looked not an hour older than when he had come aboard the *Cotton Blossom* almost fifteen years before. To the irate widow he spoke briefly but with finality.

"You're Hawks' widow. That's why I said I'd take her same's if Andy was alive. I thought Nollie's husband would boss this boat, but seems you're running it. Well, ma'am, I ain't no petticoat-pilot. I'm off the end of this trip down. Young Tanner'll come aboard there and pilot you."

"Tanner! Who's he? How d'you know I want him? I'm running this boat."

"You better take him, Mrs. Hawks, ma'am. He's young, and not set in his ways, and likely won't mind your nagging. I'm too old. Lost my taste for the rivers, anyway, since Cap went. Lost my nerve, too, seems like. . . . Well, ma'am, I'm going."

And he went.

Changes came then, tripping on each other's heels. Mis' Means stayed, and little weak-chested Mr. Means. Frank had gone after Magnolia's marriage. Ralph left.

Parthy met these difficulties and defeats with magnificent generalship. She seemed actually to thrive on them. Do this. Do that. Ravenal's right eyebrow was cocked in a perpetual circumflex of disdain. One could feel the impact of opposition whenever the two came together. Every fibre of Ravenal's silent secretive nature was taut in rejection of this managerial mother-in-law. Every nerve and muscle of that energetic female's frame tingled with enmity toward this suave soft-spoken contemptuous husband of her daughter.

Finally, "Choose," said Gaylord Ravenal, "between your mother and me."

Magnolia chose. Her decision met with such terrific opposition from Parthy as would have shaken any woman less determined and less in love.

"Where you going with that fine husband of yours? Tell me that!"

"I don't know."

"I'll warrant you don't. No more does he. Why're you going? You've got a good home on the boat."

"Kim . . . school . . ."

"Fiddlesticks!"

Magnolia took the plunge. "We're not—I'm not— Gay's not happy any more on the rivers."

"You'll be a sight unhappier on land before you're through, make no mistake about that, young lady. Where'll you go? Chicago, h'm? What'll you do there? Starve, and worse. I know. Many's the time you'll wish yourself back here."

Magnolia, nervous, apprehensive, torn, now burst into sudden rebellion against the iron hand that had gripped her all these years.

"How do you know? How can you be so sure? And even if you are right, what of it? You're always trying to keep people from doing the things they want to do. You're always wanting people to live cautiously. You fought to keep Papa from buying the *Cotton Blossom* in the first place, and made his life a hell. And now you won't leave it. You didn't want me to act. You didn't want me to marry Gay. You didn't want me to have Kim. Maybe you were right. Maybe I shouldn't

have done any of those things.   But how do you know?
You can't twist people's lives around like that, even
if you twist them right.   Because how do you know that
even when you're right you mayn't be wrong?   If Papa
had listened to you, we'd be living in Thebes.   He'd
be alive, probably.   I'd be married to the butcher,
maybe.   You can't do it.   Even God lets people have
their own way, though they have to fall down and break
their necks to find out they were wrong.   . . .   You
can't do it . . .   and you're glad when it turns out
badly . . ."

She was growing incoherent.

Back of Parthy's opposition to their going was a
deep relief of which even she was unaware, and whose
existence she would have denied had she been informed
of it.   Her business talent, so long dormant, was leaping
into life.   Her energy was cataclysmic.   One would
almost have said she was happy.   She discharged actors,
crew; engaged actors, crew.   Ordered supplies.   Spoke
of shifting to an entirely new territory the following
year—perhaps to the rivers of North Carolina and
Maryland.   She actually did this, though not until
much later.   Magnolia, years afterward reading her
mother's terse and maddening letters, would be seized
with a nostalgia not for the writer but for the lovely-
sounding places of which she wrote—though they
probably were as barren and unpicturesque as the river
towns of the Mississippi and Ohio and Big Sandy and
Kanawha.   "We're playing the town of Bath, on the
Pamlico River," Parthy's letter would say.   Or, "We
had a good week at Queenstown, on the Sassafras."

Magnolia, looking out into the gray Chicago streets, slippery with black ice, thick with the Lake Michigan fog, would repeat the names over to herself. Bath on the Pamlico. Queenstown on the Sassafras.

Mrs. Hawks, at parting, was all for Magnolia's retaining her financial share in the *Cotton Blossom*, the money accruing therefrom to be paid at regular intervals. In this she was right. She knew Ravenal. In her hard and managing way she loved her daughter; wished to insure her best interests. But Magnolia and Ravenal preferred to sell their share outright if she would buy. Ravenal would probably invest it in some business, Magnolia said.

"Yes—monkey business," retorted Mrs. Hawks. Then added, earnestly, "Now mind, don't you come snivelling to me when it's gone and you and your child haven't a penny to bless yourselves with. For that's what it'll come to in the end. Mark my words. I don't say I wouldn't be happy to see you and Kim back. But not him. When he's run through every penny of your money, he needn't look to me for more. You can come back to the boat; you and Kim. I'll look for you. But him! Never!"

The two women faced each other, and they were no longer mother and daughter but two forces opposing each other with all the strength that lay in the deep and powerful nature of both.

Magnolia made one of those fine speeches. "I wouldn't come to you for help—not if I were starving to death, and Kim too."

"Oh, there's worse things than starving to death."

"I wouldn't come to you no matter what."

"You will, just the same.   I'd take my oath on that."

"I never will."

Secretly she was filled with terror at leaving the rivers; for the rivers, and the little inaccessible river towns, and the indolent and naïve people of those towns whose very presence in them confessed them failures, had with the years taken on in Magnolia's eyes the friendly aspect of the accustomed.   Here was comfort assured; here were friends; here the ease that goes with familiarity. Even her mother's bristling generalship had in it a protective quality.   The very show boat was a second mother, shielding her from the problems and cares that beset the land-dweller.   The *Cotton Blossom* had been a little world in itself on which life was a thing detached, dream-like, narcotic.

As Magnolia Ravenal, with her husband and her child, turned from this existence of ease to the outside world of which she already had had one bitter taste, she was beset by hordes of fears and doubts.   Yet opposing these, and all but vanquishing them, was the strong love of adventure—the eager curiosity about the unknown— which had always characterized her and her dead father, the little captain, and caused them both to triumph, thus far, over the clutching cautious admonitions of Parthenia Ann Hawks.

Fright and anticipation; nostalgia and curiosity; a soaring sense of freedom at leaving her mother's too-protective wing; a pang of compunction that she should feel this unfilial surge of relief.

They were going.   You saw the three of them scrambling up the steep river bank to the levee (perhaps for the last time, Magnolia thought with a great pang. And within herself a voice cried no! no!) Ravenal slim, cool, contained; Magnolia whiter than usual, and frankly tearful; the child Kim waving an insouciant farewell with both small fists. They carried no bundles, no parcels, no valises. Ravenal disdained to carry parcels; he did not permit those of his party to carry them. Two Negroes in tattered and faded blue overalls made much of the luggage, stowing it inefficiently under the seats and over the floor of the livery rig which had been hired to take the three to the nearest railway station, a good twelve miles distant.

The *Cotton Blossom* troupe was grouped on the forward deck to see them off. The *Cotton Blossom* lay, smug, safe, plump, at the water's edge. A passing side-wheeler, flopping ponderously downstream, sent little flirty waves across the calm waters to her, and set her to palpitating coyly. Good-bye! Good-bye! Write, now. Mis' Means' face distorted in a ridiculous pucker of woe. Ravenal in the front seat with the driver. Magnolia and Kim in the back seat with the luggage protruding at uncomfortable angles all about them. Parthenia Ann Hawks, the better to see them, had stationed herself on the little protruding upper deck, forward—the deck that resembled a balcony much like that on the old *Cotton Blossom*. The livery nags started with a lurch up the dusty village street. They clattered across the bridge toward the upper road. Magnolia turned for a last glimpse through her tears. There stood Parthenia Ann Hawks, silhouetted against sky and water, a massive and almost menacing figure in her robes of black—tall, erect, indomitable. Her face was set. The keen eyes gazed, unblinking, across the sunlit waters. One arm was raised in a gesture of farewell. Ruthless, unconquerable, headstrong, untamed, terrible.

"She's like the River," Magnolia thought, through her grief, in a sudden flash of vision. "She's the one, after all, who's like the Mississippi."

A bend in the upper road. A clump of sycamores. The river, the show boat, the silent black-robed figure were lost to view.

XIII

THE most casual onlooker could gauge the fluctuations of the Ravenal fortunes by any one of three signs. There was Magnolia Ravenal's sealskin sacque; there was Magnolia Ravenal's diamond ring; there was Gaylord Ravenal's malacca cane. Any or all of these had a way of vanishing and reappearing in a manner that would have been baffling to one not an habitué of South Clark Street, Chicago. Of the three, the malacca stick, though of almost no tangible value, disappeared first and oftenest, for it came to be recognized as an I O U by every reputable Clark Street pawnbroker. Deep in a losing game of faro at Jeff Hankins or Mike McDonald's, Ravenal would summon a Negro boy to him. He would hand him the little ivory-topped cane. "Here—take this down to Abe Lipman's, corner Clark and Monroe. Tell him I want two hundred dollars. Hurry." Or: "Run over to Goldsmith's with this. Tell him a hundred."

The black boy would understand. In ten minutes he would return minus the stick and bearing a wilted sheaf of ten-dollar bills. If Ravenal's luck turned, the cane was redeemed. If it still stayed stubborn, the diamond ring must go; that failing, then the sealskin sacque. Ravenal, contrary to the custom of his confrères, wore no jewellery; possessed none. There were certain sinister aspects of these outward signs, as when, for example, the reigning sealskin sacque was known to skip an entire winter.

Perhaps none of these three symbols was as significant a betrayal of the Ravenal finances as was Gay Ravenal's choice of a breakfasting place. He almost never breakfasted at home. This was a reversion to one of the habits of his bachelor days; was, doubtless, a tardy rebellion, too, against the years spent under Mrs. Hawks' harsh régime. He always had hated those *Cotton Blossom* nine o'clock family breakfasts ominously presided over by Parthy in cap and curl papers.

Since their coming to Chicago Gay liked to breakfast between eleven and twelve, and certainly never rose before ten. If the Ravenal luck was high, the meal was eaten in leisurely luxury at Billy Boyle's Chop House between Clark and Dearborn streets. This was most agreeable, for at Billy Boyle's, during the noon hour, you encountered Chicago's sporting blood—political overlords, gamblers, jockeys, actors, reporters—these last mere nobodies—lean and somewhat morose young fellows vaguely known as George Ade, Brand Whitlock, John McCutcheon, Pete Dunne. Here the news and gossip of the day went round. Here you saw the Prince Albert coat, the silk hat, the rattling cuffs, the glittering collar, the diamond stud of the professional gamester. Old Carter Harrison, Mayor of Chicago, would drop in daily, a good twenty-five-cent cigar waggling between his lips as he greeted this friend and that. In came the brokers from the Board of Trade across the way.

Smoke-blue air. The rich heavy smell of thick steaks cut from prime Western beef. Massive glasses of beer through which shone the pale amber of light brew, or the seal-brown of dark. The scent of strong black coffee. Rye bread pungent with caraway. Little crisp round breakfast rolls sprinkled with poppy-seed.

Calories, high blood pressure, vegetable luncheons, golf, were words not yet included in the American everyday vocabulary. Fried potatoes were still considered a breakfast dish, and a meatless meal was a snack.

Here it was, then, that Gay Ravenal, slim, pale, quiet, elegant, liked best to begin his day; listening charmingly and attentively to the talk that swirled about him—talk of yesterday's lucky winners in Gamblers' Alley, at Prince Varnell's place, or Jeff Hankins' or Mike McDonald's; of the Washington Park racetrack entries; of the new blonde girl at Hetty Chilson's, of politics in their simplest terms. Occasionally he took part in this talk, but like most professional gamblers, his was not the conversational gift. He was given credit for the astuteness he did not possess merely on the strength of his cool evasive glance, his habit of listening and saying little, and his bland poker face.

"Ravenal doesn't say much but there's damned little he misses. Watch him an hour straight and you can't make out from his face whether he's cleaning up a thousand or losing his shirt." An enviable Clark Street reputation.

Still, this availed him nothing when funds were low. At such times he eschewed Billy Boyle's and breakfasted meagrely instead at the Cockeyed Bakery just east of Clark. That famous refuge for the temporarily insolvent was so named because of the optical peculiarity of the lady who owned it and who dispensed its coffee and sinkers. This refreshment cost ten cents. The coffee was hot, strong, revivifying; the sinkers crisp and fresh. Every Clark Street gambler was, at one time or another, through the vagaries of Lady Luck, to be found moodily munching the plain fare that made up the limited menu to be had at the Cockeyed Bakery. For that matter lacking even the modest sum required for this sustenance, he knew that there he would be allowed to "throw up a tab" until luck should turn.

Many a morning Gaylord Ravenal, dapper, nonchalant, sartorially exquisite, fared forth at eleven with but fifty cents in the pocket of his excellently tailored pants. Usually, on these occasions, the malacca stick was significantly absent. Of the fifty cents, ten went for the glassy shoeshine; twenty-five for a boutonnière; ten for coffee and sinkers at the Cockeyed Bakery. The remaining five cents stayed in his pocket as a sop to the superstition that no coin breeds no more coins. Stopping first to look in a moment at Weeping Willy Mangler's, or at Reilly's pool room for a glance at the racing chart, or to hear a bit of the talk missed through his enforced absence from Boyle's, he would end at Hankins' or McDonald's, there to woo fortune with nothing at all to offer as oblation. But affairs did not reach this pass until after the first year.

It was incredible that Magnolia Ravenal could so

soon have adapted herself to the life in which she now
moved. Yet it was explicable, perhaps, when one
took into consideration her inclusive nature. She was
interested, alert, eager—and still in love with Gaylord
Ravenal. Her life on the rivers had accustomed her
to all that was bizarre in humanity. Queenie and Jo
had been as much a part of her existence as Elly and
Schultzy. The housewives in the little towns, the
Negroes lounging on the wharves, the gamblers in the
river-front saloons, the miners of the coal belt, the
Northern fruit-pickers, the boatmen, the Southern
poor whites, the Louisiana aristocracy, all had passed
in fantastic parade before her ambient eyes. And she,
too, had marched in a parade, a figure as gorgeous, as
colourful as the rest.

Now, in this new life, she accepted everything,
enjoyed everything with a naïveté that was, perhaps,
her greatest charm. It was, doubtless, the thing that
held the roving Ravenal to her. Nothing shocked her;
this was her singularly pure and open mind. She
brought to this new life an interest and a curiosity as
fresh as that which had characterized the little girl who
had so eagerly and companionably sat with Mr. Pepper,
the pilot, in the bright cosy glass-enclosed pilot house
atop the old *Creole Belle* on that first enchanting trip
down the Mississippi to New Orleans.

To him she had said, "What's around that bend?
. . . Now what's coming? . . . How deep is
it here? . . . What used to be there? . . .
What island is that?"

Mr. Pepper, the pilot, had answered her questions

amply and with a feeling of satisfaction to himself as he
beheld her childish hunger for knowledge being ap-
peased.

Now she said to her husband with equal eagerness:
"Who is that stout woman with the pretty yellow-
haired girl? What queer eyes they have! . ˙. .
What does it mean when it says odds are two to one?
. . . Why do they call him Bath House John?
. . . Who is that large woman in the victoria, with
the lovely sunshade? How rich her dress is, yet it's
plain. Why don't you introduce me to—— Oh! That!
Hetty Chilson! Oh! . . . Why do they call him
Bad Jimmy Connerton? . . . But why do they
call it the Levee? It's really Clark Street, and no
water anywhere near, so why do they call it the Levee?
. . . What's a percentage game? . . . Hier-
onymus! What a funny word! . . . Mike
McDonald? That! Why, he looks like a farmer,
doesn't he? A farmer in his Sunday-best black clothes
that don't fit him. The Boss of the Gamblers. Why
do they call his place 'The Store'? . . . Oh, Gay
darling, I wish you wouldn't. . . . Now don't
frown like that. I just mean I—when I think of Kim,
I get scared because, how about Kim—I mean when
she grows up? . . . Why are they called owl cars?
. . . But I don't understand why Lipman lets you
have money just for a cane that isn't worth more than
ten or twenty . . . How do pawnbrokers . . .
Mont Tennes—what a queer name! . . . Al
Hankins? Oh, you're joking now. Really killed by
having a folding bed close up on him! Oh, I'll never

again sleep in a . . . Boiler Avenue? . . . Hooley's
Theatre? . . . Cinquevalli? . . . Fanny Davenport?
. . . Derby Day? . . . Weber and Fields? . . . Sau-
terne? . . . Rector's? . . .

Quite another world about which to be curious—a
world as sordid and colourful and crude and passionate and cruel and rich and varied as that other had
been.

It had taken Ravenal little more than a year to
dissipate the tidy fortune which had been Magnolia's
share of Captain Andy's estate, including the *Cotton
Blossom* interest. He had, of course, meant to double
the sum—to multiply it many times so that the plump
thousands should increase to tens—to hundreds of
thousands. Once you had money—a really respectable
amount of it—it was simple enough to manipulate that
money so as to make it magically produce more and
more money.

They had made straight for Chicago, at that period
the gamblers' paradise. When Ravenal announced
this step, a little look of panic had come into Magnolia's
eyes. She was reluctant to demur at his plans. It was
the thing her mother always had done when her father
had proposed a new move. Always Captain Andy's
enthusiasm had suffered the cold douche of Parthy's
disapproval. At the prospect of Chicago, the old
haunts, congenial companions, the restaurants, the
theatres, the races, Ravenal had been more elated than
she had ever seen him. He had become almost lo-
quacious. He could even be charming to Mrs. Hawks,
now that he was so nearly free of her. That iron woman

had regarded him as her enemy to the last and, in making over to Magnolia the goodish sum of money which was due her, had uttered dire predictions, all of which promptly came true.

That first year in Chicago was a picture so kaleidoscopic, so extravagant, so ridiculous that even the child Kim retained in her memory's eye something of its colour and pageantry. This father and mother in their twenties seemed really little older than their child. Certainly there was something pathetically childish in their evident belief that they could at once spend their money and keep it intact. Just a fur coat—what was that! Bonnets. A smart high yellow trap. Horses. The races. Suppers. A nursemaid for Kim. Magnolia knew nothing of money. She never had had any. On the *Cotton Blossom* money was a commodity of which one had little need.

On coming to Chicago they had gone directly to the Sherman House. Compared with this, that first visit to Chicago before Kim's birth had been a mere picnic jaunt. Ravenal was proud of his young wife and of his quiet, grave big-eyed child; of the nursemaid in a smart uniform; of the pair of English hackneys which he sometimes allowed Magnolia to drive, to her exquisite delight. Magnolia had her first real evening dress, cut décolleté; tasted champagne; went to the races at the Washington Park race track; sat in a box at Hooley's; was horrified at witnessing the hootchie-kootchie dance on the Midway Plaisance at the World's Fair.

The first fur coat was worthy of note. The wives

of the well-to-do wore sealskin sacques as proof of their
husband's prosperity. Magnolia descended to these
later. But the pelts which warmed her during that
first winter of Chicago lake blasts and numbing cold
had been cunningly matched in Paris, and French
fingers had fashioned them into a wrap.

Ravenal had selected it for her, of course. He always
accompanied her on her shopping trips. He liked to
loll elegantly at ease like a pasha while the keen-eyed
saleswomen brought out this gown and that for his expert
inspection. To these alert ladies it was plain to see
that Magnolia knew little enough about chic attire.
The gentleman, though—he knew what was what.
Magnolia had been aghast at the cost of that first fur
coat, but then, how should she know of such things?
Between them, she and Parthy had made most of the
costumes she had worn in her *Cotton Blossom* days, both
for stage and private use. The new coat was a black
astrakhan jacket; the fur lay in large smooth waves
known as baby lamb. Magnolia said it made her feel
like a cannibal to wear a thing like that. The sales-
ladies did not smile at this, but that was all right because Magnolia had not intended that they should. The
revers and cuffs were of Russian sable, dark and rich and
deep; and it had large mutton-leg sleeves—large enough
to contain her dress sleeves comfortably, with a little
expert aid in the way of stuffing. "Stuff my sleeves in,"
was one of the directions always given a gentleman
when he assisted a lady with her wrap.

This royal garment had cost——"Oh, Gay!" Magnolia had protested, in a low shocked voice (but not so

low that the sharp-eared saleswomen failed to hear it)
—"Oh, Gay! I honestly don't think we ought——"

"Mrs. Potter Palmer," spoke up the chief sales-
woman in a voice at once sharp and suave, "has a coat
identically similar. They are the only two of the kind
in the whole country. To tell you the truth, I think
the sable skins on this garment of madam's are just a
little finer than Mrs. Palmer's. Though perhaps it's
just that madam sets it off better, being so young and
all."

He liked her to wear, nestling in the rich depths of
the sable revers, a bunch of violets. For the theatre
she had one of those new winged bonnets, representing
a butterfly, cunningly contrived of mousseline de soie
wired and brilliantly spangled so that it quivered and
trembled with the movements of her head and sparkled
enchantingly. Kim adored the smell of the violet-
scented creature who kissed her good-night and swept
out, glittering. The impression must have gone deep,
deep into the childish mind, for twenty years later she
still retained a sort of story-book mental picture of this
black-haired creamy mother who would come in late
of a winter afternoon laughing and bright-eyed after a
drive up Grand Boulevard in the sleigh behind the
swift English hackneys. This vision would seem to
fill the warm room with a delightful mixture of violets,
and fur, and cold fresh air and velvet and spangles and
love and laughter. Kim would plunge her face deep
into the soft scented bosom.

"Oh, Gay, do see how she loves the violets! You
won't mind if I take them off and put them here in this

glass so she—— No, you mustn't buy me any fresh ones. Please! I wish she didn't look quite so much like me . . . her mouth . . . but it's going to be a great wide one, like mine. . . . Oh, Bernhardt! Who wants her little girl to look like Bernhardt! Besides, Kim isn't going to be an actress."

At the end of a year or so of this the money was gone —simply gone. Of course, it hadn't been only the hackneys, and the races, and the trap, and the furs, and the suppers and the theatres and dresses and Gay's fine garments and the nurse and the hotel. For, as Ravenal explained, the hackneys hadn't even been pure-blooded, which would have brought them up to one thousand each. He had never been really happy about them, because of a slight blot on their family escutcheon which had brought them down to a mere six hundred apiece. This flaw was apparent, surely, to no one who was not an accredited judge at a horse show. Yet when Ravenal and Magnolia on Derby Day joined the gay stream of tallyhos, wagonettes, coaches, phaetons, tandems, cocking carts, and dog-carts sweeping up Michigan Avenue and Grand Boulevard toward the Washington Park race track he was likely to fall into one of his moody silences and to flick the hackneys with little contemptuous cuts of the long lithe whip in a way that only they—and Magnolia—understood. On such occasions he called them nags.

"Ah! That off nag broke again. That's because they're not thoroughbreds."

"But, Gay, you're hurting their mouths, sawing like that."

"Please, Nola. This isn't a Mississippi barge I'm driving."

She learned many things that first year, and saw so much that part of what she saw was mercifully soon forgotten. You said Darby Day, very English. You pretended not to mind when your husband went down to speak to Hetty Chilson and her girls in their box. For that matter, you pretended not to see Hetty Chilson and her girls at all, though they had driven out in a sort of private procession of victorias, landaus, broughams, and were by far the best-dressed women at the races. They actually set the styles, Gay had told her. Hetty Chilson's girls wore rich, quiet, almost sedate clothes; and no paint on their faces. They seemed an accepted part of the world in which Gaylord Ravenal moved. Even in the rough life of the rivers, Magnolia had always understood that women of Hetty Chilson's calling simply did not exist in the public sense. They were not of the substance of everyday life, but were shadows, sinister, menacing, evil. But with this new life of Magnolia's came the startling knowledge that these ladies played an important part in the social and political life of this huge sprawling Mid-western city. This stout, blonde, rather handsome woman who carried herself with an air of prosperous assurance; whose shrewd keen glance and hearty laugh rather attracted you—this one was Hetty Chilson. The horsewomen you saw riding in the Lincoln Park bridle path, handsomely habited in black close-fitting riding clothes, were, likely as not, Hetty Chilson's girls. She was actually a power in her way. When strangers were

shown places of interest in Chicago—the Potter Palmer
castle on Lake Shore Drive, the Art Museum, the
Stockyards, the Auditorium Hotel, the great mansions
of Phil Armour and his son on Michigan Avenue, with
the garden embracing an entire city block—Hetty
Chilson's place, too, was pointed out (with a lowering
of the voice, of course, and a little leer, and perhaps an
elbow dug into the ribs). A substantial brick house on
Clark Street, near Polk, with two lions, carved in stone,
absurdly guarding its profane portals.

"Hetty Chilson's place," Gay explained to his wide-
eyed young wife, "is like a club. You're likely to find
every prominent politician in Chicago there, smoking
and having a sociable drink. And half the political
plots that you read about in the newspapers later are
hatched at Hetty's. She's as smart as they make 'em.
Bought a farm, fifteen acres, out at Ninetieth and
State, for her father and mother. And she's got a
country place out on the Kankakee River, near Mo-
mence—about sixty miles south of here—that's known
to have one of the finest libraries in the country.
Cervantes—Balzac—rare editions. Stable full of
horses—rose garden——"

"But, Gay dear!"

You saw Hetty driving down State Street during the
shopping hour in her Kimball-made Victoria, an equi-
page such as royalty might have used, its ebony body
fashioned by master craftsmen, its enamel as rich and
deep and shining as a piano top. Her ample skirts
would be spread upon the plum-coloured cushions.
If it was summer the lace ruffles of her sunshade would

plume gently in the breeze. In winter her mink coat swathed her full firm figure. One of her girls sat beside her, faultlessly dressed, pale, unvivacious. Two men in livery on the box. Harness that shone with polished metal and jingled splendidly. Two slim, quivering, high-stepping chestnuts. Queen of her world—Chicago's underworld.

"But, Gay dear!"

"Well, how about France!"

"France?"

"How about the women you used to read about—learned about them in your history books, for that matter, at school? Pompadour and Maintenon and Du Barry! Didn't they mix up in the politics of their day—and weren't they recognized? Courtesans, every one of them. You think just because they wore white wigs and flowered silk hoops and patches——"

A little unaccustomed flush surged over Magnolia's pallor—the deep, almost painful red of indignation. She was an inexperienced woman, but she was no fool. These last few months had taught her many things. Also the teachings of her school-teacher mother had not, after all, been quite forgotten, it appeared.

"She's a common woman of the town, Gaylord Ravenal. All the wigs and patches and silks in the world wouldn't make her anything else. She's no more a Du Barry than your Hinky Dink is a—uh—Mazarin."

It was as though he took a sort of perverse pleasure in thus startling her. It wasn't that she was shocked in the prim sense of the word. She was bewildered and a

little frightened. At such times the austere form and
the grim visage of Parthenia Ann Hawks would rise up
before her puzzled eyes. What would Parthy have said
of these unsavoury figures now passing in parade before
Magnolia's confused vision—Hetty Chilson, Doc Haggerty, Mike McDonald, "Prince" Varnell, Effie Hankins? Uneasy though she was, Magnolia could manage
to smile at the thought of her mother's verbal de-
struction of this raffish crew. There were no half tones
in Parthy's vocabulary. A hussy was a hussy; a rake
a rake. But her father, she thought, would have been
interested in all this, and more than a little amused.
His bright brown eyes would have missed nothing; the
little nimble figure would have scampered inquisitively
up and down the narrow and somewhat sinister lane
that lay between Washington and Madison streets,
known as Gamblers' Alley; he would have taken a turn
at faro; appraised the Levee ladies at their worth;
visited Sam T. Jack's Burlesque Show over on Madison,
and Kohl & Middleton's Museum, probably, and
Hooley's Theatre certainly. Nothing in Chicago's
Levee life would have escaped little Captain Andy, and
nothing would have changed him.

"See it all, Nollie," he had said to her in the old
Cotton Blossom days, when Parthy would object to their
taking this or that jaunt ashore between shows. "Don't
you believe 'em when they say that what you don't
know won't hurt you. Biggest lie ever was. See it
all and go your own way and nothing'll hurt you. If
what you see ain't pretty, what's the odds! See it

anyway. Then next time you don't have to look."

Magnolia, gazing about her, decided that she was seeing it all.

The bulk of the money had gone at faro. The suckers played roulette, stud poker, hazard, the bird-cage, chuck-a-luck (the old army game). But your gambler played faro. Faro was Gaylord Ravenal's game, and he played at Hankins'—not at George Hankins' where they catered to the cheap trade who played percentage games—but at Jeff Hankins' or Mike McDonald's where were found the highest stakes in Chicago. Faro was not a game with Ravenal—it was for him at once his profession, his science, his drug, his drink, his mistress. He had, unhappily, as was so often the case with your confirmed gambler, no other vice. He rarely drank, and then abstemiously; smoked little and then a mild cigar, ate sparingly and fastidiously; eschewed even the diamond ring and shirt-stud of his kind.

The two did not, of course, watch the money go, or despair because it would soon be gone. There seemed to be plenty of it. There always would be enough. Next week they would invest it securely. Ravenal had inside tips on the market. He had heard of a Good Thing. This was not the right time, but They would let him know when the magic moment was at hand. In the meantime there was faro. And there were the luxurious hotel rooms with their soft thick carpets, and their big comfortable beds; ice water tinkling at the door in answer to your ring; special dishes to tempt the taste of Mr. Ravenal and his lady. The sharp-eyed gentleman in evening clothes who stood near the little ticket box as you entered the theatre said, "Good-evening, Mr. Ravenal," when they went to Hooley's or McVicker's or the Grand Opera House, or Kohl and Castle's. The heads of departments in Mandel's or Carson Pirie's or even Marshall Field's said, "I have something rather special to show you, Mrs. Ravenal. I thought of you the minute it came in."

Sometimes it seemed to Magnolia that the *Cotton Blossom* had been only a phantom ship—the rivers a dream—a legend.

It was all very pleasant and luxurious and strange. And Magnolia tried not to mind the clang of Clark Street by day and by night. The hideous cacophony of noise invaded their hotel apartment and filled its every corner. She wondered why the street-car motormen jangled their warning bells so persistently. Did they do it as an antidote to relieve their own jangled nerves? *Pay*-pes! MO'-nin' *pay*-pes! Crack! Crack! Crackcrackcrack! The shooting gallery across the street. Someone passing the bedroom door, walking heavily and clanking the metal disk of his room key. The sound of voices, laughter, from the street, and the unceasing shuffle of footsteps on stone. Whee-e-e-e-e! Whoop-a! Ye-e-eow! A drunkard. She knew about that, too. Part of her recently acquired knowledge. Ravenal had told her about Big Steve Rowan, the three-hundred-pound policeman, who, partly because of his goatee and moustache, and partly because of his expert manipulation of his official weapon, was called the Jack of Clubs.

"You'll never see Big Steve arrest a drunk at night,"

Gay had explained to her, laughing. "No, sir! Nor
any other Clark Street cop if he can help it. If they
arrest a man they have to appear against him next
morning at the nine o'clock police court. That means
getting up early. So if he's able to navigate at all,
they pass him on down the street from corner to corner
until they get him headed west somewhere, or north
across the bridge. Great system."

All this was amusing and colourful, perhaps, but
scarcely conducive to tranquillity and repose. Often
Magnolia, lying awake by the side of the sleeping man,
or lying awake awaiting his late return, would close her
stinging eyelids the better to visualize and sense the
deep velvet silence of the rivers of her girlhood—the
black velvet nights, quiet, quiet. The lisping cluck-
suck of the water against the hull.

Clang! MO'nin' *pay*-pes! Crack! E-e-eee-yow!

And then, suddenly, one day: "But, Gay dear, how
do you mean you haven't one hundred dollars? It's for
that bronze-green velvet that you like so much, though I
always think it makes me look sallow. You did urge
me to get it, you know, dear. And now this is the third
time they've sent the bill. So if you'll give me the
money—or write a check, if you'd rather."

"I tell you I haven't got it, Nola."

"Oh, well, to-morrow'll do. But please be sure to-
morrow, because I hate——"

"I can't be any surer to-morrow than I am to-day.
I haven't got a hundred dollars in the world. And
that's a fact."

Even after he had finished explaining, she did not

understand; could not believe it; continued to stare at him with those great dark startled eyes.

Bad luck. At what? Faro. But, Gay—thousands! Well, thousands don't last for ever. Took a flyer. Flyer? Yes. A tip on the market. Market? The stock market. Stock? Oh, you wouldn't understand. But all of it, Gay? Well, some of it lost at faro. Where? Hankins'. How much? What does it matter? —it's gone. But, Gay, how much at faro? Oh, a few thousands. Five? Y-y-yes. Yes, five. More than that? Well, nearer ten, probably.

She noticed then that the malacca cane was gone. She slipped her diamond ring off her finger. Gave it to him. With the years, that became an automatic gesture.

Thus the change in their mode of living did not come about gradually. They were wafted, with Cinderella-like celerity, from the coach-and-four to the kitchen ashes. They left the plush and ice water and fresh linen and rich food and luxurious service of the Sherman House for a grubby little family hotel that was really a sort of actors' boarding house, on the north side, just across the Clark Street bridge, on Ontario Street. It was, Ravenal said, within convenient walking distance of places.

"What places?" Magnolia asked. But she knew. A ten minutes' saunter brought you to Gamblers' Alley. In the next fifteen years there was never a morning when Gaylord Ravenal failed to prove this interesting geographical fact.

XIV

THE Ravenal reverses, if they were noticed at all in Gamblers' Alley, went politely unremarked. There was a curious and definite code of honour among the frequenters of Chicago's Levee. You paid your gambling debts. You never revealed your own financial status by way of conversation. You talked little. You maintained a certain physical, sartorial, and social standard in the face of all reverses. There were, of course, always unmistakable signs to be read even at the most passing glance. You drew your conclusions; made no comment. If you were seen to breakfast for days—a week—two weeks—at the Cockeyed Bakery, you were greeted by your confrères with the same suavity that would have been accorded you had you been standing treat at Billy Boyle's or the Palmer House. Your shoe might be cracked, but it must shine. Your linen might be frayed, but it must be clean. Your cheeks were perhaps a trifle hollow, but they must be shaven and smell pleasantly of bay rum. You might dine at Burkey and Milan's (Full Meal 15c.) with ravenous preliminary onslaughts upon the bread-and-butter and piccalilli. But you consumed, delicately and fastidiously, just so much and no more of the bountiful and rich repast spread out for your taking at Jeff Hankins' or at Mike McDonald's. Though your suit was shabby, it must bear the mark of that tailor to the well-dressed sporting man—Billy McLean. If you were too impecunious for Hetty Chilson's you disdained the window-tapping dives on Boiler Avenue and lower Clark Street and State; the sinister and foul shanties of Big Maud and her ilk. You bathed, shaved, dressed, ate, smoked with the same exotic care when you were broke as when luck was running your way. Your cigar was a mild one (also part of the code), and this mild one usually a dead one as you played. And no one is too broke for one cigar a day. Twelve o'clock —noon—found you awake. Twelve o'clock—midnight—found you awake. Somewhere between those hours you slept the deep sweet sleep of the abstemious. You were, in short, a gambler—and a gentleman.

Thus, when the Ravenals moved, perforce, from the comfort of the Sherman to the threadbare shabbiness of the Ontario Street boarding house, there was nothing in Gaylord Ravenal's appearance to tell the tale. If his cronies knew of his financial straits, they said nothing. Magnolia had no women friends. During the year or more of their residence in Chicago she had been richly content with Kim and Gay. The child had a prim and winning gravity that gave her a curiously grown-up air.

"Do you know, Gay," Magnolia frequently said, "Kim sometimes makes me feel so gawky and foolish and young. When she looks at me after I've been amused about something, or am enthusiastic or excited or—you know—anyway, she looks at me out of those big eyes of hers, very solemn, and I feel—— Oh, Gay, you don't think she resembles—that is—do you think she is much like Mama?"

"God forbid!" ejaculated Ravenal, piously.

Kim had been Magnolia's delight during the late morning hours and the early afternoon. In company with the stolid nurse, they had fared forth in search of such amusement as the city provided for a child brought up amidst tne unnatural surroundings of this one. The child had grown accustomed to seeing her nurse stand finger on lips, eyes commanding silence, before the closed door of her parents' room at ten in the morning —at eleven, even—and she got it into her baby head that this attitude, then, was the proper and normal one in which to approach the closed door of that hushed chamber. Late one morning Magnolia, in nightgown and silken wrapper, had opened this door suddenly to find the child stationed there, silent, grave-eyed, admonitory, while in one corner, against the door case, reposed the favourite doll of her collection—a lymphatic blonde whose eyes had met with some unfortunate interior mishap which gave them a dying-calf look. This sprawling and inert lady was being shushed in a threatening and dramatic manner by the sternly maternal Kim. There was, at sight of this, that which brought the quick sting of tears to Magnolia's eyes. She gathered the child up in her arms, kissed her passionately, held her close, brought her to Ravenal as he lay yawning.

"Gay, look at her! She was standing by the door telling her doll not to make any noise. She's only a baby. We don't pay enough attention to her. Do you think I neglect her? Standing there by the door! And it's nearly noon. Oh, Gay, we oughtn't to be living here. We ought to be living in a house—a little house where it's quiet and peaceful and she can play."

"Lovely," said Gay. "Thebes, for example. Now don't get dramatic, Nola, for God's sake. I thought we'd finished with that."

With the change in their fortunes the English nurse had vanished with the rest. She had gone, together with the hackneys, the high smart yellow cart, the violets, the green velvets, the box seats at the theatre, the champagne. She, or her counterpart, never returned, but many of the lost luxuries did, from time to time. There were better days to come, and worse. Their real fortune gone, there now was something almost humdrum and methodical about the regularity of their ups and downs. There rarely was an intermediate state. It was feast or famine, always. They actually settled down to the life of a professional gambler and his family. Ravenal would have a run of luck at faro. Presto! Rooms at the Palmer House. A box at the races. The theatre. Supper at Rector's after the theatre. Hello, Gay! Evening, Mrs. Ravenal. Somebody's looking mighty lovely to-night. A new sealskin sacque. Her diamond ring on her finger. Two new suits of clothes for Ravenal, made by Billy McLean. A little dinner for Gay's friends at Cardinal Bemis's famous place on Michigan Avenue. You couldn't fool the Cardinal.

He would ask suavely, "What kind of a dinner, Mr. Ravenal?"

If Gay replied, "Oh—uh—a cocktail and a little red wine," Cardinal Bemis knew that luck was only so-so, and that the dinner was to be good, but plainish. But if, in reply to the tactful question, Gay said, magnificently, "A cocktail, Cardinal; claret, sauterne, champagne, and liqueurs," Bemis knew that Ravenal had had a real run of luck and prepared the canvasbacks boiled in champagne; or there were squabs or plover, with all sorts of delicacies, and the famous frozen watermelon that had been plugged, filled with champagne, put on ice for a day, and served in such chunks of scarlet fragrance as made the nectar and ambrosia of the gods seem poor, flavourless fare indeed.

Magnolia, when luck was high, tried to put a little money by as she had instinctively been prompted to do during those first months of their marriage, when they still were on the *Cotton Blossom*. But she rarely had money of her own. Gay, when he had ready cash, was generous—but not with the handing over of the actual coin itself.

"Buy yourself some decent clothes, Nola; and the kid. Tell them to send me the bill. That thing you're wearing is a terrible sight. It seems to me you haven't worn anything else for months." Which was true enough. There was something fantastic about the magnificence with which he ignored the reason for her not having worn anything else for months. It had been, certainly, her one decent garment during the lean period just passed, and she had cleaned and darned and refurbished to keep it so. Her experience in sewing during the old *Cotton Blossom* days stood her in good stead now.

There were times when even the Ontario Street hotel
took on the aspect of unattainable luxury. That meant
rock bottom. Then it was that the Ravenals took a
room at three dollars a week in a frowzy rooming
house on Ohio or Indiana or Erie; the Bloomsbury of
Chicago. There you saw unshaven men, their coat
collars turned up in artless attempt to conceal the
absence of linen, sallying forth, pail in hand, at ten or
eleven in the morning in search of the matutinal milk
and rolls to accompany the coffee that was even now
cooking over the gas jet. Morning was a musty jade
on these streets; nothing fresh and dewy and sparkling
about her. The ladies of the neighbourhood lolled
huge, unwieldy, flaccid, in wrappers. In the afternoon
you saw them amazingly transformed into plump and
pinkly powdered persons, snugly corseted, high-heeled,
rustling in silk petticoats, giving out a heady scent.
They were friendly voluble ladies who beamed on the
pale slim Magnolia, and said, "Won't you smile for me
just a little bit? H'm?" to the sedate and solemn-eyed
Kim.

Magnolia, too, boiled coffee and eggs over the gas jet
in these lean times. Gravely she counted out the two
nickels that would bring her and Kim home from
Lincoln Park on the street car. Lincoln Park was an
oasis—a life-giving breathing spot to the mother and
child. They sallied forth in the afternoon; left the gas
jet, the three-dollar room, the musty halls, the stout
females behind them. There was the zoo; there was the
lake; there was the grass. If the lake was their choice
it led inevitably to tales of the rivers. It was in this

way that the background of her mother's life was first
etched upon Kim's mind. The sight of the water
always filled Magnolia with a nostalgia so acute as to
amount to an actual physical pain.

The childish treble would repeat the words as the
two sat on a park bench facing the great blue sea that
was Lake Michigan.

"You remember the boat, don't you, Kim?"

"Do I?" Kim's diction was curiously adult, due,
doubtless, to the fact that she had known almost no
children.

"Of course you do, darling. Don't you remember
the river, and Grandma and Grandpa——"

"Cap'n!"

"Yes! I knew you remembered. And all the little
darkies on the landing. And the band. And the steam
organ. You used to put your hands over your ears and
run and hide, because it frightened you. And Jo and
Queenie."

"Tell me about it."

And Magnolia would assuage her own longing by
telling and retelling the things she liked to remember.
The stories, with the years, became a saga. Figures
appeared, vanished, reappeared. The rivers wound
through the whole. Elly, Schultzy, Julie, Steve; the
man in the box with the gun; the old *Creole Belle* and
Magnolia's first trip on the Mississippi; Mr. Pepper and
the pilot house; all these became familiar and yet
legendary figures and incidents to the child. They
were her Three Bears, her Bo-peep, her Red Riding
Hood, her Cinderella. Magnolia must have painted

these stories with the colour of life itself, for the child never wearied of them.

"Tell me the one about the time you were a little girl and Gra'ma locked you in the bedroom because she didn't want you to see the show and you climbed out of the window in your nightie . . . ."

Kim Ravenal was probably the only white child north of the Mason and Dixon line who was sung to sleep to the tune of those plaintive, wistful Negro plantation songs which later were to come into such vogue as spirituals. They were the songs that Magnolia had learned from black Jo and from Queenie, the erstwhile rulers of the *Cotton Blossom* galley. Swing Low Sweet Chariot, she sang. O, Wasn't Dat a Wide River! And, of course, All God's Chillun Got Wings. Kim loved them. When she happened to be ill with some childhood ailment, they soothed her. Magnolia sang these songs, always, as she had learned to sing them in unconscious imitation of the soft husky Negro voice of her teacher. Through the years of Kim's early childhood, Magnolia's voice might have been heard thus wherever the shifting Ravenal fortunes had tossed the three, whether the red-plush luxury of the Sherman House, the respectable dulness of the family hotel, or the sordid fustiness of the cheap rooming house. Once, when they were living at the Sherman, Magnolia, seated in a rocking chair with Kim in her arms, had stopped suddenly in her song at a curious sound in the corridor. She had gone swiftly to the door, had opened it, and had been unable to stifle a little shriek of surprise and terror mingled. There stood a knot of black faces, teeth gleaming, eyes rolling. Attracted by the songs so rarely heard in the North, the Sherman House bell boys and waiters had eagerly gathered outside the closed door in what was, perhaps, as flattering and sincere a compliment as ever a singer received.

Never did child know such ups and downs as did this daughter of the Chicago gambler and the show-boat actress. She came to take quite for granted sudden and complete changes that would have disorganized any one more conventionally bred. One week she would find herself living in grubby quarters where the clammy fetid ghost of cabbage lurked always in the halls; the next would be a gay panorama of whisking waiters, new lace petticoats, drives along the lake front, ice cream for dessert, front seats at the matinée. The theatre bulked large in the life of the Ravenals. Magnolia loved it without being possessed of much discrimination with regard to it. Farce, comedy, melodrama—the whole gamut as outlined by Polonius—all held her interested, enthralled. Ravenal was much more critical than she. You saw him smoking in the lobby, bored, dégagé. It might be the opening of the rebuilt Lincoln Theatre on Clark near Division, with Gustave Frohman's company playing The Charity Ball.

"Oh, Gay, isn't it exciting!"

"I don't think much of it. Cheap-looking theatre, too, isn't it? They might better have left it alone after it burned down."

Kim's introduction to the metropolitan theatre was when she was taken, a mere baby, to see the spectacle America at the Auditorium. Before she was ten she had seen everyone from Julia Marlowe to Anna Held; from Bernhardt to Lillian Russell. Gravely she beheld the antics of the Rogers Brothers. As gravely saw Klaw and Erlanger's company in Foxey Quiller.

"It isn't that she doesn't see the joke," Magnolia confided to Ravenal, almost worriedly. "She actually doesn't seem to approve. Of course, I suppose I ought to be glad that she prefers the more serious things, but I wish she wouldn't seem quite so grown-up at ten. By the time she's twenty she'll probably be spanking me and putting me to bed."

Certainly Magnolia was young enough for two. She was the sort of theatre-goer who clutches the hand of her neighbour when stirred. When Ravenal was absent Kim learned to sustain her mother at such emotional moments. They two frequently attended the theatre together. Their precarious mode of living cut them off from sustained human friendships. But the theatre was always there to stimulate them, to amuse them, to make them forget or remember. There were long afternoons to be filled, and many evenings as Ravenal became more and more deeply involved in the intricacies of Chicago's night world.

There was, curiously enough, a pendulum-like regularity about his irregular life. His comings and goings could be depended on almost as though he were a clerk or a humdrum bookkeeper. Though his fortunes changed with bewildering rapidity, his habits remained the same. Indeed, he felt these changes much less than did Magnolia and Kim. No matter what their habitation—cheap rooming house or expensive hotel—he left

at about the same hour each morning, took the same
leisurely course toward town, returned richer or poorer
—but unruffled—well after midnight. On his off nights
he and Magnolia went to the theatre. Curiously, they
seemed always to have enough money for that.

Usually they dwelt somewhere north, just the other
side of the Chicago River, at that time a foul-smelling
and viscid stream, with no drainage canal to deodorize
it. Ravenal, in lean times, emerging from his dingy
hotel or rooming house on Ontario or Ohio, was as
dapper, as suave, as elegant as that younger Ravenal
had been who, leaning against the packing case on the
wharf at New Orleans, had managed to triumph over
the handicap of a cracked boot. He would stand a
moment, much as he had stood that southern spring
morning, coolly surveying the world about him. That
his viewpoint was the dingy front stoop of a run-down
Chicago rooming house and his view the sordid street
that held it, apparently disturbed his equanimity not at
all. On rising he had observed exactly the same niceties that would have been his had he enjoyed the ser-
vices of a hotel valet. He bathed, shaved, dressed
meticulously. Magnolia had early learned that the
slatternly morning habits which she had taken for
granted in the *Cotton Blossom* wives—Julie, Mis'
Means, Mrs. Soaper, even the rather fastidious Elly—
would be found inexcusable in the wife of Ravenal.
The sternly utilitarian undergarments of Parthy's
choosing had soon enough been done away with, to be
replaced with a froth of lace and tucks and embroidery

and batiste. The laundering of these was a pretty problem when faro's frown decreed Ohio Street.

Ravenal was spared these worrisome details. Once out of the dingy boarding house, he could take his day in his two hands and turn it over, like a bright, fresh-minted coin. Each day was a new start. How could you know that you would not break the bank! It had been done on a dollar.

Down the street Ravenal would stroll past the ship chandlers' and commission houses south of Ontario, to the swinging bridge that spanned the slimy river. There he would slacken his already leisurely pace, or even pause a moment, perhaps, to glance at the steamers tied up at the docks. There was an occasional sailboat. A three-masted schooner, *The Finney*, a grain boat, was in from up North. Over to Clark and Lake. You could sniff in the air the pleasant scent of coffee. That was Reid & Murdock's big warehouse a little to the east. He sometimes went a block out of his way just to sniff this delicious odour. A glittering shoeshine at the Sherman House or the Tremont.

"Good-morning, George."

"Mawnin' Mist' Ravenal! Mawnin'! Papah, suh?"

"Ah—n-n-no. No. H'm!" His fifty cents, budgeted, did not include the dispensing of those extra pennies for the *Times-Herald*, the *Inter-Ocean*, or the *Tribune*. They could be seen at McDonald's for nothing. A fine Chicago morning. The lake mist had lifted. That was one of the advantages of never rising early. Into the Cockeyed Bakery for breakfast. To-morrow it would be Boyle's. Surely his bad luck would break to-day. He felt it. Had felt it the moment he opened his eyes.

"Terrapin and champagne to-morrow, Nola. Feel it in my bones. I woke up with my palm itching, and passed a hunchback at Clark and Randolph last night."

"Why don't you let me give you your coffee and toast here this morning, Gay dear? It'll only take a minute. And it's so much better than the coffee you get at the—uh—downtown."

Ravenal, after surveying his necktie critically in the mirror of the crazy little bureau, would shrug himself into his well-made coat. "You know I never eat in a room in which I have slept."

Past the Court House; corner of Washington reached. Cut flowers in the glass case outside the basement florist's. A tapping on the glass with a coin, or a rapping on the pavement with his stick—if the malacca stick was in evidence. "Heh, Joe!"

Joe clattering up the wooden steps.

"Here you are, sir. All ready for you. Just came in fresh." A white carnation. Ravenal would sniff the spicy bloom, snap the brittle stem, thrust it through the buttonhole of his lapel.

A fine figure of a man from his boots to his hat. Young, handsome, well-dressed, leisurely. Joe, the Greek florist, pocketing his quarter, would reflect gloomily on luck—his own and that of others.

Ravenal might drop in a moment at Weeping Willy Mangler's, thence to Reilly's pool room near Madison, for a look at the racing odds. But no matter how low

his finances, he scorned the cheaper gambling rooms
that catered to the clerks and the working men. There
was a great difference between Jeff Hankins' place and
that of his brother, George. At George's place, and
others of that class, barkers stood outside. "Game
upstairs, gentlemen! Game upstairs! Come in and
try your luck! Ten cents can make you a millionaire."

At George Hankins' the faro checks actually were
ten cents. You saw there labouring men with their
tin dinner pails, their boots lime-spattered, their garments reeking of cheap pipe tobacco. There, too, you
found stud poker, roulette, hazard—percentage games.
None of these for Ravenal. He played a gentleman's
game, broke or flush.

This game he found at Mike McDonald's "The
Store." Here he was at home. Here were excitement,
luxury, companionship. Here he was Gaylord Ravenal.
Fortune lurked just around the corner. At McDonald's
his credit always was good for enough to start the play.
On the first floor was the saloon, with its rich walnut
panelling, its great mirrors, its tables of teakwood and
ivory inlay, its paintings of lolling ladies. Chicago's
saloons and gambling resorts vied with each other in
rich and massive decoration. None of your soap-
scrawled mirrors and fancy bottle structures for these.
"Prince" Varnell's place had, for years, been famous for
its magnificent built-in mantel of Mexican onyx, its
great marble statue of the death of Cleopatra, its enormous Sèvres vases.

The second floor was Ravenal's goal. He did not
even glance at the whirling of the elaborately inlaid rou-

lette wheels.   He nodded to the dealers and his greeting
was deferentially returned.   It was said that most of
these men had come of fine old Southern families.
They dressed the part.   But McDonald himself looked
like a farmer.   His black clothes, though well made,
never seemed to fit him.   His black string tie never
varied.   Thin, short, gray-haired, Mike McDonald the
Boss of the gamblers would have passed anywhere for a
kindly rustic.

"Playing to-day, Mr. Ravenal?"

"Why, yes.   Yes, I thought I'd play a while."

"Anything we can do to make you comfortable?"

"Well—uh—yes——"

McDonald would raise a benevolent though authori-
tative hand.   His finger would summon a menial.
"Dave, take care of Mr. Ravenal."

Ravenal joined the others then, a gentleman gambler
among gentleman gamblers.   A group smartly dressed
like himself, well groomed, quiet, almost elegant.   Most
of them wore jewellery—a diamond scarf pin, a diamond
ring, sometimes even a diamond stud, though this was
frowned on by players of Ravenal's class.   A dead cigar
in the mouth of each.   Little fine lines etched about
their eyes.   They addressed each other as "sir."
Thank you, sir.   . . .   Yours I believe, sir.   . . .
They were quiet, quiet.   Yet there was an electric vibra-
tion in the air above and about the faro table.   Only
the dealer seemed remote, detached, unmoved.   An
hour passed; two, three, four, five.   The Negro waiters
in very white starched aprons moved deferentially
from group to group.   One would have said that no

favouritism was being shown, but they knew the piker from the plunger. Soft-voiced, coaxing: "Something to drink, suh? A little whisky, suh? Cigar? Might be you'd relish a little chicken white meat and a bottle of wine?"

Ravenal would glance up abstractedly. "Time is it?"

"Pushin' six o'clock, suh."

Ravenal might interrupt his game to eat something, but this was not his rule. He ate usually after he had finished his play for the day. It was understood that he and others of his stamp were the guests of McDonald or of Hankins. Twenty-five-cent cigars were to be had for the taking. Drinks of every description. Hot food of the choicest sort and of almost any variety could be ordered and eaten as though this were one's own house, and the servants at one's command. Hot soups and broths. Steaks. Chops. Hot birds. You could eat this at a little white-spread table alone, or with your companions, or you could have it brought to you as you played. On long tables in the adjoining room were spread the cold viands—roast chickens, tongue, sausages, cheese, joints of roast beef, salads. Everything about the place gave to its habitués the illusion of plenty, of ease, of luxury. Soft red carpets; great prism-hung chandeliers; the clink of ice; the scent of sappy cigars and rich food; the soft slap-slap of the cards; the low voices of the dealers. It was all friendly, relaxed, soothing. Yet when the dealer opened the little drawer that was so cleverly concealed under his side of the table —the money drawer with its orderly stacks of yellow-backs, and green-backs and gold and silver—you saw, if your glance was quick and sharp enough, the gleam of still another metal: the glittering, sinister blue-gray of steel.

A hundred superstitions swayed their play. Luck was a creature to be wooed, flattered, coaxed, feared. No jungle voodoo worshipper ever lent himself to simpler or more childish practices and beliefs than did these hard-faced men.

Sometimes Ravenal left the faro table penniless or even deeper in Mike McDonald's debt. His face at such times was not more impassive than the bucolic host's own. "Better luck next time, Mr. Ravenal."

"She's due to turn to-morrow, Mike. Watch out for me to-morrow. I'll probably clean you."

And if not to-morrow, to-morrow. Luck must turn, sooner or later. There! Five hundred! A thousand! Five thousand! Did you hear about Ravenal? Yes, he had a wonderful run. It happened in an hour. He walked out with ten thousand. More, some say.

On these nights Ravenal would stroll coolly home as on losing nights. Up Clark Street, the money in neat rolls in his pocket. There were almost no street robberies in those simpler Chicago days. If you were, like Ravenal, a well-dressed sporting looking man, strolling up Clark Street at midnight or thereabouts, you were likely to be stopped for the price of a meal. You gave it as a matter of course, unwrapping a bill, perhaps, from the roll you carried in your pocket.

They might be living in modest comfort at the Revere House on Clark and Austin. They might be liv-

ing in decent discomfort at the little theatrical boarding
house on Ontario. They might be huddled in actual
discomfort in the sordid room of the Ohio Street rooming house. Be that as it may, Ravenal would take high-
handed possession, but in a way so blithe, so gay, so
charming that no one could have withstood him, least
of all his wife who, though she knew him and understood him as well as any one could understand this secretive and baffling nature, frequently despised him,
often hated him, still was in love with him and always
would be.

The child would be asleep in her corner, but Magnolia
would be wide awake, reading or sewing or simply sitting
there waiting. She never reproached him for the hours
he kept. Though they quarrelled frequently it was
never about this. Sometimes, as she sat there, half
dozing, her mind would go back to the rivers and gently
float there. An hour—two hours—would slip by.
Now the curtain would be going down on the last act.
Now the crowd staying for the after-piece and concert
would be moving down to occupy the seats nearer the
stage. A song number by the ingénue, finishing with a
clog or a soft-shoe dance. The comic tramp. The
character team in a patter act, with a song. The after-
piece now; probably Red Hot Coffee, or some similar
stand-by. Now the crowd was leaving. The band
struck up its last number. Up the river bank scrambled
the last straggler. You never threw me my line at all.
There I was like a stuck pig. Well, how did I know
you was going to leave out that business with the door.
Why'n't you tell me? Say, Ed, will you go over my

song with me a minute? You know, that place where it goes TUM-ty-ty TUM-ty-ty TUM-TUM-TUM and then I vamp. It kind of went sour to-night, seemed to me. A bit of supper. Coffee cooked over a spirit lamp. Lumps of yellow cheese, a bite of ham. Relaxation after strain. A daubing with cold cream. A sloshing of water. Quieter. More quiet. Quiet. Darkness. Security. No sound but that of the river flowing by. Sometimes if she dozed she was wakened by the familiar hoot of a steamer whistle—some big lake boat, perhaps, bound for Michigan or Minnesota; or a river barge or tug on the Chicago River near by. She would start up, bewildered, scarcely knowing whether she had heard this hoarse blast or whether it was only, after all, part of her dream about the river and the *Cotton Blossom*.

Ravenal coming swiftly up the stairs. Ravenal's quick light tread in the hall.

"Come on, Nola! We're leaving this rat's nest."

"Gay, dear! Not now. You don't mean to-night."

"Now It'll only take a minute. I'll wake up the slavey. She'll help."

"No! No! I'd rather do it myself. Oh, Gay, Kim's asleep. Can't we wait until morning?"

But somehow the fantastic procedure appealed tremendously to her love of the unexpected. Packing up and moving on. The irresponsible gaiety of it. The gas turned high. Out tumbled the contents of bureau drawers and boxes and trunks. Finery saved from just such another lucky day. Froth and foam of lace and silk strewn incongruously about this murky little chamber with its frayed carpet and stained walls and crazy chairs. They spoke in half whispers so as not to wake the child. They were themselves like two children, eager, excited, laughing.

"Where are we going, Gay?"

"Sherman. Or how would you like to try the Auditorium for a change? Rooms looking out over the lake."

"Gay!" Her hands clasped as she knelt in front of a trunk.

"Next week we'll run down to West Baden. Do us good. During the day we can walk and drive or ride. You ought to learn to ride, Nola. In the evening we can take a whirl at Tom Taggart's layout."

"Oh, don't play there—not much, I mean. Let's try to keep what we have for a little while."

"After all, we may as well give Tom a chance to pay our expenses. Remember the last time we were down I won a thousand at roulette alone—and roulette isn't my game."

He awoke the landlady and paid his bill in the middle of the night. She did not resent being thus disturbed. Women rarely resented Gaylord Ravenal's lack of consideration. They were off in a hack fetched by Ravenal from the near-by cab stand. It was no novelty for Kim to fall asleep in the dingy discomfort of a north side rooming house and to wake up amidst the bright luxuriousness of a hotel suite, without ever having been conscious of the events which had wrought this change. Instead of milk out of the bottle and an egg cooked over the gas jet, there was a shining breakfast tray bearing mysterious round-domed dishes whose covers you whip-

ped off to disclose what not of savoury delights! Crisp
curls of bacon, parsley-decked; eggs baked and actually
bubbling in a brown crockery container; hot golden buttered toast.   And her mother calling gaily in from the
next room, "Drink your milk with your breakfast, Kim
darling! Don't gulp it all down in one swallow at the
end."

It was easy enough for Kim to believe in those fairy
tales that had to do with kindly sprites who worked
miracles overnight.   A whole staff of such good crea-
tures seemed pretty regularly occupied with the Ravenal
affairs.

Once a month there came a letter from Mrs. Hawks.
No more and no less.   That indomitable woman was
making a great success of her business.   Her letters
bristled with complaint, but between the lines Magnolia
could read satisfaction and even a certain grim happiness.   She was boss of her world, such as it was.   Her
word was final.   The modern business woman had not
yet begun her almost universal battle against the male in
his own field.   She was considered unique.   Tales of her
prowess became river lore.   Parthy Ann Hawks, owner
and manager of the Cotton Blossom Floating Palace
Theatre, strong, erect, massive, her eyebrows black
above her keen cold eyes, her abundant hair scarcely
touched with gray, was now a well-known and important
figure on the rivers.   She ran her boat like a pirate
captain.   He who displeased her walked the plank.   It
was said that the more religious rivermen who hailed
from the Louisiana parishes always crossed themselves
fearfully at her approach and considered a meeting with

the *Cotton Blossom* a bad omen. The towering black-garbed form standing like a ship's figurehead, grim and portentous, as the boat swept downstream, had been known to give a really devout Catholic captain a severe and instantaneous case of chills and fever.

Her letters to Magnolia were characteristic:

Well, Maggie, I hope you and the child are in good health. Often and often I think land knows what kind of a bringing up she is getting with the life you are leading. I can imagine. Well, you made your own bed and now you can lie in it. I have no doubt that he has run through every penny of your money that your poor father worked so hard to get as I predicted he would. I suppose you heard all about French's *New Sensation*. French has the worst luck it does seem. She sank six weeks ago at Medley's just above New Madrid. The fault of the pilot it was. Carelessness if ever I heard it. He got caught in the down draft of a gravel bar and snagged her they say. I think of your poor pa and how he met his end. It took two weeks to raise her though she was only in six feet of water. On top of that his other boat the *Golden Rod* you remember went down about four weeks ago in the Illinois near Hardin. A total loss. Did you ever hear of such luck. Business is pretty good. I can't complain. But I have to be right on hand every minute or they would steal me blind and that's the truth. I have got a new heavy. No great shakes as an actor but handy enough and a pretty good black face in the concert and they seem to like him. We had a pretty rough audience all through the coal country but whenever it looked like a fight starting I'd come out in front and stand there a minute and say if anybody started anything I would have the boat run out into the middle of the river and sink her. That I'd never had a fight on my boat and wasn't going to begin any such low life shenanigans now.

(Magnolia got a swift mental picture of this menacing, black-garbed figure standing before the gay crude curtain, the footlights throwing grim shadows on her stern face. That implacable woman was capable of cowering even a tough coal-belt audience bent on a fight.)

Crops are pretty good so business is according. I put up grape jell last week. A terrible job but I can't abide this store stuff made of gelatine or something and no real grapes in it. Well I suppose you are too stylish for the *Cotton Blossom* by now and Kim never hears of it. I got the picture you sent. I think she looks kind of peaked. Up all hours of the night I suppose and no proper food. What kind of an education is she getting? You wrote about how you were going to send her to a convent school. I never heard of such a thing. Well I will close as goodness knows I have enough to do besides writing letters where they are probably not wanted. Still I like to know how you and the child are doing and all.

Your mother,
PARTHENIA ANN HAWKS.

These epistles always filled Magnolia with an emotion that was a poisonous mixture of rage and tenderness and nostalgia. She knew that her mother, in her harsh way, loved her, loved her grandchild, often longed to see both of them. Parthy's perverse and inhibited nature would not permit her to confess this. She would help them with money, Magnolia knew, if they needed help. But first she must know the grisly satisfaction of having them say so. This Magnolia would not do, though there were many times when her need was great. There was Kim, no longer a baby. This feverish and irregular life could not go on for her. Magnolia's letters to her mother, especially in lean times, were triumphs of lying pride. Sentimental Tommy's mother, writing boastfully home about her black silks and her gold chain, was never more stiff-necked than she.

Gay is more than good to me. . . . I have only

to wish for a thing . . . Everyone says Kim is unusually tall and bright for her age. . . . He speaks of a trip to Europe next year . . . new fur coat . . . never an unkind word . . . very happy . . .

Still, if Magnolia was clever at reading between the lines of her mother's bald letters, so, too, was Parthenia at hers. In fact, Parthy took many a random shot that struck home, as when once she wrote, tartly, "Fur coat one day and none the next I'll be bound."

XV

THE problem of Kim's education, of Kim's future, was more and more insistently borne in upon her. She wanted money—money of her own with which to provide security for the child. Ravenal's improvident method was that of Paddy and the leaky roof. When luck was high and he was showering her and Kim with luxuries, he would say, "But, good God, haven't you got everything you want? There's no satisfying you any more, Nola."

When he had nothing he would throw out his hands, palms upward, in a gesture of despair. "I haven't got it, I tell you. I give you everything I can think of when I am flush. And now, when I'm broke, you nag me."

"But, Gay, that's just it. Everything one day and nothing the next. Couldn't we live like other people, in between? Enough, and none of this horrible worrying about to-morrow. I can't bear it."

"You should have married a plumber."

She found herself casting about in her mind for ways in which she could earn money of her own. She took stock of her talents: a slim array. There was her experience on the show-boat stage. She could play the piano a little. She could strum the banjo (relic of Jo's and Queenie's days in the old *Cotton Blossom* low-raftered kitchen). She had an untrained, true, and rather moving voice of mediocre quality.

Timidly, with a little nervous spot of red showing in either cheek, she broached this to Ravenal one fine afternoon when they were driving out to the Sunnyside Hotel for dinner. Gaylord had had a run of luck the week before. Two sleek handsome chestnuts seemed barely to flick the road with their hoofs as they flew along. The smart high cart glittered with yellow varnish. None of your cheap livery rigs for Ravenal. Magnolia was exhilarated, happy. Above all else she loved to drive into the country or the suburbs behind a swift pair of horses. Ravenal was charming; pleased with himself; with his handsome, well-dressed young wife; with the cart, the horses, the weather, the prospect of one of Old Man Dowling's excellent dinners. They sped through Lincoln Park. Their destination was a two-hours' drive north, outside the city limits: a favourite rendezvous for Chicago's sporting world. At Dowling's one had supper at a dollar a head—and such a supper! The beefsteak could be cut with a fork. Old Man Dowling bred his own fine fat cattle. Old Lady Dowling raised the plump broilers that followed the beefsteak. There was green corn grown in the Dowling garden; fresh-plucked tomatoes, young onions. There was homemade ice cream. There was a huge chocolate cake, each slice a gigantic edifice alternating layers of black and white.

"Can't I drive a while, Gay dear?"

"They're pretty frisky. You'd better wait till we get out a ways, where there aren't so many rigs." The

fine cool late summer day had brought out all manner of
vehicles. "By that time the nags'll have some of the
skittishness worked out of them, too."

"But I like to have them when they're skittish.
Papa always used to let me take them."

"Yes—well, these aren't canal-boat mules, you know.
Why can't you be content just to sit back and enjoy
the drive? You're getting to be like one of those
bloomer girls they joke about. You'll be wanting to
wear the family pants next."

"I am enjoying it, only——"

"Only don't be like your mother, Nola."

She lapsed into silence. During one of their many
sojourns at the Ontario Street hotel she had struck up
a passing acquaintance with a large, over-friendly blonde
actress with green-gold hair and the tightest of black
bodices stretched over an imposing shelf of bosom.
This one had surveyed the Ravenal ménage with a
shrewd and kindly though slightly bleary eye, and had
given Magnolia some sound advice.

"Why'n't you go out more, dearie?" she had asked
one evening when she herself was arrayed for festivity
in such a bewilderment of flounces, bugles, jets, plumes,
bracelets, and chains as to give the effect of a lighted
Christmas tree in the narrow dim hallway. She had
encountered Magnolia in the corridor and Nola had
returned the woman's gusty greeting with a shy and
faintly wistful smile. "Out more, evenin's. Young
thing like you. I notice you're home with the little girl
most the time. I guess you think that run, run is about
all I do."

Magnolia resented this somewhat. But she reflected instantly this was a friendly and well-meaning creature. She reminded her faintly of Elly, somehow; Elly as she might be now, perhaps; blowsy, over-blown, middle-aged. "Oh, I go out a great deal," she said, politely.

"Husband home?" demanded the woman, bluntly. She was engaged in the apparently hopeless task of pulling a black kid glove over her massive arm.

Magnolia's fine eyebrows came up in a look of hauteur that she unconsciously had borrowed from Ravenal. "Mr. Ravenal is out." And started on toward her room.

The woman caught her hand. "Now don't get huffy, dear. I'm a older woman than you and I've seen a good deal. You stay home with the kid and your husband goes out, and will he like you any better for it? Nit! Now leave me tell you when he asks you to go out somewheres with him you go, want to or not, because if you don't there's those that will, and pretty soon he'll quit asking you."

She had waddled stiffly down the hallway then, in her absurdly high-heeled slippers, leaving a miasma of perfume in the passage. Magnolia had been furious, then amused, then thoughtful, then grateful. In the last few years she had met or seen the wives of professional gamblers. It was strange: they were all quiet, rather sad-faced women, home-loving and usually accompanied by a well-dressed and serious child. Much like herself and Kim, she thought. Sometimes she met them on Ohio Street. She thought she could recognize the wife of a gambler by the look in her face.

Frequently she saw them coming hurriedly out of one of the many pawnshops on North Clark, near the river. The windows of these shops fascinated her. They held, often, such intimate, revealing, and mutely appealing things—a doll, a wedding ring, a cornet, a meerschaum pipe, a Masonic emblem, a Bible, a piece of lace, a pair of gold-rimmed spectacles.

She thought of these things now as she sat so straight and smartly dressed beside Ravenal in the high yellow cart. She stole a glance at him. The colour was high in his cheeks. His box-cut covert coat with the big pearl buttons was a dashingly becoming garment. In the buttonhole bloomed a great pompon of a chrysanthemum. He looked very handsome. Magnolia's head came up spiritedly.

"I don't want to wear the pants. But I would like to have some say-so about things. There's Kim. She isn't getting the right kind of schooling. Half the time she goes to private schools and half the time to public and half the time to no school at all—oh, well, I know there aren't three halves, but anyway . . . and it isn't fair. It's because half the time we've got money and half the time we haven't any."

"Oh, God, here we are, driving out for pleasure——"

"But, Gay dear, you've got to think of those things. And so I thought—I wondered—Gay, I'd like to earn some money of my own."

Ravenal cut the chestnuts sharply with his whip.

"Pooh!" thought Magnolia. "He can't scare me that way. How like a man—to take it out on the horses just because he's angry." She slipped her hand through his arm.

"Don't! Don't jerk my arm like that. You'll have them running away in a minute."

"I should think they would, after the way you slashed them. Sometimes I think you don't care about horses—as horses—any more than you do about——" She stopped, aghast. She had almost said, "than you do about me as a wife." A long breath. Then, "Gay darling, I'd like to go back on the stage. I'd like to act again. Here, I mean. In Chicago."

She was braced for a storm and could have weathered it. But his shouts of laughter startled and bewildered her and the sensitive chestnuts as well. At this final affront they bolted, and for the next fifteen minutes Magnolia clutched the little iron rod at the end of the seat with one hand and clung to her hat with the other as the outraged horses stretched their length down the rutty country road, eyes flaming, nostrils distended, hoofs clattering, the light high cart rocking and leaping behind them. Ravenal's slender weight was braced against the footboard. The veins in his wrists shone blue against dead white. With a tearing sound his right sleeve ripped from his coat. Little beads of moisture stood out about his mouth and chin. Magnolia, white-lipped, tense, and terribly frightened, magnificently uttered no sound. If she had been one of your screamers there probably would have been a sad end. Slowly, gradually, the chestnuts slowed a trifle, slackened, resumed a normal pace, stood panting as Ravenal drew up at the side of the road. They actually essayed to nibble innocently at some sprigs of grass growing by the roadside while Ravenal wiped his face and neck and hands, slowly, with his fine perfumed linen handkerchief. He took off his black derby hat and mopped his forehead and the headband of his hat's splendid white satin lining. He fell to swearing, softly, this being the form in which the male, relieved after fright, tries to deny that he has been frightened.

He turned to look at her, his eyes narrow. She turned to look at him, her great eyes wide. She leaned toward him a little, her hand over her heart. And then, suddenly, they both began to laugh, so that the chestnuts pricked up their ears again and Ravenal grabbed the reins. They laughed because they were young, and had been terribly frightened, and were now a little hysterical following the strain. And because they loved each other, so that their fear of injury and possible death had been for each a double horror.

"That's what happens when you talk about going on the stage," said Ravenal. "Even the horses run at the thought. I hope this will be a lesson to you." He gathered up the reins.

"A person would think I'd never been an actress and knew nothing of the stage."

"You don't think that catch-as-catch-can performance was acting, do you? Or that hole in the wall a stage! Or that old tub a theatre! Or those plays—— Good God! Do you remember . . . 'Sue, if he loves yuh, go with him. Ef he ain't good to yuh——'"

"But I do!" cried Magnolia. "I do think so. I

loved it. Everybody in the company was acting because they liked it. They'd rather do it than anything
in the world. Maybe we weren't very good but the
audiences thought we were; and they cried in the places
where they were supposed to cry, and laughed when
they should have laughed, and believed it all, and were
happy, and if that isn't the theatre then what is?"

"Chicago isn't a river dump; and Chicago audiences
aren't rubes. You've seen Modjeska and Mansfield
and Bernhardt and Jefferson and Ada Rehan since then.
Surely you know the difference."

"That's the funny part of it. I don't, much. Oh,
I don't mean they haven't got genius. And they've
been beautifully directed. And the scenery and costumes and all. But—I don't know—they do exactly
the same things—do them better, but the same things
that Schultzy told us to do—and the audiences laugh at
the same things and cry at the same things—and they
go trouping around the country, on land instead of
water, but trouping just the same. They play heroes
and heroines in plays all about love and adventure; and
the audiences go out blinking with the same kind of
look on their faces that the river-town audiences used
to have, as though somebody had just waked them
up."

"Don't be silly, darling. . . . Ah, here we are!"

And here they were. They had arrived in ample
time, so that Magnolia chatted shyly and Ravenal
chatted charmingly with Pa and Ma Dowling; and
Magnolia was reminded of Thebes as she examined the
shells and paper roses and china figurines in the parlour.

The dinner was excellent, abundant, appetizing. Scarcely were they seated at the long table near the window when there was heard a great fanfare and hulla-baloo outside. Up the winding driveway swept a tallyho, and out of it spilled a party of Chicago bloods in fawn covert coats and derby hats and ascot ties and shiny pointed shoes; and they gallantly assisted the very fashionable ladies who descended the perilous steps with much shrill squealing and shrieking and maidenly clutching at skirts, which clutchings failed satisfactorily of their purpose. Some of the young men carried banjos and mandolins. The four horses jangled their metal-trimmed harness and curveted magnificently. Up the steps swarmed the gay young men and the shrill young women. On closer sight Magnolia noticed that some of these were not, after all, so young.

"Good God!" Ravenal had exclaimed; and had frowned portentously.

"Do you know them, Gay?"

"It's Bliss Chapin's gang. He's giving a party. He's going to be married day after to-morrow. They're making a night of it."

"Really! How lovely! Which one's the girl he's to marry? Point her out."

And for the second time Ravenal said, "Don't be silly, darling."

They entered the big dining room on a wave of sound and colour. They swarmed the table. They snatched up bits of bread and pickles and celery, and munched them before they were seated. They caught sight of Ravenal.

"Gay! Well, I'm damned! Gay, you old Foxey Quiller, so that's why you wouldn't come out! Heh, Blanche, look! Here's Gay, the bad boy. Look who's here!"

"I thought you were going out to Cramp's place," Gay said, sullenly, in a low voice, to one of the men.

He chose the wrong confidant, the gentleman being neither reticent nor ebriate. He raised his voice to a shout. "That's a good 'un! Listen! Foxey Gay thought we were going out to Cramp's place, so what does he do? He brings his lady here. Heh, Blanche, d'you hear that? Now you know why he couldn't come." He bent upon Magnolia a look of melting admiration. "And can you blame him? All together! NO!"

"You go to hell," said the lady named Blanche from the far end of the table, though without anger; rather in the manner of one who is ready with a choice bit of repartee. Indeed it must have been so considered, for at its utterance Mr. Bliss Chapin's pre-nuptial group uttered shouts of approbation.

"Shut up, you jackass," said Ravenal then, sotto voce.

And "Oho!" bellowed the teaser. "Little Gay's afraid he'll get in trouble with his lady friend."

Gay's lady friend now disproved for all time her gentleman friend's recent accusation that she knew nothing about the art of acting. She raised her head and gazed upon the roistering crew about the long table. Her face was very white, her dark eyes were enormous; she was smiling.

"Won't you introduce me to your friends, Gay?"
she said, in her clear and lovely voice.

"Don't be a fool," whispered Ravenal, at her side.

The host, Bliss Chapin, stood up rather red-faced
and fumbling with his napkin. He was not sober,
but his manner was formal—deferential, even. "Mrs.
—uh—Rav'nal—I—uh—charmed. I rem'ber seeing
you—someone pointed you out in a box at th—th—
th—" he gave it up and decided to run the two words
together—"ththeatre. Chapin's my name. Bliss
Chapin. Call me Bliss. Ever'body calls me Bliss.
Uh—" he decided to do the honours. He indicated
each guest with a graceful though vague wave of the
hand. "'S Tantine . . . Fifi . . . Gerty
. . . Vi'let . . . Blanche . . . Mignon.
Lovely girls. Lovely. But—we'll let that pass. Uh
. . . Georgie Skiff. . . . Tom Haggerty . . .
Billy Little—Li'l' Billee we call him. Pretty cute,
huh? . . . Know what I mean? . . . Dave
Lansing . . . Jerry Darling—that's his actu-al
name. Can you 'mazhine what the girls can do with
name like that! Boys 'n girls, this's Mrs. Gaylord
Ravenal, wife of the well-known faro expert. An' a
lucky dog he is, too. No offense, I hope. Jus' my rough
way. I'm going to be married to-morr'. An'thing
goes 'sevening."

Prolonged applause and shouting. A twanging of
mandolins and banjos.

"Speech!" shouted the man who had first called
attention to Magnolia. "Speech by Mrs. Ravenal!"

They took it up shrilly, hoarsely, the Fifis, the Violets,

the Billys, the Gertys, the Jerrys. Speech! Speech!

Ravenal got to his feet. "We've got to go," he began. "Sorry——"

"Sit down! Throw him out! Foxey Gay! Shut up, Gay!"

Ravenal turned to Magnolia. "We'll have to get out of this," he said. He put a hand on her arm. His hand was trembling. She turned her head slowly and looked up at him, her eyes blank, the smile still on her face. "Oh, no," she said, and shook her head. "Oh, no. I like it here, Gay dear."

"Speech!" yelled the Tantines, the Mignons, the Daves, beating on their plates with their spoons.

Magnolia brought one hand up to her throat in a little involuntary gesture that betokened breathlessness. There was nothing else to indicate how her heart was hammering. "I—I can't make a speech," she began in her lovely voice.

"Speech! Speech!"

She looked at Ravenal. She felt a little sorry for him.

"But I'll sing you a song if you'll lend me a banjo, someone."

She took the first of a half-dozen instruments thrust toward her.

"Magnolia!"

"Do sit down, Gay dear, and stop fidgeting about so. It's all right. I'm glad to entertain your friends." She still wore the little set smile. "I'm going to sing a song I learned from the Negroes when I was a little girl and lived on a show boat on the Mississippi River." She

bent her head above the banjo and began to thumb it
softly. Then she threw her head back slightly. One
foot tapped emphasis to the music's cadence. Her
lids came down over her eyes—closed down over them.
She swayed a little, gently. It was an unconscious
imitation of old Jo's attitude. "It's called Deep River.
It doesn't mean—anything. It's just a song the niggers
used to——" She began to sing, softly. "Deep——
river——"

When she had finished there was polite applause.

"I think it's real sweet," announced the one they
called Violet. And began to snivel, unbecomingly.

Mr. Tom Haggerty now voiced the puzzlement which
had been clouding his normally cheerful countenance.

"You call that a coon song and maybe it is. I don't
dispute you, mind. But I never heard any song like
that called a coon song, and I heard a good many coon
songs in my day. I Want Them Presents Back, and A
Hot Time, and Mistah Johnson, Turn Me Loose."

"Sing another," they said, still more politely.
"Maybe something not quite so sad. You'll have us
thinking we're at prayer meeting next. First thing you
know Violet here will start to repent her sins."

So she sang All God's Chillun Got Wings. They
wagged their heads and tapped their feet to that. I got
a wings. You got a wings. All o' God's chillun got
a wings. When I get to heab'n I'm goin' to put on my
wings, I'm goin' to fly all ovah God's heab'n . . .
heab'n . . .

Well, that, they agreed, was better. That was more
like it. The red-faced cut-up rose on imaginary wings

to show how he, too, was going to fly all over God's heab'n. The forthright Blanche refused to be drawn into the polite acclaim. "If you ask me," she announced, moodily, "I think they're rotten." "I like somepin' a little more lively, myself," said the girl they called Fifi. "Do you know What! Marry Dat Gal! I heard May Irwin sing it. She was grand."

"No," said Magnolia. "That's the only kind of song I know, really." She stood up. "I think we must be going now." She looked across the table, her great dark eyes fixed on the red-faced bridegroom. "I hope you will be very happy."

"A toast to the Ravenals! To Gaylord Ravenal and Mrs. Ravenal!" She acknowledged that too, charmingly. Ravenal bowed stiffly and glowered and for the second time that day wiped his forehead and chin and wrists with his fine linen handkerchief.

The chestnuts were brought round. Bliss Chapin's crew crowded out to the veranda off the dining room. Magnolia stepped lightly up to the seat beside Ravenal in the high dog-cart. It was dusk. A sudden sharpness had come into the evening air as always, toward autumn, in that Lake Michigan region. Magnolia shivered a little and drew about her the little absurd flounced shoulder cape so recently purchased. The crowd on the veranda had caught the last tune and were strumming it now on their banjos and mandolins. The kindly light behind them threw their foolish faces into shadow. You heard their voices, plaintive, even sweet; the raucous note fled for the moment. Fifi's voice and Jerry's; Gerty's voice and little Billee's. I got a wings. You got a wings. All God's chillun got a wings. When I get to heab'n I'm goin' to put on my wings, I'm goin' to fly . . .

Magnolia turned to wave to them as the chestnuts made the final curve in the driveway and stretched eagerly toward home.

Silence between the two for a long half hour. Then Ravenal, almost humbly: "Well—I suppose I'm in for it, Nola. Shoot!"

But she had been thinking, "I must take things in hand now. I have been like a foolish young girl when I'm really quite an old married woman. I suppose being bossed by Mama so much did that. I must take Kim in hand now. What a fool I've been. 'Don't be silly, darling.' He was right. I have been——" Aloud she said, only half conscious that he had spoken, "What did you say?"

"You know very well what I said. I suppose I'm in for one of your mother's curtain lectures. Go on. Shoot and get it over."

"Don't be silly, darling," said Magnolia, a trifle maliciously. "What a lovely starlight night it is! . . ." She laughed a little. "Do you know, those dough-faced Fifis and Tantines and Mignons were just like the Ohio and Illinois farm girls, dressed up. The ignorant girls who used to come to see the show. I'll bet that when they were on the farm, barefooted, poor things, they were Annie and Jenny and Tillie and Emma right enough."

XVI

A ND this," said Sister Cecilia, "is the chapel."
She took still another key from the great bunch
on her key chain and unlocked the big gloomy
double doors. It was incredible that doors and floors
and wainscotings so shining with varnish could still
diffuse such an atmosphere of gloom. She entered
ahead of them with the air of a cicerone. It seemed to
Magnolia that the corridors were tunnels of murk.
It was like a prison. Magnolia took advantage of this
moment to draw closer still to Kim. She whispered
hurriedly in her ear:

"Kim darling, you don't need to stay. If you don't
like it we'll slip away and you needn't come back.
It's so gloomy."

"But I do like it," said Kim in her clear, decisive
voice. "It's so shiny and clean and quiet." In spite
of her lovely Ravenal features, which still retained something of their infantile curves, she looked at that moment startlingly like her grandmother, Parthenia Ann
Hawks. They followed Sister Cecilia into the chapel.
Magnolia shivered a little.

In giving Kim a convent education it was not in
Magnolia's mind to prepare her for those Sunday
theatrical page interviews beginning, "I was brought
up by the dear Sisters in the Convent." For that mat-

ter, the theatre as having any part in Kim's future never once entered Magnolia's mind. Why this should have been true it is difficult to say, considering the child's background, together with the fact that she was seeing Camille and Ben Hur, and the Rogers Brothers in Central Park at an age when other little girls were barely permitted to go to cocoa parties in white muslin and blue sashes where they might, if they were lucky, see the funny man take the rabbit out of the hat.

The non-sectarian girls' schools of good standing looked askance at would-be entrants whose parentage was as socially questionable, not to say bizarre, as that represented by Ravenal mère and père. The daughter of a professional gambler and an ex-show-boat actress would have received short shrift at the hands of the head mistress of Miss Dignam's School for Girls at Somethingorother-on-the-Hudson. The convent school, then, opened its gloomy portals to as motley a collection of *jeunes filles* as could be imagined under one roof. In the prim dim corridors and cubicles of St. Agatha's on Wabash Avenue, south, you might see a score of girlish pupils who, in spite of the demure face, the sleek braids, the severe uniform, the modest manner, the prunes-and-prism expression, still resembled in a startling degree this or that vivacious lady whose name was associated with the notorious Everleigh Club, or with the music halls and museums thriving along Clark Street or Madison or Dearborn. Visiting day at St. Agatha's saw an impressive line of smart broughams outside the great solemn brick building; and the ladies who emerged therefrom, while invariably dressed in garments of sombre colour and restrained cut, still produced the effect of being attired in what is known as fast black. They gave forth a heady musky scent. And the mould of their features, even when transformed by the expression that crept over them as they gazed upon those girlish faces so markedly resembling their own, had a look as though the potter had used a heavy thumb.

The convent had been Magnolia's idea. Ravenal had laughed when she broached the subject to him. "She'll be well fed and housed and generally cared for there," he agreed. "And she'll learn French and embroidery and deportment and maybe some arithmetic, if she's lucky. But every t—uh—every shady lady on Clark Street sends her daughter there."

"She's got to go somewhere, Gay. This pillar-to-post life we're leading is terrible for a child."

"What about your own life when you were a child? I suppose you led a prissy existence."

"It was routine compared to Kim's. When I went to bed in my little room on the *Cotton Blossom* I at least woke up in it next morning. Kim goes to sleep on north Clark and wakes up on Michigan Avenue. She never sees a child her own age. She knows more bell boys and chambermaids and waiters than a travelling man. She thinks a dollar bill is something to buy candy with and that when a stocking has a hole in it you throw it away. She can't do the simplest problem in arithmetic, and yesterday I found her leaning over the second floor rotunda rail spitting on the heads of people in the——"

"Did she hit anybody?"

"It isn't funny, Gay."

"It is, too.   I've always wanted to do it."

"Well, so have I—but, anyway, it won't be funny five years from now."

St. Agatha's occupied half of one of Chicago's huge square blocks.   Its great flight of front steps was flush with the street, but at the back was a garden discreetly protected by a thick brick wall fully ten feet high and belligerently spiked.   St. Agatha herself and a whole host of attendant cherubim looked critically down upon Magnolia and Kim as they ascended the long broad flight of steps that led to the elaborately (and lumpily) carved front door.   Of the two Magnolia was the more terrified.   The windows glittered so sharply.   The stairs were so clean.   The bell, as they rang it, seemed to echo so hollowly through endless unseen halls and halls and halls.   The hand that opened the door had been preceded by no sound of human footsteps.   The door had loomed before them seemingly as immovable as the building itself.   There was the effect of black magic in its sudden and noiseless opening.   The great entrance hall waited still and dim.   The black-robed figure before them was vaguely surmounted by a round white face that had the look of being no face at all but a flat circular surface on which features had been clumsily daubed.

"I came to see about placing my little girl in school."

The flat surface broke up surprisingly into a smile. She was no longer a mysterious and sombre figure but a middle-aged person, kindly, but not especially bright. "This way."

This way led to a small and shiny office presided over by another flat circular surface. This, in turn, gave way to a large and almost startlingly sunny room, one flight up, where sat at a desk a black-robed figure different from the rest. A large pink face. Penetrating shrewd blue eyes behind gold-rimmed spectacles. A voice that was deep without resonance. A woman with the look of the ruler. ·Parthy, practically, in the garb of a Mother Superior.

"Oh, my goodness!" thought Magnolia, in a panic. She held Kim's cool little hand tight in her own agitated fingers. Of the two, she was incalculably the younger. The classrooms. The sewing room. Sister This. Sister That. The garden. Little hard benches. Prim gravel paths. Holy figures in stone brooding down upon the well-kept flower beds. Saints and angels and apostles. When all those glittering windows were dark, and the black-robed figures within lay in slumber, their hands (surely) crossed on their barren breasts and the flat circular surfaces reposed exactly in the centre of the hard pillows, and the moonlight flooded this cloistered garden spot with the same wanton witchery that enveloped a Sicilian bower, did these pious stone images turn suddenly into fauns and nymphs and dryads, Magnolia wondered, wickedly.

Aloud: "I see . . . I see . . . Oh, the refectory . . . I see. . . . Prayers . . . seven o'clock . . dark blue dresses . . . every Thursday from two to five . . . and sewing and music and painting as well. . . ."

And this was the chapel. I see. And this was her

bedroom to be shared with another pupil. But she has always had her own. It is the rule. I see. I'll let you know. It's Kim. I know it is, but that's her name, really. It's—she was born—in Kentucky and Illinois and Missouri—that is—yes, it does sound—no, I don't think she'd like to have you call her anything else, she's so used—I'll let you know, may I? I'd like to talk it over with her to see if she thinks she'd be happy . . .

In the garden, in various classrooms, in the corridors, and on the stairs they had encountered girls from ten to sixteen or even eighteen years of age, and they were all dressed exactly alike, and they had all flashed a quick prim look at the visitors from beneath demure lids. Magnolia had sensed a curious undercurrent of plot, of mischief. Hidden secret thoughts scurried up the bare varnished halls, lurked grinning in the stairway niches.

They were back in the big sunny second-floor room after their tour of inspection. The pink-faced Parthy person was regarding them with level brows. Magnolia was clinging more tightly than ever to Kim's hand. It was as though the child were supporting her, not she the child.

"But I know now whether I like it or not," Kim had spoken up, astonishingly. "I like it."

Magnolia was horrified to find that she had almost cried, "Oh, no! No, Kim!" aloud. She said, instead, "Are you sure, darling? You needn't stay unless you want to. Mother just brought you to see if you might like it."

"I do," repeated Kim, patiently, as one speaks to an irritating child.

Magnolia was conscious of a sinking sense of disappointment. She had hoped, perversely enough, that Kim would stamp her feet, throw herself screaming on the floor, and demand to be carried out of the bare clean orderly place back to the delightful welter of Clark Street. She could not overcome the feeling that in thus bestowing upon Kim a ladylike education and background she was depriving her of something rich and precious and colourful. She thought of her own childhood. She shut her eyes so as to see more clearly the pictures passing in her mind. Deep rivers. Wide rivers. Willows by the water's edge trailing gray-green. Dogwood in fairy bloom. Darkies on the landing. Plinketty-plunk-plunk-plunk, plinketty-plunk-plunk-plunk. Cotton bales. Sweating black bodies. Sue, ef he loves yuh, go with him. To-morrow night, ladies and gentlemen, that magnificent comedy-drama, Honest Hearts and Willing Hands. The band, red-coated, its brass screaming defiance at the noonday sun.

The steely blue eyes in the pink face surrounded by the white wimple and the black coif seemed to be boring into her own eyes. "If you yourself would rather not have her here with us we would prefer not to take her."

"Oh, but I would! I do!" Magnolia cried hastily.

So it was arranged. Next week. Monday. Half a dozen woollen this. Half a dozen cotton that.

Descending the great broad flight of outside steps Magnolia said, like a child, "From now until Monday we'll do things, shall we? Fun. What would you like to do?"

"Oh, a matinée on Saturday——" began Kim eagerly. Magnolia was enormously relieved. She had been afraid that this brief glimpse into the more spiritual life might already have had a chastening effect upon the cosmopolitan Kim.

Thus the child was removed from the pernicious atmosphere of the Chicago Levee just when the Levee itself began to feel the chastening hand of reform. Suddenly, overnight, Chicago went civic. For a quarter of a century she had been a strident, ample-bosomed, loud-mouthed Rabelaisian giantess in red satin and diamonds, who kept open house day and night and welcomed all comers. There were food and drink and cheer. Her great muscular arms embraced ranchers from Montana and farmers from Indiana and bankers from New York. At Bath House John's Workingmen's Exchange you got a tub of beer for a nickel; the stubble-faced bums lined the curb outside his ceaselessly swinging door on Clark Street. The visiting ranchers and farmers and bankers were told to go over to the Palmer House and see the real silver dollars sunk in the tiled floor of that hostelry's barroom. The garrulous Coughlin, known as The Bath, and the silent little Hinky Dink Mike Kenna were Chicago's First Ward aldermen and her favourite naughty sons. The faro wheels in Gamblers' Alley spun merrily by day and by night. The Mayor of the city called a genial, "Hope you're all winning, boys!" as he dropped in for a sociable drink and a look at the play; or even to take a hand. "What'll you have?" was Chicago's greeting, and "Don't care if I do," her catch phrase. Hetty Chilson was the recognized leader of her sinister world, and that this world happened to be prefaced by the qualifying word, "under" made little difference in Chicago's eyes. Pawnshops, saloons, dives, and gambling houses lined Clark Street from Twelfth to the river, and dotted the near-by streets for blocks around. The wind-burned ranchmen in bearskin coats and sombreros at Polk and Clark were as common a sight as the suave white-fingered gentry in Prince Alberts and diamonds at Clark and Madison. It was all one to Chicago. "Game up-stairs, gentlemen! Game upstairs!"

New York, eyeing her Western cousin through dis-approving lorgnettes, said, "What a crude and vulgar person!"

"Me!" blustered Chicago, dabbing futilely at the food and wine spots on her broad satin bosom. "Me! I'll learn you I'm a lady."

The names of University of Chicago professors (Economics Department) began to appear on the lists of aldermanic candidates. Earnest young men and women with notebooks and fountain pens knocked at barred doors, stated that they were occupied in compiling a Survey, and asked intimate questions. Down came whole blocks of rats' nests on Clark and Dearborn, with the rats scuttling frantically to cover. Up went office buildings that actually sneered down upon the Masonic Temple's boasted height. Brisk gentlemen in eye-glasses and sack suits whisked in and out of these chaste edifices. The clicking sound to be heard on Clark Street was no longer that of the faro wheel but of the stock market ticker and the Western Union transmitter.

It was rumoured that they were going to close Jeff Hankins'. They were going to close Mike McDonald's. They were going to banish the Washington Park race track.

"They can't do it," declared Gaylord Ravenal.

"Oh, can't we!" sneered the reformers. Snick-snack, went the bars on Hankins' doors and on Mike McDonald's. It actually began to be difficult to find an open game. It began to be well-nigh impossible. It came to such a pass that you had to know the signal knock. You had to submit to a silent scrutiny from unseen eyes peering through a slit somewhere behind a bland closed door. The Prince Alberts grew shiny. The fine linen showed frayed edges. The diamonds reposed unredeemed for longer and longer periods at Lipman's or Goldsmith's. The Ravenal ring and the succession of sealskin sacques seemed permanently to have passed out of the Ravenal possession. The malacca stick, on the other hand, was now a fixture. It had lost its magic. It was no longer a symbol of security. The day was past when its appearance at Lipman's or Goldsmith's meant an I O U for whatever sum Gay Ravenal's messenger might demand. There actually were mornings when even the Cockeyed Bakery represented luxury. As for breakfast at Billy Boyle's! An event.

The Ravenals' past experience in Chicago seemed, in comparison with their present precarious position, a secure and even humdrum existence. Ohio and Ontario streets knew them for longer and longer periods. Now when Magnolia looked into the motley assemblage of objects in the more obscure pawnshop windows, she was likely to avert her eyes quickly at recognition of some object not only intimate but familiar. Magnolia thought of Kim, safe, secure, comfortable, in the convent on Wabash Avenue.

"I must have felt this thing coming," she said to Ravenal. "Felt it in my bones. She's out of all this. It makes me happy just to think of it; to think of her there."

"How're you going to keep her there?" demanded Ravenal, gloomily. "I'm strapped. You might as well know it, if you don't already. I've had the damnedest run of luck."

Magnolia's eyes grew wide with horror. "Keep her there! Gay! We've got to. I wouldn't have her knocking around here with us. Gay, can't you do something? Something real, I mean. Some kind of work like other—I mean, you're so wonderful. Aren't there things—positions—you know—with banks or—uh—those offices where they buy stocks and sell them and make money in wheat and—wheat and things?" Lamely.

Ravenal kissed her. "What a darling you are, Nola. A darling simpleton."

It was a curious and rather terrible thing, this love bond between them. All that Parthy had grimly predicted had come to pass. Magnolia knew him for what he was. Often she hated him. Often he hated her. Often he hated her because she shamed him with her gaiety, her loyalty, her courage, her tenderness. He was not true to her. She knew this now. He knew she knew this. She was a one-man woman. Frequently they quarrelled hideously. Tied to you. . . . Tied! God knows I'd be happier without you. You've never brought me anything but misery. . . . Always finding fault. . . . Put on those fine lady airs with me. What'd I take you out of! . . . An honest living, anyway. Look people in the face. Accusations. Bitterness. Longing. Passion. The long periods of living in sordid surroundings made impossible most of the finer reticences. Garments washed out in the basin. Food cooked over the gas jet. One room. One bed. Badly balanced meals. Reproaches. Tears. Sneers. Laughter. Understanding. Reconciliation.

They loved each other. Over and above and through and beneath it all, thick and thin, warp and woof, they loved each other.

It was when their fortunes were at lowest ebb; when the convent tuition had now been two terms unpaid; when the rent on the Ontario Street lodgings was over-due; when even Ravenal, handsome and morose, was forced to content himself with the coffee and rolls of the bedroom breakfast; when a stroll up Clark Street meant meeting a dozen McLean suits as shabby as his own—it was at this unpropitious time that Parthenia Ann Hawks was seized with the idea of visiting her daughter, her son-in-law, and her grandchild in Chicago. Her letters always came to the Sherman House—had been called for there through these years though the fluctuations of fortune had carried the Ravenals away from the hotel and back again with a tide-like regularity. Twice Magnolia had taken Kim to see her grim grandmamma at Thebes when the *Cotton Blossom* was in for repairs during the winter season. These visits had always been timed when the Ravenal tide was high. Magnolia and Kim had come back to Thebes on the crest of a wave foaming with silks and laces and plumes and furs. The visits could not, however, be said to have been a success. Magnolia always came prepared to be the fond and dutiful daughter. Invariably she left seething between humorous rage and angry laughter.

"It wasn't anything she actually did," she would explain afterward, ruefully, to Ravenal. "It's just that she treats me with such disrespect." She pondered this a moment. "I honestly think Mama's the vainest woman I have ever met."

Strangely enough, Kim and her grandmother did not get on very satisfactorily, either. It dawned on Magnolia that the two were much alike. Their methods were different, but the result was the same. Each was possessed of an iron determination; boundless vitality; enormous resistance; canny foresight; definite ambition. Parthy was the blustering sort; Kim the quietly stubborn. When the two met in opposition they stood braced, horn to horn, like bulls.

On both occasions these visits had terminated abruptly in less than a week. The bare, wind-swept little town, winter-locked, had seemed unspeakably dreary to Magnolia. In the chill parlour of the cottage there was a wooden portrait of her father done in crayon. It was an enlargement which Parthy had had done from a small photograph of Andy in his blue coat and

visored cap and baggy wrinkled pants.   An atrocious
thing, but the artist, clumsy though he was, had somehow happened to catch the alert and fun-loving bright-
ness of the keen brown eyes.   The mutton-chop whiskers
looked like tufts of dirty cotton; the cheeks were
pink as a chorus girl's.   But the eyes were Andy's.
Magnolia wandered into the parlour to stand before
this picture, looking up at it with a smile.   She wandered,
too, down to the river to gaze at the sluggish yellow
flood thick now with ice, but as enthralling as ever to
her.   She stood on the river bank in her rich furs, a
lonely, wind-swept figure, gazing down the river, down
the river, and her eyes that had grown so weary with
looking always at great gray buildings and grim gray
streets and swarming gray crowds now lost their look
of strain, of unrepose, as they beheld in the far still
distance the lazy Southern wharves, the sleepy Southern
bayous—Cairo, Memphis, Vicksburg, Natchez, New
Orleans—Queenie, Jo, Elly, Schultzy, Andy, Julie,
Steve.

She took Kim eagerly to the water's edge—gave her
the river with a sweep of her arm.   Kim did not like it.

"Is that the river?" she asked.

"Why, yes, darling.   Don't you remember!   The
river!"

"The river you told me about?"

"Of course!"

"It's all dirty and ugly.   You said it was beautiful."

"Oh, Kim, isn't it?"

"No."

She showed her the picture of Captain Andy.

"Grampa?"

"Yes."

"Cap'n?"

"Yes, dear. He used to laugh so when you called him that when you were a little baby. Look at his eyes, Kim. Aren't they nice? He's laughing."

"He's funny-looking," said Kim.

Parthy asked blunt questions. "Sherman House? What do you go living in a hotel for all these years, with the way they charge for food and all! You and that husband of yours must have money to throw away. Why don't you live in a house, with your own things, like civilized people?"

"Gay likes hotels."

"Shiftless way to live. It must cost a mint of money."

"It does," agreed Magnolia, amiably.

"Like to know where you get it, that's what."

"Gay is very successful."

A snort as maddening as it was expressive from Parthy. The widow Hawks did not hesitate to catechize the child in the temporary absence of her mother. From these sessions Parthy must have gained some knowledge of the Ohio and Ontario street interludes, for she emerged from them with a look of grim satisfaction.

And now Parthenia Ann Hawks was coming to Chicago. She had never seen it. The letter announced her arrival as two weeks distant. The show-boat season was at an end. She would stay at the Sherman House where they were, if it wasn't too expensive. They were not to pay. She wouldn't be beholden to any one. She might stay a week, she might stay two weeks or longer, if she liked it. She wanted to see the Stock-yards, the Grand Opera House, the Masonic Temple, Marshall Field's, Lincoln Park, and the Chicago River.

"My God!" said Gaylord Ravenal, almost piously. "My GOD!"

Stricken, they looked at each other. Stared. It was a thing beyond laughter. Every inch of space about them spelled failure. Just such failure as had been predicted for them by the woman who was now coming, and whose coming would prove to her the triumph of that prediction. They were living in a huddle of dis-comfort on Ontario Street. Magnolia, on her visits to Kim at the convent, was hard put to it to manage the little surprise gift planned to bring to the girl's face the flashing look of gay expectancy. A Henrici cake elaborately iced, to share with her intimates; a book; a pair of matinée tickets as a special treat; flowers for the Mother Superior; chocolates. Now the Christmas holidays were approaching. Kim would expect to spend them with her parents. But where? They would not bring her to this sordid lodging. And some-how, before the new term began, the unpaid tuition fee must be got together. Still, the Ravenals had faced such problems as these before now. They could have met them, they assured each other, as they always had. Luck always turned when things looked blackest. Life did that to tease you. But this was different. Gay-lord Ravenal's world was crumbling. And Parthy!

Parthy! Here was a situation fraught with what of horror! Here was humiliation. Here was acknowledged defeat.

"Borrow," suggested Magnolia.

"On what security?"

"I don't mean that kind of—I don't mean businesslike borrowing. I mean borrowing from friends. Friends. All these men——"

"Men! What men?"

"The men at the—at the places." She had always pretended that she did not actually know he came by his livelihood as he did. She never said, "Gamblers' Alley." She refused to admit that daily he had disappeared within the narrow slit of lane that was really a Clark Street alley; that he had spent the hours there watching bits of pasteboard for a living. "The men you have known so many years."

Grimly: "They've all been trying to borrow of me."

"But Mike McDonald. Hankins. Varnell." She cast pretense aside now. "Thousands. They've had thousands of dollars. All the money we brought with us to Chicago. Won't they give some of it back?"

This he found engaging rather than irritating, as well he might have. He shouted with laughter as he always did at a fresh proof of her almost incredible naïveté. At times such as these he invariably would be impelled to caress her much as one laughs at a child and then fondles it delightedly after it has surprised one with an unexpected and charming trick. He would kiss the back of her neck and then her wide, flexible mouth, and she would push him away, bewildered and annoyed that this should be his reaction to what she had meant so seriously.

"Nola, you're priceless! You're a darling. There's no one like you." He went off again into a shout of laughter. "Give it back! McDonald, h'm? There's an idea for you."

"How can you act like that when you know how serious it is!"

"Serious! Why, damn it, it's desperate. I tell you I'll never have her come here and see us living like this. We'll get out, first. . . . Say, Nola, what's to prevent us getting out, anyway? Chicago's no good any more. Why not get out of this! I'm sick of this town."

"We haven't any money to get out with, for one reason. And Kim's at school and she's going to stay there. She's going to stay there if I have to——"

"Have to what?"

"Ask Mama for the money." She said this mischievously, troubled though she was. Out he flew into a rage.

"I'll see her in—— I've been in deeper holes than this and managed to crawl out." He sat a moment in silence, staring with unseeing eyes at the shabby sticks of furniture that emphasized the room's dreariness. Magnolia, seated as quietly opposite him, sewing on a petticoat for Kim, suddenly let her hands sink in her lap. She realized, with a sort of fright, that he was as completely outside the room as though his body had been wafted magically through the window. And for him she, too, had vanished. He was deep in thought.

The mask was off. She sat looking at him. She saw, clearly, the man her mother had so bitterly fought her marrying. The face of this man now in his late thirties was singularly unlined. Perhaps that was what you missed in it. The skin and hair and eyes, the set of the shoulders, the lead of the hand from the wrist, bespoke a virile man. But vigour—vigorous —no, he was not that. This was a fencer, not a fighter. But he had fought for her, years ago. The shambling preacher in the little river town whose name she had forgotten. That simple ignorant soul who preached hell fire and thought that play actors were damned. He had not expected to be knocked down in his own musty little shop. Not much of a victory, that. Gay had opposed that iron woman, her mother. But the soft life since then. Red plush, rich food, Clark Street. Weak. What was it? No lines about the mouth. Why was it weak? Why was it weak now if it had not been twelve years ago? A handsome man. Hard. But you couldn't be hard and weak at the same time, could you? What was he thinking of so intently? His face was so exposed, so defenceless, as sometimes when she awoke in the early morning and looked at him, asleep. Almost ashamed to look at his face, so naked was it of the customary daytime covering.

Now resolve suddenly tightened it. He stood up. He adjusted the smart and shabby hat at an angle that defied its shabbiness. He reached for the malacca stick. It was nine o'clock in the evening. They had had a frugal and unappetizing meal at a little near-by lunch room. Ravenal had eaten nothing. He had, for the most part, stared at the dishes with a detached and slightly amused air as though they had been served him by mistake and soon would be apologetically reclaimed by the slovenly waitress who had placed them before him.

She had never been one to say, "Where are you going?" Yet now her face was so moving in its appeal that he answered its unspoken question.

"Cheer up, old girl! I know somebody."

"Who? Who, Gay?"

"Somebody I've done favours for. She owes me a good turn." He was thinking aloud.

"She?"

"Never mind."

"She, Gay?"

"Did I say—now never mind, Nola. I'll do the worrying."

He was off.

She had become accustomed, through these years, to taking money without question when there was money; to doing without, uncomplainingly, when there was none. They had had to scheme before now, and scurry this way and that, seeking a way out of a tight corner. They had had to borrow as they had often lent. It had all been part of the Clark Street life—the gay, wasteful, lax, improvident sporting life of a crude new Mid-west city. But that life was vanishing now. That city was vanishing with it. In its place a newer, harder, more sophisticated metropolis was rearing its ambitious head.

Magnolia, inured to money crises, realized that the

situation to-night was different. This was not a crisis. It was an impasse.

"Let's get out of here," Gay had said. There was no way out. The men from whom he had borrowed in the past were themselves as harried as he. The sources from which he had gained his precarious livelihood were drying up; had almost ceased to exist, except furtively. I know somebody. Somebody who would like to do me a favour. Somebody—who—would—like—— A horrid suspicion darted through her mind, released from the subconscious. Appalled at its ugliness, she tried to send it back to its hiding place. It would not go. It stayed there before her mind's eye, grinning, evil, unspeakably repulsive. She took up her sewing again. She endeavoured to fix her mind on Kim. Kim asleep in the cold calm quiet of the great walled convent on South Wabash. French and embroidery and deportment and china painting and wimples and black wings and long dark shining halls and round white faces and slim white tapers and statues of the saints that turned into fauns and why was that not surprising? A clatter. One of the saints had dropped her rosary on the bare shining floor. It wasn't a rosary. It was an anchor ringing against the metal stanchion of the *Cotton Blossom*.

Magnolia awoke. Her sewing scissors had fallen from her lap. Her face felt stiff and drawn. She hugged herself a little, and shivered, and looked about her. Her little gold watch on the dresser—no, of course not. That was gone. She folded her sewing. It was late, she knew. She was accustomed to being up until twelve, one, two. But this was later. Something told

her that this was later. The black hush of the city outside. The feel of the room in which she sat. The
sinister quiet of the very walls about her. The cheap
clock on the shelf had stopped. The hands said twenty
minutes after two. Twenty-one minutes after, she
told herself in a foolish triumph of precision.

She took down her fine long black hair. Brushed it.
Plaited it. One of the lacy nightgowns so absurd in
the sordid shabbiness of the rooming-house bedroom;
so alien to the coarse gray sheets. She had no other
kind. She went to bed. She fell asleep.

It was just before dawn when he returned. The
black of the window panes showed the promise of gray.
His step had an unaccustomed sound. He fumbled for
the gas jet. His very presence was strange in the dark.
The light flared blue, but she knew; she knew even before it illumined his face that bore queer slack lines she
had never before seen there. For the first time in their
life together Gaylord Ravenal was drunk.

She sat up; reached for her wrapper at the foot of
the bed and bunched it about her shivering shoulders.
He was immensely serious and dignified. He swayed a
little. The slack look on his face. That was all.

"I'll do the worrying," he said, as though continuing
the conversation that had held them at nine o'clock.
He placed the malacca stick carefully in its corner. He
removed his coat, keeping his hat on. The effect was
startlingly rowdy, perhaps because he had always so
meticulously observed the niceties. Standing thus,
weaving back and forth ever so slightly, he pulled from
his left vest pocket, where it fitted much too snugly, a

plump bill-folder. Custom probably cautioned him to retain this, merely widening its open side to reveal the sheaf of notes within. But his condition, and all that had gone to bring it about, caused him to forego his cunning. With a vague, but successful, gesture, and a little lurch as he stood, he tossed the leather folder to the counterpane. "Coun' it!" he commanded, very distinctly. "Ten one hun'er' dollar bills and ten one hun'er' dollar bills makes twen'y one hun'er' dollar bills an' anybody says it doesn' is a liar. Two thousan' dollars. Would you kin'ly count 'em, Mrs. Rav'nal? I believe"—with businesslike dignity—"I b'lieve you'll find that correc'."

Magnolia Ravenal in her nightgown with her wrapper hunched about her shoulders sat staring at the little leather booklet on the bed. Its gaping mouth mocked her. She did not touch it.

"Two thousand dollars?" she said.

"I b'lieve you'll fin' tha's correc'." He seemed to be growing less distinct.

"Where did you get this, Gay?"

"Never min'. I'll do th' worrying."

He unbuttoned his vest with some difficulty. Yawned prodigiously, like one who has earned his rest after a good day's work.

She looked at him. She was like a drawing in French ink—her face so white, her eyes so enormous, her hair so black.

"You got this from Hetty Chilson."

His collar came off with a crack-snap. He held it in the hand that pointed toward the money. He seemed offended at something. Not angry, but hurt. "How can you say that, M'nolia! I got one thousan' from good ol' Het and not cen' more. Wha' do I do then! Marsh up to Sheedy's and win a thousan' more at roulette. Ha! That's a great joke on Sheedy because, look, roulette isn' my game. Nev' has been. Faro's my game. Tha's a gen'leman's game, faro. One thousan' Hetty, and marsh ri' up . . . roulette . . . win . . . 'nother . . . Thous. . ." He lurched to the bed.

He was asleep at once, heavily, deeply, beside her on the bed, his fine long head lolling off the pillow. She knelt in her place and tried to lift the inert figure to a more comfortable position; succeeded, finally, after some tugging. She drew the lumpy coverlet over him. Then she sat as before, hunched in her nightgown and the wrapper, staring at the open wallet with its many leaves. It was dawn now. The room was gray with it. She ought to turn out the gas. She arose. She picked up the wallet. Before extinguishing the light she counted out ten one-hundred-dollar bills from the sheaf within the wallet. One thousand dollars. Her fingers touched the bills gingerly, fastidiously, and a little wrinkle of disgust curled her lip. She placed the bills on the dresser. She folded the leather holder and tucked it, with its remaining contents, under his pillow. He did not waken. She turned out the light then, and coming back to the bedside drew on the slippers that lay on the floor. She got her shirtwaist—a fresh white one with a Gibson tuck—from the drawer, and her skirt and jacket from the hooks covered over with a protect-

ing length of calico against the wall. She heated a
little water, and washed; combed and dressed her hair;
put on her clothes, laid her hat on the dresser. Then
she sat in the one comfortable chair that the room
afforded—a crazy and decayed armchair done in dingy
red plush, relic of some past grandeur—and waited.
She even slept a little there in the sagging old chair,
with the morning light glaring pitilessly in upon her
face. When she awoke it must have been nearly noon.
A dour day, but she had grown accustomed to the half-
lights of the Chicago fogs. She glanced sharply at him.
He had not moved. He had not stirred. He looked,
somehow, young, helpless, innocent, pathetic. She
busied herself in making a cup of coffee as quietly as
might be. This might rouse him, but it would make
little difference. She knew what she had to do. She
drank the hot revivifying liquid in great gulps. Then
she put on her jacket, pinned on her hat, took up the
bills and placed them neatly in her handbag. She
glanced at herself in the mirror.

"My, you're plain!" she thought, meaninglessly.
She went down the dim stairway. The fusty landlady
was flapping a gray rag in the outer doorway as her
contribution to the grime of the street.

"What's taking you out so bright and early, Mis'
Ravenal? Business or pleasure?" She liked her little
joke.

"Business," said Magnolia.

XVII

THE knell had sounded for the red brick house with the lions guarding its portals. The Chicago soot hung like a pall over it. The front steps sagged. Even the stone lions had a mangy look. The lemon-water sunshine of a Chicago winter day despoiled the dwelling of any sinister exterior aspect. That light, filtering through the lake mist, gave to the house-front the look of a pock-marked, wrinkled, and evil old hag who squats in the market place with her face to the sun and thinks of her purple past and does not regret it.

It was half-past one. Magnolia Ravenal had figured this out nicely. That part of Clark Street would be astir by now. As she approached the house on Clark, near Polk, her courage had momentarily failed her, and she had passed it, hurriedly. She had walked a block south, wretchedly. But the feel of the bills in her bag gave her new resolve. She opened the handbag to look at them, turned and walked swiftly back to the house. She rang the bell this time, firmly, demandingly; stood looking down at its clean-scrubbed doorstep and tried to ignore the prickling sensation that ran up and down her spine and the weak and trembling feeling in her legs. The people passing by could see her. She was knocking at Hetty Chilson's notorious door, and the people passing by could see her: Magnolia Ravenal.

Well, what of it! Don't be silly. She rang again.

The door was opened by a Negro in a clean starched white house coat. Magnolia did not know why the sight of this rather sad-eyed looking black man should have reassured her; but it did. She knew exactly what she wanted to say.

"My name is Mrs. Ravenal. I want to speak to Hetty Chilson."

"Mis' Chilson is busy, ma'am," he said, as though repeating a lesson. Still, something about the pale, well-dressed, earnest woman evidently impressed him. Of late, when he opened the door there had been frequent surprises for him in the shape of similar earnest and well-dressed young women who, when you refused them admittance, flashed an official-looking badge, whipped out notebook and pencil and insisted pleasantly but firmly that he make quite sure Miss Chilson was not in. "You-all one them Suhveys?"

Uncomprehending, she shook her head. He made as though to shut the door, gently. Magnolia had not spent years in the South for nothing. "Don't you shut that door on me! I want to see Hetty Chilson."

The man recognized the tone of white authority. "Wha' you want?"

Magnolia recovered herself. After all, this was not the front door of a home, but of a House. "Tell her Mrs. Gaylord Ravenal wants to speak to her. Tell her that I have one thousand dollars that belongs to her, and I want to give it to her." Foolishly she opened her bag and he saw the neat sheaf of bills. His eyes popped a little.

"Yes'm. Ah tell huh. Step in, ma'am."

Magnolia entered Hetty Chilson's house. She was frightened. The trembling had taken hold of her knees again. But she clutched the handbag and looked about her, frankly curious. A dim hallway, richly carpeted, its walls covered with a red satin brocade. There were deep soft cushioned chairs, and others of carved wood, high-backed. A lighted lamp on the stairway newel post cast a rosy glow over the whole. Huge Sèvres vases stood in the stained-glass window niches. It was an entrance hall such as might have been seen in the Prairie Avenue or Michigan Avenue house of a new rich Chicago packer. The place was quiet. Now and then you heard a door shut. There was the scent of coffee in the air. No footfall on the soft carpet, even though the tread were heavy. Hetty Chilson descended the stairs, a massive, imposing figure in a black-and-white patterned foulard dress. She gave the effect of activity hampered by some physical impediment. Her descent was one of impatient deliberateness. One hand clung to the railing. She appeared a stout, middle-aged, well-to-do householder summoned from some domestic task abovestairs. She had aged much in the last ten years. Magnolia, startled, realized that the distortion of her stout figure was due to a tumour.

"How do you do?" said Hetty Chilson. Her keen eyes searched her visitor's face. The Negro hovered near by in the dim hallway. "Are you Mrs. Ravenal?"

"Yes."

"What is it, please?"

Magnolia felt like a schoolgirl interrogated by a stern

but well-intentioned preceptress. Her cheeks were
burning as she opened her handbag, took out the sheaf
of hundred-dollar bills, tendered them to this woman.
"The money," she stammered, "the money you gave
my—you gave my husband. Here it is."

Hetty Chilson looked at the bills. "I didn't give it
to him. I loaned it to him. He said he'd pay it back
and I believe he will. Ravenal's got the name for being
square."

Magnolia touched Hetty Chilson's hand with the
folded bills; pressed them on her so that the hand opened
automatically to take them. "We don't want it."

"Don't want it! Well, what'd he come asking me
for it for, then? I'm no bank that you can take money
out and put money in."

"I'm sorry. He didn't know. I can't—we don't—
I can't take it."

Hetty Chilson looked down at the bills. Her eye-
glasses hung on the bodice of her dress, near the right
shoulder, attached to a patent gold chain. This she
pulled out now with a businesslike gesture and adjusted
the eyeglasses to her nose. "Oh, you're that kind,
huh?" She counted the bills once and then again;
folded them. "Does your husband know about this?"
Magnolia did not answer. She looked dignified and
felt foolish. The very matter-of-factness of this world-
hardened woman made this thing Magnolia had done
seem overdramatic and silly. Hetty Chilson glanced
over her shoulder to where the white-coated Negro
stood. "Mose, tell Jule I want her. Tell her to bring
her receipt book and a pen." Mose ran up the

soft-carpeted stairs. You heard a deferential rap at an upper door; voices. Hetty turned again to Magnolia. "You'll want a receipt for this. Anyway, you'll have that to show him when he kicks up a fuss." She moved ponderously to the foot of the stairway; waited a moment there, looking up. Magnolia's eyes followed her gaze. Mose had vanished, evidently, down some rear passage and stairway, for he again appeared mysteriously at the back of the lower hall though he had not descended the stairway up which he had gone a moment before. Down this stair came a straight slim gray-haired figure. Genteel, was the word that popped into Magnolia's mind. A genteel figure in decent black silk, plain and good. It rustled discreetly. A white fine turnover collar finished it at the throat. Narrow cuffs at the wrist. It was difficult to see her face in the dim light. She paused a moment in the glow of the hall lamp as Hetty Chilson instructed her. A white face— no, not white—ivory. Like something dead. White hair still faintly streaked with black. In this clearer light the woman seemed almost gaunt. The eyes were incredibly black in that ivory face; like dull coals, Magnolia thought, staring at her, fascinated. Something in her memory stirred at sight of this woman in the garb of a companion-secretary and with a face like burned-out ashes. Perhaps she had seen her with Hetty Chilson at the theatre or the races. She could not remember.

"Make out a receipt for one thousand dollars received from Mrs. Gaylord Ravenal. R-a-v-e-n-a-l. Yes, that's right. Here; I'll sign it." Hetty Chilson penned her name swiftly as the woman held the book for her. She turned to Magnolia. "Excuse me," she said. "I have to be at the bank at two. Jule, give this receipt to Mrs. Ravenal. Come up as soon as you're through."

With a kind of ponderous dignity this strange and terrible woman ascended her infamous stairway. Magnolia stood, watching her. Her plump, well-shaped hand clung to the railing. An old woman, her sins heavy upon her. She had somehow made Magnolia feel a fool.

The companion tore the slip of paper from the booklet, advanced to Magnolia and held it out to her. "One thousand dollars," she said. Her voice was deep and rich and strange. "Mrs. Gaylord Ravenal. Correct?" Magnolia put out her hand, blindly. Unaccountably she was trembling again. The slip of paper dropped from her hand. The woman uttered a little exclamation of apology. They both stooped to pick it up as the paper fluttered to the floor. They bumped awkwardly, actually laughed a little, ruefully, and straightening, looked at each other, smiling. And as Magnolia smiled, shyly, she saw the smile on the face of the woman freeze into a terrible contortion of horror. Horror stamped itself on her every feature. Her eyes were wild and enormous with it; her mouth gaped with it. So the two stood staring at each other for one hideous moment. Then the woman turned, blindly, and vanished up the stairs like a black ghost. Magnolia stood staring after her. Then, with a little cry, she made as though to follow her up the stairway. Strangely she cried, "Julie! Julie, wait for me!" Mose, the

Negro, came swiftly forward. "This way out, miss,"
he said, deferentially. He held the street door open.
Magnolia passed through it, down the steps of the brick
house with the lions couchant, into the midday bright-
ness of Clark Street. Suddenly she was crying, who
so rarely wept. South Clark Street paid little attention
to her, inured as it was to queer sights. And if a
passer-by had stopped and said, "What is it? Can I
help you?" she would have been at a loss to reply.
Certainly she could not have said, "I think I have just
seen the ghost of a woman I knew when I was a little
girl—a woman I first saw when I was swinging on the
gate of our house at Thebes, and she went by in a long-
tailed flounced black dress and a lace veil tied around
her hat. And I last saw her—oh, I can't be sure. I
can't be sure. It might not——"

Clark Street, even if it had understood (which is impossible), would not have been interested. And presently, as she walked along, she composed herself. She
dabbed at her face with her handkerchief and pulled
down her neat veil. She had still another task to perform. But the day seemed already so old. She was
not sleepy, but her mind felt thick and slow. The
·events of the past night and of the morning did not
stand out clearly. It was as if they had happened long
ago. Perhaps she should eat something. She had had
only that cup of coffee; had eaten almost nothing the
night before.

She had a little silver in her purse. She counted
it as it lay next to the carefully folded thousand-dollar
receipt signed in Hetty Chilson's firm businesslike

hand. Twenty-five—thirty-five—forty—fifty—seventy-three cents. Ample. She stopped at a lunch room on Harrison, near Wabash; ate a sandwich and drank two cups of coffee. She felt much better. On leaving she caught a glimpse of herself in a wall mirror—a haggard woman with a skin blotched from tears, and a shiny nose and with little untidy wisps of hair showing beneath her hat. Her shoes—she remembered having heard or read somewhere that neat shoes were the first requisite for an applicant seeking work. Furtively and childishly she rubbed the toe of either shoe on the back of each stocking. She decided to go to one of the department-store rest rooms for women and there repair her toilette. Field's was the nicest; the Boston store the nearest. She went up State Street to Field's. The white marble mirrored room was full of women. It was warm and bright and smelled pleasantly of powder and soap and perfume. Magnolia took off her hat, bathed her face, tidied her hair, powdered. Now she felt less alien to these others about her—these comfortable chattering shopping women; wives of husbands who worked in offices, who worked in shops, who worked in factories. She wondered about them. She was standing before a mirror adjusting her veil, and a woman was standing beside her, peering into the same glass, each seemingly oblivious of the other. "I wonder," Magnolia thought, fancifully, "what she would say if I were to turn to her and tell her that I used to be a show-boat actress, and that my father was drowned in the Mississippi, and my mother, at sixty, runs a show boat all alone, and that my husband is a gambler and we have

no money, and that I have just come from the most
notorious brothel in Chicago, where I returned a thousand dollars my husband had got there, and that I'm on
my way to try to get work in a variety theatre." She
was smiling a little at this absurd thought. The other
woman saw the smile, met it with a frozen stare of utter
respectability, and walked away.

There were few theatrical booking offices in Chicago
and these were of doubtful reputation. Magnolia knew
nothing of their location, though she thought, vaguely,
that they probably would be somewhere in the vicinity
of Clark, Madison, Randolph. She was wise enough
in the ways of the theatre to realize that these shoddy
agencies could do little for her. She had heard Ravenal
speak of the variety houses and museums on State
Street and Clark and Madison. The word "vaudeville"
was just coming into use. In company with her husband she had even visited Kohl & Middleton's Museum
—that smoke-filled comfortable shabby variety house
on Clark, where the admission was ten cents. It had
been during that first Chicago trip, before Kim's birth.
Women seldom were seen in the audience, but Ravenal,
for some reason, had wanted her to get a glimpse of this
form of theatrical entertainment. Here Weber and
Fields had played for fifteen dollars a week. Here you
saw the funny Irishman, Eddie Foy; and May Howard
had sung and danced.

"They'll probably build big expensive theatres some
day for variety shows," Ravenal had predicted.

The performance was, Magnolia thought, much like
that given as the concert after the evening's bill on the

Cotton Blossom. "A whole evening of that?" she said. Years later the Masonic Temple Roof was opened for vaudeville.

"There!" Ravenal had triumphantly exclaimed. "What did I tell you! Some of those people get three and four hundred a week, and even more." Here the juggling Agoust family threw plates and lighted lamps and tables and chairs and ended by keeping aloft a whole dinner service and parlour suite, with lamps, soup tureens, and plush chairs passing each other affably in midair without mishap. Jessie Bartlett Davis sang, sentimentally, Tuh-rue LOVE, That's The Simple Charm That Opens Every Woman's Heart.

At the other end of the scale were the all-night restaurants with a stage at the rear where the waiters did an occasional song and dance, or where some amateur tried to prove his talent. Between these were two or three variety shows of decent enough reputation though frequented by the sporting world of Chicago. Chief of these was Jopper's Varieties, a basement theatre on Wabash supposed to be copied after the Criterion in London. There was a restaurant on the ground floor. A flight of marble steps led down to the underground auditorium. Here new acts were sometimes tried out. Lillian Russell, it was said, had got her first hearing at Jopper's. For some reason, Magnolia had her mind fixed on this place. She made straight for it, probably as unbusinesslike a performer as ever presented herself for a hearing. It was now well on toward mid-afternoon. Already the early December dusk was gathering, aided by the Chicago smoke and the lake fog.

Her fright at Hetty Chilson's door was as nothing compared to the sickening fear that filled her now. She was physically and nervously exhausted. The false energy of the morning had vanished. She tried to goad herself into fresh courage by thoughts of Kim at the convent; of Parthy's impending visitation. As she approached the place on Wabash she resolved not to pass it, weakly. If she passed it but once she never would have the bravery to turn and go in. She and Ravenal had driven by many times on their way to the South Side races. It was in this block. It was four doors away. It was here. She wheeled stiffly, like a soldier, and went in. The restaurant was dark and deserted. One dim light showed at the far end. The tablecloths were white patches in the grayness. But a yellow path of light flowed up the stairway that led to the basement, and she heard the sound of a piano. She descended the swimming marble steps, aware of the most alarming sensation in her legs—rather, of no sensation in them. It was as though no solid structure of bone and flesh and muscle lay in the region between her faltering feet and her pounding heart.

There was a red-carpeted foyer; a little ticket window; the doors of the auditorium stood open. She put out a hand, blindly, to steady herself against the door jamb. She looked into the theatre; the badly lighted empty theatre, with its rows and rows of vacant seats; its stage at the far end, the curtain half raised, the set a crudely painted interior. As she looked there came over her—flowed over her like balm—a feeling of security, of peace, of home-coming. Here were ac-

customed surroundings. Here were the very sights and
smells and sounds she knew best. Those men with their
hats on the backs of their heads and their cigars waggling comfortably and their feet on the chair in front of
them might have been Schultzy, Frank, Ralph, Pa
Means. Evidently a song was being tried out in rehearsal. The man at the piano was hammering it and
speaking the words in a voice as hoarse and unmusical
as a boat whistle coming through the fog. It was a coon
song full of mah babys and choo-choos and Alabam's.

Magnolia waited quietly until he had come to a full
stop.

A thin pale young man in a striped shirt and a surprising gray derby who had been sitting with his wooden
kitchen chair tipped up against the proscenium now
brought his chair down on all fours.

"You was with Haverly's, you say?"

"I cer'nly was. Ask Jim. Ask Sam. Ask anybody."

"Well, go back to 'em is what I say. If you ever
was more than a singin' waiter then I'm new to the
show business." He took his coat from where it lay on
top of the piano. "That's all for to-day, ain't it, Jo?"
He addressed a large huddle whose thick shoulders and
round head could just be seen above the back of a
second-row centre seat. The fat huddle rose and
stretched and yawned, and grunted an affirmative.

Magnolia came swiftly down the aisle. She looked
up at the thin young man; he stared at her across the
footlight gutter.

"Will you let me try some songs?" she said.

"Who're you?" demanded the young man.

"My name is Magnolia Ravenal."

"Never heard of it. What do you do?"

"I sing. I sing Negro songs with a banjo."

"All right," said the thin young man, resignedly. "Get out your banjo and sing us one."

"I haven't got one."

"Haven't got one what?"

"One—a banjo."

"Well, you said you—didn' you just say you sung nigger songs with a banjo!"

"I haven't got it with me. Isn't there one?" Actually, until this moment, she had not given the banjo a thought. She looked about her in the orchestra pit.

"Well, for God's sakes!" said the gray derby.

The hoarse-voiced singer who had just met with rebuff and who was shrugging himself into a shabby overcoat now showed himself a knight. He took an instrument case from the piano top. "Here," he said. "Take mine, sister."

Magnolia looked to left, to right. "There." The fat man in the second row jerked a thumb toward the right stage box back of which was the stage door. Magnolia passed swiftly up the aisle; was on the stage. She was quite at ease, relaxed, at home. She seated herself in one of the deal chairs; crossed her knees.

"Take your hat off," commanded the pasty young man.

She removed her veil and hat. A sallow big-eyed young woman, too thin, in a well-made suit and a modish rather crumpled shirtwaist and nothing of the look of the stage about her. She thumbed the instrument again. She remembered something dimly, dimly, far, far back; far back and yet very recent; this morning. "Don't smile too often. But if you ever want anything . . ."

She smiled. The thin young man did not appear overwhelmed. She threw back her head then as Jo had taught her, half closed her eyes, tapped time with the right foot, smartly. Imitative in this, she managed, too, to get into her voice that soft and husky Negro quality which for years she had heard on river boats, bayous, landings. I got a wings. You got a wings. All God's chillun got a wings.

"Sing another," said the old young man. She sang the one she had always liked best.

> "Go down, Moses,
>   'Way down in Egypt land,
>   Tell ole Pharaoh,
>   To let my people go."

Husky, mournful, melodious voice. Tapping foot. Rolling eye.

Silence.

"What kind of a coon song do you call that?" inquired the gray derby.

"Why, it's a Negro melody—they sing them in the South."

"Sounds like a church hymn to me." He paused. His pale shrewd eyes searched her face. "You a nigger?"

The unaccustomed red surged into Magnolia's cheeks, dyed her forehead, her throat, painfully. "No, I'm not a—nigger."

"Well, you cer'nly sing like one. Voice and—I don't know—way you sing. Ain't that right, Jo?"

"Cer'nly is," agreed Jo.

The young man appeared a trifle embarrassed, which made him look all the younger. Years later, in New York, Kim was to know him as one of the most powerful theatrical producers of his day. And he was to say to Kim, "Ravenal, h'm? Why, say, I knew your mother when she was better-looking than you'll ever be. And smart! Say, she tried to sell me a coon song turn down in Jopper's in the old days, long before your time. I thought they were hymns and wouldn't touch them. Seems they're hot stuff now. Spirituals, they call them. You hear 'em in every show on Broadway. 'S fact! Got to go to church to get away from 'em. Well, live and learn's what I say."

It was through this shrewd, tough, stage-wise boy that Magnolia had her chance. He did not understand or like her Negro folk songs then, but he did recognize the quality she possessed. And it was due to this precociousness in him that Magnolia, a little more than a year later, was singing American coon songs in the Masonic Roof bill, her name on the programme with those of Cissie Loftus and Marshall Wilder and the Four Cohans.

But now she stood up, the scarlet receding from her face, leaving it paler than before. Silently she handed the husky singer his banjo; tried to murmur a word of thanks; choked. She put on her hat, adjusted her veil.

"Here, wait a minute, sister. No offense. I've seen 'em lighter'n you. Your voice sounds like a—

ain't that the truth, Jo?" Actually distressed, he appealed again to his unloquacious ally in the third row.

"Sure does," agreed Jo.

The unfortunate hoarse-voiced man who had loaned her the banjo now departed. He seemed to bear no rancour. Magnolia, seeing this, tried again to smile on the theory that, if he could be game, then so, too, could she. And this time, it was the real Magnolia Ravenal smile of which the newspapers made much in the years to come. The ravishing Ravenal smile, they said (someone having considered that alliterative phrase rather neat).

Seeing it now the young showman exclaimed, without too much elegance, "Lookit that, Jo!" Then, to Magnolia: "Listen, sister. You won't get far with those. Your songs are too much like church tunes, see? They're for a funeral, not a theaytre. And that's a fact. But I like the way you got of singing them. How about singing me a real coon song? You know. Hello, Mah Baby! or something like that."

"I don't know any. These are the only songs I know."

"Well, for——! Listen. You learn some real coon songs and come back, see, in a week. Here. Try these over at home, see." He selected some song sheets from the accommodating piano top. She took them, numbly.

She was again in the cold moist winter street. Quite dark now. She walked over to State Street and took a northbound car. The door of their room on the third floor was locked, and when she had opened it she felt that the room was empty. Not empty merely; de-

serted. Before she had lighted the gas jet she had an
icy feeling of desolation, of impending and piled-up
tragedy at the close of a day that already toppled with
it. Her gaze went straight to the dresser.

An envelope was there. Her name on it in Ravenal's
neat delicate hand. Magnolia. Darling, I am going
away for a few weeks . . . return when your
mother is gone . . . or send for you . . . six
hundred dollars for you on shelf under clock . . .
Kim . . . convent . . . enough . . . weeks . . .
darling . . . love . . . best . . . always . . .

She never saw him again.

She must have been a little light-headed by this time,
for certainly no deserted wife in her right senses would
have followed the course that Magnolia Ravenal now
took. She read the note again, her lips forming some
of the words aloud. She walked to the little painted
shelf over the wash stand. Six hundred. That was
right. Six hundred. Perhaps this really belonged to
that woman, too. She couldn't go there again. Even
if it did, she couldn't go there again.

She left the room, the gas flaring. She hurried down
Clark Street, going a few blocks south. Into one of the
pawnshops. That was nothing new. The man actually
greeted her by name. "Good-evening, Mrs. Ravenal.
And what can I do for you?"

"A banjo."

"What?"

"I want to buy a banjo."

She bargained for it, shrewdly. When she tendered
a hundred-dollar bill in payment the man's face fell.

"Oh, now, Mrs. Ravenal, I gave you that special price because you——"

"I'll go somewhere else."

She got it. Hurried back with it. Into her room again. She had not even locked the door. Five of the six one-hundred-dollar bills lay as she had tossed them on the dresser. A little crazy, certainly. Years, years afterward she actually could relate the fantastic demoniac events of this day that had begun at four in the morning and ended almost twenty hours later. It made a very good story, dramatic, humorous, tragic. Kim's crowd thought it was wonderful.

She took off her veil and hat and jacket. Her black hair lay in loose limp ugly loops about her face. She opened one of the sheets of music—Whose Black Baby Are You?—and propped it up against the centre section of the old-fashioned dresser. She crossed her knees. Cradled the banjo. One foot tapped the time rhythmically. An hour. Two hours.

A knock at the door. The landlady, twelve hours fustier than she had been that morning. "It ain't me, Mis' Ravenal, but Downstairs says she can't sleep for the noise. She's that sickly one. She says she pounded but you didn't——"

"I'll stop. I didn't hear her. I'm sorry."

"For me you could go on all night." The landlady leaned bulkily and sociably against the door. "I'm crazy about music. I never knew you was musical."

"Oh, yes," said Magnolia. "Very."

XVIII

I WAS educated," began Kim Ravenal, studying her
reflection in the mirror, and deftly placing a dab of
rouge on either ear lobe, "in Chicago, by the dear
Sisters there in St. Agatha's Convent."

She then had the grace to snigger, knowing well what
the young second assistant dramatic critic would say to
that. She was being interviewed in her dressing room
at the Booth between the second and third acts of
Needles and Pins. She had opened in this English
comedy in October. Now it was April. Her play before this had run a year. Her play before that had run
two years. Her play—well, there was nothing new to
be said in an interview with Kim Ravenal, no matter
how young or how dramatic the interviewer. There
was, therefore, a touch of mischievous malice in this
trite statement of hers. She knew what the bright
young man would say in protest.

He said it. He said: "Oh, now, Pete's sake, Miss
Ravenal! Quit kidding."

"But I was. I can't help it. I was! Ask my
mother. Ask my husband. Ask anybody. Educated
by the dear Sisters in the con——"

"Oh, I know it! So does everybody else who reads
the papers. And you know as well as I do that that
educated-in-a-convent stuff is rubber-stamp. It ceased

to be readable publicity when Mrs. Siddons was a gal. Now be reasonable. Kaufman wants a bright piece about you for the Sunday page."

"All right. You ask intelligent questions and I'll answer them." Kim then leaned forward to peer intently at her own reflection in the dressing-room mirror with its brilliant border of amber lights. She reached for the rabbit's foot and applied to her cheeks that nervous and redundant film of rouge which means that the next curtain is four minutes away.

He was a very cagey New York second assistant dramatic critic, who did not confine his talents to second-assistant dramatic criticism. The pages of *Vanity Fair* and *The New Yorker* (locally known as the Fly Papers) frequently accepted first (assistant dramatic) aid from his pen. And, naturally, he had written one of those expressionistic plays so daringly different that three intrepid managers had decided not to put it on after all. Embittered, the second assistant dramatic critic threatened sardonically to get a production through the ruse of taking up residence in Prague or Budapest, changing his name to Capek or Vajda, and sending his manuscript back to New York as a foreign play for them to fight over.

Though she had now known New York for many years, there were phases of its theatrical life that still puzzled Kim's mother, Magnolia Ravenal; and this was one of them. "The critics all seem to write plays," she complained. "It makes the life of a successful actress like Kim so complicated. And the actors and actresses all lecture on the Trend of the Modern Drama at League Luncheons given at the Astor. I went to one once, with Kim. Blue voile ladies from Englewood. In my day critics criticized and actors acted."

Her suave and gifted son-in-law, Kenneth Cameron, himself a producer of plays of the more precious pattern (The Road to Sunrise, 1921; Jock o' Dreams, 1924), teased her gently about this attitude of intolerance. "Why, Nola! And you a famous stage mama! You ought to know that even Kim occasionally has to do things for publicity."

"In my *Cotton Blossom* days we were more subtle. The band marched down Main Street and played on the corner and Papa gave out handbills. That was our publicity. I didn't have to turn handsprings up the levee."

There was little that the public did not know about Kim Ravenal. There was nothing that the cagey young assistant critic did not know. He now assumed a tone of deep bitterness.

"All right, my fine lady. I'll go back and write a pattern piece. Started in stock in Chicago. Went to New York National Theatre School. Star pupil and Teacher's Pet while there. Got a bit in—uh—Mufti, wasn't it?—and walked away with the play just like the aspiring young actress in a bum short story. Born on a show boat in Kentucky and Illinois and Missouri simultaneously—say, explain that to me some time, will you?—hence name of Kim. Also mother was a show-boat actress and later famous singer of coon—— Say, where is your mother these days, anyway? Gosh, I think she's grand! I'm stuck on her. She's the burn-

ing passion of my youth. No kidding. I don't know.
She's got that kind of haunted hungry et-up look, like
Bernhardt or Duse or one of them. You've got a little
of it, yourself."

"Oh, sir!" murmured Kim, gratefully.

"Cultivate it, is my advice. And when she smiles!...
Boy! I work like a dawg to get her to smile whenever I
see her. She thinks I'm one of those cut-ups. I'm
really a professional suicide at heart, but I'd wiggle my
ears if it would win one of those slow, dazzling——"

"Listen! Who—or whom—are you interviewing,
young man? Me or my mama?"

"She around?"

"No. She's at the Shaw opening with Ken."

"Well, then, you'll do."

"Just for that I think I'll turn elegant on you and
not grant any more interviews. Maude Adams never
did. Look at Mrs. Fiske! And Duse. Anyway, interviews always sound so dumb when they appear in
print. Dignified silence is the thing. Mystery. Everybody knows too much about the stage, nowadays."

"Believe me, *I* do!" said the young second assistant
dramatic critic, in a tone of intense acerbity.

A neat little triple tap at the dressing-room door.
"Curtain already!" exclaimed Kim in a kind of panic.
You would have thought this was her first stage summons. Another hasty application with the rabbit's
foot.

A mulatto girl in black silk so crisp, and white batiste cap and apron so correct that she might have
doubled as stage and practical maid, now opened the

door outside which she had been discreetly stationed. "Curtain, Blanche?"

"Half a minute more, Miss Ravenal. Telegram." She handed a yellow envelope to Kim.

As Kim read it there settled over her face the rigidity of shock, so plain that the second assistant dramatic critic almost was guilty of, "No bad news, I hope?" But as though he had said it Kim Ravenal handed him the slip of paper.

"They've misspelled it," she said, irrelevantly. "It ought to be Parthenia."

He read:

Mrs. Parthna A. Hawks died suddenly eight o'clock before evening show Cotton Blossom playing Cold Spring Tennessee advise sympathy company.

CHAS. K. BARNATO.

"Hawks?"

"My grandmother."

"I'm sorry." Lamely. "Is there anything——"

"I haven't seen her in years. She was very old—eighty. I can't quite realize. She was famous on the rivers. A sort of legendary figure. She owned and managed the *Cotton Blossom*. There was a curious kind of feud between her and Mother and my father. She was really a pretty terrible—I wonder—Mother——"

"Curtain, Miss Ravenal!"

She went swiftly toward the door.

"Can I do anything? Fetch your mother from the theatre?"

"She'll be back here with Ken after the play. Half an hour. No use——"

He followed her as she went swiftly toward the door from which she made her third-act entrance. "I don't want to be offensive, Miss Ravenal. But if there's a story in this—your grandmother, I mean—eighty, you know——"

Over her shoulder, in a whisper, "There is. See Ken." She stood a moment; seemed to set her whole figure; relaxed it then; vanished. You heard her lovely but synthetic voice as the American wife of the English husband in the opening lines of the third act:

"I'm so sick of soggy British breakfast. Devilled kidneys! Ugh! Who but the English could face food so visceral at nine A. M.!"

She was thinking as she played the third act for the three hundredth time that she must tuck the telegram under a cold cream jar or back of her mirror as soon as she returned to her dressing room. What if Magnolia should take it into her head to leave the Shaw play early and find it there on her dressing table! She must tell her gently. Magnolia never had learned to take telegrams calmly. They always threw her into a panic. Ever since that one about Gaylord Ravenal's death in San Francisco. Gaylord Ravenal. A lovely name. What a tin-horn sport he must have been. Charming though, probably.

Curtain. Bows. Curtain. Bows. Curtain. Bows. Curtain.

She was back in her dressing room, had removed her make-up, was almost dressed when Ken returned with her mother. She had made desperate haste, aided expertly by her maid.

The two entered laughing, talking, bickering good-naturedly. Kim heard her husband's jejune plangent voice outside her dressing-room door.

"I'm going to tell your daughter on you, Nola! Yes, I am."

"I don't care. He started it."

Kim looked round at them. Why need they be so horribly high-spirited just to-night? It was like comedy relief in a clumsily written play, put in to make the tragedy seem deeper. Still, this news was hardly tragic. Yet her mother might——

For years, now, Kim Ravenal had shielded her mother; protected her; spoiled her, Magnolia said, almost resentfully.

She stood now with her son-in-law in the cruel glare of the dressing-room lights. Her face was animated, almost flushed. Her fine head rose splendidly from the furred frame of her luxurious coat collar. Her breast and throat were firm and creamy above the square-cut décolletage of her black gown. Her brows looked the blacker and more startling for the wing of white that crossed the black of her straight thick hair. There was about this woman of nearly sixty a breath-taking vitality. Her distinguished young son-in-law appeared rather anæmic in contrast.

"How was the play?" Kim asked, possibly in the hope of changing their ebullient mood.

"Nice production," said Cameron. "Lunt was flawless. Fontanne's turned just a shade cute on us. She'd better stop that. Shaw, revived, tastes a little mouldy. Westley yelled. Simonson's sets were—uh

—meticulous I think the word is. . . . And I want
to inform you, my dear Mrs. C., that your mama has
been a very naughty girl."

This would never do, thought Kim, her mind on the
yellow envelope. She put an arm about her mother.
"Kiss me and I'll forgive you," she said.

"You don't know what she's done."

"Whatever it is——"

"Woollcott started it, anyway," protested Magnolia
Ravenal, lighting her cigarette. "I should think a man
who's dramatic critic of the New York *World* would
have more consideration for the dignity of his——"

Cameron took up the story. "Our seats turned out
to be next to his. Nola sat between us. You know
how she always clutches somebody's hand during the
emotional scenes."

"The last time I went to the theatre with Woollcott
he said he'd slap my hands hard if I ever again——"
put in Magnolia. But Cameron once more interrupted.

"Then in the second act she clutched him instead
of me and he slapped her hand——"

"And pinched——"

"And Nola gave him a sharp dig in the stomach, I'm
afraid, with her elbow, and there was quite a commotion.
Mothers-in-law are a terrible responsibility."

"Mother *dear!* A first night of a Shaw revival at
the National!"

"He started it. And anyway, you've brought me
up wrong."

There was about her suddenly a curious effect of
weariness. It was as though, until now, she had been

acting, and had discarded her rôle. She stood up. "Ken, if you'll get me a taxi I'll run along home. I'm tired. You two are going to the Swopes', aren't you? That means three o'clock."

"I'm not going," said Kim. "Wait a minute, Ken." She came over to Magnolia. "Mother, I just got a telegram."

"Mama?" She uttered the word as though she were a little girl.

"Yes."

"Where is it?"

Kim indicated it. "There, Ken. Get it for me, will you? Under the make-up tray."

"Dead?" Magnolia had not unfolded the yellow slip.

"Yes."

She read it. She looked up. The last shadow had vanished of that mood in which she had entered ten minutes earlier. She looked, suddenly, sallow and sixty. "Let me see. Tennessee. Trains."

"But not to-night, Mother!"

"Yes. Ken, there's something to St. Louis— Memphis—I'm sure. And then from there to-morrow morning."

"Ken will go with you."

"No!" sharply. "No!"

She had her way in the end; left that night, and alone, over Kim's protests and Ken's. "If I need you, Ken dear, I'll telegraph. All those people in the troupe, you know. Some of them have been with her for ten years—fifteen."

All sorts of trains before you reached this remote

little town. Little dusty red-plush trains with sociable brakemen and passengers whose clothes and bearing now seemed almost grotesque to the eyes that once had looked upon them without criticism. A long, hard, trying journey. Little towns at which you left this train and waited long hours for the next. Cinderstrewn junctions whose stations were little better than sheds.

Mile after mile the years had receded as New York was left behind. The sandy soil of the South. Little straggling villages. Unpainted weather-stained cabins, black as the faces that peered from their doorways. When Magnolia Ravenal caught the first gleam of April dogwood flashing white in the forest depths as the train bumbled by, her heart gave a great leap. In a curious and dreamlike way the years of her life with Ravenal in Chicago, the years following Ravenal's desertion of her there, the years of Magnolia's sudden success in New York seemed to fade into unreality; they became unimportant fragmentary interludes. This was her life. She had never left it. They would be there— Julie, and Steve, and Windy, and Doc, and Parthy, and Andy, and Schultzy—somehow, they would be there. They were real. The others were dream people: Mike McDonald, Hankins, Hetty Chilson, all that raffish Chicago crew; the New York group—Kim's gay, fly, brittle brilliant crowd with which Magnolia had always assumed an ease she did not feel.

She decided, sensibly, that she was tired, a little dazed, even. She had slept scarcely at all the night before. Perhaps this news of her mother's death had been, after all, more of a shock than she thought. She would not pretend to be grief-stricken. The breach between her and the indomitable old woman had been a thing of many years' standing, and it had grown wider and wider with the years following that day when, descending upon her daughter in Chicago, Mrs. Hawks had learned that the handsome dashing Gaylord Ravenal had flown. She had been unable to resist her triumphant, "What did I tell you!" It had been the last straw.

She had wondered, vaguely, what sort of conveyance she might hire to carry her to Cold Spring, for she knew no railroad passed through this little river town. But when she descended from the train at this, the last stage but one in her wearisome journey, there was a little group at the red brick station to meet her. A man came toward her (he turned out to be the Chas. K. Barnato of the telegram). He was the general manager and press agent. Doc's old job, modernized. "How did you know me?" she had asked, and was startled when he replied:

"You look like your ma." Then, before she could recover from this: "But Elly told me it was you."

A rather amazing old lady came toward her. She looked like the ancient ruins of a bisque doll. Her cheeks were pink, her eyes bright, her skin parchment, her hat incredible.

"Don't you remember me, Nollie?" she said. And pouted her withered old lips. Then, as Magnolia stared, bewildered, she had chirped like an annoyed cockatoo, "Elly Chipley—Lenore La Verne."

"But it isn't possible!" Magnolia had cried.

This had appeared to annoy Miss Chipley afresh. "Why not, I'd like to know! I've been back with the *Cotton Blossom* the last ten years. Your ma advertised in the *Billboard* for a general utility team. My husband answered the ad, giving his name——"

"Not——?"

"Schultzy? Oh, no, dearie. I buried poor Schultzy in Douglas, Wyoming, twenty-two years ago. Yes, indeed. Clyde!" She wheeled briskly. "Clyde!" The man came forward. He was, perhaps, fifty. Surely twenty years younger than the erstwhile ingénue lead. A sheepish, grizzled man whose mouth looked as if a drawstring had been pulled out of it, leaving it limp and sprawling. "Meet my husband, Mr. Clyde Mellhop. This is Nollie. Mrs. Ravenal, it is, ain't it? Seems funny, you being married and got a famous daughter and all. Last time I saw you you was just a skinny little girl, dark-complected—— Well, your ma was hoity-toity with me when she seen it was me was the other half of the Mellhop General Utility Team. Wasn't going to let me stay, would you believe it! Well, she was glad enough to have me, in the end."

This, Magnolia realized, must be stopped. She met the understanding look of the man Barnato. He nodded. "I guess you must be pretty tuckered out, Mrs. Ravenal. Now, if you'll just step over to the car there." He indicated an important-looking closed car that stood at the far end of the station platform.

Gratefully Magnolia moved toward it. She was a little impressed with its appearance. "Your car!

That was thoughtful of you.   I was wondering how I'd
get——"

"No, ma'am.   That ain't mine.   I got a little car of
my own, but this is your ma's—that is—well, it's yours,
now, I reckon."   He helped her into the back seat with
Elly.   He seated himself before the wheel, with Mellhop
beside him.   He turned to her, solemnly.   "I suppose
you'd like to go right over to see your—to view the re-
mains.   She's—they're at Breitweiler's Undertaking
Parlours.   I kind of tended to everything, like your
son-in-law's telegram said.   I hope everything will suit
you.   Of course, if you'd like to go over to the hotel
first.   I took a room for you—best they had.   It's real
comfortable.   To-morrow morning we take her—we go
to Thebes on the ten-fifteen——"

"The hotel!" cried Magnolia.   "But I want to sleep
on the boat to-night.   I want to go back to the boat."

"It's a good three-quarters of an hour run from here,
even in this car."

"I know it.   But I want to stay on the boat to-night."

"It's for you to say, ma'am."

The main business street of the little town was bustling and prosperous-looking.   Where, in her childhood
river-town days the farm wagons and buggies had stood
hitched at the curb, she now saw rows of automobiles
parked, side by side.   Five-and-Ten-Cent Stores.   Motion Pictures.   Piggly-Wiggly.   Popular magazines in
the drug-store window.   She had thought that everything would be the same.

Breitweiler's Undertaking Parlours.   Quite a little
throng outside; and within an actual crowd, close-

packed. They made way respectfully for Barnato and his party. "What is it?" whispered Magnolia. "What are all these people here for? What has happened?"

"Your ma was quite a famous person in these parts, Mrs. Ravenal. Up and down the rivers and around she was quite a character. I've saved the pieces for you in the paper."

"You don't mean these people—all these people have come here to see——"

"Yes, ma'am. In state. I hope you don't object, ma'am. I wouldn't want to feel I'd done something you wouldn't like."

She felt a little faint. "I'd like them to go away now."

Parthenia Ann Hawks in her best black silk. Her strong black eyebrows punctuated the implacable old face with a kind of surprised resentment. She had not succumbed to the Conqueror without a battle. Magnolia, gazing down upon the stern waxen features, the competent hands crossed in unwilling submission upon her breast, could read the message of revolt that was stamped, even in death, upon that strong and terrible brow. Here! I'm mistress of this craft. You can't do this to me! I'm Parthenia Ann Hawks! Death? Fiddlesticks and nonsense! For others, perhaps. But not for me.

Presently they were driving swiftly out along the smooth asphalt road toward Cold Spring. Elly Chipley was telling her tale with relish, palpably for the hundredth time.

". . . seven o'clock in the evening or maybe a few minutes past and her standing in front of the looking-glass in her room doing her hair. Clyde and me, we had the room next to hers, for'ard, the last few years, on account I used to do for her, little ways. Not that she was feeble or like that. But she needed somebody younger to do for her, now and then"—with the bridling self-consciousness of a girlish seventy, as compared to Parthy's eighty and over. "Well, I was in the next room, and just thinking I'd better be making up for the evening show when I hear a funny sound, and then a voice I didn't hardly recognize sort of squeaks, 'Elly! A stroke!' And then a crash."

Magnolia was surprised to find herself weeping: not for grief; in almost unwilling admiration of this powerful mind and will that had recognized the Enemy even as he stole up on her and struck the blow from behind.

"There, there!" cooed Elly Chipley, pleased that her recital had at last moved this handsome silent woman to proper tears. "There, there!" She patted her hand. "Look, Nollie dear. There's the boat. Seems funny not to see her lighted up for the show this time of night."

Magnolia peered through the dusk, a kind of dread in her heart. Would this, too, be changed beyond recognition? A great white long craft docked at the water's edge. Larger, yes. But much the same. In the gloom she could just make out the enormous letters painted in black against the white upper deck.

COTTON BLOSSOM FLOATING PALACE THEATRE
Parthenia Ann Hawks, Prop.

And there was the River. It was high with the April rains and the snows that nourished it from all the hundreds of miles of its vast domain—the Mississippi Basin.

Vaguely she heard Barnato—"Just started out and promised to be the biggest paying season we had for years. Yessir! Crops what they were last fall, and the country so prosperous. . . . Course, we don't aim to bother you with such details now. . . . Troupe wondering—ain't no more'n natural—what's to become of 'em now. . . . Finest show boat on the rivers. . . . Our own electric power plant. . . . Ice machine. . . . Seats fifteen hundred, easy. . . ."

And there was the River. Broad, yellow, turbulent. Magnolia was trembling. Down the embankment, across the gangplank, to the lower forward deck that was like a comfortable front porch. The bright semi-circle of the little ticket window. A little group of Negro loungers and dock-hands making way respectfully, gently for the white folks. The sound of a banjo tinkling somewhere ashore, or perhaps on an old side-wheeler docked a short distance downstream. A play-bill in the lobby. She stared at it. Tempest and Sunshine. The letters began to go oddly askew. A voice, far away—"Look out! She's going to faint!"

A tremendous effort. "No, I'm not. I'm—all right. I don't think I've eaten anything since early morning."

She was up in the bedroom. Dimity curtains at the windows, fresh and crisp. Clean. Shining. Orderly. Quiet. "Now you just get into bed. A hot-water bag. We'll fix you a tray and a good cup of tea. To-morrow morning you'll be feeling fine again. We got to get an early start."

She ate, gratefully. Anything I can do for you now, Nollie? No, nothing, thanks. Well, I'm kind of beat, myself. It's been a day, I can tell you. Good-night. Good-night. Now I'll leave my door open, so's if you call me——

Nine o'clock. Ten. The hoarse hoot of a boat whistle. The clank of anchor chains. Swish. Swash. Fainter. Cluck-suck against the hull. Quieter. More quiet. Quiet. Black velvet. The River. Home.

XIX

KIM RAVENAL'S tenth letter to her mother was the decisive one. It arrived late in May, when the Cotton Blossom Floating Palace Theatre was playing Lulu, Mississippi. From where the show boat lay just below the landing there was little enough to indicate that a town was situated near by. Lulu, Mississippi, in May, was humid and drowsy and dusty and fly-ridden. The Negroes lolled in the shade of their cabins and loafed at the water's edge. Thick-petalled white flowers amidst glossy dark green foliage filled the air with a drugging sweetness, and scarlet-petalled flowers stuck their wicked yellow tongues out at the passer-by.

Magnolia, on the *Cotton Blossom* upper deck that was like a cosy veranda, sat half in the shade and half in the sun and let the moist heat envelop her. The little nervous lines that New York had etched about her eyes and mouth seemed to vanish magically under the languorous touch of the saturant Southern air. She was again like the lovely creamy blossom for which she had been named; a little drooping, perhaps; a little faded; but Magnolia.

Elly Chipley, setting to rights her privileged bedroom on the boat's port side, came to the screen door in cotton morning frock and boudoir cap. The frock was a gay gingham of girlish cut, its colour a delicate pink. The cap was a trifle of lace and ribbon. From this frame her withered life-scarred old mask looked out, almost fascinating in its grotesquerie.

"Beats me how you can sit out there in the heat like a lizard or a cat or something and not get a stroke. Will, too, one these fine days."

Magnolia, glancing up from the perusal of her letter, stretched her arms above her head luxuriously. "I love it."

Elly Chipley's sharp old eyes snapped at the type-written sheets of the letter in Magnolia's hand. "Heard from your daughter again, did you?"

"Yes."

"I never seen anybody such a hand at writing letters. You got one about every stand since you started with the boat, seems. I was saying to Clyde only yesterday, I says, what's she find to write about!"

This, Magnolia knew, was not a mere figure of speech. In some mysterious way the knowledge had seeped through the *Cotton Blossom* company that in these frequent letters between mother and daughter a battle was being waged. They sensed, too, that in the outcome of this battle lay their own future.

The erstwhile ingénue now assumed an elaborate carelessness of manner which, to the doubting onlooker, would forever have decided the question of her dramatic ability. "What's she got to say, h'm? What——" here she giggled in shrill falsetto appreciation of her own wit—"what news on the Rialto?"

Magnolia glanced down again at the letter. "I think

Kim may come down for a few days to visit us, in June. With her husband."

The ribbons of Elly's cap trembled. The little withered well-kept hand in which she still took such pride went to her lips that were working nervously. "You don't say! Well, that'll be nice." After which triumph of simulated casualness you heard her incautious steps clattering down the stairs and up the aisle to the lesser dressing rooms and bedrooms at the rear of the stage.

Magnolia picked up the letter again. Kim hated to write letters. The number that she had written her mother in the past month testified her perturbation.

Nola darling, you've just gone gaga, that's all. What do you mean by staying down there in that wretched malarial heat! Now listen to me. We close June first. They plan to open in Boston in September, then Philadelphia, Chicago. My contract, of course, doesn't call for the road. Cruger offered me an increase and a house percentage if I'd go when the road season opens, but you know how I hate touring. You're the trouper of this family. Besides, I wouldn't leave Andy. He misses you as much as Ken and I do. If he could talk, he would demand his grandmother's immediate presence. If you aren't in New York by June third I shall come and get you. I mean this. Ken and I sail on the *Olympic* June tenth. There's a play in London that Cruger wants me to see for next season. You know. Casualty. We'll go to Paris, Vienna, Budapest, and back August first. Come along or stay in the country with Andy. Nate Fried says he'll settle up your business affairs if that's what's bothering you. What is there to do except sell the old tub or give it away or something, and take the next train for New York? Your bookings say Lazare, Mississippi, June fourth, fifth and sixth. Nate looked it up and reports it's twenty miles from a railroad. Now, Nola, that's just too mad. Come on home.

KIM.

The hand that held the letter dropped to her lap again. Magnolia lay relaxed in the low deck chair and surveyed through half-closed lids the turgid, swift-flowing stream that led on to Louisiana and the sea. Above the clay banks that rose from the river lay the scrubby little settlement shimmering in the noonday heat. A mule team toiled along the river road drawing a decrepit cart on whose sagging seat a Negro sat slumped, the rope lines slack in his listless hands, his body swaying with the motion of the vehicle. From the cook's galley, aft, came the yee-yah-yah-yah of Negro laughter. Then a sudden crash of piano, drum, horn, and cymbals. The band was rehearsing. The porcine squeal and bleat and grunt of the saxophone. Mississippi Blues they were playing. Ort Hanley, of the Character Team, sang it in the concert after the show. I got the blues. I said the blues. I got the M-i-s-, I said the s-i-s, I said the s-i-pp-i, Mississippi, I got them Miss-is-*sippi blu*-hoo-hoos.

The heat and the music and the laughter and the squeak of the mule cart up the road blended and made a colourful background against which the woman in the chair viewed the procession of the last twenty-five years.

It had turned out well enough. She had gone on, blindly, and it had turned out well enough. Kim. Kim was different. Nothing blind about Kim. She had emerged from the cloistral calm of the Chicago convent with her competent mind quite made up. I am going to be an actress. Oh, no, Kim! Not you! But Kim had gone about it as she went about everything. Clear-headed. Thoughtful. Deliberate. But actresses were

not made in this way, Magnolia argued. Oh, yes, they
were. Five years in stock on Chicago's North Side.
A tiny part in musical comedy. Kim decided that she
knew nothing. She would go to the National Theatre
School of Acting in New York and start all over again.
Magnolia's vaudeville days were drawing to an end.
A middle-aged woman, still able to hold her audience,
still possessing a haunting kind of melancholy beauty.
But more than this was needed to hold one's head above
the roaring tide of ragtime jazz-time youngsters surging
now toward the footlights. She had known what it
was to be a headliner, but she had never commanded the
fantastic figures of the more spectacular acts. She had
been thrifty, though, and canny. She easily saw Kim
through the National Theatre School. The idea of Kim
in a school of acting struck her as being absurd, though
Kim gravely explained to her its uses. Finally she took
a tiny apartment in New York so that she and Kim
might have a home together. Kim worked slavishly,
ferociously. The idea of the school did not amuse
Magnolia as much as it had at first.

Fencing lessons. Gymnastic dancing. Interpretive
dancing. Singing lessons. Voice placing. French
lessons.

"Are you studying to be an acrobat or a singer or a
dancer? I can't make it out."

"Now, Nola, don't be an old-fashioned frumpy darling. Spend a day at the school and you'll know what
I'm getting at."

The dancing class. A big bright bare room. A
phonograph. Ten girls bare-legged, bare-footed,

dressed in wisps. A sturdy, bare-legged woman teacher in a hard-worked green chiffon wisp. They stood in a circle, perhaps five feet apart, and jumped on one foot and swung the other leg behind them, and kept this up, alternating right leg and left, for ten minutes. It looked ridiculously simple. Magnolia tried it when she got home and found she couldn't do it at all. Bar work. Make a straight line of that leg. Back! Back! Stretch! Stretch! Stretch! Some of it was too precious. The girls in line formation and the green chiffon person facing them, saying, idiotically, and suiting actions to words:

"Reach down into the valley! Gather handfuls of mist. Up, up, facing the sun! Oh, how lovely!"

The Voice class. The Instructor, wearing a hat with an imposing façade and clanking with plaques of arts-and-crafts jewellery, resembled, as she sat at her table fronting the seated semi-circle of young men and women, the chairman of a woman's club during the business session of a committee meeting.

Her voice was "placed." Magnolia, listening and beholding, would not have been surprised to see her remove her voice, an entity, from her throat and hold it up for inspection. It was a thing so artificial, so studied, so manufactured. She articulated carefully and with great elegance.

"I don't need to go into the wide-open throat to-day. We will start with the jaw exercises. Down! To the side! Side! Rotate!"

With immense gravity and earnestness twelve young men and women took hold of their respective jaws and pulled these down; from side to side; around. They showed no embarrassment.

"Now then! The sound of *b*. Bub-ub-ub-ub. *They bribed Bob with a bib*. Sound of *t*. *It isn't a bit hot*. Sound of *d*. *Dad did the deed*. Sound of *n*. *None of the nine nuns came at noon*."

Singly and en masse they disposed of Bob and Dad and the nine nuns. Pharynx resonance. Say, "Clear and free, Miss Ravenal." Miss Ravenal said clear-and-free, distinctly. No, no, no! Not clear-and-free, but clear—and free. Do you see what I mean? Good. Now take it again. Miss Ravenal took it again. Clear—and free. *That's* better.

Now then. Words that differ in the *wh* sound. Mr. Karel, let us hear your list. Mr. Karel obliges. Whether-weather, when-wen, whinny-winnow, whither-wither; why do you spell it with a y?

Miss Rogers, *l* sounds. Miss Rogers, enormously solemn (fated for Lady Macbeth at the lightest)—level, loyal, lull, lily, lentil, love, lust, liberty, boil, coral——

Now then! The nerve vitalizing breath! We'll all stand. Hold the breath. Stretch out arms. Arms in —and IN—AND IN—out—in—head up—mouth open——

Shades of Modjeska, Duse, Rachel, Mrs. Siddons, Bernhardt! Was this the way an actress was made!

"You wait and see," said Kim, grimly. Dancing, singing, fencing, voice, French. One year. Two. Three. Magnolia had waited, and she had seen.

Kim had had none of those preliminary hardships and terrors and temptations, then, that are supposed to be-

set the path of the attractive young woman who would
travel the road to theatrical achievement. Her success
actually had been instantaneous and sustained. She
had been given the part of the daughter of a worldly
mother in a new piece by Ford Salter and had taken the
play away from the star who did the mother. Her
performance had been clear-cut, modern, deft, convincing. She was fresh, but finished.

She was intelligent, successful, workmanlike, intuitive, vigorous, adaptable. She was almost the first
of this new crop of intelligent, successful, deft, workmanlike, intuitive, vigorous, adaptable young women
of the theatre. There was about her—or them—
nothing of genius, of greatness, of the divine fire. But
the dramatic critics of the younger school who were too
late to have seen past genius in its heyday and for whom
the theatrical genius of their day was yet to come,
viewed her performance and waxed hysterical, mistaking
talent and intelligence and hard work and ambition for
something more rare. It became the thing to proclaim
each smart young woman the Duse of her day if she
had a decent feeling for stage tempo, could sustain a
character throughout three acts, speak the English
language intelligibly, cross a stage or sit in a chair
naturally. By the time Kim had been five years out of
the National Theatre School there were Duses by the
dozen, and a Broadway Bernhardt was born at least
once a season.

These gave, invariably, what is known as a fine performance. As you stood in the lobby between the acts,

smoking your cigarette, you said, "She's giving a fine performance."

"A fine performance!" Magnolia echoed one evening, rather irritably, after she and Kim had returned from the opening of a play in which one of Kim's friends was featured. "But she doesn't act. Everything she did and everything she said was right. And I was as carried out of myself as though I were listening to a clock strike. When I go to the theatre I want to care. In the old days maybe they didn't know so much about tempo and rhythm, but in the audience strong men wept and women fainted——"

"Now listen, Nola darling. One of your old-day gals would last about four seconds on Broadway. I've heard about Clara Morris and Mrs. Siddons, and Modjeska, and Bernhardt all my life. If the sentimental old dears were to come back in an all-star revival to-day the intelligent modern theatre-going audience would walk out on them."

The new-school actresses went in for the smarter teas, eschewed cocktails, visited the art exhibits, had their portraits painted in the new manner, never were seen at night clubs, were glimpsed coming out of Scribner's with a thick volume of modern biography, used practically no make-up when in mufti, kept their names out of the New York telephone directory, wore flat-heeled shoes and woollen stockings while walking briskly in Central Park, went to Symphony Concerts; were, in short, figures as glamorous and romantic as a pint of milk. Everything they did on the stage was right.

Intelligent, well thought out, and right. Watching
them, you knew it was right—tempo, tone, mood,
character. Right. As right as an engineering blue-
print. Your pulses, as you sat in the theatre, were
normal.

Usually, their third season, you saw them unwisely
lunching too often at the Algonquin Round Table and
wise-cracking with the critics there. The fourth they
took a bit in that new English comedy just until O'Neill
should have finished the play he was doing for them.
The fifth they married that little Whatshisname. The
sixth they said, mysteriously, that they were Writing.

Kim kept away from the Algonquin, did not attend
first nights with Woollcott or Broun, had a full-
page Steichen picture in *Vanity Fair*, and married
Kenneth Cameron. She went out rarely. Sunday
night dinners, sometimes; or she had people in (ham *à la*
Queenie part of the cold buffet). Her list of Sunday
night guests or engagements read like a roster of the
New York Telephone Company's Exchanges. Stuy-
vesant, Beekman, Bleeker, Murray, Rhinelander, Van-
derbilt, Jerome, Wadsworth, Tremont. She learned
to say, "It's just one of those things——" She finished
an unfinished sentence with, "I *mean*——!" and a
throwing up of the open palms.

Kenneth Cameron. Her marriage with Kenneth
Cameron was successful and happy and very nice.
Separate bedrooms and those lovely negligées—velvet
with Venetian sleeves and square neck-line. Excellent
friends. Nothing sordid. Personal liberty and privacy
of thought and action—those were the things that made

for happiness in marriage.   Magnolia wondered, sometimes, but certainly it was not for her to venture opinion.   Her own marriage had been no such glittering
example of perfection.   Yet she wondered, seeing this
well-ordered and respectful union, if Kim was not, after
all, missing something.   Wasn't marriage, like life, un-
stimulating and unprofitable and somewhat empty
when too well ordered and protected and guarded?
Wasn't it finer, more splendid, more nourishing, when
it was, like life itself, a mixture of the sordid and the
magnificent; of mud and stars; of earth and flowers;
of love and hate and laughter and tears and ugliness and
beauty and hurt?   She was wrong, of course.   Ken's
manner toward Kim was polite, tender, thoughtful.
Kim's manner toward Ken was polite, tender, thoughtful.   Are you free next Thursday, dear?   The Paynes
are having those Russians.   It might be rather interesting. . . . Sorry.   Ken's voice.   Soft, light.   It
was the—well, Magnolia never acknowledged this, even
to herself, but it was what she called the male interior
decorator's voice.   You heard it a good deal at teas,
and at the Algonquin, and in the lobby between the
acts on first nights and in those fascinating shops on
Madison Avenue where furniture and old glass and
brasses and pictures were shown you by slim young
men with delicate hands.   I *mean*——!   It's just one
of those things. . . .

There was no Mississippi in Kim.   Kim was like the
Illinois River of Magnolia's childhood days.   Kim's
life flowed tranquilly between gentle green-clad shores,
orderly, well regulated, dependable.

"For the land's sakes, Magnolia Hawks, you sitting out there yet! Here it's after three and nearly dinner time!" Elly Chipley at the screen door. "And in the blazing sun, too. You need somebody to look after you worse than your ma did."

Elly was justified, for Magnolia had a headache that night.

Kim and Ken arrived unexpectedly together on June second, clattering up to the boat landing in a scarecrow Ford driven by a stout Negro in khaki pants, puttees, and an army shirt.

Kim was breathless, but exhilarated. "He says he drove in France in '17, and I believe it. Good God! Every bolt, screw, bar, nut, curtain, and door in the thing rattled and flapped and opened and fell in and fell out. I've been working like a Swiss bell-ringer try-ing to keep things together there in the back seat. Nola darling, what do you mean by staying down in this miserable hole all these weeks! Ken, dear, take another aspirin and a pinch of bicarb and lie down a minute. . . . Ken's got a headache from the heat and the awful trip. . . . We're going back to-night, and we sail on the tenth, and, Nola darling, for heaven's sake . . ."

They had a talk. The customary four o'clock dinner was delayed until nearly five because of it. They sat in Magnolia's green-shaded bedroom with its frilled white bedspread and dimity curtains—rather, Kim and Magnolia sat and Ken sprawled his lean length on the bed, looking a little yellow and haggard, what with the heat and the headache. And in the cook's galley, and on the stage, and in the little dressing rooms that looked out on the river, and on deck, and in the box office, the company and crew of the Cotton Blossom Floating Palace Theatre lounged and waited, played pinochle and waited, sewed and napped and read and wondered and waited.

"You can't mean it, Nola darling. Flopping up and down these muddy wretched rivers in this heat! You could be out at the Bay with Andy. Or in London with Ken and me—Ken, dear, isn't it any better?—or even in New York, in the lovely airy apartment, it's cooler than——"

Magnolia sat forward.

"Listen, Kim. I love it. The rivers. And the people. And the show boat. And the life. I don't know why. It's bred in me, I suppose. Yes, I do know why. Your grandpa died when you were too little to remember him, really. Or you'd know why. Now, if you two are set on going back on the night train, you'll have to listen to me for a minute. I went over things with the lawyer and the banker in Thebes when we took Mama back there. Your grandmother left a fortune. I don't mean a few thousand dollars. She left half a million, made out of this boat in the last twenty-five years. I'm giving it to you, Kim, and Ken."

Refusal, of course. Protest. Consideration. Acquiescence. Agreement. Acceptance. Ken was sitting up now, pallidly. Kim was lyric. "Half a million! Mother! Ken! It means the plays I want, and Ken to produce them. It means that I can establish a real American theatre in New York. I can do the plays

I've been longing to do—Ibsen and Hauptmann, and
Werfel, and Schnitzler, and Molnar, and Chekhov, and
Shakespeare even. Ken! We'll call it the American
Theatre!"

"The American Theatre," Magnolia repeated after
her, thoughtfully. And smiled then. "The American
Theatre." She looked a trifle uncomfortable, as one
who has heard a good joke, and has no one with whom
to share it.

A loud-tongued bell clanged and reverberated through
the show boat's length. Dinner.

Kim and Ken pretended not to notice the heat and
flies and the molten state of the butter. They met
everyone from the captain to the cook; from the ingénue
lead to the drum.

"Well, Miss Ravenal, this is an—or Mrs. Cameron,
I suppose I should say—an honour. We know all about
you, even if you don't know about us." Not one of
them had ever seen her.

A little tour of the show boat after dinner. Ken, still
pale, but refreshed by tea, was moved to exclamations
of admiration. Look at that, Kim! Ingenious. Oh,
say, we must stay over and see a performance. I'd
no idea! And these combination dressing rooms and
bedrooms, eh? Well, I'll be damned!

Elly Chipley was making up in her special dressing
room, infinitesimal in size, just off the stage. Her part
for to-night was that of a grande dame in black silk and
lace cap and fichu. The play was The Planter's Daughter. She had been rather sniffy in her attitude toward
the distinguished visitors. They couldn't patronize

her. She applied the rouge to her withered cheeks in little pettish dabs, and leaned critically forward to scrutinize her old mask of a face. What did she see there? Kim wondered, watching her, fascinated.

"Mother tells me you played Juliet, years ago. How marvellous!"

Elly Chipley tossed her head skittishly. "Yes, indeed! Played Juliet, and was known as the Western Favourite. I wasn't always on a show boat, I promise you."

"What a thrill—to play Juliet when you were so young! Usually we have to wait until we're fifty. Tell me, dear Miss La Verne"—elaborately polite, and determined to mollify this old harridan—"tell me, who was your Romeo?"

And then Life laughed at Elly Chipley (Lenore La Verne on the bills) and at Kim Ravenal, and the institution known as the Stage. For Elly Chipley tapped her cheek thoughtfully with her powder puff, and blinked her old eyes, and screwed up her tremulous old mouth, and pondered, and finally shook her head. "My Romeo? Let me see. Let—me—see. Who *was* my Romeo?"

They must go now. Oh, Nola darling, half a million! It's too fantastic. Mother, I can't bear to leave you down in this God-forsaken hole. Flies and Negroes and mud and all this yellow terrible river that you love more than me. Stand up there—high up—where we can see you as long as possible.

The usual crowd was drifting down to the landing as the show-boat lights began to glow. Twilight was

coming on. On the landing, up the river bank, sauntering down the road, came the Negroes, and the hangers-
on, the farm-hands, the river folk, the curious, the idle,
the amusement-hungry. Snatches of song. Feet shuffling upon the wharf boards. A banjo twanging.

They were being taken back to the nearest railroad
connection, but not in the Ford that had brought them.
They sat luxuriously in the car that had been Parthy's
and that was Magnolia's now.

"Mother, dearest, you'll be back in New York in
October or November at the latest, won't you? Promise me. When the boat closes? You will!"

Kim was weeping. The car started smoothly. She
turned for a last glimpse through her tears. "Oh, Ken,
do you think I ought to leave her like this?"

"She'll be all right, dear. Look at her! Jove!"

There stood Magnolia Ravenal on the upper deck
of the Cotton Blossom Floating Palace Theatre, silhouetted against sunset sky and water—tall, erect, indomitable. Her mouth was smiling but her great eyes
were wide and sombre. They gazed, unwinking, across
the sunlit waters. One arm was raised in a gesture of
farewell.

"Isn't she splendid, Ken!" cried Kim, through her
tears. "There's something about her that's eternal and
unconquerable—like the River."

A bend in the upper road. A clump of sycamores.
The river, the show boat, the straight silent figure were
lost to view.

THE END